I0699017

I dedicate this book to my ARC Team.
Thank you so much for your dedication to my author journey.

RESOLVE OF A MIDLIFE WITCH

J.C. YEAMANS

RSP

REED SHORE PRESS

Resolve of a Midlife Witch

Copyright © 2025 by J.C. Yeamans

All rights reserved. Except as permitted under the US Copyright Act, no part of this publication may be reproduced, distributed, or transmitted in any form or by any means, or stored in a database or retrieval system, without the prior written permission of the author and publisher.

Published by Reed Shore Press under the Imprint Broomstick & Lace.

Long Beach, CA 90814

ISBN: 979-8-88652-018-7

If you're reading this book and did not purchase it, or it was not purchased for your use only, please delete it and purchase your own copy from an authorized retailer. Thank you for respecting the hours of labor and investment of this author.

This is a work of fiction. Names, characters, places, and incidents either are the product of the author's imagination or are used fictitiously, and any resemblance to actual persons, living or dead, business establishments, events, or locales is entirely coincidental. The publisher does not have any control over and does not assume any responsibility for the author or third-party websites, social media, or their content.

For content elements, visit the J.C. Yeamans website: https://jcyeamans.com/content-elements/. Please visit the link if you would like more information on the contents before reading this book. There are spoilers.

Cover: Charles W. Clark, Reed Shore Press.
The cover design uses Rosarivo font (designed by Pablo Ugerman) and Photoshop brushes by Brusheezy.com.

Content/Line Editor: Sarah Faeth Sanders

Proofreader: Reed Shore Press

PRONUNCIATION GUIDE

Gwynedd: GWYN-eth
Cockburn: CO-burn
Gorawen: GOHR-a-when
Nain: NINE
Taid: TIDE
Shailagh: SHAY-la
Aonghas: ANG-us
Tuatha Dé Danann: TOO-a-day-DAN-ann
Cat sith: CAT shee
Crabbit: KRAB-it
Cariad: kar-EE-ahd
Diwrnod da: dee-UR-nod da

CONTENTS

CHAPTER ONE

NEW BEGINNINGS

STREAMS OF HAZY WHITE magic snake between the sparkling amethyst geode in one palm and the clear crystal quartz in the other as I chant, disappearing with a pop when I set them on the wooden table. I relish in my success, a grin of immense satisfaction forming on my face.

The process of strengthening my witch's intuition is second nature to me now. But enhancing my prognostication using the crystal grid requires me to trudge along on a steady yet labored path of drudgery. One way to safeguard myself from the family of Nuada, the Tuatha Dé Danann fairy who failed to whisk me away to his kingdom in the Otherworld, is to expand my vision of the gray-skinned Fomorian—the enemy of the Tuatha Dé.

I jump when the door to the magic room in the chilly basement creaks open. Soon after, muscular arms wrap around my torso from behind. Firm hands press against my abdomen through my long-sleeved T-shirt, and I embrace them. A warm breath caresses my ear as my Scottish lover, Professor Archibald Cockburn, plants a kiss on my neck. A whiff of his woodsy cologne relaxes me.

"Gwynedd, I hope I didn't interrupt you," he says in a breathy voice. "I sensed you were finished."

"For now, I am. Archie, I should get ready for work. It's my last shift at Mystic Sage before we leave for Scotland and Wales."

"Under the circumstances, you should have asked for the day off. Shane and Jeff would have understood."

He's right. My bosses Shane Murphy and Jeff Williams would gladly have given me the time off, but it's the Sunday after the Christmas holiday. New Year's Eve is two days away. How busy could it be?

I spin around to face him, mesmerized as always by his icy blue eyes. A few more strands of silver hair have sprouted in his ash-blond locks after all we've been through together. I lay my hands on his toned chest, protruding through his black tee. He brushes my chestnut-brown strands behind an ear.

"You should eat before you go. What would you like for lunch, Ms. Crowther?"

I chuckle. "So formal. It's been over a week since I moved in. I expected the newness to have worn off by now."

A corner of his mouth curls. "I'll never tire of you, my love." He kisses me and gestures to the crystals on the table. "You've become adept at melding them. Has the practice increased your intuition enough to point to anything more? Since the aura you experienced on the Winter Solstice in Agnes's library?"

"No," I reply, my frustration apparent in the sharp huff of air that passes through my lips. "But it was powerful. I'm sure one of Nuada's family has crossed over through the portal."

A wrinkle creases between Archie's eyes. "I wish you would consider carrying the dirk again. You should be prepared."

"I'll think about it. I understand your concern, but Nuada's family may pick up on Tyler's magic in the area, too. Although his last name is Wolfe, they could still find him through me. You only have one dirk. How will my son remain safe?"

"Point taken. As usual, my love, you win. Should I train Tyler to use the dirk so he can keep it in his possession? Would that calm your concerns?"

"I doubt it. Nuada fooled everyone with his cover." Who would have ever guessed the young assistant professor, Dr. Nick Evans, was masking his true identity? "Plus, he glamoured us to suppress our suspicions. We may not detect them coming any more this time than the last."

"Aye," he says, swiping my cheek with a finger. "But we'll be leaving for the UK soon. I'm glad Tyler is coming. He'll be safer with us. If Nuada's family is in Bearsden, our exit should throw them off both of your magic scents."

"My intuition merely hinted at them crossing over. They could be anywhere. Courtney pretty much admitted there are portals everywhere. If we're lucky, they may never find us. Nick said it took him years to track me down in Bearsden. I'll have to learn to live with the threat and move on. Carry protection pouches on me at all times to avoid future glamouring. The alternative is a life full of what could have been."

"Aye. Let's hope for that scenario. We should all carry protection. I'll recommend it to Trinity."

Courtney Erickson, a Tylwyth Teg fairy in hiding, is married to John Erickson, one of the new city councilmen. We discovered her secret recently when she helped us retrieve abducted children from Alys Morgan, another Tylwyth Teg who covered her true identify by serving on the city council.

I move the crystals to the shelf where he stores his herbs, bowls, candles, and grimoires. "In the meantime, I've started to use the crystal grid again."

Archie motions toward the door and begins walking. "I noticed."

"Thanks for not asking me about it," I say, turning off the magic room light as I exit. "If my vision of the monster returns, you'll be the first to know."

I should call the supernatural being by its proper name now that I've discovered its identity—a Fomorian—the enemy of the Tuatha Dé Danann. Having this in common, I'd like to think we could be friends. But that huge, bulbous eye glared at me as if I was his next meal.

Archie shuts the basement door of his two-bedroom cottage residence on Duncan Street and we enter the small kitchen—technically, mine, too. Tyler and Zoe are purchasing the home of Dr. Lelsie Hughes, the Chair of the Celtic Studies department and the Bearsden Coven Elder. I rented a room there prior to learning of Tyler's intentions to buy the house. After the initial shock of the sudden change, I adjusted to living with Archie faster than I expected. I'm elated to be here now. But there's so much left to unpack and no time to do it in. Instead, I've been packing a suitcase all afternoon. We visit the UK in a few days.

"Why don't you sit for a wee bit while I make us salads," he says. "You're the one who has work."

"Thank you, honey." After I pour some iced tea, I sit down at the tiny kitchen table. "I'll return the favor with dinner sometime this week."

He grins as he cuts the carrots. "I'm chuffed to bits you moved in. Change whatever you want to make it your home, too."

"I doubt you'd like my idea of organization. You're so..." I snicker as I point at the perfectly aligned row of sliced carrots. "Anal."

His smile falls flat. "Are you trying to start something, witch? You haven't even lived here for two weeks."

"No," I say with a snort. "Just stating the obvious. I hope I don't get on your nerves."

He smiles lovingly. "You're not so bad. If I have to live with a few garments strewn on the furniture and floor, I'll gladly adapt."

He tosses a few cherry tomatoes to top off the kale salad, sets the bowls and dressing on the table, and sits across from me. His phone vibrates and he reads a text.

"Who's contacting you on a Sunday?" I ask.

"It's Leslie. She's more than a wee bit blowing a fuse over Seamus Duffy's letter of resignation, although it doesn't take effect until the end of Spring Semester. She brought some mail home yesterday from her office and opened it. I didn't tell you because she asked me not to."

"Actually, I already knew. Seamus told me, but he preferred I not say anything." I jab my fork into some kale.

Archie takes a sip of tea. "Of course he confided in you."

I'm sure the Elder wasn't expecting the visiting Irish professor to bail on them.

"You know Seamus has deep feelings for me. Anyway, I knew you would find out soon enough. Why is Leslie so upset?"

He stares down at his salad. "The Dean of Arts and Sciences already refused to renew one position. She's worried they won't allow another visiting professor to replace him."

"What about Ashley Lewis? Certainly she could move into a tenure track position now?"

The young instructor of Welsh literature and folklore just started in the Fall Semester. She's a single mom of a half human, half Tylwyth Teg fairy son and is in a loving relationship with my younger boss, Jeff Williams. Why wouldn't the college allow her to become a permanent fixture in the department? She has multiple degrees, and besides, the students love her.

"The college would have to approve the search and it wouldn't start until next year." He picks at his salad. "Ashley loves working in the Celtic Studies department, but she needs stability. Leslie found out she applied for a tenure-track position in the English department. The Elder flipped her lid. With Seamus leaving in May and the disappearance of Nick Evans, the dean is questioning the longevity of Celtic Studies degrees. Frankly, I hope Ashley gets it."

I drop my fork. "Where would that leave you and Leslie?"

"I don't know." He looks away for a minute but returns his gaze to me, smiling. "You have enough to fret about. We've been in this situation before. Something will come through at the last minute. Let's enjoy the rest of the Yule season while we can. Trinity's idea to celebrate New Year's Eve together was brilliant. We need to unwind."

Our coven leader and the Director of Family for All, the local LGBTQ support group, thought a party would take our minds off the recent trauma. After Alys Morgan kidnapped my best friend Ronnie Baldwin's baby, Luna, the Bearsden Coven had to fight to see her returned safely. The battle with the formidable Tylwyth Teg left its mark on even the most skilled members of the coven. Her partner Derek Young is an Unremarkable, but he wasn't afraid to help. She hit the jackpot with that man.

"I wish we'd taken Agnes up on her offer to have it at her farm-house," I say. "She has more space than the Pumpkin House."

"True, but she would have complained the entire time we were there, asking when we were going to leave. Now that Leslie moved in with her, the old hedge witch is content to spend the evening alone with her sweetheart."

"She'll complain anyway. It'll probably start an hour after she arrives."

Archie is right. My mentor, Agnes Pritchard, won't admit how happy she is now. But I remember what a curmudgeon she was when she was living as a hermit on that farm, having lived there for years after breaking up with Leslie in the '60s. When I first started working at Mystic sage, she would skulk around the store with a scowl etched on her face—embedded from the decades of heartache.

"I haven't seen Mr. Yeats in a while," I say. "I'm sure he's lonely. He saw me daily at Leslie's and we'd become closer in the last year."

He arches an eyebrow. "If I didn't know you loved me, I'd be jealous of that cat familiar."

I chuckle. "I'll visit him when I return. Are Ronnie and Derek coming? Luna is only a few weeks old."

"Yeah, but they'll stay for a couple of hours and go home. Trinity invited the Ericksons to the party. I think that was a wonderful idea. Jeff and Ashley would like to build their friendship with them. This provides a jovial time to do that."

"A shared desire to protect their children, I'm sure."

After discovering Courtney was a Tylwyth Teg fairy, it makes perfect sense for Ashley to want a close friendship with her. Courtney is pregnant and they probably share the same fears of their children's identities being discovered by Unremarkables—those who aren't *in the knowing* of all things supernatural.

A notification dings on my phone. It's an alert about a missing person. Archie's cell vibrates right after.

"This says an older woman with dementia is missing. Oh, my gods." I peer up at Archie. "It's Riley Shaw."

He cocks his head. "That name is familiar."

"It should be. Riley is the old crone witch from Middletown who helped the coven several times, including the banishment of the Unseelie Sluagh fairy back to the Otherworld."

"Ahhh," he says, nodding. "Sad she has lost her faculties. Her family and the Middletown Coven must be sick with worry. Very dangerous for such a powerful witch to be on the loose."

"Yeah, I suppose. I sure hope they find her. She is fairly old and frail. Certainly, she couldn't win a marathon. But her mind was as quick as a wink last time I saw her. Her health must have deteriorated recently."

"Unusual for such a talented witch. But everyone's time comes to an end eventually, no matter how much witchcraft we cast to delay it."

"Speak for yourself. I plan to live forever."

Archie chuckles. "As stubborn as you are, I have no doubt you'll discover a long-lost ancestral spell to achieve that goal."

I throw him a glower. "Now who's starting something?"

"Only stating the facts, my love." He blows me a kiss. "You know you have my heart."

"Yes, I do." I finish the last of my iced tea and take my dishes to the sink. "I'm supposed to train Shane's girlfriend on the register today. Be right back. My jacket is hanging on the oak hall tree in the foyer."

As I grab my coat, the mantle clock in the living room dings the first of twelve. I glance at the painting of my mom, Lowri Crowther, hanging over the fireplace. The wind blows her chestnut hair into snake-like strands while her arms stretch out toward gloomy skies. Did a vision influence my Great-Aunt Gorawen's artistry? She never mentioned the possibility.

I haven't conferenced with Mom and Dad in the Otherworld for Yule. Neither has Tyler. I wasn't ready to tell them about my realization on the solstice when my intuition flooded me with the knowledge the Tuatha Dé Danann had crossed over—well, at least one. They would panic unnecessarily. But I have to share the news before we depart for the UK. I owe them that.

I slip on my fleece jacket as I walk back to the mudroom to put on my sneakers. "See you for dinner when I get home, honey. I don't thank you enough for all the cooking you do."

Archie follows and kisses me goodbye. "It's a pleasure, my love, and I enjoy it. Please, be aware of your surroundings walking home. And don't brush me off for being concerned. I understand you're quite able to defend yourself, but I still worry about you."

"I know. Thank you, honey," I say, hugging him. "I'll text you on the way home."

As I stroll toward Main Street with my hood up, gray skies unnerve me with their rolling, billowy clouds. Like the painting of my mother forewarns—a storm is coming.

CHAPTER TWO

AN UNREMARKABLE LOVE

I GESTURE AT THE cash register. "Why don't I talk you through logging in again? Remember to always have the key to open the drawer on you. Make sure to lock it whenever you walk away from the register."

Julia Harding, Shane's new lady friend, lays her hand on the computer mouse, trembling. She's a sweet woman with a head full of fluffy, silver curls and a broad smile that shines even on the gloomiest of days. A petite lady in her upper-60s, she is near my boss's age. But she must have never worked a day outside the home. Tech-savvy, she isn't.

"Click your finger on the left side of the mouse to highlight the employee ID number box and type it in," I say. "Now, type your password in the box below. Then hit enter."

Julia picks a pen from the skull mug on the counter and grabs a notepad from her purse. "Can I write this down? I'm sure I'll forget." Her nasal vowels hint at a Midwest upbringing.

"Of course," I say, forcing a smile. "You probably don't need to. Once you've done it a few times, you'll remember. But I wouldn't leave your login and password sitting around ever. A customer may notice it and copy down the information. That's certain to get Shane robbed."

"It's all so much to remember. Thank you for being so patient with me. I don't know a lot about using a computer. This is all new to me."

"I understand. But you don't have to thank me. It's my job. I'm happy to teach you."

"You're so understanding, Gwyn. I don't want my prior life to keep me from succeeding with new things. My heart burst with joy when Shane asked me to work at Mystic Sage. I just hope I learn the job well enough to take over for you when you leave."

"I'm sure you will. That's not for a few weeks." But at this rate, she may still be at the login stage. "While the store is empty, why don't we practice ringing up some merchandise? I can void the sales once we're done. Go grab a few items from the shelves."

Julia shuffles around and scans the walls, settling on some spell jars and candles. She returns to the cash register and places the witchy objects on the counter.

"When Shane told me he was the owner of this store, I was a little wary. I mean, I'm fine with his pagan beliefs and the community group the Fellowship. You all are so welcoming." She points at the items on the counter. "But to sell all this...witch stuff. I couldn't imagine he'd have so many customers who think these things work. Do you believe in all this hocus-pocus?"

How do I answer her without lying? "It doesn't matter what I think. The power is with those who do."

Her eyes widen and she whispers, "Are there actual witches in Bearsden? I've heard rumors about that old woman on the farm on the edge of town. She's in your pagan group."

"You're talking about Agnes Pritchard." I swallow and clear my throat. "She spouts off about a lot of things. If I were you, I'd take anything she says with a grain of salt. Don't give her another thought. We should get on with your training."

"Yes. I don't want to let Shane down."

"He hasn't shared much about you. Have you always lived in Bearsden? Were you married before?"

She turns her attention to the scanner, angling it toward the tarot cards. "I'm a widow. I moved here a few months ago."

"My condolences. Losing a loved one is difficult, especially losing a spouse. Where did you used to live? A city or a rural area? What brought you to Bearsden?"

She peers out the store window. "I'd rather not say. That was a different life."

"I'm sorry for being so nosey. My curiosity makes an ass out of me sometimes. Small talk isn't my forte."

"No worries, Gwyn. I'm a private person. I haven't even told Shane yet. He seems to understand."

"Well, you're entitled to your privacy. I apologize for putting you on the spot." I can't believe my boss is dating this woman and knows nothing about her past. "Let's continue."

I spend the next hour teaching Julia how to ring up merchandise using the scanner and how to void a sale if she makes a mistake. Her hands shake as she scans each item, double-checking each time. She observes customers using the credit card reader as if she's never seen one before...or used one, for that matter.

My white-haired boss walks into the front of the store carrying a large box. New stock for the games section, I guess. The Yule sale left the shelves bare. He sets the merchandise on the floor and pulls up his cargo pants, which were hanging low on his bit of a paunch. His beard and ponytail have grown a little longer. I glance back at Julia and wonder how such a strait-laced woman became so interested in an aging hippie. But who doesn't fall in love with Shane at their first meeting? My boss exemplifies all the good in this world.

"How's the training going?" he asks in his North Carolinian accent.

"Everyone learns at their own pace," I say. "In a few weeks, she'll be ordering you around here."

He chuckles. "No doubt about that."

The sparkle has returned to Shane's emerald-green eyes. I'm so happy he found a woman to love after his prior relationship with Cordelia Davenport—a narcissistic witch who cared more about herself than the lives of Unremarkables in our town. She left my boss with an empty heart. If I ever come in contact with her again, it will be too soon. He had a fulfilling life with his first wife, who was an Unremarkable. Perhaps that's the secret sauce to a joyful existence for him, keeping his witch status hidden. How did he ever pull it off?

"Sugar, are you ready to learn the tedious part of the job?" Shane asks. "Unboxing inventory and tagging it is mundane."

"Actually, sounds like fun." Julia grabs her purse from under the counter. "Thank you, Gwyn. I hope I remember everything for the next time."

"Well, Jeff Williams will mentor you on your future shifts. I'll be leaving for the UK with my partner, Archie Cockburn, soon."

The door swings in and Jeff enters. He pulls off his Delaware University at Bearsden beanie and fingers his taffy-brown hair into place.

"Good afternoon." He removes his jacket and shakes off the drops of rain. "It's drizzling. Hopefully, the storm will move out by closing."

I wave to my boss. "Are your ears burning? I was just telling Julia you're going to take over her training since I'm leaving for a month."

"I hope you don't have to start from the beginning again," she says, wringing her hands.

"And that's fine if he has to, sugar." Shane gestures to the doorway. "Let's go to the back and I'll teach you all you need to know about tagging merchandise."

Julia smiles sweetly at my boss and follows him to the back through the crystals room. Jeff hangs his jacket on a hook and comes behind the counter.

"How did she do?" he whispers, glancing back at the doorway.

I wrinkle my nose. "Well..."

He chuckles softly. "That good, huh? Come on, she couldn't be that bad."

"She acts like she's never used a computer before. I don't think she even owns a cell phone. Shane mentioned buying her one. He thinks she's too poor to afford one. It's why he offered her a job."

"He also said she's a widow. She may have been a stay-at-home parent all her life and never learned. Lots of Boomers can't use tech. Do you think she can still learn?"

"Yeah, but you'll have to be patient with her. She trembles with every new task and double-checks everything she does. At least she's conscientious." I lower my voice to a barely audible level. "She asked if I believe in witchcraft and if the rumors about Agnes are true."

He leans into me, whispering, "Oh, what did you say?"

"I told her not to believe everything she hears; that power resides in those who believe."

"You didn't lie. By the way, thanks for asking Trinity to invite us and the Ericksons to the Fellowship's New Year's Eve party. I think it will help to normalize fairies living here if the coven includes them at social gatherings."

"How are Ashley and Courtney getting along?" I ask.

"Awesome. Courtney has been such a help. She's taught Aidan how to stop his magic from releasing. Of course, he's still a two-year-old with a mind of his own. But Ashley is much less stressed about his budding skills."

The door dings and a blast of cool air enters with a customer. Jeff gestures to the back of the store.

"I'm going to go help them. Call if you need anything."

"Will do, boss."

The front of Mystic Sage is quiet as a tomb for the next couple of hours, except for a sprinkling of shoppers. To stay busy, I roam around, dusting the shelves and organizing the disarray from the frenzy of the holiday sales. Shane and Julia's laughter trickles in from the back of the store, the expression of new love. I recall the newness of my early days with Archie and a smile erupts. Closing time arrives and we put on our coats to prepare for the chilly temperature. At least the rain stopped. Jeff sets the alarm and locks up the store.

"Ashley is expecting me, so I'm gonna run. Goodnight, every-one."

"Goodnight," we reply as he rushes off.

"Enjoy your dinner at the Raven Pub, you two," I say, slipping on my gloves.

"Thank you, darling," Shane replies. "Let's go, Julia. I can smell the fresh popcorn from here."

"I'm salivating over their signature seafood chowder already. Thank you for your help today, Gwyn. I hope you have a wonder-ful time in the UK."

"Won't you be attending the New Year's Eve party?" I ask.

Shane peers at me with a raise of his chin. "I thought it would be better if we celebrated this one at home this year."

I get his drift. She'd be the single Unremarkable there. He must want us to have the freedom to talk without the danger of slipping up.

"Well, you enjoy your evening together. Everyone deserves alone time. And if I don't see you before I leave, Happy New Year."

"To you, too, darling. Give Archie my best."

Julia and Shane follow the red paver sidewalk toward the Raven Pub and I head for the Green. It's a roundabout way to get to

Archie's, my new home, but the lampposts illuminate the maze of walkways better than the high streetlights. As I approach the Old Men oak trees with their arm-like branches, my body buzzes with the alert of a nearby witch. I stop and survey the area but find no one.

"Is someone there? Seamus?" My voice reverberates off the stately DUB buildings, but no one replies.

A twinge of panic builds inside as I inspect the shadows of the red-brick buildings flanking the Green, sending my heart into overdrive. But the sensation disappears. What if it's not a witch's magic I am detecting? I've made that mistake before.

I pick up my pace until I'm jogging in my sneakers toward the alleyway to Douglas Street. When I turn the corner into the alley—BAM—I run into Dr. Seamus Duffy. His long black hair is tied behind his head as always and his sea-green eyes appear to glow in the dark—the nature of a cat sith witch.

"I'm so sorry. I wasn't expecting anyone to be in the alley."

"No harm done, Gwynedd," he says in a soft Irish brogue. "If I may ask. Why were you running? Attempting to get in some exercise before dinner?" He picks up the canvas bag full of books he dropped.

I laugh as I pant. "No. I sensed there was a witch nearby. When I didn't find anyone there, I got the heebie-jeebies."

"With all this worry about the Tuatha Dé and a Fomorian crossing over, I'd expect you to be wary. I was on the way to the library to return these books, but it wouldn't be a bother to walk you home."

"Nah. I'm jumpy, that's all. I haven't seen you since the solstice. How are you, Seamus?"

"Sound as a pound," he says, grinning.

I'm not convinced. A yearning remains in his eyes. It's clear he laments what can never be. It pains me to watch him suffer silently; a part of me wishes I could reciprocate. I cherish his friendship, but Archie will always hold my heart.

"Well, it was nice to chat. I should go. Archie probably has dinner ready. See you at the New Year's Eve party at the Pumpkin House?"

"Yes. I'm delighted to attend. Goodnight, Gwynedd."

I smile and hurry through the alleyway as the clicking of Seamus's cane echoes behind me. I was quite a distance from Seamus when I sensed his presence. Have my skills become so advanced I could detect him at such a distance?

CHAPTER THREE

A MESSAGE CUT SHORT

I PULL OFF THE bubble wrap from a framed photo and place it on the fireplace mantle. It's a selfie of Tyler and me he snapped on our first Yule without his dad. The abrasions from fighting the Sluagh are slightly visible, but I don't care. It represents the transition from our old life to this one. I didn't think it would be appropriate to display one with my husband, Richard. Archie wouldn't mind at all. But why would I want to have an image of my cheating husband glaring at me every day? Not to mention, Tyler has had mixed feelings about him since hearing what his father said to me at that initial Samhain ritual.

"The picture looks wonderful there." Archie enters the living room with an odd stride, as if there's a broomstick up his back. "Hang some of your paintings from storage wherever you want. All I ask is, please don't touch my weaponry display. There are dirks on the wall I cherish."

I shimmy to him and stroke his goatee. "I would never touch your *dirk* without your permission."

"As a matter of fact, I can remember many times you helped yourself to my dirk," he says, winking.

I snicker. "Don't worry. I won't mess with your antiques...unless you ask me to."

"You're welcome to examine them anytime. But keep them on the wall." He reaches behind his back and pulls out his family dirk, protected in its sheath.

"You're not gonna let it go, are you?" I ask, stepping back.

"You can't be certain it was Seamus you sensed on the Green. I'll remind you Nick Evans found you by tracking your magic scent. His Tuatha Dé family will do the same. You may need this again to defend yourself."

"Maybe, but Nuada's relatives would have to find me first, and the body is buried in California by now. Wherever they are, they're not in Bearsden yet."

"As far as you're able to discern. Please oblige me. I don't want to lose you, Gwynedd."

He passes the dirk to me and I recall when he came to my house on Mulberry Lane. It was moving day. I hadn't seen him since the night we banished the Sluagh and I wasn't ready to deal with the revelation of his womanizing past. But when he handed me his most prized heirloom, he had tears in his eyes. I knew in that moment he loved me, even if he couldn't express himself with words.

I peer up at his pleading icy blues. "Sure, I'll carry the dirk tonight. But then I want you to train Tyler on how to use it. I'd sleep better knowing he had your family's heirloom in his possession."

"Thank you for indulging me, my love," he says, kissing me on the cheek. "I'll invite him over for a quick session before we leave the country."

"Speaking of Seamus, I'm happy he's coming to the New Year's Eve Party. He needs to socialize more."

Archie's eyes wander. "Actually, he said he was staying in for the night. Said he wasn't up to a large gathering."

"Oh, he told me the other day he was going."

"Most of the coven are aware he is leaving at the end of the semester. He probably doesn't want them to fuss over him. Remember, he's a cat sith witch—solitary in his practice. The same for his friendships, I imagine. Although he has a few that remain close to his heart."

He curls a corner of his mouth. Of course, I understand his reference. But I can't do anything about Seamus's love for me. My cell phone plays *Don't Stop Believin'*. "I don't recognize the number. Hello?"

"Gwynedd Crowther?" The voice sounds thin and raspy, cracking as she speaks.

"Yes. This is Gwyn. Who is this?"

Archie turns an ear to me and I shrug.

"This is Riley Shaw. I'm a member of the Middletown Coven. Do you remember me?"

"It's Riley Shaw," I say, covering the phone microphone. "Of course I do. We are indebted to you. Mrs. Shaw, a plethora of people are searching for you. The media said you have dementia. You should go home. Tell me where you are. Archie Cockburn and I will come and pick you up."

A crackling laugh fills my ear. "My family will say anything to find me. My mind is as sound as the day I was born. I don't want to talk about this on the phone. There's so much I need to tell you. Can you meet me tonight?"

"Tonight? It's New Year's Eve, Riley. The Bearsden Coven is having a party."

"This is of utmost importance to your safety, Gwyn. Meet me in the Celestial Gardens at Mitchell Mansion. Be there at 11:30 p.m. You'll be back to the party in time for your New Year's kiss."

"I'll meet you then, I guess. But you should return home after we talk. Your family and coven are worried about you."

"They have reason." She clears her throat of phlegm. "See you soon." The connection disappears.

"That was fucking weird," I say, putting my phone in my purse. "Riley wants to meet me at 11:30 p.m. in the Celestial Gardens."

"What do you think she has to tell you?" Archie asks.

"No clue. But she says she has information about my safety. I'll find out soon enough. She sounded lucid to me. The dementia may come and go."

He rubs the whiskers of his goatee. "Should I walk there with you?"

"I don't think so. It could scare her off. I'll convince her to walk back to the Pumpkin House and we can call one of her children or a member of her coven."

The doorbell rings and I glance over at the foyer. "That's the lovebirds now. We shouldn't talk about this with them." I rush to the oak hall tree and shove the dirk into my backpack.

Tyler and his partner, Zoe Wu, enter. His facial structure resembles his father, but he inherited my chestnut hair and hazel eyes. He gets more handsome with each passing year, but it's the growth in his magic skills I admire the most.

Zoe is bubbly as ever, her warm brown eyes glowing with the zest of life. Her witchcraft skills were barely functional when I met her and she was so disorganized. But now, she's as competent as any other witch in the Bearsden Coven—the Fellowship of the Associated Pagans to Unremarkables. The neophytes are gone, replaced with skilled level three witches.

She pats her mittens together. "The temperature is dropping. You may want to wear a coat with a hood."

"I plan to." I grab my fleece jacket off the hall tree. "Hi, dear."

"Hi, Mom," Tyler says. "Are you guys ready to go?"

Archie slips on his leather coat and dons a plaid cap. "Aye. I'm looking forward to a night of festivities after the *battle at the bog*."

We head to the Pumpkin House via the Green under the luminescence of the waxing crescent moon. Archie, Tyler, and Zoe discuss the upcoming trip while my mind remains preoccupied with Riley Shaw's phone call.

Tyler waves a hand in front of my face. "Hel-looo. Why are you so quiet, Mom? We usually can't shut you up about visiting the UK."

"I'm just tired," I say, brushing off his concern. "Zoe, you must be excited. This is your first time visiting the area."

"I can't wait. Since the showdown at the bog, I've been too wound up to sleep through the night—dreaming about meeting *the hand*." Her signature wide grin brightens her face as she splays the fingers of her right hand.

I chuckle. "Yes. Aunt Gorawen's *magic butler* is amazing."

"How about you, Tyler?" Archie asks. "You must be chuffed to bits to meet your great-aunt in person finally."

"It's a little surreal. Only a couple of years ago, I didn't even know she existed. Or that I was an ancestral witch. Mom, shouldn't we conference with Nain and Taid before we go? Catch them up on what's happened?"

"Yeah. Why don't I come to your house on New Year's Day after lunch to conference? But let's not blow things out of proportion. My intuition might have signaled a Tuatha Dé crossed over, but I don't sense they're anywhere nearby. I won't worry my parents over the threat when Nuada's family may never find me."

Tyler nods. "Don't you mean us? They could discover my magic scent, too."

"That would suck," Zoe blurts out. "Could that really happen?"

I glance at Archie. "Let's not lose sleep over it. We don't know what's gonna transpire."

"Your mum and I spoke about training you on the use of my family's dirk. Witches need not fret about such things when they're well-prepared."

"Sounds good, Archie," Tyler says.

Zoe wraps her arm around my son's, peering up at him with soulful eyes. I want to tell her not to stress about all this talk of dirks and evil fairies. But the truth is—she should be concerned.

Nuada threatened to take Tyler with him to the Otherworld if I didn't go with him freely. She must remember that night.

When we arrive at the Pumpkin House, the festivities are in full gear. Tyler and Zoe rush off to hang with the young witches in the dining room. The Ericksons are there as well. As Archie and I move to the parlor, the older witches are making googly eyes at Luna, Ronnie and Derek's baby. Jasmine Moore is holding the infant while my best friend and her partner relish the attention. A woman with an amiable disposition, Jasmine is engaged to Elijah Jackson, a social worker and director of the Bearsden shelter. He also serves on the Bearsden City Council. The gentle giant of a man gazes at his love while she soaks up a few minutes of mothering the infant in her arms.

"I can't wait to begin a family," she says as she puts a pacifier in Luna's mouth. "Elijah and I want to start soon after we're married."

Ronnie's azure eyes sparkle with joy. "Becoming a mother is the most magical thing to happen to me in my life. I endorse it wholeheartedly."

"I felt incomplete before meeting Ronnie and having Luna." Derek nudges Elijah. "Good luck to you both."

"Thank you, my man," Elijah replies.

Leslie pushes her silver side-swept bangs from her copper eyes. "I, for one, feel blessed. I can die an extremely happy woman knowing the coven will prosper for years to come with the infusion of new offspring."

"Always about the survival of the fucking coven," Agnes says, frowning. "But Luna is cute with all those strawberry blond curls." She leans over the infant, rubbing her belly, and her salt-and-pepper hair falls like a curtain on either side of her face. "Coochie-coochie-coo."

Our coven leader squeezes next to her. "Don't hog the baby. Aunty Trinity wants to get her loving in."

Elijah's deep belly laugh fills the space. "You would make a fantastic grandmother, Agnes."

"Are you fucking with me?" she asks, scowling.

"No, I mean it," he replies. "You're hiding honey inside your curmudgeon exterior, and you know it."

I chime in. "Hello, everyone. Agnes, you and I both are aware you're hiding a sweet old lady under that bitchy facade."

She twists her face into a knot. "Aww, fuck you."

Laughter takes over the parlor and the young witches send us glares of annoyance from the dining room.

"Agnes, I can truthfully say one thing about you," Archie says. "You would make quite the unconventional grandmother."

Trinity guffaws. "No lies told. Agnes, we both know you'd be devoted. You certainly helped me out when I was younger. As much as you don't want to admit it, you have a loving streak underneath all that gruff."

"Now you're just insulting me." She flips us the bird.

"Oh, Agnes." Leslie hugs her partner. "Accept the compliments, dear. You can show your soft side on occasion."

The hedge witch attempts to quash a smile, but she isn't fooling anyone. "OK, sweetheart."

"Trinity, where's Charlie?" Archie asks.

"She's coming later with more desserts. Had to work late."

Our coven leader's wife, Charlie, is an Unremarkable but is *in the knowing*. She's charming, and her calm demeanor compliments Trinity's boisterous personality. They have an adult daughter who lives out of state.

"It's so nice to spend time with everyone away from what's been going on." I attempt to hide my continuing concerns with small talk, especially the recent phone call with Riley Shaw. "This was a wonderful idea to take our minds off the recent events." I glance at Archie and back to our coven leader.

"Is that right?" she replies, her jade eyes squinting. "Would you two mind helping me in the kitchen for a minute? I told Charlie I'd have some plates ready for her Yule cookies."

"Sure," Archie replies. "We'd be happy to."

I glare at him as we make our way to the small kitchen in the back, following the echo of Trinity's spike heels clicking on the wooden floor. When we pass through the doorway, the questions fly out of her mouth.

"What are you hiding? Has something happened I should know about? Your twitchy eyes and fidgeting always give you away, lady."

"Was I fidgeting?" I glance down at my fingers, tapping a mile a minute on my thigh, and fold them together. "I'm not hiding anything. Tonight was supposed to be a celebration to loosen up, not add more knots to the rope. I was going to fill you in later, after the party."

"What the hell are you talking about?" she asks.

Archie interjects. "Are you aware of the missing person from Middletown—Riley Shaw?"

"Yeah. That crone witch who helped us to banish the Sluagh, the one who has dementia. They hadn't found her yet the last I heard." She tilts her head. "Did they find her?"

"No," I say. "She called me right before we left the house."

"What? She had a cell with her? Or did she call from a police station?"

"She had a phone. I tried to get her to tell me where she was so we could pick her up, but she wouldn't. She asked me to meet her in the Celestial Gardens at 11:30 p.m. She said she has information regarding my safety."

"What the hell," Trinity says. "How is she even functioning?"

"She sounded fine to me. As coherent as she ever was."

Archie runs a hand through his hair. "Riley probably has lucid moments, but the mention of Gwyn's safety is alarming."

Trinity puts a hand on her hip. "If she has dementia, she could be confusing past dangers with the present day. But I note your concerns, Archie. Are you going alone?"

"Yes," I say. "I don't want to scare her off. If you're right, she could be confusing many memories. I need to convince her to come back to the party. Then we can call the Bearsden Police and her family."

Trinity nods. "Sounds good. I'll share this with the older witches later. No need to concern the youngins. Let's each grab a platter. I don't want anyone questioning why we came back empty-hand-ed."

We carry the serving plates to the dining room and place them on the dessert table just as Charlie arrives. Trinity rushes to the door to help her with the bags of cookies. Archie and I catch the end of a conversation among the young witches and Unremarkables as we rearrange the desserts. Spence Huxley, my old classmate and current DUB teaching assistant, appears perplexed, his hands flailing all over as he talks to Courtney and John Erickson.

"Let me get this straight. There are portals all over in random places. Why even bother closing the one in Bearsden?"

"Lots of reasons," she says. "The Bearsden portal provides easier access for other beings to come through here and wreak havoc on the town. The most important one—it's a front door for Nuada's family to find Gwyn."

John takes a sip of wine. "He has a point, though. We can close this portal, and they could cross over through another one and come here."

"So, don't bother at all?" Spence's partner, Tanner Jones, cocks his head. "That seems fatalist."

"Does it matter right now?" Skye McGowen asks in her husky voice. "Gwyn's intuition revealed Nuada's family is already here somewhere."

I turn my head to find Tyler staring at me.

"Oops," Zoe says, clenching her teeth.

My son states the obvious. "Sorry, Mom. We were debating the actual necessity of closing the portal in the mound now that...you know."

"You may as well say it. Since the fairies trying to kill her have already crossed over through it?" Zach Ward blurts out. Skye's boyfriend is an Unremarkable, but the supernatural world never appears to faze him. "No offense, Courtney."

"No offense taken," she says. "Entirely different fairies with tremendous egos."

Archie raises a corner of his mouth. "Zach, I applaud you for not tip-toeing around the subject."

"And you don't have to. I'm very aware of the threat," I say. "But let's try to forget about it for one night. We'll deal with the problem *if* Nuada's family ever shows up. My intuition pointed to the possibility. That's all." But the vision of the gray-skinned monster still lurks in my brain.

Spence gives me a one-armed hug. "Sis, I'm proud of you. I say let's get this party rolling."

"I agree," Archie says. "Only positives thoughts the rest of the night. Who needs a drink?"

Jeff Williams and Ashley Lewis arrive sans Aidan. They rush over to join us while Archie retrieves some drinks.

"Sorry we're late," Ashley says, removing her coat. "We had to wait for the babysitter. A grad student who Aidan adores."

"What? He loves someone more than me?" I ask.

Jeff pats my arm. "Don't worry. You're still his favorite babysitter because you have *invisible hands*." He waves his fingers around.

"I'm kidding," I say. "It's great you found a student who was willing to give up a night of fun so you could enjoy the evening."

Archie returns with a platter of half full wine glasses. I wave to the older witches in the parlor to join us and they amble over, grabbing a drink at the refreshment table when they arrive. Trinity encourages everyone to form a small circle and she begins.

"I know it's not midnight yet, but I want to say something to all of you now. We had a very trying time this Yule season. When one of our own was snatched from her cradle, we all rose to the occasion as usual." She searches for Ronnie and grasps her gaze with a nod. "Luckily, we have much to celebrate with the rescue of all the children from Alys Morgan, the Tylwyth Teg fairy who fooled us all. Let's drink to our witch family and supportive friends, even those from the Otherworld. If we can't accept them, too, who are we?"

Agnes grimaces and I nudge her. Leslie sends her partner a judgy scowl. Everyone takes a sip of their drink of choice and we all respond with cheers of "here's to a New Year" and "blessed Yule."

The rest of the evening disappears as we reminisce about past Yules. I recall that Winter Solstice morning where Archie gave me my mortar and pestle—and the dragon necklace—the calm before the storm. Ronnie and Derek are the first to depart the festivities. Ashley and Jeff follow soon after. When I finally glance at my cell phone, it reads 11:15 p.m.

I whisper to Archie, "I need to go. If anyone asks, tell them I went to check on the Seelie Fae."

"As good an excuse as any," he says, kissing me on the cheek. "Make it back by midnight, my love. I want you here for Auld Lang Syne."

"Of course, honey. See you soon."

I put on my fleece jacket, grab my backpack, and slip out the back door. The chill in the air encourages me to walk briskly to Mitchell Mansion. As I hurry through the Green, a buzzing prompts me to stop. I survey the area, sparsely lit by lampposts. All I find are eerie shadows created by the stately oak trees guarding the paver walkways and the white vapors of my steamy breath. I shake off my witch alarm and proceed hastily to the Celestial Gardens.

When I arrive, I admire the stately Federalist house once owned by Rose and Alistair Mitchell. Protected by an iron fence, the mansion harks to bygone days when the couple lived here, hoping to start a family. But the fertility spell cast by Leslie, Agnes, and my mom had unintended consequences, opening the portal in the mound.

I rush through the gate and call out, "Riley, are you here? Mrs. Shaw." Only the echo of my voice resounds in the winter's tomb of barren limbs and frosted greenery.

The portal lights up with magic swirls, rotating left and right. The fae children, Shailagh and Aonghas, cross over and skip to me, their long golden hair flying behind them. Moonbeams spot their mint-green eyes.

"Aunt Gwyn! You came to play with us!" They rub their peachy skin. "It's so cold here."

"I don't have time to play tonight," I say, wrapping my arms around them. "Did you see an old woman in here?"

"No, Aunty Gwyn," they reply in unison. "We sensed your presence and came to play."

"I'm sorry I can't tonight. You should cross back over. Humans are up late this evening. They may come in here." I turn my curious gaze to the gate. "I have to go. The person I was meeting hasn't arrived, and I have to return to my friends. Be careful."

"Goodnight, Aunt Gwyn." They dart off, skipping around a few of the fairy fountains in the gardens, and return to the Other-world.

I peek past the iron gate before I exit and dart to the paver sidewalk in front of Mitchell Mansion. To my right, a few patrons at the Raven Pub spill out onto the porch in the distance, their laughter traveling down the road to me. I scan Main Street on my left. A group of townies stagger on the sidewalk before entering the next bar. Riley still isn't here. My phone screen reads 11:45 p.m. I can't wait any longer. If her dementia comes and goes, she likely forgot she had scheduled to meet me here.

I jaywalk across Main Street toward the Green. When I reach the Old Men oak trees, lit by the hazy glow of a lamppost, my body buzzes with the warning of a witch nearby. The petite figure of a pale, old woman emerges from behind the trunks—Riley Shaw of Middletown. She's frail and trembling in a thin sweater that's barely enough to warm anyone in fall temperatures, let alone the winter chill. I dart to her.

"Riley, are you OK? You're shaking. You must be freezing in that cardigan. Please, come with me to the Pumpkin House. We have hot chocolate to warm you up."

She struggles to speak, the words tripping over her tongue. "I...I...need...to warn you. You're in...danger."

"What are you talking about, Riley? How am I in danger?" I ask, warming her shoulders with my hands.

The old crone witch passes out. I try to break her fall by shoving my arms between her body and the ground, but she slides past them and lands on the grassy area underneath the Old Men oaks. I kneel next to her and place my backpack under her feet.

"Mrs. Shaw! Riley!"

She opens her eyes and stares into my soul, a sense of fear painted across her ghostly face. "She seeks...to harm you. You must—"

Riley's eyelids slowly close and her body goes limp. I lay a hand over her nose—no signs of breathing. I press my ear against her chest to check for a pulse. Nothing. I chant to summon my amber magic and apply my radiating hand to heal her. But I'm zapped—a hex. I snatch my cell phone from my purse and call 911.

"An old woman has collapsed on the Green under the oak trees. Send an ambulance!"

I hang up, not wanting to give them my information, and send Archie a text.

Me: *Come quick! I'm with Riley Shaw near the Old Men oaks!*
Archie: *What happened? Why are you on the Green?*
Me: *I think Riley is dead.*

Chapter Four

A WITCH'S WARNING

THE AMBULANCE SIRENS SCREECH like banshees in the far-off distance as I attempt to revive Riley Shaw. I chant different spells, applying my magic, but I have no access to herbs or crystals to implement them effectively. The air around us turns foggy with my erratic breathing as I attempt over and over to revive the Middletown crone.

"Oh, Mrs. Shaw. Please, come back. It's not time for you to cross over to the Otherworld. I need you to tell me who wants to harm me."

With each application of my magic, the hex on Riley pushes back, stinging me several times. As footsteps approach, I try one more time to remove the malevolent spell, but collapse on my butt with exhaustion. I've failed the old crone—and myself.

"Gwynedd!" Archie's voice appears distant, muffled by the increasing volume of the sirens.

Trinity's distinct tone breaks through the piercing noise. "Gwyn!"

"Mom?" Tyler asks, tapping me on the shoulder. "Are you OK?"

My son catches his breath as Archie and Trinity arrive. My partner drops to the ground to examine Riley. Our coven leader bends over, leaning on her knees. She's holding her spiked heels in one hand.

"I'm getting way too old for this shit," she says, gasping for air.

"If we can remove the hex in time, we may be able to revive her," Archie says.

"Sounds good to me, but I can't help with something like this." Tyler kneels next to me, wrapping an arm around my shoulder.

"Archie can handle this." Trinity stands upright. "Do it."

My partner floats his palm over the crone witch, amber emanating from his skin. He chants a spell I don't recognize, but the hex repels him. Trinity joins him and they perform another and another, working diligently as one to remove the wicked spell as the sirens grow louder. Tyler continues to embrace me, as I have no energy left. They try one last time. With the final attempt, there is no pushback.

Trinity shakes her head at us. "I'm calling it. The paramedics are almost here. We did our best."

Archie pushes off the ground and walks around the body to Tyler and me. He kneels down and takes my hand in his. "What happened here, my love?" he asks.

My eyes bounce among them before I speak. "I hung out in the Celestial Gardens for Riley, but she didn't turn up on time. I waited another five minutes and left. When I approached the Old Men oak trees, I sensed the presence of a witch. She stepped out. I tried to convince her to go back to the Pumpkin House with me, but she said she had to warn me about something."

"About what?" Tyler asks, a wrinkle creasing between his eyes.

I stare at Riley's lifeless body. "She said a woman seeks to harm me."

Archie flinches. "What? How?"

"And who is this mysterious woman?" Trinity asks.

"I don't know. Riley passed out before she could tell me."

"Well, that sucks," Tyler says. "What if the woman is a member of Nuada's family? She could have gotten involved in the Middletown coven—masked herself as a witch. Aunt Gorawen said the Tuatha Dé Danann were cunning."

Trinity nods. "Nick Evans certainly was."

"Shit. What if the woman who caused this is his mother?" my son asks.

"You're forgetting one thing." I stand with Archie's help. "If a hex killed Riley—kept her from warning me—the woman must be a witch."

Archie examines Riley's body again. "It's like no hex I have ever experienced."

"Me neither," Trinity says as the emergency medical vehicles approach. "Tyler, we should get the hell out of dodge. We don't need the cops asking us questions, too. Everyone being here may spark suspicion. Archie, you stay with Gwyn. It would make sense she called you."

"Aye, I agree," he replies.

Tyler hugs me. "Good thing we're leaving for Great Britain soon. I'll call you later."

"Bye, dear. You better get going."

I pat his back and he rushes off with Trinity to the Pumpkin House. The chill nips at my nose and cheeks as people dressed in heavy winter coats run toward us. Their shadows flicker under the light of the lampposts. I sure hope they didn't catch Trinity and Tyler leaving. Archie takes off his coat and lays it over Riley's cold body. My eyes well up.

"She risked her life for me and I couldn't do anything to save her."

He stands and wraps an arm around my shoulder. "The local covens have always had our backs. No one will hold this against you."

"It never occurred to me her message would contain anything more than an incoherent bundle of blather, a symptom of her dementia." I wipe a tear from my cheek.

"The Bearsden Police and EMTs are here. We should be vague about what happened."

"You know I'm terrible at lying. I'll do my best."

We move a few feet away from Riley while the EMTs check her vitals. Officer Braddock Wilson approaches us. I'm always taken aback by his extreme height. He has a few inches on Elijah Jackson. Officer Quinn O'Connor, not even five-feet tall, is his street partner. She kneels next to Mrs. Shaw's lifeless body. Seeing these two city servants together usually prompts me to chuckle, but not tonight.

"Good evening. I know you. Gwynedd Crowther, right?" he asks, taking out his cell phone.

"Yes," I reply. "You can call me Gwyn."

"A woman called 911. Was that you?"

"Yeah, I didn't leave my name because I was trying to revive her."

"I see." But his rapidly blinking eyes hint he may not. "You administered CPR to the old wo—"

"Her name is Riley Shaw. She's the woman with dementia in the news who was missing. But no. I didn't administer CPR. I haven't had training for years." How do I tell this Unremarkable the truth without spilling the beans? "I did what I could to revive her, but it didn't work."

He types onto his phone screen and addresses Archie. "Were you with her? I remember you, too. You're a professor at DUB."

"I am. Dr. Archibald Cockburn. No, I wasn't here when Mrs. Shaw passed. Gwyn sent me a text and I came running. The Fellowship of Associated Pagans is having a New Year's Eve party nearby."

I glance over at Riley's body. She's in the Otherworld now. All because she was trying to protect me from someone. But who?

Officer Wilson adjusts his cap. "Ma'am, I have to ask. What in the hell were you doing out here on the Green? Were you super late for the party?"

Fuck. I peer at Archie, my heart taking off like a jet. I can't lie to Officer Wilson, but I don't have to divulge everything, either.

"Mrs. Shaw called me and said she needed to talk to me, so I left the party to meet her. Not wanting to scare her off, I decided I should convince her to return to the Pumpkin House." My gaze floats back to the officer. "When I got to the Old Men oaks, I told her she should come back with me. She barely spoke to me before she collapsed. That's when I called 911."

"You should have called them immediately, ma'am. Maybe the EMTs—"

"Getting here sooner wouldn't have made a wee bit of difference," Archie interjects. "Mrs. Shaw wasn't dressed for the weather. My guess is hypothermia affected her. Gwyn did the best she could to help Mrs. Shaw."

Oh, I could kiss you, Archie. By all means, officer, blame me without knowing all the facts. To be fair, I can't tell him the truth.

"I understand what you're saying," Officer Wilson replies. "Be prepared for lots of questions. What did Mrs. Shaw say to you?"

No lying needed for this response. "Nothing really. She passed out before she could tell me."

"Probably nonsense. Sounds like the dementia was far gone if she was wearing a thin sweater. If the department has any more questions, we'll contact you."

The EMTs have loaded Riley Shaw's body onto a gurney and are rolling it into the back of the ambulance. As the doors slam shut, the campus carillon begins playing Auld Lang Syne. Quinn O'Connor joins us.

"They couldn't revive Mrs. Shaw. She was gone by the time the EMTs arrived," she says in her mouse-like voice. "What a terrible way to ring in the New Year. Did you finish interviewing them?"

Officer Wilson nods. "For now. The medical examiner may have some questions in a couple of days, Ms. Crowther."

"Oh. I'm leaving for the UK on January 2nd. I'll be gone for most of the month."

"We're heading there to visit my family," Archie says, wrapping an arm around me to limit my fidgeting.

"But I can give you my email address. I usually check it regularly."

"I'll pass that on." Braddock Wilson puts his cell away and pulls on his cap.

"We're sorry you had to deal with this," Officer O'Connor says. "We'll contact the family. I recommend you go home now. Nothing more to celebrate tonight."

She's right about that. My midnight kiss evaporated into the frigid air with the chiming of the carillon. This New Year has begun with the death of a respected and beloved crone witch—one who gave her life to save me. I stare at the back of the ambulance and my stomach churns like curdled milk.

Officer Wilson tips his cap. "A Happy New Year to you both."

"To you as well," Archie replies. "And thank you for working on this dismal night."

The campus carillon finishes playing as they rush to their car and the ambulance takes off toward the city morgue.

"Do you think Officer Wilson believed me?" I ask.

Archie shrugs. "You didn't lie, but be prepared to give the examiner more specific answers. You may have to stretch the truth. But if you do...keep that rubber band of statements straight. Once you contradict yourself, they'll suspect foul play."

"We should get back to the party, although I'm not in the mood to talk about Riley and what she said right now."

He kisses the top of my head. "Why don't you go home? I'll help the others tear down. They've cleaned up already, more than likely, anyway. We can talk when I get back. You have the dirk?"

"Yes. It's in my backpack."

He presses on my bag until he feels the point of the leather sheath.

"Don't worry about me. I'm not the weak, demure woman you first met."

"No, you aren't, my love." He kisses me. "I miss that naïve Unremarkable occasionally, but I love the powerful witch you've become. It doesn't mean I won't fret about your safety every waking moment you're not with me."

I caress his cheek. "See you when you get home. I'll be waiting in bed for a proper midnight kiss."

"If the evening hadn't taken this grave turn, I'd give you more than that," he says with a wink.

"I know you're joking, but I'm not in the mood."

"I expect not. See you at home, my love."

Archie hugs me and takes off toward the Pumpkin House while I follow the red-brick pavers to the shortcut to Douglas Street. When I turn into the creepy alley, I spy a tall, thin man leaning against the exterior wall of Menzies Hall, cane in hand. He blends in with the shadows in his long winter coat and jet-black hair. I smile as I approach him.

"Have you been waiting here for me, Seamus?"

He shifts from the wall to his cane. "A few minutes. I heard the sirens and came to investigate. I observed what transpired from afar. Did you lose a friend tonight?"

"More of an acquaintance. Riley Shaw was a member of the Middletown Coven. She guided us through opening a large portal a couple of years ago so we could banish an evil Sluagh back to the Otherworld."

"Why don't we converse as we walk," he says, motioning forward with a hand. "This was the Sluagh that tried to kill you if I'm not mistaken."

"Yes. Thanks to Riley and the Bearsden Coven, I am here. But Mrs. Shaw assisted us many times. And she was trying to help again."

His cane clicks on the pavement as we stroll toward his house. He hesitates for a moment. "If I may ask, what transpired tonight?"

"There was a missing person alert announced for the whereabouts of Riley. Her family said she was experiencing dementia. Then, out of nowhere, I got a call from her. She asked me to meet her in the Celestial Gardens at 11:30 p.m. Sounded as coherent as anyone I know. I waited for fifteen minutes and gave up. When I arrived at the Old Men oaks, she emerged from behind the trunks. She tried to tell me something, but words were garbled in her throat, like someone was stopping her from speaking."

"Interesting. What did she manage to convey to you?"

"That she needed to warn me about a woman who wants to harm me. I don't know what to think. Her family said she had dementia, so the threat could all be in her head. But..."

Seamus lays a comforting hand on my arm. "I sense there's more to this. If you believe Mrs. Shaw had dementia, why be concerned?"

"When I tried to revive her, I was zapped by magic."

"Ah," he says, nodding. "You suspect a hex."

"Yes. Malevolent magic that killed her with every stab of her spoken words. I believe she knew it would kill her, but she felt compelled to warn me of the danger. A true and dependable witch. She gave her life for me."

We have arrived at Seamus's brown bungalow and stop at the flagstone walkway that leads to the front door.

"Gwynedd, do not let guilt eat away at your soul. Mrs. Shaw would not have wanted you to blame yourself. You would do the same if your loved ones were in danger. She must have cared about you more than you realize."

"I suppose. I'm exhausted and need to get to bed. Thank you for talking."

He smiles warmly. "Gwynedd, I am happy to listen anytime."

"Seamus, can I ask you something?"

"Of course. Anything."

"Why didn't you attend the party tonight? You said you were coming?" Archie told me, but I need to hear it from him.

He taps his cane nervously. "I'm leaving Bearsden at the end of this semester. Maintaining multiple friendships is difficult for cat sith witches. It's why we are solitary in our craft—one of many reasons. I will fare better if I prepare for my exit on my own terms."

Exit? That's a rather final way to describe his moving. "But you're not saying goodbye, Seamus. We'll meet up with you in Buckley occasionally, I hope."

"Perhaps," he says as his eyes fall to the pavement.

"Seamus, you know I care about what happens to you, don't you? I consider our close relationship something...special."

He lifts his head and smiles faintly. "Yes. I value our friendship highly as well. My life would be less without having met you, Gwynedd."

"I feel the same," I reply, a grin erupting. "Goodnight, good friend."

"May you find a quick path to slumber."

Seamus turns and walks up the flagstone path, his cane clicking until he reaches the front door. I continue on to Duncan Street.

On my stroll home, the image of Riley Shaw dying in my arms returns to me. I swallow to hold back the tears. Why did she sacrifice herself to warn me? And who is this evil woman who seeks to harm me?

CHAPTER FIVE

SUSPICIONS

I stir with the bounce of the bed and roll over. Archie is leaning against the Walnut Victorian headboard and browsing his cell phone. I caress his arm and he leans down to kiss me.

"Good morning, my love. I'm sorry. Did I wake you when I got back into bed? I waited as long as I could, but the bladder called."

"It's OK. I slept like a log. Didn't hear you come in. What time is it? I told Ronnie I would stop by this morning."

He glances at his cell. "Quarter to nine. I understand you want to visit her before we go, but the day is packed now."

"Well, I didn't plan on the death of a local witch snatching a spot on my agenda. I chose not to practice with the crystal grid. No energy left to deal with the possible visions—like they're ever going to return at this rate. Even my intuition seems to be stunted. Lack of focus, I guess." I sit up on my elbow and rest my head on his arm. "Any news about Riley on there?"

"Several articles, actually. They are stating her death was most likely due to natural causes and hypothermia, but the incident is being investigated."

"Hmph. We know better. But what will a medical examination show? They have no skills to test for a malevolent spell."

"She was a witch, but she had a decade on Agnes. The hex may have finished her off, but it was the elements of the earth that started her decline."

"You told everyone at the party about Mrs. Shaw?"

"Only the members of the Fellowship. The guests had left. Trinity and Leslie want to convene a circle tonight before we depart for Scotland. I suggested they take the leftovers from the party to the farm, so we can eat dinner during our discussion. A text notification is probably waiting on your phone. They were going to contact the Middletown Coven leader to find out more information regarding Riley—whether there is any truth to the dementia story."

"That's good. What if Tyler is right? That this *woman* who's after me is Nuada's mother? I know what I'd do if I found the witch who killed my fairy son." I slice my neck with an index finger.

He chuckles. "Oh, I think she'd do more than slit your throat, Gwyn. I suspect she'd want you to suffer a long and excruciating death."

"Aren't you comforting," I say, frowning. "I won't let it dictate how I live. Until Nuada's family shows up, I'm living my life. But I will maintain a list of possible suspects going forward. I have to approach the future with a level head and prepare. And we all need to create protection pouches to avoid being glamoured. I refuse to go through that again."

He strokes the tip of his goatee. "Aye. We should investigate spells while we're visiting my kin. Much older grimoires in Scotland. We are bound to find one. Meanwhile, you and Tyler will be safe across the pond."

My cell vibrates on the nightstand and I flip it over to see the screen—a phone call. "Unknown number. Could be spam, but the prefix is a city number, I think." I swipe the green icon. "Hello?"

"Good morning," the familiar, gruff male voice responds. "Am I speaking with Gwynedd Crowther?"

"Yeah, this is Gwyn. Can I help you?" I peer up at Archie and shrug.

"Yes, Detective Jack Schmidt from the Bearsden Police Department. Good to speak with you again, Gwyn. We've spoken a few times in the past. I know it's New Year's Day, but I have a few questions regarding the passing of Riley Shaw. Officer Braddock Wilson told me you were there."

Archie whispers, "Who is it?"

I mouth the words, "It's Jack Schmidt."

"Ms. Crowther, are you there?"

"Yes. Sorry. I'm still in bed. It's New Year's Day after all. I'm surprised to hear from you today."

"And I apologize. But some of us don't take off. Not when an unusual death occurs."

I sit up straight in bed, my heart thumping in my chest. "What do you mean, *unusual death*? Didn't Riley pass away from natural causes?"

Archie silently shouts, "What?!"

"I'm not at liberty to discuss the case. Officer Wilson said you are leaving for Great Britain tomorrow. Would you mind answering some questions this afternoon?"

Archie shakes his head nervously. But how do I say no?

"Sure, but my availability is slim. I still need to pack some things, and I'm spending time with family before we leave for the airport." It's not a lie. The Fellowship is my family.

"I can work with that," he replies. "How about I stop by at 1 p.m.?"

"Sure," I say, swallowing my panic.

"You're on Drummond Lane, correct?" he asks.

"No, I live on Duncan Street. Dr. Archie Cockburn's house. You probably have his address."

"Oh, I see." He clears his throat. "In that case, if the professor doesn't mind, I'll ask him some questions as well. Thank you for cooperating, Gwynedd—I mean, Ms. Crowther. We'll talk at one."

The cell signal disconnects and I throw my phone down. "I don't have time to deal with this. My day is full. I'm stopping by Ronnie's and then I have to conference with my parents at Tyler and Zoe's."

"You should have told him you'd speak with him when you got back from the UK," Archie says.

"Like the detective was going to wait a month for me to return?" I puff a breath in frustration. "I don't think so."

"Aye. You're right, as always. Better to nip it in the bud." He wraps his arms around me. "Nothing to fret about. Tell him what happened, but keep the magic part of the equation to yourself."

I kiss him and slide out of bed. "Better get in the shower."

"I'll start breakfast." He heads out the door.

While I'm basking in the warmth of the hot water, it occurs to me. No one should ever be on a first name basis with the local detective.

I sip my Earl Grey tea while Ronnie nurses Luna. She drinks a nutritious glass of milk. My heart overflows with emotion, absorbing the scene. My best friend wanted a baby for so long, and now her little one is here, despite the evil desires of Alys Morgan. Her crimson curls fall off her shoulder, covering the infant's head, and she pushes the locks aside.

"I'm so happy for you, Ronnie. You deserve this life with Derek and Luna."

She removes Luna from her nipple and rests Luna's head on her shoulder, patting her back lightly. "I just wish she would sleep better. The trauma of the kidnapping messed up her sleeping. She was doing so well before. Other than that, she appears to be OK. I can't thank you and the coven enough."

"Whether or not we want to, the thanks should go to Courtney Erickson. I can't believe we owe her anything."

I grimace inwardly, thinking of the false accusations Courtney made against Archie the night of the Winter Solstice Celebration. "She saved Luna and the other children. She has earned my respect. But I understand if you have issues trusting her."

"She's moving on with her life. I can, too."

Derek shuffles in wearing his pajama pants and a T-shirt. "Morning, ladies." He kisses Ronnie and bends down to place a kiss on Luna's head. "You, too, my little witch."

He must have gotten past his reservations about raising Luna with magic until she's older.

"Good morning," I say. "Seems like you've warmed up to the idea of raising a witch." I take another sip of tea. "Tough night?"

Ronnie answers for him. "Except for her middle of the night feeding, he entertained her all night. That's why he slept in. Good thing today is New Year's Day. The fitness center is closed."

"It's not so bad," he says, pouring himself a cup of coffee. "I get to spend special dad time with her. Just me and you, Luna." He sits down next to his love and gulps down his morning caffeine. "Thanks for making the coffee, babe. It must kill you to smell it."

She inhales the aroma and cackles. "At least I can suck it in through my nostrils. He's so good with her, Gwyn." She wipes drool off Luna's mouth and cradles her in her arms. "I admit my stress level hasn't receded yet. She has to sense it."

"You need sleep, babe. That's all." He finishes the last of his coffee and sets the mug on the table. "Why don't I take Luna back for her nap? You girls can chat. I'll catch a few more winks."

Derek lifts Luna from Ronnie's arms and returns to the bedroom. I glance at the mountain of dishes in the sink and on the counter.

"Why don't I load the dishwasher while we chat? You put your feet up and rest."

"Thanks. I meant to load it last night, but I decided I want to spend as much time with Luna as possible. She's already grown. Besides, my parents are coming tomorrow to visit again."

The plates clink as I place them in the slots. "I'm glad they're visiting. Have you ever told them you're a witch?"

"Nah. They know I follow pagan holidays, though. They said it was weird at first, but they saw how well I was doing with the new friendships and support. After my abusive ex, they want me to be happy. Are you excited about the trip to Scotland and Wales?"

"Yeah. I wish I weren't leaving Bearsden with the uncertainty concerning Riley Shaw." I wipe down the counters with a sponge and toss it in the sink.

"It's scary not knowing who cast a hex on her...and why? Do you have any hunches?"

I plop into the kitchen chair. "No clue. Tyler thinks it's Nuada's mother. Archie says it would explain the strange magic he discovered. So, it could be a fairy. Who knows? But it may have nothing to do with Nick's family at all. I'm relieved Tyler is going with us, though. Gets him away from here for a couple of weeks while the coven pokes around."

"He's probably excited to go. He gets to meet his great-aunt." Ronnie shifts on her sitting donut, flinching.

"I couldn't have survived without my donut for the first few weeks. Use it as long as you have to and carry it with you everywhere."

"You know it. Was Shane upset you'll be gone so long?"

"No. He's too excited about training Julia to take over for me at the end of the semester." I recall Julia's less than adequate skills. "I don't want to judge, but what do you think of Shane's new girlfriend?"

Ronnie swallows the last of her milk. "I thought she was sweet. Why? Please, tell me you don't have a problem with Julia. What could you possibly not like about her?"

"Oh, I think she's great. She's so nice, and Shane loves her. I get the impression she reminds him of his first wife. But..."

"But what?"

"She's not very tech savvy. She doesn't seem to know anything about tech, not even how to use a cell phone. Shane has been teaching her, though. I've been instructing her on how to work a cash register. It's as if she has never used them before—ever."

Ronnie cocks her head. "That's weird. Even older Boomers usually know how to check their email."

"Yeah. It's odd, but Shane floats on a cloud when Julia is around." I glance at my watch and grab my purse. "I have to go. This day is way too packed. I'm conferencing with my parents at Tyler's home before lunch, and Detective Jack Schmidt is coming to the house afterward to talk to me about what happened last night."

"Oh, no. Are you concerned?"

"Not really, but I have to tiptoe around the entire incident. The Bearsden Police are a bit upset I didn't call them immediately after Riley called. I may have to explain myself more in detail. That's where it gets complicated. If Jack Schmidt is involved, the medical examiner must have noticed the death was odd."

"Good luck. Don't let it worry you. You'll be fine. Excuse me if I don't get up."

"Don't you dare," I say, wrapping her in a tight hug. "We'll do lunch when I return in a month. Luna will be so big! You'll need to send me pictures while I'm there."

"Thanks, and I will. Thanks for filling me in since I won't be at the circle. Have a wonderful time."

"It's more work than a visit on this trip, but it will be great to see Aunt Gorawen again. Relish your leave with Luna. Bye."

I rush out of the house, eager to get to Tyler's. As I drive to Drummond Lane, I run dialogue in my head of Jack's expected questions. I'll answer with limited facts and maybe—a pinch of magic.

As I pull into the driveway of Leslie's former quaint Tudor home, I recall my stay here. When I first moved in, it was to spy on her. When I discovered she'd been hiding the secret of the Tuatha Dé prophecy, I didn't think I'd ever have it in me to forgive her. But now? I miss my time with her and Mr. Yeats, her old busybody familiar. I rush to the front door and knock. Zoe answers the door.

"Hi, Gwyn! Tyler is in the magic room getting things set up for the conference. Is it OK for me to join you? His Nain and Taid are so nice—for dead people, I mean."

"Sure," I say, walking down the hallway. "The session can't be long. I have to get back to the house by one."

We enter the magic room where Tyler has the photo of my parents propped up. He's ground star anise and mugwort in a bowl. I am so proud of the man he has grown into—the witch he's become.

"Hey, Mom. All I have to do is burn the herbs and we can begin. I love having a house with a magic room. Zoe and I have been practicing new spells."

She grabs the lighter. "It's so much fun to experiment."

"Please don't bring a gnome to life again, OK?" I ask.

She grins as she lights the divination mixture. "I wasn't as skilled as I am now. That was a huge oops."

"You're doing well," Tyler says, kissing her cheek. "Are we ready?"

I remove my winter coat and throw it on the chair. "Yes. I only have a few minutes. That Bearsden detective is coming by the house around 1 p.m."

"What?" he asks. "What does he want? Is this about Riley Shaw?"

"Yes, but don't stress over it. Even though she was old, the medical examiner probably can't explain everything."

I raise my hand, chanting, and Tyler taps my shoulder.

"Do you mind if I call on them?" he asks in a tentative voice.

"No, dear. It's your house—your magic room," I reply, smiling.

Tyler raises his hand, summoning his witch energy, and the amber glow appears. He chants softly, calling for Mom and Dad to appear. My heart swells with pride while my son performs his witchcraft skills as adeptly as any seasoned ancestral witch. My parents' golden image projects from the photo, glistening.

"Hi, Nain and Taid," he says. "You remember Zoe, don't you?"

Mom smiles at his love. "Oh, yes. How wonderful to conference with you again."

"Lovely to spend time with you, Zoe," Dad says. "Our grandson has chosen well."

Zoe snickers. "Actually, I really chose him. He didn't have a chance."

We all laugh and my parents' image glitters in gold.

"This has to be brief, Mom and Dad," I say. "We have a plane to catch. But before we leave, I wanted to fill you in on what's transpired. Since we spoke last, I had another vision—fairies and other beings crossing over. My witch's intuition hints the Tuatha Dé are already here. For all I know, they could have been here for a while, trying to find Nuada."

My parents' faces contort, breaking up the fluid outlines of their faces. I shouldn't have told them, but I may need their help from the other side.

"Oh, Gwynedd," Mom says. "What will you do?"

Dad's image wavers. "They must prepare themselves, Lowri."

Tyler jumps in, attempting to allay their fears. "Nain and Taid, no need to worry. We're going to Scotland and Wales to search for a spell to close the portal for good."

"And we're gonna search for an incantation to protect us from glamouring, too," Zoe says. "We're on top of this."

I laugh and hug them both. "I'm in excellent hands, Mom and Dad. And there are portals all over the country. Nuada's family could be anywhere. But I wanted you to know. Because...no more secrets."

"We appreciate your honesty, Gwynedd." Mom's image fades in and out. "Be careful, daughter."

"Yes. Don't trust anyone," Dad says. "Even the most trustworthy could be a Tuatha Dé in disguise. Heed Aunt Gorawen's warnings. We love you, Gwyn."

Their images dissipate until the photo is all that remains. Tyler covers the burning herbs and squints at me.

"You didn't tell them about the old crone witch from Middletown. Isn't that keeping a secret?"

"What happened to Riley has nothing to do with the fae. We're fairly certain she was hexed." I put the picture of Mom and Dad on a shelf.

"But how can you be sure, Gwyn?" Zoe asks, cleaning the bowl. "Archie told us the witch energy was unusual. What if it's fairy magic?"

I glare at them both. "That's how it's gonna be? You two ganging up on me?"

Zoe clenches her teeth. "Who? Me? I'm just an innocent witch bystander."

Tyler laughs as he turns out the light. "You do you, Mom. You always do."

I slip on my jacket and exit the magic room. It appears less full of life without Mr. Yeats there giving orders. Tyler and Zoe follow me. When I reach the front door, I slip on my gloves.

"Come to the house around 2:00 p.m. Don't be late. We need to get to Agnes's farm by 2:30 for the circle."

"Sounds good," he replies. "We'll roll our luggage over with us."

"Remember to bring your neck pillow," Zoe adds.

I smile at my son's love, so sweet and caring. "You've never taken a red-eye flight, have you?"

Tyler chuckles. "Zoe could sleep upside down, Mom."

"Lucky you. See you at two."

I prepare myself mentally for Jack Schmidt's inquisition on the way back to Archie's house—*my* home. I smile. You'll be on my turf, Jack.

Chapter Six

MOURNING A WITCH

"EAT, WITCH," ARCHIE SAYS from across the kitchen table. "Detective Schmidt will arrive soon."

I pick at my kale salad. "Why is he even talking to me about what happened? I told Officer Wilson everything. If they believe she died from natural causes, why bring in a detective? Does he think I had something to do with her demise?"

"Probably following up. Her family may have questions."

The mantle clock on the fireplace dings once with the knocking on the door. Jack is certainly punctual. I drop my fork onto the plate and stand with a twinge in my gut. Is it nerves or my intuition?

"I'll get it. He's mostly here to talk to me."

Archie follows me into the foyer and I straighten out my long-sleeved tee over my jeans. I open the door. Jack is standing on the other side of the screen door in casual attire, a puffy winter coat over a flannel shirt and denim jeans. He always appears angry with that Cro-magnon forehead of his.

"Good afternoon," he says. "May I come in?"

"Oh, yes. Please, come in," I reply.

I open the screen door and he wipes his shoes on the welcome mat before he enters.

"Would you like to sit in the living room?" Archie asks.

"That won't be necessary," he replies. "I only have a couple of questions. Officer Wilson said you were leaving the country and I didn't want this hanging over all our heads. The family is pressing us to check everything out. I figured better to get this done now, so Mrs. Shaw can be laid to rest."

"Oh, OK. Sure. That makes sense. Ask away." Am I worrying about this for nothing?

Jack removes a notepad from his back pocket and flips through a couple of pages. "Officer Wilson took these notes. Dr. Cockburn, if you have something to add, jump in. If I've got anything wrong, let me know. Wilson reports Mrs. Shaw called you to ask you to meet her?"

"Yes. She seemed coherent, so I thought I should. I planned on convincing her to go back with me to the party."

"She asked you to meet her on the Green?"

"No, the Celestial Gardens." Wait? What did I tell Officer Wilson?

"And what time was it when Mrs. Shaw called you?"

Fuck. I glance at Archie and he averts his eyes. Thanks, honey. You're a lot of help. Surely, I can answer him without being specific.

"I didn't check my phone when she called. I don't know what time it was."

Jack stares at me with a skeptical expression. "A close approximation will do."

Will it be? I can't bring myself to lie to him. "Let me think." I stare at my phone screen.

"How about you, Dr. Cockburn?" Detective Schmidt asks. "Were you there when she received the phone call from Riley Shaw?"

In the words of Agnes, fuck me. Why not tell him? He could get my cell records, anyway. I peer at Archie out of the corner of my eye and he runs a hand through his hair.

"It was before we left for the party," he says. "I would guess around half-past six?"

Jack glares at me, one eyebrow arched. "Does that ring a bell, Ms. Crowther?"

I swallow as heart beats climb up my throat. "Yes. That sounds right."

Archie rubs my back while Jack jots a few notes on his pad. "And she didn't tell you why she wanted to meet with you?"

I hesitate. "No. She said she had information for me." I grab Archie's hand and squeeze. "She never got to say what. She passed out and then..." My gaze falls to the floor.

"Right," Jack replies. "Very odd, don't you think? How well did you know Mrs. Shaw?"

When I peer up at him, he's squinting, a look of doubt shrouding his question. "Not very well. She's a pagan but she belongs to another community group. We saw her at conferences." I hope this is enough to send him on his way.

"Riley Shaw was a respected woman in our faith," Archie says. "I know it's not mainstream, but we support each other just like other religions."

"If she was merely an acquaintance, what could she possibly have wanted to tell you, Ms. Crowther?" Jack asks.

"I don't have any idea. I hadn't seen her for a long time. If she had dementia, her message for me was probably nonsense."

"Could be," he replies. "Dr. Cockburn, was Mrs. Shaw still alive when you arrived?"

"No. She was on the ground with Gwyn," Archie says. "I checked her pulse, but she was gone."

Jack writes a few more notes on his pad. "I have one more question. Why didn't you contact the police when Mrs. Shaw first called? There was an alert sent out. The family was distraught."

Archie squeezes my hand. I stare blankly at the detective. I have no good excuse. Not one he won't question. All I can do is bullshit an answer.

"I don't know. I suppose I thought it would be better to meet her alone and talk her into coming back with me to the party. It wasn't the best choice in hindsight." What else can I say without telling this Unremarkable the truth? That she was a witch trying to warn me I was in danger. He'll surely think I've lost my marbles.

Detective Schmidt stares at me as if he's trying to suck the truth out of me, and for a moment, I'm mesmerized by his dark eyes. But I shake it off and glance at Archie.

Jack closes his pad and shoves it in his back pocket. "Thank you for your time. If anything comes to you, call me." He hands me his work card with his phone number. "Enjoy your trip. Officer Wilson says you're off to Great Britain."

"Aye. We're visiting my family in Edinburgh," Archie replies. "A post-holiday celebration. I don't teach during Winter Session this year."

"If I have any more questions, I'll contact you when you return. Happy New Year."

Detective Schmidt exits the house and I expel the longest sigh of relief when Archie shuts the front door.

"He knows I'm hiding something," I say, biting a nail. "I saw it in his eyes. He has an expression I can't put my finger on. He's good at what he does."

Archie wraps his arms around me. "I doubt the caliber of his investigative skills. He never figured out you killed Nick Evans."

"Well, it was close for a while. I imagined he would arrest me at any moment. All we can do is hope this blows over while we're in Scotland and Wales."

"You worry too much, my love. Besides, Trinity should have more information for us at the circle." He kisses me and the knots in my stomach loosen a bit.

"We should make sure our luggage is down here, ready to go. Tyler and Zoe will arrive soon with theirs, too. The shuttle picks us up at five to go to the airport."

"Aye. I'll get them. Why don't you check the back door and make sure it's locked?"

Archie rushes upstairs and I lock the deadbolt on the backdoor. I scuttle back to the foyer and the mantle clock dings one for the half hour. Instinctively, I gaze up at my mom in the painting and clutch at the sudden twinge in my stomach. What does this signal mean?

Archie pulls up to Agnes's house and we rush inside. We tear off our coats and shoes. The hedge witch is not pleased.

"You'd think you would fucking arrive on time, having a flight to catch."

Leslie shuffles in, rolling her eyes. "Oh, Agnes. They're fine. Don't take out your pot hangover on them."

"Yeah, yeah," she says, rubbing the side of her head. "Let's get this circle over with. I want to go back to bed."

My fellow witches are in the living room, the older witches standing or sitting on the sofas and chairs, the young ones squished together on the floor. Tyler and Zoe join them while Archie and I stand near the fireplace. Leslie nods to start the meeting and Trinity addresses us.

"Thank you all for attending this impromptu circle."

Agnes interrupts her. "Yeah. Happy Fucking New Year."

The young witches do a poor job of suppressing their laughter. Trinity glares at the hedge witch.

"You knew we were going to have a circle today. Couldn't you have laid off the Bearsden Poison for one New Year's Eve?"

"And break a tradition?" she asks, leaning on Leslie's shoulder. "No fucking way."

Chuckles make the rounds and our coven leader continues.

"Onto a more somber note. I've heard from the Middletown Coven. They confirmed Riley Shaw was suffering from a hex or another form of magic. Unfortunately, Riley took off before they could investigate. The family recommended they file a missing person report, saying she was suffering from symptoms of dementia. Basically, that's how the negative witchcraft appeared to affect her. It mimicked aphasia."

"But Riley spoke to me on the phone as if she was fine," I say. "Later, when she attempted to share her warning, she had trouble speaking."

Skye interjects. "Maybe the hex, if that's what it was, affected her when she tried to tell Gwyn the specifics of the warning."

"Makes sense," Tanner says. "And the closer she got to spilling the tea, the more that magic clamped down on her."

Spence frowns. "Poor Riley. She was one of the best witches around here. Her magic was dank."

"One of the most dedicated I've known," Shane says.

Elijah rubs his jaw. "The question is, what do we do now?"

"What can we do?" Archie asks. "We don't have enough information. Trinity, did the family share any other clues as to who could have cast the spell?"

"Nothing much," she replies. "They said Riley went to meet a new witch in the area who wanted to join their coven. When she returned, she wasn't herself."

Agnes rubs her temples. "Well, that fucking blows."

"It sure does," Shane says. "If we had time to inspect the body, we might have detected the quality of the magic—pinpointed the source."

"The only way to do that now is to break into the morgue," Tyler says.

Zoe jumps up. "I'm game!"

Tyler's mouth falls open. "I was kidding."

"I mean, we can use a masking spell," she says, shrugging.

Agnes raises her head with a snort. "Now you're talking. When do we go?"

Leslie scowls at her partner. "We will not sneak into the morgue, Agnes. It's too risky, even with a masking spell."

"Sometimes you're just no fun, sweetheart." The hedge witch plops her head back onto Leslie's shoulder.

"I agree with Leslie," Trinity says. "And the family admits Riley was making no sense. Whoever this witch or being was—is—they could have cast a hex to seek revenge on Riley by messing with her faculties. There may be no valid warning for Gwyn. Mrs. Shaw was an old witch. We all make enemies along the way."

Spence grimaces. "So, we do nothing?"

"What do you suggest we do?" Skye asks. "Until something else happens, we have no leads."

"As usual, Skye is level-headed," Leslie says. "We proceed with our eyes and ears—and witch senses—on alert."

Trinity catches my gaze. "Are you OK with this, Gwyn?"

"Sure. Who knows? Maybe Detective Jack Schmidt will discover something. Not that he would share those findings with us." I glance at Archie. "He stopped by the house today to ask questions."

"That's interesting, isn't it?" Tanner asks. "He suspects foul play, then?"

"I don't know," I reply. "I think the medical examiner must have discovered something unusual."

Spence sits up straight. "That's disturbing. Does he suspect you did something?"

"I don't think so," I say, but I'm not really certain. "But you know him. He always has a question mark plastered on his face."

"He sure does." Trinity puts a hand on her hip. "We can't do anything, but if I know Detective Schmidt, he'll pound the pavement until he finds some answers."

I don't agree with her. Jack never really found an explanation for the disappearance of Nick Evans. He came after me with a vengeance. I'm a little befuddled by his decision to remove me as a suspect. But Archie did cast those spells of confusion on him. They must have worked.

"We will remain in contact with the Middletown Coven," Leslie says. "For now, let us go in peace. But remain vigilant."

A notification dings on Trinity's phone and she raises her hand in a stopping motion. "Hold your horses! It's the Greenville Coven leader." She scans the circle, her eyes dripping with trepidation. "Elizabeth Wang is dead. She had the same symptoms as Riley Shaw, and Elizabeth was far from her dementia years."

Archie and I lock eyes as the others stare in disbelief. Tyler jumps up from the floor.

"We need to go, Mom. Once Detective Schmidt gets word of this, he'll have more questions, even if it isn't his jurisdiction. I'm sure he has friends."

"Oh, fuck Jack Schmidt," Agnes says. "He can't pin this on Gwyn."

"No," Archie replies. "But that won't stop him. And Gwyn is a terrible liar."

"You should go—now," Trinity says. "Cancel the shuttle and hire a driver to get you to the airport. You can deal with the detective when you return."

Agnes waves her hands. "Get a move on! It's more important you make it to the UK and search for a spell to close the portal. We'll handle Jack Schmidt. I've dealt with the cops my entire life."

Tyler and Zoe rush to the foyer. Archie and I dart after them. We throw on our coats and shoes in record time while our fellow witches wish us well, but their wrinkled faces convey distress.

Once we're in the Tesla and on our way to the house, Zoe blurts out, "Isn't this exciting? It's like a movie thriller, and we are the hunted."

CHAPTER SEVEN

A WELSH REUNION

"We're here! We're here!" an excited Zoe shouts in my ear.

The wheels of the plane have just touched down and the pilot is taxiing us on the tarmac to the terminal.

I lift one eyelid, most likely resembling the gray-skinned monster in my visions, and glare at her. "How are you so peppy? I barely slept with that giant man back there snoring like an ogre half the flight."

"I told you she sleeps like the dead," Tyler says. "He is big, but I doubt he deserves to be called an ogre, Mom."

Archie leans forward to address my son. "Your mother is simply being colorful with her descriptions."

"No, I'm not." I stretch and rub my aching lower back. "When I went to the bathroom in the middle of the night, he blocked me in the aisle. Thought he was being oh so funny. I threw an Agnes scowl at him and he let me by. If he hadn't, I would have introduced his balls to my knees next."

Zoe snickers. "Would you have really done that?"

"Maybe not a few years ago," Tyler says. "But now? You bet she would."

"Aye," Archie replies, laughing. "He'd have been laid up on the floor, no doubt, blocking your mum from the loo. So, he would have won, anyway."

"Very funny, professor." I frown at him and pick up my carry-on bag. "I'll have to catch a nap in the rental car on the way to Buckley. Do you think you guys can give me a break and keep the chatting to a whisper? I really want to be chipper when we arrive at Aunt Gorawen's house."

"Sure," Tyler says, grabbing their luggage. "But I can't speak for Zoe."

She grimaces at her love. "Hey. I can be quiet when I need to be."

I squint at her and Archie chuckles.

"Whaaat?" she replies, grinning. "I can. But I may have a teensy-weensy problem with containing myself. I'm so excited to meet your great-aunt—and the hand." She flashes her spread fingers in front of her face.

"I can't wait to see her in person," Tyler says as we shuffle up the center aisle. "Video chat is great, but it's not like being there physically in the room with her. You can't hug someone through a computer screen. You probably feel the same about your family, don't you, Archie?"

He nods. "Aye. Although there was a time I didn't appreciate those moments as much as I do now."

I smile at him, recalling our first visit to the Cockburn household. "Archie had a difficult relationship with his dad before. But now, they're good."

After entering the Manchester terminal, we proceed through the customs area, which doesn't take long at all. Great Britain has TSA lines down to an art. American airports could learn a thing or two. When we exit the terminal, even the blast of cool air doesn't jar me. The gloomy clouds reflect my fatigue. I hope I can get enough sleep on the drive to Buckley, or Aunt Gorawen may think I'm not thrilled to be here.

Once we arrive at the rental car, I am wavering like a drunkard. I fall into the passenger seat on the left side of the vehicle. Tyler helps Archie load the luggage into the trunk, and I pull up the hood of my fleece jacket and lean against the window. When they get into their seats, I close my eyes. The last thing I remember is Zoe shushing Tyler as I nod off into slumber.

When the sedan comes to a stop, I wake and peer out the window. I smile at the brown stone house and the sheep in the distance—my Great-Aunt Gorawen's estate. I'm home.

Tyler whispers close to my head, "Mom, are you awake? We're here."

I sit up and stretch my arms, yawning. "Yeah, I'm rested and ready to introduce you to your great-aunt."

"I wonder if Ellie Jones will be here?" Archie asks, opening the driver's side door.

Zoe pulls the car handle and exits. "Who's Ellie?"

"She's the woman who helps Aunt Gorawen with the farm." Tyler gets out of the car. "Her husband Owen tends to the property, too. They'll be inheriting the estate when my great-aunt passes away."

"Well, that doesn't seem fair," Zoe says, frowning. "Shouldn't your mom inherit her property? She's her flesh and blood."

I roll out of my seat and arch my aching back. "Aunt Gorawen felt the same way after she learned of my existence, but she had already willed the property to Ellie and Owen. Wouldn't have been fair to them to change the will. They took care of her and the farm for years. They earned it. Besides, what would I do with a sheep farm? Or either of you?"

Zoe scans the green pastures dotted with sheep as we walk on the stone path to my aunt's front entry. "I don't know. I think herding sheep would be fun."

Archie raises a corner of his mouth. "I expect you would take a liking to sheep husbandry."

"Well, I'm a tech guy," Tyler says. "Not a sheep farmer."

Zoe fakes a pout. "But they're so cute." Her foot squishes into a glob of crusted brown substance.

"Until they get scared and jump at you or...you step in their poop," I say with a snort.

"Ewww," she says, grimacing. "What am I going to do? I don't want to meet your aunt smelling like shit."

Tyler chuckles. "I doubt she'll notice. The odor permeates the air here."

"I never told Tyler what happened during my initial visit with Aunt Gorawen," I say. "I slipped into a pile of shit just before I went into her house. Made quite the first impression."

"But that was an emotional meeting for your mum," Archie says, smiling at me. "It's not every day you meet a distant relative you assumed had passed on."

"To meet the only surviving extended family I have in this world changed my entire outlook on life." I recall the conference with my mom and the tearful reunion she had with Aunt Gorawen. "My heart spilled over with love that day. Of course, I would have never increased my ancestral magic skills without her guidance, either. I learned to conference with Nain and Taid anytime I want." I glance at my son. "And now, so can you, thanks to Archie's training."

Tyler fist bumps Archie as I hammer the heavy knocker. A Yule wreath made of evergreen, pine cones, and berries welcomes us. The thick wooden door creaks open and a woman with a head full of short, frizzy gray curls grins from ear to ear behind the threshold.

"Ms. Thomas, they're here!" She embraces me and continues in her soft Welsh accent. "I'm so chuffed you've arrived, Gwynedd.

Your aunt has been chattering all morning about you. Please, come in. Tyler, right? I recognize you from your mother's photos."

"Yeah, and this is my girlfriend, Zoe Wu," he replies. "Great to meet you finally. Mom has talked a lot about you and what you've done for my great-aunt."

"It has been my pleasure. She's a wonderful woman, even if she is a bit eccentric."

We enter the house, which has a familiarity now after my prior visits. Its stone floors and ceilings with wood beams give forth a worn, homey feeling after hundreds of years of occupants—my ancestors. Ellie shuts the door behind us as Aunt Gorawen enters the foyer, hobbling with the use of a cane. She's wearing a long-sleeved cardigan over a knee-length gray wool dress, her white hair gathered in a bun on the back of her head.

"It's happy days when you are here, Gwynedd," she says, hugging me. "Hello, Dr. Cockburn. Always a pleasure to have you visit."

My aunt's voice no longer cracks as she speaks in her soft-spoken Welsh accent. Even pushing one hundred years of age doesn't dampen her spirits anymore. Knowing she has living family is all she needed to add a few more to her longevity. I hope the universe blesses me with a decade more of her immeasurable wisdom.

Aunt Gorawen clasps Tyler's hand. "This handsome young man must be my nephew, no doubt. Your pictures do not do you justice. Exquisite hazel eyes like your grandmother, Lowri."

He bends down, embracing her as if he's afraid he'll break a bone on her delicate, wrinkled body. "Thank you. It's so awesome to meet you finally. Video chat is great, but it can't replace meeting you in person." He gestures to his love. "This is my S.O., Zoe. You met her online."

"Yes, I remember." She tilts her head to the right. "But what is this 'S.O.'? American slang?"

Zoe jumps in and shakes her hand. "It means significant other, Aunt Gorawen. Can I call you that?"

My aunt chuckles. "Ahhh, you're his *cariad*—sweetheart. You are most welcome to call me aunt. I hope you will make it official one day." She wiggles the ring finger of her left hand. "I'm not long for this world. Don't wait too many years."

A teasing smile graces her face and she chuckles under her breath. Tyler presses his lips together and Zoe's eyes spread wide. Ellie grabs her coat from a hook on the wall.

"Owen expects me for lunch. I hope to see you all again during your visit. Ms. Thomas, call me if you need me. Diwrnod da."

"Good day to you as well. Thank you for getting the house ready for my guests," Aunt Gorawen says.

"Croeso, Ms. Thomas." She nods and exits.

When the door shuts, Aunt Gorawen's secret butler dashes up the hallway from her magic room, leaving a trail of golden glitter in its path. Zoe perks up as my aunt's personal helper flies around her. Tyler stands mesmerized while it scrutinizes them.

"Meet my treasured assistant, my magic butler," Aunt Gorawen says. "He is my *right hand*." She snickers. "I made a little joke."

We chuckle at her old lady humor as we remove our coats and hang them on the wall hooks in the entry. The magic butler hops around in the air like a bunny, demanding our attention. He taps my aunt's shoulder and points his index finger down the hallway.

"Ah, yes," she says. "My helper is reminding me of the spell I found. Follow me to the magic room."

Aunt Gorawen shuffles down the hallway with her cane, her enchanted butler flitting around her, and we follow slowly behind. When she arrives, she removes an old skeleton key from her sweater pocket and unlocks the door. The room doesn't appear as disheveled as I remember. The stacks of paintings of my mother that lined the walls are gone. Her wooden altar and worktable remain along with the shelves housing her herb jars, crystals, animal bones, bowls, mortar and pestles, etc. A pile of decaying grimoires sits on the surface of the table.

"You keep your magic room locked up," Tyler says. "Does Ellie have any idea what's in here?"

My aunt's head quivers. "Ah, no. If she were to get a glimpse of the items in this room, she'd believe I've lost my senses for good."

"Witches have hidden their magic rooms for centuries," Archie says. "Self-preservation."

"But won't she find out when...you know?" Zoe asks, clenching her teeth.

"Once I'm gone, it'll hardly matter," she replies. "She already considers me eccentric. This will surely add to my mystery. But I have been sorting through my most cherished magic belongings and placing them in a locked trunk for you, Gwynedd. Not as big as our family's steamer trunk that you have in the States, but it's big enough to house what I want you to have."

My heart pains, thinking about the day my great-aunt crosses over. I've had so little time to spend with her. "Can we not talk about this now? You're doing well. Let's celebrate that."

Aunt Gorawen clasps my hand, her cold, boney fingers reminding me she has finite days on this earth. "My day will arrive soon enough, niece. That is for certain. But while I still breathe, I'll do what I can to make sure you remain unharmed." She waves to her magic butler. "Off to the greenhouse. You have work to do." He flies through the double patio doors, prompting a giggle from Zoe.

My great-aunt leans her cane against the table and slides a heavy grimoire across the surface. She flips it open to a copy of the portal-closing spell from the family tome, holding a place in the pages. Archie, Tyler, Zoe, and I huddle together to examine the two spells. I pick up the loose paper I sent her via snail mail, comparing it with the one in the decaying book.

"It's almost written verbatim in our ancestral tome, with one major exception," I say.

Archie inspects the two spells more closely. "Aye. It resembles another we've seen."

"That's curious, isn't it?" Aunt Gorawen asks. "Where else have you seen this incantation written?"

"In Bearsden." Tyler pushes past me and puts a finger on the familiar phrase. "There must be a human sacrifice. That's what Archie was referring to."

"A hedge witch in our coven wanted us to use that spell," Zoe says. "Cringeworthy, but I think she was serious."

Aunt Gorawen's eyes pop out like two white golf balls. "We don't do that now. It would violate the do-no-harm rule. Who would even suggest such a thing?"

I laugh and drop the paper onto the grimoire. "Agnes Pritchard. You've heard me talk about her. She is a tad unconventional."

Zoe snorts. "That's a mild way to describe her. Her body is covered in tattoos and she grows pot. But she has never hidden from the fact she practices witchcraft, either. The town just thinks she's a loon."

My aunt chuckles as she closes the grimoire. "I've been called worse in my lifetime. Every witch has to follow their own path, my dear. I admire this Agnes Pritchard for being true to herself. But she was right. That ingredient is required to close the portal—the passing of a soul through the opening."

"Why would your family tome leave out that necessary item?" Archie asks, rubbing his goatee.

"I can't answer that," Aunt Gorawen replies, clutching her cane. "A prior ancestor must have copied the incantation from another spell book, leaving it out intentionally—or not. Perhaps they wanted to deter a witch from trying to do exactly what you are attempting. When one is desperate, they'll consider any solution. Even the most moral witch can become hopeless in a dire situation."

"Except we told her no," Tyler adds. "And Dr. Hughes got angry with Agnes. It's been off the table since."

"Well, of course. But that leaves us in a tough situation, doesn't it?" I ask, glancing at Archie, Tyler, and Zoe. "Aunt Gorawen, I have to be honest with you. My intuition tells me a Tuatha Dé fairy has crossed over and is searching for me."

She grabs my hand as if she's clinging to life. "Oh, Gwynedd. Are you certain? A witch's intuition is a tricky skill to interpret."

I lock eyes with Archie and hesitate. I have to tell her, but she'll worry herself into a stroke. Zoe solves my dilemma and blurts it out.

"Tyler found a sketch of that gray-skinned monster in one of Agnes's old books some crone gave her."

"Zoeee," my son says, exhaling. "Dr. Duffy said it's a Fomorian. He translated the old Irish Gaelic written underneath the picture."

"A Fomorian?" Aunt Gorawen asks, tapping her cane on the floor. "Yes. I trust Seamus's analysis. He must believe the presence of a Fomorian confirms the existence of a Tuatha Dé. But does your intuition signal his presence?"

"I don't think so," I reply. "My sixth sense could be alerting me of a future crossing as well. I don't have solid evidence of anything. All I can do is continue to work on increasing the crystals in the grid when I return home to further the vision I had. I'll also continue to increase the intensity of my witch's intuition using the two crystals Agnes and Seamus gifted me. These skills are still new to me."

Archie caresses my hand. "We'll continue to monitor our surroundings as we move forward, but we have other issues to attend to when we return."

I toss a glower at him. "I wasn't going to share what's going on in Bearsden."

"What has come to pass in your hometown, Gwynedd?" Aunt Gorawen asks with a tilt of her head.

Tyler glances at Zoe and she shrugs. "Don't look at me. I didn't say anything this time."

"Nothing for you to worry about, Aunt Gorawen," I say, tapping her hand. "But two witches have died, and we don't know what happened."

Archie shoves his hand in his pockets. "Gwyn, you have to share more than a general statement like that." He addresses my aunt. "Malevolent magic may have been used on the first witch—Riley Shaw. We don't know about the second because we needed to get out of the country before the local detective came asking Gwyn questions. She was with the poor witch when the hex took her life."

"Oh, dear. Oh, dear," my aunt says, shaking her head. She scans her shelves, tapping her cane on the floor again. "Tyler and Zoe, Ellie left a cart in the kitchen with sandwiches and tea. Could you both take them to the living room?"

"Sure," Tyler says. "Come on, Zoe."

"I can't wait." Her stomach growls like a starved animal. "I'm so hungry."

My son and his love exit the magic room. Aunt Gorawen shuts the magic room door behind them.

"I didn't want to discuss this in front of Tyler. Does this detective suspect you were involved, Gwynedd?"

"Who knows?" I ask, shrugging. "He suspected I knew something surrounding Nick Evans's death, but it went nowhere. He had no proof because the body was missing. We'll deal with him when we return. I just didn't want it to delay my visit with you and Archie's family. Please, don't fret over this."

"You and Tyler are my flesh and blood," she says. "I will concern myself with your well-being until my dying days."

Archie lays a comforting hand on her shoulder. "As you can see, we have more issues to occupy our minds than the presence of a vengeful fairy, but we'll stay alert. I promise to watch after Gwynedd, although she has done a smashing job of that herself. She's a strong ancestral witch."

Aunt Gorawen takes a breath and holds it briefly, a distressed expression gripping her face. "That may be, but I so worry about you, Gwynedd. Even coming here, you open yourself to danger. The portal in the mound near the old castle. The Tuatha Dé could find you here as well as in Bearsden—anywhere there is an opening to the Otherworld. Seamus saved you from walking into the portal, remember?"

I recall that day when Seamus Duffy knocked me to the ground, presenting in his cat sith persona. But I wasn't as skilled a witch then. I am ready to defend myself against the vengeful family of Nick Evans—Nuada.

"Don't stress yourself into a tizzy," I say. "I'll be ready for them."

A chuckle breaks free from Archie's mouth. "May the gods help the fairy who comes after Gwyn now. She's no neophyte."

"Well, then," Aunt Gorawen says. "Let's eat lunch. The tea is cooling while we babble on about the dangers of fairies. We should at least fill our bellies to fuel another day to fight them off."

We follow her down the dark hallway toward the living room and a slight twinge snaps in my gut. Am I not safe here? Or anywhere?

Chapter Eight

FAMILY MAGIC

When I wake in my aunt's antique Welsh bed, I touch the spot next to me to find it's empty and cold. This historic manor house has a cozy atmosphere, but a dampness chills the rooms within. The lumpy mattress left an ache in my lower back I thought I had sent packing. I pull my knees to my chest and stretch, but nature calls. After my visit to the porcelain throne in the ensuite bathroom, I throw on the white fuzzy robe hanging in the wardrobe and head down to the kitchen.

Chatter echoes down the hallway as I descend the dark-stained wood steps, my hand tracing the thick railing with ornate carvings. Even after four hundred years, they are as sturdy as ever. But the creaking makes it impossible to sneak down, not that they can hear me anyway above the clamor of their voices.

When I enter the spacious kitchen, everyone except Archie is seated around the thick pine table, munching down cockles and laverbread, which is made from seaweed sourced off the West Coast of Wales. Some people call it Welsh caviar, but you can make the laver into cakes, too. Tyler and Zoe are inhaling them as Aunt Gorawen shoves more onto their plates. Eat it all. I can't get past the dark-green color and texture.

An antique clock hanging over the enormous, open fireplace hearth reads half past ten. Archie breaks an egg into an iron skillet partially filled with sausage, then fiddles with the contents of another pan. The aroma of sauteed mushrooms fills my nose and my stomach groans as loud as a lion, alerting them to my presence.

"Good morning," I say, grabbing a teacup and saucer. "Why didn't someone wake me?"

"You're on holiday, niece," Aunt Gorawen replies. "No need to keep hours."

Archie flips an egg. "You tossed and turned all night. We decided it was best to let you sleep. Would you like an egg, my love?"

"Thanks, but how will I adjust now?" I ask, pouring hot water from the teakettle. "And I'd love an egg."

"If you're going to complain," Tyler says, chewing on his scrambled eggs. "We'll sick the hand on you tomorrow morning. Aunt Gorawen taught me how to summon him and make a request."

I throw a scowl in my aunt's direction as I sit with my cup. "I think I'd rather have Zoe jump on my bed."

She snaps her back straight. "I can do that! Want me to come pounce on your bed tomorrow morning?"

"I was kidding." I wave my hand and the spoon stirs the sweetener in my cup.

Zoe chuckles. "Can we do magic in here, too?"

Aunt Gorawen pats her hand. "My dear, when we're alone in the house, you may exhibit the craft as much as you wish. You, too, nephew."

My son and his love pour themselves another cup of tea and commence stirring with a splash of magic. The spoons twirl as the steam rises with swirls of amber. My aunt calls on her enchanting butler to join us, and he dances in the air above, leaving a trail of golden glitter as he jumps from one side of the table to the next. Zoe laughs and shimmies in her chair, humming a song I don't recognize. Archie continues to cook our breakfast, chuckling at the spectacle.

"I really love your house, Aunt Gorawen," she says, her signature wide grin shining. "Can Tyler and I practice with spells from your grimoires in the magic room?"

"Of course, my dear. Tyler, if you're finished, why don't you and Zoe go ahead? I'll stay here and keep company with your mom and Dr. Cockburn."

"Thank you," my son says, standing. "I promise we'll clean up when we're finished."

Zoe pushes up from her chair and hugs my aunt. "Thank you, Aunt Gorawen."

She grabs Tyler's hand and they dart down the hallway. The magic butler races through the air after them, leaving a trail of golden exhaust. Archie places a plate of food in front of me and my aunt, taking a seat next to me with his own.

"This smells wonderful, Dr. Cockburn," Aunt Gorawen says. "Thank you for cooking this magnificent breakfast."

"You're most welcome. After all this time, I expect you can call me Archie." He takes a sip of tea.

"Old habit. An academic deserves the recognition," she says, taking a bite of egg. "Gwynedd, you were clever to hold on to this man. Handsome *and* a superb cook."

"Well, you charmed that painting of his and sent him to me, didn't you? Don't I owe you the credit?" That slight doubt pinches me again, not knowing if his love has been authentic all this time or the result of the spell she attached to the picture of my mom.

Archie peers at me and squints. "I've told you many times her painting had nothing to do with my love for you."

"Please, no lover's quarrel here." Aunt Gorawen takes my hand. "Gwynedd, the charm was to find you protectors, not lovers. The love Archie has for you is genuine, not the result of the spell attached to the painting." She smiles at me with a twinkle in her hazel eyes. "If he was charmed, you cast that on him, not I."

Archie chuckles. "Aye. I've been telling her the same since we first met. I never planned on falling in love with her." He squeezes my hand. "But I had no chance from the start."

"Neither did I," I say, sipping my Earl Grey. "Now we're living together. I hadn't told you because I just moved in with him."

She drops her cup on the saucer with a clink. "Tidy, tidy. That means brilliant, fantastic. Why not make it official?" She taps her ring finger.

Archie averts his eyes back to his plate. I take another sip of tea. My aunt eats a bite of laverbread, an expression of I-should-mind-my-own-business lingering on her face.

"We're taking our relationship one step at a time," I say. "It was hard for me after what Richard did."

An awkward silence permeates the room as we finish the last morsels of food. A notification vibrates on Archie's phone. He reads the text.

"It's Trinity. She says Detective Schmidt has been asking her about the pagan Fellowship. He's questioned a few of the other coven leaders as well, though he believes he's talking to the heads of local pagan community groups. Have you checked your email since we've arrived? She thinks you should."

I retrieve my cell from the pocket in my robe and take a peek at my DUB email. "Aw, shit. There's an email from Jack Schmidt."

"Don't click on it," Archie says. "If there is no return receipt, he'll think you've been too busy on holiday to check your email."

"But I told Officer Wilson I would be checking."

"What is this about?" Aunt Gorawen asks, her eyes twitching. "Who is this Jack man?"

I lay my cell on the table. "He's the head Bearsden detective. The police force there is small, so he shows up to most of the severe crimes in the town—when unusual deaths occur. He wasn't there the night Riley Shaw passed away. He showed up at the house on New Year's Day to ask us questions."

Archie stands and collects our plates. "Nothing to worry about. He has to follow up whenever there are irregularities. The medical examiner must have noticed an oddity in her demise, we suspect. But they're Unremarkables. No way to discern a hex."

My aunt taps her fingers on the pine table. "Or a fairy's curse for unwillingness to share knowledge. Gwynedd, I fear for you. A Tuatha Dé could be seeking out other witches to syphon information about you. This detective is the least of your worries."

"I understand," I say. "But we're here now. Let's try to enjoy our visit. We can't do anything about the death of those local witches while we're in the UK. Certainly, Jack Schmidt will have to wait his turn for me because I'm on vacation."

"Sounds like a brilliant idea," Archie says, loading the dishwasher. "I'll send a text to Trinity and let her know we're too absorbed with family for emails. She needn't tell the detective she's spoken with us at all."

Aunt Gorawen grabs her cane and pushes up from the table. "Why don't we move to the magic room to see what my nephew and his *cariad* are up to?"

"You go ahead." I amble toward the door. "Archie and I should get cleaned up and dressed first, in case Ellie or Owen stop by."

"I am curious," Archie says. "When you're casting spells outside the magic room, how do you protect yourself from unexpected entries? Ellie has keys to the house."

Aunt Gorawen hobbles next to us down the hallway. "Oh, I make use of the old door bolt, of course. No key to the old mechanism. Ellie believes it's rusted open. Well, in fact, it is. But an easy incantation moves the metal."

He chuckles. "Brilliant thinking. Is it bolted now?"

I glance over my shoulder at the front door. "No, it's not, and the hand has been flying around. Pretty risky."

"I should remedy that, no?" She chants an incantation and passes her bony hand in front of the bolt, prompting it to shut with a clank. "I'm getting forgetful in my older years. I fret about the day

I forget to slide it shut. If Ellie walked in on me while I was in the midst of casting a spell, I'd have much to explain. And she'd march me straight downtown to Dr. Evans."

Archie chuckles. "No doubt, but you have nothing to fret over. Your mind is as quick as ever."

"We'll be down in a few minutes," I say, heading up the stairs.

Once Archie and I have changed into our day clothes, we head downstairs to the magic room. Aunt Gorawen is standing at her worktable with a few short candles, partially burned. Tyler and Zoe stand mesmerized as she chants and lights a white candle to promote peace, truth, sincerity, and cleansing. It's a fabulous spell to promote new beginnings. We shuffle over to them.

"Candle magic." Archie raises a corner of his mouth. "I don't use it nearly enough. Too time consuming for a professor with a heavy class schedule."

I pick up a yellow candle used for wisdom, clarity, vision, and many other situations. "And it requires a lot of time and focus. I don't possess either of those prerequisites."

"Aunt Gorawen said you would say that," Tyler says. "But I told her how busy you were with school last semester."

Zoe leans on the table, inspecting the variety of colors. "She also said it's probably why you're having trouble with the crystal grid and your visions."

"Zoeee." My son nudges her.

My aunt perks up. "That was supposed to be *our* little secret, my dear."

She clenches her teeth. "Oops."

I laugh at their gaffes. "Oh, it's OK. I don't think it's a huge secret I have a problem with concentration. Maybe if I had practiced the craft since my childhood, I would have an easier time finding my center. But I endeavor to achieve that goal one day."

"Don't be so hard on yourself, Gwyn," Archie says, kissing me on the cheek. "You saved my life, remember? Just allow yourself the time to perfect the skill."

Tyler picks up the red candle, representing power, passion, and love—some say lust.

Zoe snickers at him. "I don't think we need that one. Choose the green one. We're gonna need extra money now that we're buying Dr. Hughes's house. Our love life is doing just fiiine." She waggles her eyebrows at him.

Laughter rumbles in the room until Archie receives a notification on his cell phone. As he reads the text on his phone, his demeanor turns sullen. He types on the screen and presses send.

"That was Leslie," he says. His Scottish brogue breaks through as he continues. "Trinity heard back from the Greenville Coven. It's not encouraging news. She wants the coven to convene."

"How?" I ask, my brow crinkling. "We aren't there. We certainly can't meet in a circle if we're almost 3,500 miles away."

"Group video chat," Tyler says. "I mean, it'll be weird. But we can do it."

Zoe shoots her hands in the air. "Yes! We should set up in pairs. Aunt Gorawen can join Tyler and me."

"Aye," Archie replies. "That's her plan. But she has to co-ordinate times with all the members of the Fellowship. Many are back to regular work hours. Leslie is working Winter Session because she is the chair. But she's planning on tomorrow afternoon, our time zone."

Aunt Gorawen shakes her head. "I appreciate the invitation, but I am not a member of your coven. I should not join your circle."

"You're a part of Tyler and me." I hug her. "They will want you there. And you can shed some light on what they tell us."

"I agree for now," she says, tapping her cane. "But if they prefer I leave the circle, I will comply without judgment."

Zoe chuckles. "Well, it won't be much of a circle. More of an ellipse—a really skinny one, don't you think?"

"Very true," Aunt Gorawen replies, a titter popping out. "Why don't we return to the candle magic session tomorrow after the coven circle? We can spend the rest of today in the living room exploring our ancestors in the family photo journals."

"That sounds awesome," Tyler says. "You guys go ahead. Zoe and I will clean up."

The magic butler flits back and forth around them, pointing and directing.

"And the hand will help."

As we shuffle down the hallway, I contemplate incorporating more candle magic into my skill set and this time, apply greater effort.

CHAPTER NINE

SURPRISE!

"Where is Zoe?" I ask, glancing down the hallway toward the foyer.

There's no sign of my son's bubbly significant other. It's the next day, and we're gathered in the kitchen to prepare for the Bearsden Coven meeting online. I'm eager to hear what Trinity and Leslie have learned about Elizabeth Wang's—should we call it murder?

"Since we're leaving tonight, Zoe wanted to say goodbye to the sheep," Tyler says. "She really loves the farm."

Aunt Gorawen hugs him. "I like her, nephew. She has a sweet disposition and is so caring."

"I owe it all to the Bearsden Coven, really," he says, typing on his laptop keyboard. "If they hadn't come after Mom, I might not have met her."

Archie places my laptop on the kitchen table. "I gladly accept your thanks. But in the end, I benefitted as well." He winks at me.

The entry door opens and shuts with a thud. A few seconds pass and weighty footsteps plod down the hallway, increasing in volume until Zoe enters the kitchen. She shuffles in her socks to my son and embraces him.

"I'm here with plenty of time to spare. Did you worry I'd be late?"

"No," Tyler says. "Did the sheep cry when you said goodbye?"

"Yeah," she replies. "They went, 'Baa, baa.'"

Aunt Gorawen chuckles. "You're welcome to visit them any-time, my dear. I'd love for you both to come as often as you like. You are my only family. We should spend as much time together as you can spare."

"For sure, we'll be back," she says, flashing her signature grin.

"Tyler, are you confident the internet in Aunt Gorawen's house is adequate for us to join the video chat from two separate com-puters?" I ask, shifting chairs at the kitchen table.

"No problem at all." He slides his laptop in front of his aunt where she's sitting. "She has better fiber than many places in the US."

Archie sits down and faces my computer. "Aye. Unfortunately, the same can't be said regarding Scotland. Many of the rural areas are too remote. But most areas of Edinburgh have fiber, thankful-ly."

"I've witnessed so many advances in technology in my lifetime," Aunt Gorawen says. "But magic? It evolves to include the ways of those who aren't *in the knowing*. Witches have perfected their spells over time. A hundred years ago, they would have called these advances witchcraft."

"Isn't that the truth?" Zoe takes a seat next to my aunt. "And they would have dragged them out and prosecuted them for it. Too many of our ancestors were burned at the stake when they were simply trying to use herbs to heal. Dumbasses."

Aunt Gorawen chuckles. "Decidedly so. Nephew, I applaud your choice in a partner. A strong woman, she is—and cheeky."

"She can be," Tyler says, snickering. "But I love that about her." He kisses the top of her head and strokes it affectionately.

I sit down next to Archie and bring up the link to the video chat Trinity sent me. Tyler stands behind Zoe and my aunt, bracing himself on the back of their chairs.

"Who does that remind you of, I wonder?" Archie asks, a hint of sarcasm in his voice.

"Oh, my gods, you're right," my son replies, rolling his eyes. "I'm dating my mom."

Laughter bounces off the plaster walls as I pat him on the arm. "Is that so bad?"

"No," he says, a smile sneaking onto his face. "I'm proud of you, Mom. And all you've done for the coven and Bearsden—and me."

"It's a compliment." Zoe grins at my son. "Gwyn has always been so kind and supportive of me. When I first trained with her, I screwed up a lot and she never made fun of me. She never kept me from dating you, either, even though she knew I was a witch. And we know how that went. It triggered your magic."

"Aye. But look at the witch you've become, Tyler," Archie says, a thicker Scottish brogue seeping through. "A level three ancestral witch. You have much to celebrate on your own achievements."

Aunt Gorawen's head quivers in agreement. "I'm delighted at your progress."

"We better sign in," I say, typing onto the keyboard. "It's almost 1:00. Trinity will have a few words if we're late."

Tyler connects to the group chat on his laptop while I log in on mine. The internet connection lags a bit and my heart jumps into a mini marathon race. I tap my fingernails on the kitchen table as the little icon circles around and around. My son's laptop gets in first. After a few uneasy seconds, my fellow witches appear on the screen, trickling in as they join the session.

"Hello, world travelers," Trinity says from her video tile box on the screen.

Tyler leans into his laptop's webcam. "Before we get started, I want to introduce my Great-Aunt Gorawen Thomas."

Everyone welcomes my aunt with warm witchy salutations. She smiles at their faces. "Thank you so much for inviting me to your circle. I haven't attended one in decades. If I can assist you in any manner, I am at your service."

"I am delighted to meet you finally," Leslie says. "I came to your home years ago, but you sent me away. If I had been more persistent, we would have met sooner."

"So many have arrived at my door, claiming to be relatives. When you have an estate, thieves and rascals scurry to you like roaches."

"As our coven's leader, I formally open our circle to you," Trinity says, nodding.

Ronnie waves to me with Luna in her arms, but Derek takes their little one and walks away. The others add their greetings as well until the Elder cuts them off.

"We have no time for socializing." Leslie lifts her chin. "This circle officially begins now."

Spence snickers as he waves a finger across his screen. "Can we really call this a circle? We aren't even in the same country."

Sitting next to him in view of the webcam, Tanner grabs his partner's hand and pulls it down. "Sorry, everyone."

"He's right." Agnes shoves an eyeball at the webcam. "We're a fucking square on the screen, not a circle. Is this even safe? Someone could be spying on us?"

"It's encrypted, Agnes," Tyler says. "We're fine."

"I don't trust it," she replies. "This tech shit shouldn't be used by witches. It's not natural."

"Neither is sending supernatural beings through portals," Skye says, a titter escaping. "Yet here we are."

Ronnie throws a hand across the screen. "Even if someone casually strolled in on us by mistake, what would they think?"

"That we lost touch with reality." Zoe flashes a silly smile.

Spence chuckles. "That's true, isn't it? We've had more contact with the unreal than reality for a few years now in this town."

"Let's move on," Trinity says, throwing a hand up. "Leslie and I heard from the Coven of Greenville. Elizabeth Wang had similar symptoms to Riley. When she attempted to speak, she got sicker. The Elder said Elizabeth fought the malevolent magic back with a vengeance. She was pissed and determined to expose the miscreant."

"Has the cause of death been determined?" I ask. "I mean, what an Unremarkable would attribute it to?"

Shane leans forward and his white beard fills his video tile box. "The local news didn't report a damn thing."

"Actually, Elijah has important information regarding the deaths of Riley and Elizabeth."

"Did our council allies report to you, Elijah?" Archie asks.

"Yes," Elijah says, his deep voice distorting the audio. "John Erickson overheard two police officers talking about the forensics of the case. They said the women appeared to be victims of strangulation but have no bruising or any other markings externally, which makes sense to us but not to the Unremarkables. He says our allies are flipping out. After John told them his wife was a Tylwyth Teg fairy and Alys Morgan was the one to kidnap the children, they lost their shit more than a cow. Mayor Jessica Devine worries Detective Jack Schmidt may discover our secrets. He's been asking a boatload of questions."

Archie runs a hand through his locks. "That's disconcerting. Strangulation as an explanation could bring outside attention to Bearsden. Jack has attempted to contact Gwyn while we're here."

"I didn't open the email," I say. "Since I'm spending time with family, I thought it was better to avoid him altogether."

"Oh, fuck him." Agnes turns her nose up. "He shouldn't stick his nose where it doesn't concern him."

Tanner moves toward the screen. "He's a detective who investigates potential murder cases, Agnes. It's exactly his business."

She scowls at Tanner and the rumble of our laughter distorts the audio. But it's a nervous response to our situation. Chuckles dissipate to a restless quiet as knots tighten in my stomach. We really can't afford for Jack Schmidt to discover who and what we are.

"I wasn't going to tell you, but the detective has contacted Leslie and me several times, asking if we've spoken with you. He'll be on you like a fly to shit once you return."

I swallow my fear. "He doesn't scare me. There isn't anything to connect me to Riley's death. I'll deal with him."

Archie squeezes my hand.

"With that I am ending this circle," Leslie says. "Gorawen, if you find anything more to help us close the portal, we would gladly accept your help. Thank you for attending. Go in peace, my friends."

The video chat disconnects and Aunt Gorawen taps her cane on the wooden floor. "I like that hedge witch. She has a lot of pep. I bet we could be good friends."

Who would ever imagine my aunt having anything in common with a poor retired waitress who sells pot? But here we are.

"Now that the circle has disbanded, why don't we practice more candle magic? We should eat dinner earlier when we're finished, so you can get an early start to Edinburgh."

We close our laptops and follow Aunt Gorawen as she hobbles the short distance to her magic room. My son follows in last, shutting the door behind him. We each collect a small candle from a nearby shelf and set them on her witchcraft table. Zoe chooses green again for prosperity, Tyler picks up brown—for grounding, I guess. Archie reaches for the orange one. He must be really worried about what's happening in the Celtic Studies department. I snatch up the yellow one more time. I'm not confidant this will improve my focus, but what have I got to lose?

"Hand! We may need your help!" Aunt Gorawen's magic butler flits into the room from the greenhouse and hovers over us. She carries a small basket full of old-style matches to the table. "Take one...or two. You can strike your match on the sandpaper I have attached to the surface."

"Aren't Lucifer matches kind of dangerous?" I ask. "Wouldn't it be better to use a lighter?"

"Yes, it's more hazardous," she replies. "But I haven't burned down the house yet, and I *love* the smell of sulfur."

"I do, too," Zoe says. "I think I may have been an arsonist in a prior life."

Tyler stands back. "Good to know."

We laugh and take a match from the box, striking and lighting our candles one by one. Sulfur permeates the surrounding air and I inhale its pungent odor. I appreciate my aunt's choice of match versus a mechanical lighter. There is intention in the scraping of the slender piece of wood against the rough surface.

"This isn't an ideal situation," Aunt Gorawen says. "Expect little to materialize from this practice. I recommend you perform candle magic in solitude. But this practice session is a wonderful way for us to enjoy each other's company following the Yule season."

Archie holds his orange candle close to his heart. "Aye, but it's a wonderful way to revisit this simple magic. Some witches forget the unpretentious ways can be just as powerful."

"Your man speaks truthful words," my aunt replies. "Let's begin. Instead of performing an incantation, I will guide you through the process. Grasp the candle with both hands. Decide on your intention—the desired outcome for your spell. Take a moment to consider your options."

While we stand in a semi-circle in front of the table, my aunt's helper zips back and forth above us, making me dizzy. I attempt to stare at my candle, but the glittering hand distracts me. All I can visualize is how pretty the orange and red flame is, flickering at the top in white like a belly dancer. I glance at Archie; his icy blues are staring into the flame with a laser-sharp focus. Zoe's eyes roll left and right with the tips of the fire. Tyler stares intently. Something tells me I'm going to suck at this.

When I glance at my aunt, she's shaking her head. She grabs her cane and shifts next to me.

"Do not fret, my dear. You may need a little push. That's all. Let me help."

Aunt Gorawen raises her right hand, chanting, and summons her magic. Her fingers radiate in an amber glow as swirls of magic spread out in front of her, dancing around like the flame in Zoe's candle. She sends a spark to mine, and the flame rises two feet above my hands! It reminds me of the time I was melting wax on my stovetop and it caught fire, shooting straight up and melting the control panel on the microwave.

Zoe loses concentration. "Whoa! And you were worried about me!"

"Should I cast a water spell?!" Tyler shouts.

The door swings open and Ellie strolls in, halting the minute the amber magic and pillar of fire snatch her attention. Her jaw drops so far, her uvula flaps in clear view. Her curly gray hair appears to rise from her scalp as if she's stuck her finger in an electric socket. The loudest ear-piercing scream I've ever heard exits her mouth, and she runs down the hallway with her hands swinging in the air.

"Fuuuck," Zoe says, clenching her teeth. "I must have forgotten to bolt the front door."

"You think?" Tyler asks, blowing out his candle. "Oh, my gods, Zoe."

"I'm so sorry." She lowers her head.

"Hand!" Aunt Gorawen clutches her chest. "Stop her from leaving!"

Her magic helper darts through the doorway, golden glitter trailing behind him. The rest of us blow out our candles and fling them on the table.

Folds form in Archie's brow. "That's unfortunate."

"It sure fucking is!" My heart rate is breaking a new BPM record as I stand frozen in a panic. "What are we going to do? What do we say to her?"

"We must confess," Aunt Gorawen says as she hobbles toward the doorway. "Divulge everything."

We all head out to deal with my aunt's caretaker. When we get to the foyer, she's still screaming and trying to yank the charmed bolt open. My aunt's enchanted butler must have drizzled magic on the metal because Ellie can't budge it. The luminous assistant hovers near the entry door, waving an index finger back and forth at her. Really, hand? That's not helping.

"I'll do the talking," Aunt Gorawen says. "Ellie, dear. I implore you. Please, turn around. I need to tell you about me—and my family."

My aunt's caretaker slowly twists around to face us, her eyes wide with fear. Her entire body shakes, and she entwines her fingers together in an attempt to stop it. Her lower lip quivers as her lips part.

"I've gone completely bonkers, haven't I?" she asks. "What I imagined in your art room didn't happen."

The magic butler drops in front of her face and jumps around as if he's laughing at her and she emits a high-pitched yelp.

"That's enough, hand," I say. "Go to the magic room."

His fingers wilt and he flies down the hallway, sulking.

My aunt's caretaker hugs her torso, attempting to console herself, I suppose. Or it's my aunt's chilly historic home. "I wasn't imagining what I saw, was I?"

Aunt Gorawen approaches Ellie and she takes a step back. My aunt grasps her hands. "I am the same old woman you've known for all these years. I've been concealing some skeletons in my musty closets. Deep down, you know what that secret is, don't you?"

Ellie looks past Aunt Gorawen and scans our smiling faces. "Jesus, Mary, and Joseph. The mocking stories about you are true." She peers back at my aunt. "Many of the old town residents told me to stay away from you. They said you were a witch. I did not believe them."

Archie, Tyler, Zoe, and I move a little closer, but my aunt's most trusted life steward remains in her spot, unflinching.

"You're not evil witches, are you?" She pinches her lips together. "I could not stand by and allow you to attack my town."

We chuckle at her sudden defiance.

"No," Tyler says. "We are benevolent. Geez."

Zoe adds, "We promise to do no harm. We're the good guys...well, witches."

"That day I first came to the estate." I lay a hand on her shoulder. "I handed an old tome to you to show my aunt. It was our family grimoire."

Ellie gapes at me. "That's how Gorawen knew you were her niece."

"Yes. I'm sorry we kept all this a secret. But you see why we did."

"I am so embarrassed. I must have looked ridiculous scurrying away like an old scaredy-cat."

"No," I say, caressing her shoulder. "The news would have shocked any person who wasn't *in the knowing*—that's how we refer to those who aren't aware of the supernatural. I had a feeling you'd find out, eventually. I hoped it would happen far in the future. Now that you know, we can stop walking around on eggshells around you. But you can't tell anyone, not even Owen."

She snorts. "He'd send me straight to the town psychiatrist, you know."

"We appreciate your understanding, Ellie," Archie says. "It's important for all of us to remain in hiding. The world as a whole remains frightened of things they can't comprehend or understand."

She squints at my aunt and crosses her arms. "So, you don't need my help nearly as much as you seem to."

Aunt Gorawen embraces her. "My dear friend. I'd be lost without you. I need you more than you'll ever imagine."

"You...have my word, Gorawen." Ellie fumbles over her words. "Your secret...your secret is safe with me."

"Thank you so much." My aunt waves a splash of magic on the deadbolt and it slides open. "You should make your way home before Owen comes searching for you."

"I'll come back later to say goodbye." Ellie takes a cleansing breath and opens the door. Before exiting, she turns around and cocks her head. "Gorawen, any chance you could cast a spell on Owen to make him take out the trash?"

CHAPTER TEN

A SAD GOODBYE

I DRAG MY LUGGAGE down the old, steep wooden stairs. Archie, Tyler, and Zoe are waiting for me in the foyer, chatting with Aunt Gorawen about coming for the Summer Solstice Celebration. They already have their winter jackets on. A twinge pinches my insides as I tear up. Is this another warning? Every time I visit, my heart aches at the thought of not seeing her again, but this sends a wave of apprehension down my spine. I set my suitcase on the floor and grab my jacket from the wall hook.

"Where is Ellie?" I ask, slipping my arms into the sleeves. "Didn't she want to see us off?"

"We're getting a late start," Archie says. "Can't wait much longer. I'm sorry I left a mess in the kitchen."

"No worries. I told her not to clean up yet." Aunt Gorawen glances down the hallway. "Ellie, they need to leave soon."

Her voice travels through the hall. "I'll be there now in a minute!"

Ellie shuffles into the foyer from the kitchen, the magic butler flitting beside her. She flings her hand out at him.

"Gracious. You have to follow me everywhere now, do you?"

"Off with you. Go to the magic room." Aunt Gorawen waves him on and he flies away. "He likes you, Ellie. I also think he's wanted to meet you for quite a long time. He'd been spying on you. You'll be a fascination for the near future, I suspect."

"Well, it will take some getting used to, I tell you."

"He's fun once you get to know him," Zoe says. "And very helpful."

Tyler steps forward and hugs Ellie. "Thank you for taking care of our aunt all these years. Mom and I are indebted to you."

"You're most welcome," she replies, smiling.

Aunt Gorawen shifts closer to Tyler and Zoe. "You best get going. But before you set off on your journey, I must give you both a cwtch."

She wraps her arms around them, holding for a long moment. A puzzled expression appears on Tyler's face.

"A cwtch is a Welsh word for a very special hug," I say. "Think of it as a familial embrace you take home with you."

"I love that." Zoe helps Aunt Gorawen with her cane. "Maybe you can teach us some Welsh on our next visit."

"Of course, my dear. I'm not forgetting you two." My aunt hugs Archie and me. "Forgive me if I don't brave the cold. Ellie, could you walk out with them?"

"I'd be delighted," she replies. "I'll get my coat."

"May you have a safe journey," Aunt Gorawen says. "I love you all."

"We love you, too." I embrace her one more time, not wanting to let go. "I'll make sure we chat again soon."

We head out into the chilly air and Ellie helps load our luggage into the rental car. After a quick goodbye, she wishes us well on our trip. While everyone gets seated, I approach our newfound friend, who's *in the knowing*.

"If something should happen to my aunt, you understand what you need to do, right?" I ask. "You must hide her life as a witch."

"Gorawen will surely have a discussion with me once you leave, but I think I know what she'll ask of me. Before, I was told under no circumstances should I go through her belongings in the art room. I was to contact you directly. Now I understand why."

"I really hate to leave this time. Something in my gut—my witch's intuition—tells me I may never see her again. Being a witch, I have to take the feeling seriously."

Ellie steps forward and hugs me. "Oh, Gwynedd. Don't you worry about Gorawen. I may not be a witch. But I have instincts, too. They tell me she has a few more years in her, and it's all due to you." She pulls away. "She's making up for lost time."

"Thank you, Ellie. You're good to her. Please tell Owen we said goodbye and expect to spend time with him on our next trip."

"Will do, Gwyn. I hope your ride to Edinburgh is uneventful."

Ellie rushes back to the house, skipping over sheep poop on the way. I drop into the passenger side of the car and glance at the living room window to the left of the front door. While Aunt Gorawen waves goodbye through the window, Ellie appears. The magic butler plays with her curly gray hair and she bats him away, frowning. I chuckle. Something tells me my aunt is in capable, Unremarkable hands.

On the ride to Edinburgh, Tyler, Zoe, and I succumb to the monotonous motorway and the lingering jetlag. I'm awakened by the horn of a passing car honking, but my son and his love don't move an inch. We pass Braidburn Valley Park—not long now. Archie catches me stirring.

"Did you have a good nap, my love?" he asks.

"Yeah. I probably shouldn't have slept so long. I'll be up for hours now. Should I wake them?"

"Naw. We'll be there in a wee bit." He lays a hand on mine, grinning.

"You're excited about seeing your family now, aren't you? A lot different from the first time I traveled with you to meet them."

"Aye. I long for the trips now. Everything I'd bottled up for years came to a head during that Yule visit. The verbal beating you gave my dad didn't hurt, either. He took to you quite strongly after that. You gained his respect."

I chuckle. "It was embarrassing, losing my temper and breaking out in a hot flash. I melted all over my dinner. I blamed it on my menopausal migraines, though. And the stress of Nuada finding me." And he did.

"Dad and Quinn have spoken with other ancestral witches in the area over the last few months. So far, they've discovered no spell to close a portal. There is one witch they haven't met with yet. An old codger who lives in Dean Village."

I arch my back, aching from sitting too long. "Are we going to meet him?"

"Quinn never responded about that."

Archie turns the corner in Haymarket. After another left and a right, we arrive in the West End. He pulls up along the curb of the one-way street and parks. The Cockburn family Georgian style home stands grand under the nearly full moon. The exterior sandstone facade hides the story of its magical past, the history of a clan of ancestral witches. A single cloud floats across the shining sphere above, dulling its luminosity. Movement stirs in the back seat, and I turn around.

"Hey, sleepyheads. We're here."

Zoe gazes out the car window at the house. "Wow. You said the Cockburns owned a row home. That's a mansion!"

Tyler stretches his arms. "It's not. But a gigantic townhouse like theirs is probably worth a lot."

"Very true," I say. "And they have a corner house, which makes it even more valuable. From the top floor, there is a fabulous view of Edinburgh Castle."

We exit the sedan and move to the rear to collect our suitcases. Soon after, Archie's brother, Quinn, opens the door below the magnificent sunburst window and comes rushing down the steps. In his early 50s, he has his dad's likeness—tall and stocky with thick brown hair that's gray at the temples and eyes the color of blue steel. His dad, Harris, stands in the doorway, a beaming smile brightening his face. Despite being in his late 70s, he's as strong as his son, but his locks have turned silver.

Quinn approaches us when he reaches the walkway at the bottom of the steps. "Let me help you with the luggage. I'm sure as a witch on a broom you're too tired to lift it." He takes my suitcase.

"Thank you," I say. "It's been a long day." I touch my son's arm to get his attention. "This is my son, Tyler Wolfe, and his significant other, Zoe Wu."

Quinn grasps my son's hand and shakes it vigorously. "A right pleasure to meet you finally. Your mum never stops talking about you both."

"Awesome to meet you, too." Tyler grabs his duffel bag from the trunk. "Thank you for letting us stay in your magnificent home."

"Yeah," Zoe says. "I've never slept in a mansion before."

Quinn belly laughs. "It's a nice enough house, but don't expect servants to wait on you hand and foot. We take care of ourselves." He leans forward and whispers in a thick Scottish brogue, "Can't risk having those who aren't *in the knowing* sneaking around on us, can we?"

Zoe chuckles. "That would cause a lot of rumors."

"Aye," Archie says, rolling his suitcase. "Harris's leg is shaking like a jackhammer. We best move into the house before it falls off."

We make our way up the stairs, dragging our luggage. Harris moves aside, telling us all to come in. As always, a pine cone wreath hangs over the hall fireplace. Evergreen garland decorates the arched doorway that leads to wood and iron steps at the rear of the house. Archie's dad immediately rushes to me, wrapping me in a warm embrace.

"How is my newest daughter-in-law?" he asks in his baritone voice.

Archie clears his throat. "Dad, Gwyn moved in with me, but we didn't get married."

Harris pulls away, laughing. "Och. That will happen soon enough."

I roll my eyes. "Tyler. Zoe. I'd like to introduce you to Archie's dad."

"Chuffed to meet you," he says, nodding. "And welcome to my humble abode."

Zoe stares up toward the ornate plaster above. "Thank you for inviting us. Those cornices are beautiful, and the ceilings must be at least sixteen feet high."

"We've never been in a house this fancy," Tyler says. "We're afraid of damaging something."

Quinn pats my son on the back. "Don't worry yourself. We break stuff all the time, right, Dad?"

Harris scowls at him. "Watch yourself, son. You're never too old for me to give you a whipping out back."

Quinn laughs and it reverberates in the foyer. "He isn't serious. My brother will confirm he's just having a blether."

"He means joking around," Archie says, chuckling. "We Scots like to tease each other."

The clinking of glasses echoes in the kitchen, which is right off the foyer. Quinn motions toward the doorway. "The wife is in there setting some Scotch whisky on the table. Come sit and sip a wee bit before you start your slumber."

When we enter, I spot a head full of wavy ginger hair. Maggie darts over and hugs me. "The time between your visits is much too long, Gwyn." Her sapphire-blue eyes sparkle as she addresses my son in her light Scottish accent. "You must be Tyler. As handsome as your pictures." She's a bit younger than me—approaching her 50s.

"This is Quinn's wife, Margaret," I say. "But she goes by Maggie."

He blushes. "Thanks for the compliment. This is my partner, Zoe."

"Hi, Maggie." Tyler's love surveys their immense modern kitchen. "This room is enormous."

"Aye. But when the entire family is here, it seems not big enough," she replies. "A pleasure to meet you both. Please, sit down. Let's chat and sip some whisky."

We collapse into the chairs around the massive wood table. Quinn chants an incantation to summon his magic. A floating Scotch whisky bottle dances from witch to witch, filling our glasses. We spend the next hour catching them up on the tribulations the Tylwyth Teg fairy Alys Morgan caused for Bearsden. Maggie and Quinn share stories of their busy offspring. I haven't partaken of liquor in a long time. After a few sips, the room spins. I shove the glass away, but the others fill their glasses with a *wee* bit more.

Tyler and Zoe howl like hyenas while Harris recounts the dinner where I met the entire family and lost my cool. How we were both so angry we busted the ceiling pocket lights, and I broke out in a hot flash, dripping sweat onto the haggis. Near the end of his tale, the effect of the Scotch whisky is more apparent. His accent thickens so much, I have trouble deciphering his speech. Or am I tipsy? When the laughter dissipates to a soft chuckle, Quinn nods to Maggie.

"Tyler and Zoe," she says, getting up from the table. "Why don't I show you to your room? It's on the second floor. You'll be staying in my daughter Isla's old room. She moved out a few months ago when she found employment."

Zoe yawns as she stands. "That sounds awesome. I'm pooped."

"I shouldn't be, but I am," Tyler says, pushing up from his chair. "Night, everyone."

After a round of overlapping "goodnights," my son and his love follow Maggie out of the kitchen. The conversation quickly moves to the serious nature of this visit. Harris plops his burly arms on the wooden table.

"I thought it wise to keep this conversation between the three of us for now. You can tell your son and his girlfriend as you wish. Quinn, Maggie, and I have scoured our personal resources over the past year, as you know—even got the grandchildren involved. I reached out to local witches we trust. They confirmed what we found. Lots of incantations to open a portal, none to close. Plenty to banish malevolent beings. You may have to pick them off one by one as they cross over."

Archie slouches back in his chair. "That's all we've done for a few years—to the detriment of the community and the Bearsden Coven."

"And now local covens are being attacked," I say. "Two witches are dead, either by a hex or possibly fairy magic. We could not identify the source of the initial murder. The second happened right before we left. The first victim was an old crone who was extremely powerful, but she couldn't fight back against the nefarious witchcraft."

"Aye. Archie sent me a message." Quinn gathers several of the glasses and deposits them in the kitchen sink. "He told us the old crone said you were in danger from an unknown woman. He believes she may be Nuada's mother."

I shrug. "We don't really know. It's irrelevant. Whoever it is that wants to harm me, it doesn't supersede the threat of the open portal. We have to find a solution."

"One other possibility remains," Quinn says, peering at his father tentatively.

Harris slaps his hand on the table. "Naw. We agreed we shouldn't bother the elderly codger. He rarely leaves his house anymore. Doesn't talk with anyone."

"What old man?" I ask, leaning into the table.

"He's become quite crabbit in his later years." Archie collects the rest of the glasses. "This is one time I tend to agree with Dad."

"Because you know I'm right," Harris says, his words barely intelligible.

My shoulders fall in frustration. "Will someone please tell me who you're talking about?"

Quinn shoves the cork into the top of the Scotch whisky bottle. "A cranky old witch named Hamish Brown. He lives in Dean Village. He's a recluse. Rarely sees anyone. Gets all his food delivered by a witch neighbor. Some joke that he died years ago and his ghost orders the groceries."

"Sounds like a hedge witch I knew before I got to her to loosen up," I say. "I could try to sweet talk him?"

"No offense, Gwynedd." Harris lets out a belch so loud, I bet it wakes the neighbors. "But you should leave this to us Scots."

"We can chat about this tomorrow," Quinn says. "We should hit the sack and sleep the whisky off."

I stand and wobble. "I'm really glad I drank but half of it."

Maggie strolls back into the kitchen. "The young ones are probably dead to the world already. Archie, I made your bed as well, and I put out fresh towels for you and Gwyn."

"Thank you," he replies. "You're a dear one. Ready for sleep, my love?"

"If I can make it upstairs," I say. "Thank you, Maggie. Goodnight, everyone."

Quinn lays a hand on my shoulder. "Sleep well, Gwyn."

Harris has nodded off, his head hanging to the left and drool seeping into his shirt. As Archie and I stagger toward the stairs at the end of the hall, an aura builds in my abdomen—past visits rolling in my brain like an art movie. Even in my inebriated state, I recall what happened after that memorable Yule dinner. I woke up in the middle of the night and had a dram of Scotch whisky with Quinn in the upstairs family room. That's when I discovered their bedroom was right under Archie's. I halt and clutch my stomach.

"Go on up," I say. "I need to ask Maggie for something."

"Don't be long, my love. I'll warm up the bed for you."

He kisses me on the cheek and I get a whiff of Scotch whisky on his breath. He heads up the stairs to the attic floor and I stagger back to the kitchen.

"Maggie, do you have any cardboard scraps?" I ask. "And some duct tape?"

A perplexed expression grasps her face. "What on earth do you need that for?"

"I'll get it for you, Gwyn," Quinn says. "Wait for me at the bottom of the stairs."

I shuffle back to the stairway and he shows up a couple of minutes later. He passes me a large rectangular section of cardboard and a roll of duct tape.

"Don't have too much fun," he says, winking.

My face flushes. "Very. Funny. See you in the morning."

Quinn laughs and heads back to the kitchen to help Maggie shut down the house for the night. Laughter seeps into the hallway and I chuckle.

When I reach the second floor, I pause to steady myself. That Scotch whisky was strong—must have been a really old bottle. By the time I arrive at the top, I'm sobering up a bit. I enter the bedroom to find Archie already in bed on his cell. Probably checking his email for updates from Trinity. As I pass the dresser, I drop my phone next to the sizeable chunk of clear quartz crystal he always keeps in the room. I continue over to the register vent and kneel.

"What the fawk are you doing?" he asks.

I rip a strip of tape, place it along one edge of the cardboard, and tape it over the top of the cast iron grill. After placing three more strips, it's completely covered.

"That should do it." I walk over to his exquisite antique canopy bed and jump on.

Wrinkles form in his brow. "You do realize you cut off the single heat register that feeds this bedroom, don't you?"

I crawl to him, sporting a mischievous grin. "We'll have to make our own heat then."

"You're drunk, witch," Archie says, setting his phone on the nightstand.

"Not that much. I barely drank half the glass." I pull off my long-sleeved shirt and straddle him. "Did the whisky make you sleepy? Or are you awake enough for some recreation?"

He pulls me to him, caressing my back. "You've been too preoccupied for sex. Is it the drink?"

"It helps." I kiss him fervently and rest my forehead on his. "I feel safe here. Why do you think that is?"

He unclasps my bra and slides it off. "I don't know, but I'm chuffed you enjoy coming here. My family can be overwhelming and overbearing."

I pull his shirt off and toss it behind me. My hands fall to his chest, and I stroke his nipples, making them erect. He pulls me to him and kisses me again. The bulge in his pants pushes against me, reminding me how much I've missed our lovemaking. He bends down to kiss the red dragon tattoo on my breast before taking my nipple into his mouth.

I roll off him to remove my fleece-lined leggings and panties. He whips off his jeans and tosses them to the floor. I lie back on the bed and he crawls on top of me, positioning himself between my legs. He rubs against my wetness.

"Gwyn, we haven't made love since..."

I stroke his cheek. "I know. All this supernatural drama keeps invading our lives. I want it to end. But will it ever?"

"We'll find an incantation to close the portal. I promise."

He enters me and I wrap my legs around him. Taking his time, he makes love to me, removing the stress of the world, if only for this suspended moment in the universe. He presses a hand against mine, sparking my witch energy until an amber radiance engulfs me. I reach my peak and he moans with his release not long after. I stroke his muscular back while his panting subsides.

After a few calming breaths, he *snores* into my ear. I suppose I should be happy he lasted as long as he did. When I push him off of me, he rolls onto his side, continuing to snort and grunt into the pillow. I dash to the register vent, rip off the cardboard, and hop back into bed. As I pull the linens over us, I glimpse the clear quartz crystal on the dresser. It radiates in a white luminosity I never noticed before. Did our lovemaking spark the reaction? While I bask in the afterglow of our quickie, my mind returns to the old witch living in Dean Village.

Could he possess the knowledge we've been seeking all along?

Chapter Eleven

DEAN VILLAGE WITCH

Leslie and Agnes stand near the portal opening in the Celestial Gardens, their hair swimming in the air like snakes. I turn my head and the gray-skinned monster takes two steps toward me. He flexes his bulging muscles with each step as his gargantuan boots squish into the muddy soil, releasing a musty smell. His dark, shoulder-length hair catches a ride on a gust of wind. I get a whiff of his body odor and pinch my nose. A moonbeam highlights his disfigured face—covered in deep scars that frame a disfigured eye. He locks his one shiny coal-black eye with mine and blinks.

I wake with a gasp, my heart pumping faster than a runner at full sprint. Archie is gone. I sit up and survey the room, stopping at the dresser. The clear quartz crystal radiates a faint glow. Did the single stone spark a vision in my sleep? And Leslie and Agnes were in it. Was it a dream? Or an expanded premonition?

My phone displays 7:48 a.m., but the sun is still at rest in Edinburgh. How do the Scots deal with the late arrival of daylight? I want to crawl back under the duvet. After my morning appointment with the porcelain throne, I throw on some clothes and head downstairs. The dream disturbs me, but I can't tell Archie now. I'll have to speak with him later, when we're alone.

When I enter the kitchen, I find everyone gathered around the immense wooden table, nursing hangovers. Harris, Archie, and Quinn have cups of black tea in their hands. I thought Scots had a bit of tolerance to whisky. I mean, I expected Tyler and Zoe to be a little hungover. They're bent over, resting their heads on their limp arms. Maggie is the only one, besides me, who appears to have avoided the dreaded waking headache.

"Good morning!" I shuffle in my socks toward the forty-eight-inch range. "Looks like we may have a beautiful, sunny day."

Tyler rubs his temples. "Mom, do you have to scream?"

"I'm not talking that loud," I say. "Maggie, do you have any ibuprofen?"

Zoe lifts her head off the table. "We already took some. I remember now why I don't drink a lot. Not worth the consequences."

Harris's laughter reverberates in the spacious kitchen. "Drink your tea, lass. Lots of it. And water. You'll feel like new once you've got some food in your belly."

"I don't think I can eat anything," Tyler says, moaning. "Maybe some toast."

"Coming right up." Maggie chants a spell, sending a plate of toast through the air until it lands softly on the table. "You'll be ready for some eggs once you've got some bread in your stomach. Go on. Nibble on that." She leans into me and whispers, "Thought you should know. The cardboard didn't mask your recreational activities last night."

She chuckles as my face flushes the color of a pomegranate. I pour hot water from the teakettle into my cup and drop in a bag of Earl Grey.

"Would you like some help with breakfast?" I peer at Archie. His head hangs barely four inches from the table. "The other cook in the house appears to be out of commission. He may have sipped a bit too much whisky last night." And stayed up even later to *play*.

Harris bursts out laughing and the rest of the clan joins in on my jest. I chant and wave a splash of magic, prompting the spoon to twirl. When I glance back, Archie is glaring at me. But a slight smile erupts on one side.

He finishes the last of his tea. "I'm sure Maggie can handle breakfast without my interference."

"She loves to cook," Quinn adds, pushing up from his chair. "She rarely lets me help. Says I get in the way." He moves next to her in front of the range and kisses her on the cheek.

"Because you sneak bites of the meal." She slaps his hand as he attempts to snatch a sausage from the pan.

The front door opens and shuts with a thud, echoing in the foyer. Steps follow and Isla walks in wearing a wool coat and gloves. She possesses Maggie's wavy ginger hair and sapphire-blue eyes. Her face lights up when she sees her uncle. She rushes to where he's sitting and gives him a quick hug.

"Hey, Uncle Archie! Hi, Gwyn! I wish you could have been here for Hogmanay. The celebration was cracking this year." The unfamiliar faces catch her attention. "You must be Tyler and Zoe. Mum and Dad said you would be visiting. I thought I'd take you to the Royal Mile and show you the sights today. But you're both looking a wee peely-wally."

Tyler swallows a bite of toast. "Had a little too much Scotch whisky last night when we arrived. Feeling better now."

"So excited to meet you," Zoe says, her bubbly demeanor returning. "I can't wait to see Old Town. But I think we should eat first."

"Sit down and join us," Quinn says. "Get to know our new guests."

For the next hour, we pass conversations around the table like they're an extension of the meal. Serving plates filled with sausage, fried mushrooms, toast, and scones fly back and forth, making me as dizzy as the discourse on freely using magic in the house. Archie pushes back against his dad.

"All I'm saying is we expose ourselves to unnecessary discovery when we use witchcraft daily, as openly as all of you do. I worry you'll forget when the plumber and heating service technicians come by. It's easy to forget they aren't *in the knowing*."

"Och. Rubbish," Harris says. "We've practiced our witchcraft openly in our home for decades and have never been discovered. Yet look at your coven. Vowed to use magic on an as needed basis, yet now townspeople are in the knowing of your existence, along with the fairies and the portal they cross through."

"He has a point," Zoe says through a mouth full of scone.

"Thank you," he replies. "Your young witches are brilliant."

"They are," I say proudly. "I admit I've made a few blunders myself. Lucky for me, the Unremarkable involved turned out to be married to a Tylwyth Teg and was *in the knowing*."

Isla spits out her tea. "You have Tylwyth Teg fairies living in your town now? That's fawking hilarious."

"We have a couple," Archie says. "The coven sent one back through the portal. She was kidnapping blond-haired children in Bearsden."

"Well, I would fawking hope so." She wipes her chin with a napkin. "If they want to exist in our world, they have to live by our rules."

"It's not as simple as that," Maggie says, collecting the empty plates. "Their magic is powerful. You were lucky to send her back."

Pangs of intuition take hold in my abdomen, reminding me of my vision. The Tylwyth Teg may be the least of our worries.

Quinn gets up from the table. "I'll load the dishwasher, love. Sit down and finish your tea." He motions at our adult children. "You young witches should move like the wind if you want to make use of this bonnie but short day. Sunset arrives by 4."

"Mom, you'll let me know if you need our help?" my son asks.

"We're fine for now," I say. "Go have some fun."

Tyler and Zoe thank Maggie for breakfast and follow Isla out the front door to do some sight-seeing on the Royal Mile. Harris stands and walks toward the foyer doorway.

"I'm off to Effie's house to help her with the herbs and other plants in her nursery. I'll likely be there all day. Would you like me to bring you some?"

"We're good, Dad," Quinn says, shutting the dishwasher. "Effie Campbell is our local supplier in the winter—a talented green witch. Tell her we said hello."

"Will do. Have a pleasant day. See you at dinner."

Harris makes his way to the back of the house toward the garage. When the backdoor shuts, Quinn turns around.

"Now that Dad is gone, I can speak without the old man shutting us down. My buddy Malcom knows the witch who lives next door to Hamish Brown. His name is Lyle Murray. He spoke with his neighbor about your situation and he's agreed to meet with us. But we have to leave immediately. Hamish takes a nap after lunch."

Archie stands up and shoves his chair under the table in a huff. "I'm not comfortable going behind Dad's back. If he finds out, and he will, he'll ban us both from the family magic room for a week."

"If we set off now," Maggie says, clarity shining in her eyes, "we can make it back before he discovers we've gone. You know I'm right. Your father is as stubborn as a mule."

Archie glances at me. "Not unlike someone else I know."

"Hey," I say, frowning. "I've improved a lot."

"You have, my love." He kisses me on the cheek. "But I miss that *stubborn woman*."

Quinn laughs and pats me on the back. "You blend right in with this family, Gwyn. Well, let's go meet a witch ghost."

On the way to Dean Village, Maggie and I trail behind Quinn and Archie, chatting about dinner plans. The rest of their adult children want to meet Tyler and Zoe. To no one's surprise, they've planned an evening of enchanted games. Although Archie leans toward Leslie's rules of magic-as-needed, I embrace the daily overt use they openly embrace. It's a blast.

We're bundled up for a winter's day, but the unusual sunshine warms us as we stroll the windy path along the Water of Leith. Snow on the riverbanks melts into the rippling water as we pass the village cemetery and we stop to snap a few photos of the idyllic wintry scene with our phones. When we discover we've fallen too far behind, we quicken our pace and catch up to the men. I snatch the end of a conversation.

"Have you spoken with the University of Edinburgh since your last email to me?" Quinn asks.

"Naw," Archie replies. "I've been too busy to follow up on their invitation."

"You could lose out on an opportunity, brother."

"I've been a wee bit busy, Quinn."

A branch snaps when I step down on the path, prompting Archie and his brother to look back.

"How long have you two been sneaking behind our arses?" Quinn asks.

"Long enough to know you're about to miss the turn." Maggie points at the street sign.

We pivot right and continue down the gray cobblestone road. Archie glances at me but doesn't acknowledge their conversation. "We thought we lost you back at the cemetery."

"No," I say without questioning him. If it's something important, he'll tell me. "We took our pictures and rushed to catch up."

Archie shakes his head. "Are you sure we should go through with this? Dad will blow the cap off his crown, and you know it."

"We'll deal with that prospect should it arise," Maggie says. "This family can't make progress if we heed every single demand Harris puts forth."

"Still…I feel bad about it, too," I reply. "He'll probably stop calling me his daughter-in-law."

"At least it will be accurate." Quinn motions to cross the street. "This way. It's the door on the right at the end of the lane. Lyle Murray is waiting for us."

Lyle stands with his hands in his wool coat pockets, sporting a tweed cap. He nods to us and Quinn offers his hand. Our witch aid shakes it vigorously.

"Hamish is waiting for you in the living room," he says. "I doubted he would agree to meet with you, but he's right concerned about your plight. Let's go in."

We enter the old witch's flat into a tiny foyer that leads to a cozy living area. Lyle waves at us to follow him in. Despite the sun's rays beaming through a large window, the room has a drab appearance. The aged hardwood floors and furniture haven't seen an update since the turn of the century, I'd guess.

A man who's experienced a hundred years sits back in a wing-back chair facing a roaring fire in a small fireplace. His leathery pale skin shows signs of a long, hard life, and his white hair and beard cascade past his torso—maybe not cut for ages. His sunken, dark eyes reflect decades of unhappiness. Quinn and Archie move close to Hamish Brown while Maggie and I keep our distance. We don't want to frighten him, or worse, piss him off.

Lyle bends down next to his ear. "Hamish, these are the witches I spoke to you about. They're from the West End."

He raises his chin and scowls. "Ah, you didn't tell me they were rich arseholes. Why should I help you then? Your money isn't enough to solve your own problems, so you seek my knowledge?"

"I'm Quinn Cockburn," Archie's brother says. "We would gladly pay you for your help, Hamish."

"Fawking Cockburns, are you?" He spits into the fire. "Who are these others with you?"

Quinn gestures to his spouse. "This is my wife, Maggie."

Archie clears his throat and offers his hand, but Hamish keeps his planted on the chair arms. "I'm Archibald Cockburn." He gestures toward me. "My partner in life, Gwynedd Crowther."

"A Welsh woman, eh?" Hamish eyes me up and down.

"Actually, I'm American," I say. "My parents were born in Wales, though."

"Ah, yes. Lyle said this portal problem he spoke of is in the States. Did you open this rift to the Otherworld?"

I glance at Archie and he nods. "No. My mom and two other women opened it up in the '60s, and fae children crossed over. After a time, there wasn't any supernatural activity, but they appeared again a couple of years ago. Then other malevolent beings invaded our town. We need to shut the opening to save our city from future catastrophe. We tried to close it once, but it failed. The only promising spell we've found since requires a human sacrifice. We refuse to harm anyone."

Hamish stares at me for the longest minute, as if he disapproves. Did I share too much? Would he kill to close the portal? He examines the others, too. After a thorough inspection, he gazes into the fire.

"I've lived through many wars. Watched my village deteriorate into a rundown hellhole, and now, it's so posh they have raised my rent just to push me out. Can you spare an old witch a few quid to help me fill my landlord's greedy pocket?"

"We'd gladly pay all your rent, Hamish," Quinn says, touching his arm. "But we'll do it even if you can't assist us with our plight. Because we're Scots. We take care of our witches in need."

He raises his chin again, a slight smile poking through his layers of wrinkles. "I don't accept charity."

Hamish lifts his hand and chants a spell. Amber magic seeps from his fingertips, directed toward a bookshelf to the left of the fireplace. The amber fingers pull at a tattered leather book, carrying it toward him. He grabs the old tome and flips through the pages, stopping when he finds a loose piece of aged parchment.

"Lyle, would you pour our guests some of my best Scotch whisky?" he asks, motioning to the mismatched chairs in the room. "Please, sit and share a dram with me."

"Coming straight away," Lyle says as he darts out of the living room.

We slide chairs and set them up near the fireplace, enjoying the warmth as we sit. After a few brief minutes, Lyle returns with a tray of glasses filled with whisky. It's rather early still to be drinking hard liquor, especially after the prior night, but we don't dare insult the old witch.

"This is a map I found many years ago when I was a young lad. Never imagined I would need it. There is a legend about an old grimoire containing one-of-a-kind incantations—the Book of Dark Souls. Beware. For generations, my family warned me about the effects of its dark magic. They said for every spell one casts, you sacrifice a part of your inner soul. But the warning could have been put in place to scare witch thieves away as well. You may not find the spell that you seek, but I am willing to part with the map to cover my flat's rent. And I take no responsibility for the risks."

Archie locks eyes with Quinn and he nods. "We'll take our chances."

Hamish raises his arthritic hand and passes the parchment to Archie. He unfolds it and we lean over to inspect the contents. The map appears to depict a series of tunnels.

"What is this a map of?" Quinn asks.

"The vaults," Hamish replies. "You know of the city's underground chambers, yes?"

"Under the South Bridge?" Archie asks. "The grimoire is down there?"

"Aye. Or so legend states," Hamish says. "But you'll have to wait until mid-week to sneak into them. The tours are heavily booked—some as late as ten. I recommend you go after midnight. Lyle can take you to a back entrance."

"The vaults are privately owned now." Quinn examines the map a little closer. "We'd be taking an enormous risk for a legend written on an old piece of parchment."

Archie runs his fingers through his locks. "There's no way to get down there without breaking in using magic."

"Well, it's not like we haven't done that or worse before," I say, smirking.

Quinn, Maggie, and Archie gape at me, apparently not happy with my honest admission. I throw my hands up, clenching my teeth, and Hamish bursts out laughing. He hurls a stream of magic at the fire with his hand, stoking the flames into a red-orange blaze. We take a step back, and he shakes his index finger at me, grinning.

"I like this Yank."

CHAPTER TWELVE

A SECRET HIDING PLACE

OVER THE NEXT FEW days, we try to occupy our time with visits to Edinburgh Castle, shopping in Newtown, and dining at local pubs. But the tension is thick, like the murky fog that's moved into the city. Archie hasn't mentioned the conversation he had with Quinn on our walk to Dean Village, and I don't want to bring it up. It was a private conversation between his brother and him. I decide to let it go, but my intuition sends twinges of doubt to my gut. I know I should tell Tyler and him about the return of my vision, but we have enough on our plate. That is a battle for another day.

Wednesday, Quinn and Maggie's offspring come by for dinner sans their significant others. The plan is for them to go with all of us to the vaults. It requires some delicate timing. Harris usually passes out by midnight, but we may need to push up his bedtime by keeping his glass filled with Scotch whisky on the down-low after we eat.

After the animated meal, punctuated by shouting matches, stories, and magical flying serving platters, I'm ready to relax on the sofa in their enormous living room while the young people play games to pass the time. Finlay and Fergus, the middle twins, go to the wall shelves and collect the poker cards and chips while Quinny, the eldest, clears off the game table in the corner. Young Harris, Isla, and Zoe have their noses buried in books. They all resemble their dad and grandad except for Isla, who inherited her mom's fiery features. Tyler gets up from the sitting area where the older generation is chatting.

"I can help you collect more chairs," he says. "Zoe, will you put the book down and come play poker with us?"

"Sure," she replies. "When I'm finished with this chapter on prosperity incantations."

He rolls his eyes. "We don't need to cast spells for money. We can afford the house just fine."

"But these look more promising than the ones we have in our witchcraft database."

Isla lifts her head from the page she's reading. "It never hurts to implement one to enhance your success. The last spell pouch I made helped me snag this fabulous job I wanted."

"I'm proud of you, granddaughter," Harris says, sipping his whisky. "You learnt the craft well. But I miss having you here in the house."

"All you did was complain about me getting a job. Now that I'm gone, you whine about me moving out. Does anything make you happy?"

He raises his glass at her. "I wanted you to find gainful employment, not leave our ancestral home."

"Oh, granddad," Quinny says. "You said that about all of us."

Young Harris wrinkles his nose. "He didn't say that about me."

Finlay snorts. "That's because he wanted you to find your own place. You never cleaned your bedroom."

"Or the bathroom," Fergus says. "I always cleaned it before Finlay and I left."

I chuckle at their family banter. "It's hard to watch your children move out, but it means we did our jobs as parents when they become productive members of society."

"Archie, aren't you glad you missed out on all of this?" Quinn asks, holding an empty glass.

"Naw," he replies. "I envy you now. But I'm elated with my life as it is." He winks at me.

"You should be," Maggie says, smiling. "You found a wonderful woman to spend your life with. And she has an amazing family."

"Thank you." I gaze at my son. "He's grown into a wonderful man."

"And witch," Archie adds, toasting Tyler with his empty glass.

The young ones gather around the poker table and the rest of us eye Harris's glass. He's barely drank any of his drink. Our plan seems to be fizzling out. What the fuck are we going to do? Quinn grabs the bottle of Scotch whisky and shifts toward him.

"Would you like me to top off your drink, Dad?"

Harris yawns and stretches his arms. "I don't think so, son. I had enough last night. Didn't sleep well. Would be in my best interest to turn in for the evening." He stands up and gazes at the painting of his wife, Elspeth. "Goodnight, my love."

He exits the living room and for a couple of minutes, the whooshing sound of passing vehicles filters through the windows. Zoe is the first to break the silence.

"That's so sad," she says. "Has he ever tried to conference with her?"

"Sadly, no," Quinn replies. "He said he couldn't bear to gaze upon her beautiful face and not have the capability to touch her. He is waiting until he crosses over into the Otherworld."

"Shhh." Maggie shuffles over and shuts the door. "Sound travels in this house."

Tyler looks at me and snickers. "Right, Mom?"

I send him a side-eye. "Very. Funny."

Archie chuckles and sets his empty glass on the end table.

"How much time should we allow for him to fall asleep?" Quinny asks.

Isla puts her book back on the shelf. "I would wait for at least fifteen, twenty minutes."

"After last night," Finlay says, "I'd give him five."

Young Harris begins to pass out cards. "I think we should play a hand of poker. By the time we've finished, he'll be gone for the night, for certain."

While they play a game of magic poker, floating their cards in the air and tossing chips into a pile using amber streams, Quinn, Archie, Maggie, and I strategize our approach to combing the vaults for this legendary Book of Dark Souls. After an hour, it's nearly midnight. We sneak downstairs and throw on our winter gear, donning caps, beanies, and gloves. Archie took me on a tour when we first visited. The underground is damp and musty, not a stupendous environment for my allergies.

Quinn waves to us to follow him quietly to the entryway. When he pulls on the door, the hinges creak, and we flinch. Archie surveys the back hallway near the stairs, but there's no movement or lights shining from upstairs. We step out onto the landing and find a man with a familiar winter coat and cap sitting at the bottom of the steps. Harris stands and turns around, a glower etched on his face.

"I've been out here for a fawking hour. What took you so long?"

Taking several cars or hiring cabs would have invited unwanted attention, so we make the forty-minute trek to South Bridge through foggy streets in dead silence. Harris pounds his feet on the pavement, and we struggle to match his pace. His face is so red, I swear he's going to burst the capillaries on his skin any minute. When we pass the National Library of Scotland, Archie moves next to him.

"I'm sorry, Dad," Archie says. "I told them it was a bad idea to investigate the vaults without telling you."

Quinn scoffs at his brother. "Go ahead. Throw me under the bus. Just like when we were kids—always taking the high road."

"Enough, you two," Harris says, finally breaking his silence. "You're both on my shite list. Did you really think I wouldn't find out? I know every fawking witch in Edinburgh. Your friend Lyle needed someone privy to the hidden entrances to the vaults. I've known that person for decades."

Young Harris runs to catch up with them. "Dad asked for our help. We couldn't rightly say no. I'm sorry, Granddad."

"You should be," Harris replies. "Ungrateful grandchildren, the lot of you."

Finlay, Fergus, Quinny, and Isla spout off apologies. "We didn't have a choice." "Granddad, we're so sorry." "How can we make it up to you?"

Taking a cue from Maggie, Tyler, Zoe, and I remain silent. This is family business, and besides, it took me months to win Harris's admiration. I don't want to screw it up now.

"We'll talk about reparations when we return home," he says, anger seething in his eyes. "For now, we must prepare for our quest. Lyle Murray told me you're searching for the Book of Dark Souls. Yes, he confessed when I confronted him. I gave him little choice. So, the old codger Hamish forked over his map, did he? He's been flaunting the ownership of that hoax for fifty years, I'd estimate. How many quid did the shyster get out of you?"

Archie glances at his brother. "We agreed to pay his rent as long as he needs."

Harris bellows into the night, scornfully laughing. We snap our heads around, checking for locals. You'd think he would know better than to bring attention to us. We're already noticeable—a dozen adults roaming the streets after midnight. Clearly, he believes we're wasting our time, but at least he's willing to go. His laughter dissipates into mild snickering.

"Hamish is a talented witch with decades of experience. He also needs to make a living. At his age, that includes the occasional sale of spell jars and potions—and questionable maps, apparently. I've always wanted to search out the vaults without a tour guide, anyway. We'll go on this wild goose chase for this mysterious grimoire, but we'd be as likely to meet up with the infamous witch, Moira MacCrimmon. Legend says she *creeps* under the South Bridge." He snorts and squints at his sons. "I certainly hope you boys have a detailed plan? Because these underground tunnels are expansive, and we're almost there."

"Aye," Quinn says. "Archie and I made three copies of the map. We assigned groups to search different areas."

Lyle is waiting in the back of a local kilt store near a basement door entrance at the bottom of a set of steps, his hands in his winter coat. "Evening to you all. Sorry, Quinn. Your dad left me no choice. I had to tell him."

"Hmph. Don't worry yourself," he replies. "Water under the bridge."

"More like vaults under the bridge, no?" Harris says with a chuckle. "Let's get on with it."

Lyle chants an incantation under his breath, his palm facing the lock. Amber magic rises from his skin and the mechanism clicks open. All twelve of us shuffle in and follow Hamish's helpful neighbor into the eerie, dark basement filled with bolts of plaid wool. We stop at a rotting wooden door behind a stack of boxes. He opens it to reveal a stairway leading down—to the vaults, I assume. We pull our flashlights from our pockets.

"A bobby strolls by every couple of hours," Lyle says. "That gives you thirty minutes to search for the tome of spells you seek. Then you must exit the way you entered."

I interrupt him. "That doesn't give us a lot of time."

"We'd better be on our search, then, hadn't we?" Quinn takes out a scrap piece of paper and reads his scribbling. "Tyler, Zoe, and Young Harris, go with Archie. The second group includes

Quinny, Fergus, Gwyn, and Maggie. Isla and Finlay, you'll search with Granddad and me." He passes a copy of the map to Archie and Quinny.

"Questions, anyone, before we start?" Archie asks.

Zoe raises a hand. "What does the tome look like? How will we know if we've found it?"

"If the Book of Dark Souls exists, I imagine the tome will be in a deteriorated state," Harris replies. "Don't touch it. We have no idea what powers it has. It may be so old, it will crumble at the touch of your fingers. Best to let me examine it. *If* you find it."

Tyler checks his cell. "Everyone should make sure their phone sound is on."

"Good idea," Isla says. "If you find something, contact one person in each of the other groups. No sense in running ourselves ragged down here." She sniffs twice. "The odor is atrocious."

I fight to hold back a sneeze but fail. Huh-tschoo! "They're full of mold, too."

"Bless you, Gwynedd," Harris says. "Now let's make haste."

As we descend the worn stairway, knots tug at my insides. Is my intuition warning me of danger ahead? Or am I just creeped out by the rank odor and creepy atmosphere? We walk for a while on the flagstone floors littered with rubble before the groups split off in different directions. I trail behind my group, stopping to inspect a dark corner. The light frightens a cluster of spiders, and they scatter over the stone surface. I flinch and dash to the others.

As we meander through the labyrinth of rooms, images flash before me—cobbler's working on shoes, children in tattered clothes running, patrons in the tavern room raising their stoneware bottles, witches in centuries old garb casting spells and cackling. Or was the laughing real? Distant voices echo throughout the musty chambers, and a sudden chill overwhelms me, as if an essence is penetrating my body. I shudder and shake the sensation off as footsteps echo in the distance.

Our four flashlights beam in all directions, bouncing off the slimy walls built of sandstone and mortar. Remaining artifacts clutter the rooms: decaying shoes, cracked plates, ceramic jars, and abandoned toys. How sad that anyone had to work or live down here. The remnants of their lives are still here, as if they never left. The lack of sunlight and proper ventilation combined with seeping water from the streets above creates an environment that sends my nasal passages into revolt. I pinch my nose and nausea builds in my gut.

"A good thing we have to be out of here fast. My allergies have kicked into high gear." Or is it my intuition?

Quinny motions to pass through the archway ahead. "Imagine living down here. After industries moved out, the poor flowed in and took over the place. The stench from the lack of sanitation must have been unbearable."

"If you're poor," Maggie says, "you are happy to have a roof over your head. Remember, the Cockburns didn't always have money. Their ancestral witch line dates back to humble beginnings. They could have lived here amongst the peasants. Never forget that."

"You never let us, Mum." Fergus flashes his light at the corner of the next room. "Not to change the subject, but is that a book?"

I direct my flashlight toward the corner of the room next to what appears to be a tiny fireplace. "Yes! It's a book!"

We dash over and Quinny inspects our find a *wee* closer. He passes his hand over the item and attempts to lift it.

"Don't!" Maggie grabs his arm. "Your granddad said not to pick it up!"

But he can't budge it at all. "It's a section of stone—merely resembled a tome."

"Oh, well," I say. "Did we really expect to find the mythic grimoire this quickly?"

Shouting echoes through the tunnels accompanied by grinding and cracking sounds, ending in multiple, thunderous thuds. A rumble quakes through the ground.

"What the fawk was that?" Fergus asks, gaping.

Maggie waves her hands frantically in the air. "Let's go, children!"

My heart takes off like a racehorse as Quinny leads us back through the chambers to where we split off. As we rush through the archways, I stuff the flashlight into my coat pocket and type a text to Tyler, struggling to hit the correct letters.

Me: *Are you OK? Did you hear that? What happened?*

No response. Piercing screams travel through the corridors. Intuition pangs zap me inside. I send a text to Archie, running faster.

Me: *What is going on? Where are you?*

"They aren't getting back to me," I say, gasping for air.

"Quinny, are you sure this is the right way?" Fergus asks.

"Aye." He stops briefly to assess the area. "At least I think so."

"Remember the bottles in the corner? This is the tavern. We passed through here," Maggie says, panting. "Keep going."

A notification dings on my phone.

Tyler: *come quick*

"This is bad. Tyler sent me a text. He didn't say what happened, but my witch's intuition tells me something dreadful has transpired."

Maggie grabs my hand. "I feel it, too, Gwyn. Don't panic. We'll be there in a minute."

My abdomen pinches again and I clutch my abdomen as we run. A luminous halo shines at the end of the tunnel, created by a cluster of light beams crossing streams. The others are gathered around a body resting on the damp ground, rubble scattered around them.

My chest tightens. "Archie!"

I push past Maggie, Quinny, and Fergus, running toward the beams of light. As I get closer, a head full of ash-blond waves peeks above the huddled group. Archie motions to us and a wave of relief overwhelms me. But who is it? When the four of us reach them, Tyler and Zoe move aside. Harris lies lifeless on the wet, dirty surface, his eyes staring into nothingness. Tears stream down his grandchildren's cheeks while Quinn and Archie attempt to revive him, applying healing magic.

What the fuck happened?

Chapter Thirteen
What the Hex?

Quinny pushes past us and kneels next to Harris. "Granddad! Fawk! Is he dead?"

Archie lays a hand on his shoulder. "Naw. But he's not doing well either."

Fergus drops next to his brother. "What's wrong with him?"

Quinn's hand is radiating an amber glow. "He's been hexed. Archie and I tried to heal him—remove the malevolent spell—but no incantation we know worked. And we got electrocuted trying to do it. That's what it felt like, anyway."

"What happened?" I ask, catching my breath.

"Apparently, the mysterious Moira MacCrimmon isn't a legend at all," Archie replies. "She's a nasty witch who roams the vaults. She had white hair and her face appeared ravaged by more than time. Her eyes were like balls of shiny black glass, oozing evil. When we got near the last chamber, she attacked us with an odd magic of red and black fire. We ran here, but she followed us. I guess we pissed her off. The Book of Dark Souls may be with her in her stronghold, but we can't go back there now."

"We have to move him," Quinn says. "The bobby could arrive soon. I called Lyle. He said he'll come by with his car but can take but a few of us. The rest of you will have to run home by foot."

"Gwyn and Maggie," Archie says. "You need to take a taxi to Hamish's. Tell him what transpired and beg him to come to the house. Promise him whatever he wants."

Tyler steps forward. "I think I should go with you, Mom."

"You're not going without me," Zoe says.

Archie nods in my direction. "I know you and Maggie can defend yourselves, but it won't hurt to have them with you. In case Hamish needs more convincing."

"OK," I say. "Keep us updated on him." I scan the weepy faces of Harris's grandchildren. "We'll convince him to come. I promise." I glance back at Archie. Tears are welling up in his eyes.

"Let's be on our way," Maggie says. "Quinn, call me, if..."

Her husband grinds his teeth, fighting to hold back the tears. "Boys, help your uncle and me to carry him. It's going to be a challenge, even if we aid the lift with magic."

We rush back through the tunnel until we reach the stairs and run up to the basement. When we exit to the street, Lyle Murray is pulling up in his small van. He jumps out.

"Where are they? We have to get out of here. The bobby will surely be here soon."

"They're bringing him up now," Maggie says. "Thank you for coming. I know you're exposing yourself unnecessarily. They want us to fetch Hamish to ask if he can remove the hex."

Lyle rolls his eyes. "Good luck with that. The old witch sleeps like a log and he won't take to having his slumber disrupted."

"Too fucking bad," I say. "I'll talk to him. He seemed to warm up to me."

"I wish you well, then."

Maggie, Tyler, Zoe, and I run around the block to South Bridge to find the nearest pub. We hail a minibus taxi and head to Dean Village. On the way, my cell phone vibrates.

"It's a message from Archie. It says, 'We tried a few more times using old-fashioned spells with the herbs Lyle threw in the van at the last minute. No luck. We'll try more once we arrive at the house.' I'll text him back."

Me: *We got a cab. We're almost to Dean Village. Good luck, honey.*

Tyler shakes his head. "That sounds bad. Maggie, could the Cockburn family grimoire contain a hex reversal incantation?"

"I don't know," she replies. "We've never needed one in my lifetime with Quinn."

Zoe becomes sullen. "I hope Hamish Brown knows of a spell. If only one of us could have stopped that witch who's hiding in the vaults."

When we arrive at the end of the lane, I whisper into my son's ear, "Stay here. I'm afraid the driver will take off and leave us stranded."

"Not a bad idea," he replies into my ear. "I'll feed the meter."

"Good luck," Zoe says. "If anyone can convince him, you and Maggie can."

We dart to the flat and bang on the door. "Hamish, wake up! We need your help!"

The rushing ripples of the Water of Leith appear to mask our knocking, but we pound on the door again.

"Should we break in?" I ask.

Maggie inspects the window to the left. "A century old and painted shut, I'd wager."

I raise my fist one more time, but the door creaks open. Hamish stands bent over in plaid flannel pajamas, a disgruntled expression on his face. He slams his cane on the wooden floor.

"Why the fawk are you knocking at this hour? I was enjoying a dance with a young, pretty woman until you woke me with your obnoxious knocking." He squints at me. "You're that Yank that came with the Cockburns on Sunday. What do you want?"

Maggie answers for me. "Lyle let us into the vaults. We didn't find the grimoire, but we discovered the source of the legend of Moira MacCrimmon. A homeless witch has taken sanctuary down there, and she was none too happy they happened upon her secret living quarters in a chamber."

"She attacked part of the family and slapped a hex on Harris Cockburn." I lean into Hamish and grasp his arm. "She left him in a dreadful state. He's unresponsive. Quinn and Archie attempted to remove the wicked spell and heal him, but everything they tried failed. You have decades of witchcraft experience. I'm begging you. Can you help us?"

The old witch taps his cane on the floor while he considers our request. I glance at Maggie and recall what Archie said. I pull my hand back and look him straight in the eye.

"They'll give you whatever you want."

His bushy white eyebrows leap upward and a smile peeks through his beard. "I'll have to chew on that offer. Where is he now?"

"They took him to the house," Maggie says. "We have a large taxi waiting out front. Will you go with us?"

"What?" he asks. "Now? In the wee morning hours?" Hamish grimaces and taps his cane again. "Och. I'll need to change. Wait for me outside."

He slams the door and I sigh. "Go to Tyler and Zoe. I'll stay here and help him to the taxi."

Maggie worries her lip. "I sincerely hope he knows how to treat Harris. Otherwise, he could be stuck in this state forever. Or until we find a spell to remove the evil hex."

She darts to the car and I stand in the chilly, damp air until the door opens again. Hamish is wearing a thick wool coat and lugging a heavy tome. After helping him into the taxi, we drive the half mile to the West End through the misty fog. If it weren't for the old witch's age and need of a cane, we could have probably made better time on foot.

After we arrive, we help Hamish up several steps to the entry door. When we enter, we discover the family gathered around Harris in the kitchen. They've laid his body on the long wooden table, not wanting to carry him up the stairs to a bed, I assume. One of them has closed his eyelids. A black candle is burning.

The grandchildren console each other as their dad tosses aside the spell bowl. Maggie joins them, hugging each of her children. Tyler, Zoe and I move next to Archie. He appears sullen and defeated. I can't imagine how guilty he feels right now. I squeeze his hand.

Hamish shuffles in behind us, leaning on his cane, and drops the thick, tattered tome next to the family patriarch with a thud. "I assume this is the victim."

"Aye," Archie says. "We cast every hex reversal spell we could find. None of them were strong enough. Even general use of intention magic was useless."

Quinn moves next to the old witch. "Everyone, this is Hamish Brown of Dean Village. He's the famous witch I told you about. If any witch has the experience necessary to help us, it's him."

The grandchildren welcome him with heartfelt salutations. "Thank you for coming to save Granddad." "We have complete trust you can help him." "We're indebted to you."

"Not yet, but you will be," Hamish says, removing his coat with some difficulty and tossing it haphazardly aside. "What can you tell me regarding the magic this witch used? Were there any distinctive qualities?"

"Aye," Archie replies. "She cast magic that resembled fire, but the flames burned with hues of red and black."

"Och, aye. Effects from the overuse of the grimoire," he says. "I told you before of my family's warnings concerning the Book of Dark Souls. Many generations back, one of my ancestors was attacked by a witch who had declined into darkness. The wicked woman cast a hex on her." Hamish opens his grimoire, flips through a few pages, and stops. "This reversal spell was used to heal her. I need these ingredients."

He points at the list in the tome and Maggie gestures to the grandchildren, Tyler, and Zoe. They run to the magic room and collect herbs, returning with a fresh wooden bowl, a new mortar and pestle, and a jar of liquid. Hamish spends the next twenty minutes meticulously choosing a pinch of this and a pinch of that, grinding them with the mortar and pestle. He adds lavender oil, creating a thick paste.

"I need a sharp knife, the kind you could kill with," he says matter-of-factly.

Maggie darts to the wood block and retrieves a paring knife, passing it to him without question. I'm glad she trusts him, because this seems to be headed down a dark path. As if prompted by my thoughts, Hamish raises the blade at the grandchildren.

"Who's going first?" he asks, a soft cackle erupting. "Come on now. I need the blood of his dearest loved ones. That be you, children."

The five of them share glances between Maggie and Quinn, then Isla steps forward, shoving her arm at him.

"As usual, I am the one who has to get things started. Do it. I'm not scared."

Hamish chuckles. "I like this one. She has spunk."

"That she does," Quinn says with a curl of his mouth.

Quinny follows behind her. "I'll go next. This is for you, Granddad."

Young Harris, Fergus, and Finlay follow, offering their palms to Hamish. He slices open a wound an inch wide on each of them, allowing their blood to trickle into the mixture. Tyler and Zoe pass each of them a paper towel to stop the bleeding. While Maggie and I bandage up their slashes, the old witch places his hands over the concoction, summoning his witch energy. He chants so softly I can't make out the words. When he finishes, he stands back, an arrogant expression stamped amid his wrinkles.

"You can strip him now," he says.

We pass stares around, not sure if he's joking. Archie bends down close to him.

"You want us to remove all his clothes?"

"Are you daft?" Quinn asks, gaping at the old witch.

Hamish huffs. "His loved ones must spread the paste all over his body while casting an intention of reversal. It has to make direct contact with his skin. Do you know of another way to accomplish that?"

Quinn scratches the back of his head. "May the gods help us. Let's remove his shirt and trousers. I think we can leave his pants on." He's referring to his dad's boxer shorts, of course. That's how Scottish men refer to their underwear.

Over the next fifteen minutes, Quinn, Archie, and the boys remove Harris's clothing. Maggie and Isla lay them on the nearby chairs. They spread the reversal paste all over his arms, legs, feet, abdomen, and face, chanting their intention as they go. When they're finished, they stand back, hope rising in their eyes. Hamish bangs his cane on the floor.

"That's all we can do. You were right to burn a black candle. It will help the reversal. Let it burn all night until the flame goes out. Now, I need a comfortable chair and an ottoman brought to the kitchen. A heavy blanket, too. I'd bet you have several in this home of riches, no?"

"Young Harris and Finlay, fetch your granddad's favorite chair from the living room," Maggie says. "Isla, grab the quilt from the linen closet."

They return quickly with the requested items and set them in a corner of the kitchen. Hamish hobbles over and plops in the chair, propping his feet on the ottoman and covering himself with the blanket.

"What are you doing?" Archie asks.

"Going back to sleep," Hamish replies. "I hope that pretty woman I was dancing with is waiting for me in the dream you interrupted. Wake me when the sun comes up—not before." He pulls the quilt up over his shoulders and rolls onto his side.

We all gather around Harris, who lies motionless on the kitchen table, covered in mush. The grandchildren want to cover him with a blanket but are worried it may affect the reversal of the hex. I feel bad for the Cockburns as they gather in a hopeful embrace. Tyler and Zoe offer to clean up the witchcraft materials while I caress Archie's back.

It's going to be a long night.

I pinch my nose and the gray-skinned being blinks at me with his single black eye. His bulging muscles flex as he steps toward me. Voices shout in distress behind me. I snap my head to the right but struggle to see through the streams of white fog. Leslie and Agnes move near the portal, their long hair blowing in random directions. A large cat roars in the distance, and I scream. "NO!"

I sit up, my heart nearly bursting through my ribcage. The bedroom is dark except for the glow of the clear crystal on Archie's dresser. I feel strange since our excursion to South Bridge. As I steady my breathing, the images I viewed in the vaults fade in and out in my brain. The crystal's glow dissipates. Did something happen to me down there?

The linens next to me appear untouched. Archie never came to bed. I grab my phone from the nightstand. The screen displays 4:12 a.m. The sun won't rise for almost five hours, the tradeoff for long Scottish summer days. Two notifications appear at the top of my screen—one a group text from Trinity to Archie and me, the other from Ronnie.

Trinity: *Check your email! Lots of shit piling up here!*
Ronnie: *The Fellowship met. You need to come home!*
I respond to my friend but not our coven leader.
Me: *I just got Trinity's text. I'm opening my email now.*
Ronnie: *We're terrified, Gwyn!*

I click on my mail service icon, which I've avoided because of the correspondence from Detective Jack Schmidt. There are two more from him, but I don't touch them. I tap the email from Trinity.

I understand you all have your own issues over there, but things have escalated here quickly. We heard more about Elizabeth Wang. She reported to her coven that she sensed she was being followed, but she could never identify the source. Other witches in New Castle County are reporting similar experiences. Shit is going down and we don't know how to prepare for it. Leslie and I convened a circle. They all agreed we need you to return ASAP. Oh, to top it off? That damn Detective Schmidt won't stop bugging me. He's really pissed you haven't responded to his emails. But I'm glad you didn't. He can fuck all the way off!

Shit. Do I read Jack's emails? No fucking chance. I throw on my robe and tiptoe down a flight of stairs. The door to Isla's old bedroom where Tyler and Zoe are sleeping remains shut. A light shines in the doorway to the living room. I tiptoe down the hallway and peek in. Quinny, Fergus, Finlay, and Young Harris are sprawled out on the sofas and floor, sound asleep. I shuffle down to the first floor in my socks until Archie and Quinn's voices reach me. I stop to soak in their chat. Could it be news about their dad?

"So, that's it," Quinn says, an angry tone in his voice. "You're going to abandon Dad again. I made excuses for you when you left for that academic position in the States. It broke his heart. But he's sick now, brother. This time, you need to make the right decision regarding your family, especially when you have choices—opportunities available to you."

Archie doesn't respond for a moment. "It's not all so simple, Quinn. I have responsibilities in Bearsden. I promise I'll do whatever I can to return by the summer."

Suddenly, my stomach churns. I've been listening in on a private conversation between brothers. No way I can tell him about the change in my vision now—not with Harris's condition. I stamp down the last set of steps and walk toward the front of the house.

Quinn and Archie gaze at me from where they've been chatting near the kitchen doorway. They've ended their discussion. I glance at the open door.

"How is Harris? Has he responded at all?"

Archie shakes his head. "He's the same, but it's early. Hamish remains fast asleep. The black candle is still burning."

Snoring spills into the hallway, confirming the old witch is deep in slumber. I hope his dream restarted or he'll bitch when he wakes up.

Quinn makes eye contact with me, then averts his gaze. "I'm going to relieve Maggie and Isla. They should try to get some sleep." He strolls into the kitchen, his shoulders weighted down by guilt, I bet.

I wrap my arms around Archie's torso. "You got the text from Trinity?"

"Aye," he says. "Read the email she sent us. I told Quinn we need to leave early. We should move our flights up to tomorrow. They sound frightened. This being who is tracking the witches in the other covens has an objective."

"Riley said I was in danger. That the being was a female. It has to be someone related to Nuada—his mother, a sister. What other reason would she have for tracking down witches to get to me?"

He strokes my cheek. "I don't know, Gwyn. I'm scared for them...and us. We must go home."

"But what about your dad? What if he doesn't wake up?"

Archie's eyes tear up and I lay my head against his chest. His heart beats erratically, a sign of his uncertainty. He didn't share anything about his talk with Quinn with me. I think back on what his older brother said to him in the hallway and intuition pangs pinch me inside.

What did he mean by *opportunities available to him*?

Chapter Fourteen

DEAD SLUMBER

ARCHIE AND QUINN PACE back and forth in the kitchen all morning while Hamish sleeps like the dead. Isla shuffles in wearing her old bunny slippers and hugs her dad. As the sun splays its first rays of light through the windows, the boys stagger in, one by one. They gather around their granddad, sullen expressions morphing their faces. I haven't heard a peep from Tyler and Zoe. Maggie and I whisper as we lean against the counter a few feet away.

"The two of them are going to wear a rut on the wooden floor if they keep that up." Maggie glances at the table where Harris lies covered in a mud-like paste. "The black candle has little time left to burn out. If he doesn't wake after that...shite, I don't know what they'll do."

"Don't worry. There's still time."

Hamish stirs in the chair and throws off the quilt. "Where's my walking stick? I need to find the bog."

Isla rushes to the old witch, his cane in her hand. "Here, Mr. Brown. Why don't I help you up? Would you like me to show you the loo?"

"Turn down an escort from a pretty ginger-haired lass?" he asks with a mischievous twist of his mouth.

She chuckles. "You're bad, Mr. Brown. Let's go."

Isla takes his arm and assists him out. Twenty more grueling minutes pass, and the weary men of the Cockburn family examine their patriarch again. Young Harris bends over his granddad, inspecting his eyelids.

"Is he waking?" Fergus asks, checking his legs.

"I think you're imagining his movement," Finlay replies. "His body is as lifeless as a cadaver."

Quinny steps closer. "Don't talk like that. He's not dead."

"Not yet, anyway," Hamish says, hobbling into the kitchen. "Let me look."

He pushes Fergus and Finlay aside and hovers his palm above their granddad's flabby belly, summoning his magic. His hand radiates in an amber glow as he passes it over their granddad's corpse-like body. The black candle has melted down to a nub, and the flame glimmers, finally giving way to a swirl of smoke.

We gather around the Cockburn patriarch and wait for Hamish to finish his examination. When he retracts his magic, only the sound of apprehensive breathing remains. Harris's arms twitch, prompting soft gasps from all surrounding him.

Quinn bends over and whispers in his ear. "Dad. Can you hear me?"

Harris pops up like the return of the dead, screaming, "Aghhh! You bitch! I dare you to try that again! You'll never get past a Cockburn witch!"

He throws a bolt of amber magic at the ceiling. Sections of plaster fall, scattering all around on us and onto the floor. When the dust settles, he surveys our elated faces and scans the room with bulbous eyes.

"Why the fawk am I in the kitchen?" he asks, shuddering from the cold air, I assume. His gaze falls to the hardened paste on his arms, legs, and torso—and his boxer shorts. "Why am I in my pants? Where are my clothes? And what in all the gods of the Otherworld is this shite all over my skin?"

We burst out laughing, so overwhelmed with happiness that tears roll down our cheeks. Archie, Quinn, and the grandkids jump at Harris, smothering him with hugs while Maggie and I share a sisterly embrace. Hamish grins, proud of his accomplishment, but a splash of egotistical pride decorates his visage, too. He's earned it. Archie shakes his hand vigorously.

"Hamish, we can't thank you enough. We owe you."

"You bet your family dynasty you do," he says, waving his cane.

Quinn pats his back. "We will honor our promise. Thank you."

Harris eyes Hamish. "You're that old codger who lives in Dean Village. Why are you here? And will someone explain why I suddenly find myself on the kitchen table wearing my pants and a layer of muck?"

"Moira MacCrimmon, or whatever the fawk her name is, cast a hex on you, Granddad," Isla says. "Mr. Brown removed the evil spell. You owe him your life."

"What? The fawk I'm going to give that sleekit witch any of my money," he replies, grimacing.

Maggie approaches him. "Ah, Harris. Not but five minutes ago, you were riding with a one-way ticket to the Otherworld. Hamish brought you back to us. Now shut up and agree to pay his monthly rent!" She crosses her arms and eyes him down, squinting.

The grandkids snicker and punch their granddad's arm. Archie and Quinn join Maggie in the stare fest, but I stay out of this family disagreement.

"I'm not a sleekit—simply asking for help with my rent for the work I performed," Hamish says. "If you cover that, I'll consider the debt paid."

"I refuse to pay a monthly rent." Harris crosses his weak arms in a huff.

Quinn rolls his eyes at his father. "You will pay him."

Hamish Brown squishes his face into an epic scowl and bangs his cane on the floor. Harris cracks up and shakes his head.

"I'll not pay the rent because it's a waste of my earnings." He curls a corner of his mouth. "Give me the name of your flat owner. I bet I can negotiate a fair price to purchase it on your behalf. I'd be a crabbit old man, too, if I had to beg or barter for rent each month at your age."

The old witch tears up and presses his lips together, unable to respond. After a couple of minutes, he clears his throat. "Thank you, Mr. Cockburn. I'll never say another negative thing about your clan from this point forward. You have made this bitter witch very happy."

Harris nods. "You're welcome. Now, grandchildren. Who is going to help me off this table? I believe I need a bath."

"Come on, Granddad," Quinny says, helping him stand on his weakened legs.

"Whoa." Harris wobbles when his feet make contact with the wooden floor. "I may need more assistance, children."

"Harris," I say, darting to him. "Someone stronger needs to support you."

Archie rushes to his other side. "Let's take it slow, Quinny. Nephews, follow us up. We may need more bodies to get him into the tub."

Isla snatches her granddad's clothes from the pile. "I'll carry these up for him."

Harris growls like a tiger. "Stop talking about me as if I'm not here."

"Ah, Granddad," Isla says as she follows.

"You're sounding like yourself," I say.

Quinn grins. "He certainly is."

Before they get to the doorway, Tyler and Zoe rush in, panting.

"We're so sorry!" my son yells through gasps. "We slept in."

Tyler's love catches sight of Harris. "Hey! Mr. Cockburn is alive! I didn't expect that!"

Tyler slaps a hand to his face. Another round of laughter fills the kitchen with an air of relief. The situation is humorous to us now, yet merely a few minutes ago we thought Harris wouldn't survive the hex. The grandchildren and Archie exit with the patriarch and Hamish grabs his grimoire off the table.

"Be aware, Mr. Cockburn may suffer long-term effects for a while. He'll need daily care. I will come by again if he worsens. But now, if you don't mind. I'd like to use the loo one more time, then I'll be on my way."

"I can help you down the hall." Quinn glances at his wife and nods.

Maggie pats Hamish's shoulder warmly. "Mr. Brown, how would you like to stay and eat with us? I make a mean Scottish breakfast."

"She does," I say. "We'd love to have you share in our joy this morning."

"I am a changed witch," Hamish says. "You are too kind."

"Simply doing as we should." Quinn grasps his elbow. "You'll find a basket of guest toothbrushes in there as well, if you'd like to wash up."

As they exit, Tyler and Zoe approach us, a look of confusion contorting Tyler's face. "What in the name of the gods happened?"

"The hex reversal—removal—whatever you want to call it...worked. Harris's shouting must have woken you up. He thought he was still back in the vaults."

"I'm so happy for the Cockburns," Zoe says, sporting her signature wide grin. "Will he be OK?"

Maggie stares up at the ceiling, a furrow in her brow. "Time should tell."

"What can we do to help you?" I ask. "You have more than a house full this morning."

"Dig into the fridge and see what we've got. We may need to send the twins out for more food."

As Tyler, Zoe, and I rummage through the fridge, my witchy innards tighten. I don't need to decipher this message to recognize Harris has a long road ahead of him.

How can Archie leave now?

Early the next morning, Maggie, Quinn, and Harris follow us to the garage to say goodbye. The dark gray sky appears gloomy since the sun won't rise for another four hours, but it's par for a Scottish winter's day. I shiver in my fleece jacket as my misty white breath floats around me. Archie's dad is using a cane to walk, but he needs the added support from his brother as well. The significance of saying goodbye now hangs over all of us like a heavy fog. An aura overcomes me, reminding me we've done this many times before. But it was a patriarch as strong as an ox who said those goodbyes.

Tyler shakes Harris's hand. "Thank you so much for your hospitality. Despite everything, I had a wonderful time meeting you and your family."

"I really wish that homeless witch hadn't attacked you," Zoe says, pouting.

"Ahh, don't fret over the incident," he replies. "Too bad we didn't find you a spell."

Archie pats his dad's arm. "It's probably for the best we didn't find the grimoire, Dad. The risks of its dangerous effects are too high. We shouldn't have gone down there."

"Now don't you do that. I made the choice to go into the vaults. How were we supposed to know that witch was squatting down there? No one ever believed there was truth in the legend."

"The unknown is always dangerous," Quinn says, loading the last of our luggage into the trunk. "We take risks. You're loaded and ready to travel." He looks away, clenching his jaw.

"Bye. We hope to visit again," Tyler and Zoe say as they drop into the backseat.

I embrace Maggie. "We'll stay in touch."

"Of course. Have a safe journey, Gwyn," she says. "We will continue to search for a spell to close the portal in the meantime."

As if they have the wherewithal to concern themselves with that under the circumstances. I approach Harris and hug him. He squeezes me back tighter than any of the other times we shared goodbyes and whispers in my ear. "Marry him, Gwynedd. I want to see my baby married before I die."

When I step back, he winks at me, a faint smile curving his mouth. The request doesn't sound pushy, merely reflecting the hope of a man who cheated death. Quinn whispers in his brother's ear and Archie pats his brother on the shoulder.

"I promise I'll do what's needed." He moves next to me.

"Good luck to you all," Quinn says. "May you find a resolution to the portal."

I hug him. "Thank you. I'm so sorry we have to leave."

"Get on your way," Harris says. "You can visit when you've solved this new riddle."

I wave goodbye and get into the car. Archie embraces his dad one more time and plops into the driver's seat. Quinn and Maggie grab the patriarch's arms on each side and he shakes them off, balking at their assistance.

As we drive off, I glance at Archie. A single tear rolls from the corner of his eye. What did Quinn say to him?

The flight passes without a snag and we arrive at the Philly Airport as expected. By the time the shuttle stops at Tyler and Zoe's house, the sun has set. The plane ride caused us to miss the bright day except for a few glimpses of sunshine through the window. It's pouring now and the bitter cold chills my bones when they exit the van. We wave to them as they dart with their luggage to the side door.

When we arrive at home, Archie tips the driver and we haul our fatigued bodies to the entry, dragging our suitcases behind us. He shakes his jacket and hangs it on the oak hall tree. I remove my coat, repeating the ritual. We kick off our shoes and enter the living room, sinking into the leather loveseat. I rest my head against him and he wraps his arm around my shoulder. The mantle clock ticks for a stretched moment before either of us speaks—too spent, I suppose.

A notification vibrates my phone. It's my best friend.

Ronnie: *Welcome home, Gwyn. So glad you're back. Stop by before the circle.*

Me: *Sure. I have so much to share with you. Too pooped to type.*

Ronnie: *I bet. See you tomorrow. Get some rest.*

"That was Ronnie," I say. "She wants me to stop by the house. It's too late in the UK to check in on Harris. I know we should stay up to shift, but I want to crawl under the sheets like ten minutes ago."

"Aye, the jet lag always sucks on the return, especially during the winter."

I caress his firm abdomen. "Harris will recover. I sense it. But the road to wellness may be challenging. Please, don't feel guilty regarding the witch attack. Your father had a right to go."

"I know. Doesn't make it hurt any less." He strokes the back of my head.

"We have a circle tomorrow. Maybe we should go to sleep now. I'll wake up early and open all those emails from Jack Schmidt. I may need your advice on how I should reply."

"Sounds like a fantastic idea."

He stands up, offers me his hand, and we drag our fatigued bodies up the stairs. While Archie washes up in the bathroom, I lie in bed, contemplating how I'm going to bring up the visions I had while we were in Edinburgh. I recall my experiences in the vaults and the glow of the clear quartz crystal in Archie's bedroom back in Scotland.

Immediately, I jump out of bed and run down two flights of stairs to the basement's magic room. I flip the light switch and gaze at the crystal Seamus Duffy gave me. Did his clear quartz enhance my visions, too? I snatch the stone and dash back to the bedroom.

"Where did you go?" Archie asks. "To the loo downstairs?"

"No." I open my fist, exposing the crystal. "I almost forgot. I want to continue my training with the grid, but I decided I should start with a single clear quartz first—you know, for clarity."

"Aye. A good idea. Restart your energy." He kisses me on the cheek. "Sleep well, my love."

"You, too, honey." I set Seamus's crystal on the nightstand and lie back.

Have I been overthinking this?

CHAPTER FIFTEEN

DANGEROUS DECISIONS

Several faceless people gather in the Celestial Gardens—divided in two rows. A whoosh rings out behind me and I turn around to discover the gray-skinned Fomorian stepping in my direction. His enormous boots disappear into the squishy dirt as his dark mane catches a ride on a zephyr. The blending of musty earth and body odor turns my stomach, and I squeeze my nostrils. Several voices shout near me and I snap my head around. Strings of white haze cover the area like a veil. Leslie and Agnes yell from the portal as a gust of wind sends their hair flying toward the clouds. Nearby, a cat roars and leaps at the monster. I scream. "NO!"

I sit up in bed, gasping, and look to my left. The clear quartz crystal is radiating a white magic halo in the blackness of the night—more expansive than what I saw on Archie's dresser in Edinburgh. As my breathing calms, my racing heart slows to a pitter-patter. A hand touches my arm.

"Are you all right, Gwynedd?" Archie asks, caressing my skin. "Did you have a nightmare? About my dad?" The streetlight breaks through the curtains, shining on his crinkled brow.

"No." A few seconds pass as I consider what to tell him. "Archie, it was a dream, but more of an extension of the daytime visions I had. More like what I experienced when I was first using the grid. But it's due to a single crystal, the clear quartz."

A grin spreads his goatee. "That's cracking, Gwyn. It's been weeks since you had made any progress."

"Well..." I say with a twist of my mouth. "It might have happened before."

"What do you mean?" He shifts onto an elbow. "Have you had others you didn't share with me?"

I blink twice. "Yes. Back in Edinburgh."

He sits up and leans into me. "What happened and why didn't you tell me?"

"Oh, Archie. So many things were going on. The first time the dream returned was the morning after we got there. Everyone was hungover from drinking too much Scotch whisky the night before, except for Maggie and me. You were already gone from the bed when I woke. When I glanced at your dresser, the clear quartz crystal you keep there was glowing faintly. The second occurrence happened the night Harris was under the effects of the hex. It wasn't appropriate to share yet."

"You've had plenty of opportunities since we left." He grunts like a bear. "You stubborn witch. Must you double guess what I can handle in every situation?"

"No, but Tyler and Zoe didn't need to hear about this yet. I wanted to discuss the vision with you first."

"Well, as Spence says frequently, *spill the tea*."

"The gray-skinned giant was there in the Celestial Gardens—or will be. I always thought I was alone when he crossed over in the visions. But I wasn't. Leslie and Agnes were standing near the portal, and the wind was blowing something fierce. And that monster dude stank like the crotch of the Otherworld. I nearly vomited."

He chuckles. "You have a way with descriptions, my love."

"Trying to be accurate, honey. Leslie and Agnes yelled at me. Others, I don't know who, shouted behind me, too. A large cat roared and leaped at the gray being. And I screamed so loud I felt the pain down to my chest."

"Curious. Do you think it's Seamus?" He rubs his whiskers. "Or Leslie's familiar?"

I snort. "Mr. Yeats jumping at a gigantic Fomorian?"

He raises a corner of his mouth. "Stranger things have happened."

"I suppose. But I can't decipher what's happening at all. I get the sense the vision isn't expanding forward. In fact, the premonition showed me more of what occurred before the arrival of the Fomorian, too."

"Did you sense the presence of a Tuatha Dé fairy in the vision?"

"No. I don't even know who the others were."

"We should tell Trinity. Leslie and Agnes as well."

"Can we wait a while? I know from the visions I had about you, we can't stop what's going to happen. At least not until more of the vision reveals itself."

"Will you promise to tell me when the premonition shows more of the puzzle?"

"Of course." I glance at the crystal on the nightstand. "Why do you think a single stone is suddenly enhancing my visions? I had some creepy experiences in the vaults. Could that evil witch and others before her have left some sort of essence down there?"

"Hmph. I have no answers, Gwyn. A question for Seamus, perhaps." He kisses me tenderly and hops out of bed. "It's almost five. Why don't I make us breakfast?"

"Thanks, honey. I need the protein to tackle those emails from Jack Schmidt."

He chuckles and heads downstairs. I open my mail server and count six emails from the curious detective. He doesn't give up. That's for sure.

Ronnie finishes nursing Luna and clasps the edge of her bra. As she pats her little one's back, Derek places a cup of decaf coffee in front of her, along with a glass of milk. She takes a sip from her mug and sticks out her tongue.

"Come on, babe," he says. "The decaf can't be that bad." He chortles and passes a cup of Earl Grey to me.

"Thanks, Derek. I shouldn't drink tea this late in the day, but I need the mental boost."

"You're welcome." He pulls out a chair, takes Luna, and cradles her in his burly arms.

"Decaf is like sad, brown water," Ronnie says. "But what other choice do I have? The herbal teas are even worse. I tried regular coffee, but the caffeine had Luna waking throughout the night. Not worth it, especially after dinner."

"We're sorry about Archie's dad. Will he recover?" Derek asks.

"We don't know," I say, sipping my tea. "My intuition points to a long, drawn-out recuperation. He and Quinn harbor so much guilt, though. Archie shed a lot of tears. I'm not feeling too great about it, either. Searching the vaults for that grimoire was mostly for me."

"And the town, Gwyn." Ronnie drinks more of the decaf and grimaces. "I think I'll drink my milk instead."

Derek stands with their infant witch. "I'll put Luna down for her morning nap. You two need to talk about important coven matters." He gets to the doorway and turns around. "I'm not a witch, and the tension in this town weighs on me, too—like a ton of bricks. Maybe your witchy ways are rubbing off on me." He continues down the hall.

"He knows I haven't told him everything," Ronnie says. "But he knows enough about the witch murders to make him accompany me everywhere, even the public restroom."

"You're a mother now with a baby depending on you. You can't take risks."

"Yeah, I know. Hey, did you reply to Jack Schmidt yet?"

I rub my temples. "Yeah. Six emails. You can't blame him for doing his job. But when I didn't reply, you'd think he would wait until I got home."

"To be fair, you were supposed to be over there for two weeks. What did he ask you in the emails?"

"The same questions mostly. Like he was trying to catch me in a lie. Except, I don't have to fib. Well, minus the whole mag-ic-killed-her stuff."

Ronnie cackles. "He wouldn't believe you, anyway. What did you reply?"

"Nothing. I apologized for not replying and told him to catch me at Mystic Sage. Or I could come to the police department in the municipal building. But I'd rather he visit me on my ground—well, Shane and Jeff's domain."

"What can you tell him about Elizabeth Wang? You barely knew her."

"I'm sure it's a puzzle of mega proportions to him. He never solved Nick Evans's death. The failure probably hangs over his head, and not like mistletoe."

"Well, Yule has been over for a week, anyway." She checks her phone. "Shouldn't we leave for Agnes's farm? Trinity said she wants to start the circle early. Can I get a ride with you? Mr. Worrywart doesn't want me to drive alone at night."

"Sure. I'll wait for you in the car."

"I will kiss my two babies goodbye and be right out."

I slip on my jacket and walk to my Prius. When I touch the door handle, the beep-beep resounds, and I stop short. My body buzzes. I spin on the balls of my feet. I survey my surroundings, but the sensation has disappeared. Ronnie rushes to the car.

"It's so fucking cold. What are you staring at?"

I turn around. "Nothing, I guess. A little paranoid."

"Not like you don't have a reason to be. We're gonna be late now. Sorry. I'll text Trinity on the way."

We hop in the car and I drive to Agnes and Leslie's home near the Maryland state line. It's heartwarming to know they'll spend the remainder of their days together. They hadn't spoken to each other in fifty years—all because of my mom's secret about the Tuatha Dé Danann. That's water under the bridge now.

There are several vehicles parked in front, including Archie's Tesla. Everyone has arrived but us. Ronnie and I enter the foyer, and Mr. Yeats, Leslie's chimera cat familiar, scuttles toward me, transforming into his feline persona inches from my face.

"Aghhh! I've told you a million times not to pop up so close to me like that."

"I'm so sorry, Ms. Crowther," he says in a posh Irish accent. "It's been so long since you've come for a visit. I...I..." He steps forward and gives me a hug—the most awkward embrace I've ever encountered. "They're waiting for you in the living room. Remember to take off your shoes. Ms. Pritchard becomes unbearable to live with if you don't."

"We know." I pull off my sneakers.

"What? No hug for me?" Ronnie asks, kicking off her flats.

Mr. Yeats takes two steps and taps his hands on her arms. My best friend snickers at him. He backs away, adjusting his spectacles.

"They've already begun the circle. I recommend you join them now. I'll be in the magic room cleaning up. Ms. Pritchard left a mess in there, like always."

He rolls his eyes and darts down the hallway, transforming into his cat presentation as he scuttles off. Voices echo into the foyer from the living room, increasing in volume as Ronnie and I stroll in. Tyler and Zoe wave at me. We squeeze in behind the sofa next to Archie, soaking in the end of Trinity's announcement.

"So, from here on, no one walks at night without a partner. When it's your turn to check on the Seelie Fae children in the Celestial Gardens, grab a partner. Riley and Elizabeth were attacked on the way home alone."

"That's easy for me and Tanner," Spence says. "We live together."

Tanner raises a hand. "But I go out of town on business occasionally, so I'll need a backup."

"We'll all have to sub for others," Skye says. "We all have jobs. Some of us start classes in February. The visits could get complicated."

Spence huffs. "Our TA positions will be worse Spring Semester, too."

Ronnie bounces her leg a mile a minute. "I can't commit. Would you be upset if I bow out of this duty for now?"

"We don't expect a new mother to put herself in such danger," Trinity says. "We'll take up the slack for you."

Skye yells across the living room. "I'll back you up, Ronnie, no matter how busy the semester turns out."

"Thanks, Skye," my best friend replies.

Leslie stands. "Indeed. We should all pair up according to magic strength. Gwyn, Archie, and Tyler are ancestral witches. They should each accompany a younger witch, not each other. Agnes and I are powerful, but we are crones. We should not go together, either."

"Speak for yourself, woman," Agnes says, growling up at her. "I can fucking take care of myself."

"No doubt," Archie replies. "But we don't know what we're battling. We have to approach this pragmatically."

Spence laughs. "Agnes may not understand what the definition of pragmatically is."

"Of course I know what it fucking means." She sticks out her tongue at him. "I live with an academic. I'm saying I am ready to fight whatever it is. But I'll check out the gardens with a younger witch if I have to."

"You do," Trinity says, putting a fist on her hip. "Elijah, where do we stand with the council allies?"

He moves in front of the fireplace. "They've come to the end of the line with us. They want the murders of these two witches solved before the local police discover supernatural beings are involved, and they demand we shut the portal. John Erickson said Courtney did some of her own *fishing* but has yet to find a trail of magic from other Tylwyth Teg fairies in Bearsden. We can rule them out."

"I, for one, am a lot more comfortable knowing our ancestral witches have returned," Shane says, twisting at the strands of his beard. "I agree with Leslie. We are strong as a coven, but in pairs, we must admit when our age is a disadvantage." He glares at the hedge witch. "Even you, darling Agnes."

Her middle finger slowly rises, and he chuckles. Leslie grasps her sweetheart's hand and pushes it down.

"I'm happy you're cooperating, Agnes," Trinity says. "All of us are glad Gwyn, Archie, Tyler, and Zoe have returned, me especially. That damned detective hasn't stopped bugging me since you left—all kinds of questions regarding our pagan groups in New Castle County. But Shane speaks some serious truth. We are stronger together than apart. We're all walking targets right now."

Tyler and Zoe haven't offered their opinions. Their eyelids flutter, and they nod off occasionally. I don't know how they went to work today. They should have used the day to chill and adjust to the sudden time zone change.

A notification rings on Trinity's cell, and she reads the text. Her face tenses as she types a reply. She hits send and looks up, pressing her lips together. "That was the Hockessin Coven. I understand some of you won't shed tears over this. They said local police discovered the body of Laura Lovelace, the witch they expelled after—you know. It appears she's the product of the same evil magic."

I glance at Archie and Ronnie. "Fuck."

Chapter Sixteen

CURIOUS JACK

Archie stands at the mudroom door, his family's sharp heirloom in hand, glaring at me. "Please, humor me. Before we left for Edinburgh, we discussed training Tyler on the use of it. I agree he should learn. But carry the dirk when you must walk home in the dark after work. I could come and escort you back?"

"Oh, for fuck's sake," I say, snatching the heirloom from his hand. "Weaponry is too serious a conversation for a Saturday morning. I'm already carrying a protection pouch. What if the witch killer isn't a fairy? Your dirk will add unnecessary weight to my bag."

I shove the heavy fairy protection into my backpack and pull the zipper closed. He pulls me close and kisses me.

"Thank you, Gwyn. We'll follow through on Tyler's training, as you suggested. He's an ancestral witch. The redundancy will help us prepare for the inevitable."

"Speaking of ancestral witches, have you checked on your dad's progress?"

"Aye. Quinn says he's in good spirits, but he is weak. Walks from room to room and has to sit in a chair to rest before moving to another. Hamish told him not to attempt any witchcraft until he improves physically and mentally."

I rub his back. "Please don't beat yourself up over what happened. Harris is a powerful ancestral witch. He'll recover."

"But we're realistic. If he doesn't improve, he *will* need care—and not from Unremarkables."

"Well, let's hope for the best. I've been thinking about the most recent witch murder. Why do you think the killer went after Laura Lovelace? She wasn't a member of any coven as far as we knew. She certainly was not a friend of mine. Not after casting a love spell on you with the help of Nuada, so I would catch you in bed with her. And you know what happened after that. I'm not proud of my behavior even if he glamoured me. So why kill her to get to me? It doesn't make sense."

"It's perplexing, for sure."

I kiss him and pull away to slip on my gloves. "I need to leave for work."

Tension seizes his face. "I don't understand why you started back so soon. You already had the time off."

"You know why. My job ends when Winter Session is over, and I have to train Shane's girlfriend, Julia Harding, before I leave. Jack Schmidt said he would come by to ask more questions regarding Riley's death. I don't want him coming to the house again. Plus, I put him off for four days."

"Fair enough. Who is going with you to the Celestial Gardens tonight?"

"Skye said she would go with me. She's doubling up visits during Winter Session to help out."

"Have I ever told you she has always been one of my best students?"

"No. I suspected Spence was at the top of that list."

"He's brilliant, for sure, and an extremely talented witch." His mouth twitches. "But his undergrad days nearly drove me to drink with all his unending questions."

My brow crinkles. "But you do drink, Archie."

"Precisely," he says with a wink.

I chuckle. "You realize he looks up to you as a surrogate father. They all do. Tyler, Tanner, Spence. Bye, honey."

He kisses my cheek. "Tell Skye hello for me and hurry home after you check on the Seelie Fae."

An unexpected change in temperature makes the stroll to Mystic Sage enjoyable, surprising for a January day. Checking on the Seelie Fae will be more bearable, too. As much as I wanted this interview with Jack Schmidt out of the way, I'm regretting coming in today. Julia found out I was going to work after all and decided she should take advantage of my presence. She'll be here by three. When I arrive, Jeff is tidying up the front of the store.

"Hey, Gwyn. Thanks for coming in today, but you didn't have to. You deserve the time off."

I shove my backpack under the counter. "Oh, I wanted to. I don't have many days left here, and Julia needs the extra training, too. The last time I worked with her, she was super flustered and had trouble retaining information. Did you train her while I was in Edinburgh?"

"Yeah." He leans over the counter and whispers, "She had to repeat everything you showed her. Shane wanted to be nice by offering her this job. But I don't see how she'll work out. And I have no idea how to tell him."

"Give her some time, Jeff. Short-term memory is the first thing to go when you get older. She may need repeated training sessions, but eventually, she could run circles around the both of us. Let's see how the afternoon goes."

Shane walks into the front of the store carrying a box and drops it on the floor with a thud. "I believe my ears are burning."

Jeff and I lock eyes and freeze. Holy crystals. Did he hear us talking?

A wide grins peeks through his beard. "I was pulling a funny, friends."

"Oh," I say, relaxing. "We were talking about Julia. Jeff filled me in on how her training went while I was gone."

Jeff grabs his coat. "I'm picking up Ashley and Aidan for lunch. Again, thanks for coming in, Gwyn."

"You're welcome. Tell her I said hi and give Aidan a hug from Miss Gwyn."

"I will. Bye, Shane." Jeff waves as he exits the store.

My other boss opens the box and pulls out a stack of board games. "I didn't want to ask in front of Jeff. Are you concerned the detective thinks you had something to do with these murders?"

"Not really. But I think he suspects I'm hiding things. And I am. Obviously, I can't tell him the truth. None of us can."

"I fear he will dig so deep, he'll discover more than he bargained for. Now his ears must be burning, because here he comes." He gestures at the glass door.

Cro-Magnan Forehead Man enters the store and approaches the counter. "Good afternoon. I'd like to talk with Ms. Crowther for a few minutes. She said to come here. Is that agreeable to you, Mr. Murphy?"

"Sure. If customers should come in, send me a text. I'll be in the back."

My boss crosses his fingers and walks into the crystals room while Jack pulls out his notepad and a pen. He flips through a few pages and stops.

"Thank you for being so cooperative, Ms. Crowther. Can I call you Gwyn? Since you seem to be around when so many of these incidents occur in Bearsden."

I swallow hard. This can't be good. Is he trying to act friendly to trip me up? Should I say no? But I don't. "Sure. You know me well enough."

"Excellent. My questions will be short. By now you must have heard or read there have been two more deaths of women in New Castle County."

"Yeah. We learned about one when we returned from Scotland—the other in the local paper online."

He reads his notes and peers up at me. "Did you know the second victim, Elizabeth Wang?"

My lips part, but the words get jumbled in my brain. Why is he asking me about her? I wasn't there. "Yeah. I wouldn't call her a good friend, but I knew who she was."

"And how did you know her?"

Where is he going with this? "She was a member of a local pagan group in Greenville. I saw her at conferences, ceremonies, celebrations—monthly meetings."

"Did Elizabeth Wang contact you on New Year's Eve?"

"No. Why do you ask?" Did she send me a text? An email? If so, I didn't receive them.

He stares down at his notepad. "How about the most recent victim? Her name was..." He flips through a few more pages. "Ah, yes. Laura Lovelace. Was she a friend of yours?"

Holy crystals. I can't move—my joints lock in place, including my jaw. *This isn't helping your case, Gwyn.*

Jack leans over the counter, his eyes attaching to mine like magnets. "Gwyn, do I need to repeat the question?"

What's wrong with me? I shudder. "No. I'm sorry. The jet lag crops up at the strangest times and my brain goes blank." But how the fuck do I answer his question? "No. We weren't friends." No lies there.

"But she was also a member of a local pagan group." He glances at his notepad again. "In Hockessin, I was told. Their community leader said she was expelled. They wouldn't tell me why. I imagine the reason was probably because of breaking rules of their faith. Are you aware? Did you hear any rumors through the grapevine?"

Fuck! What do I say? I have to lie—no other choice. As I place a pen in the skull mug on the counter, I miss the cup altogether and knock them over. They splatter on the floor. "I'm sorry." While I rush around to the front to pick up the mess I made, a customer enters the store. My heart skips a few beats. "No one in their community shared anything with me. Local groups protect the privacy of their members."

The nosy young woman wearing a DUB jacket eyes us while I collect the pens and place them in their proper holder. She pretends to check out the tarot cards. As I stand, Jack takes the mug from me and sets it back on the counter.

"Are you always this clumsy or do I make you nervous, Ms. Crowther?" he asks.

So, now we're back to formalities? "If I had a dollar for every time I knocked that mug over, I could retire."

He closes his notepad and my heart finds a steady rhythm again. "That's all for now. Thank for you for your cooperation. The more information I gather, the easier path I'll have to discover the reason for these unnecessary deaths. Have a pleasant afternoon, Gwyn."

"You, too, detective," I say, feigning a pleasant expression.

Jack exits the store and Shane returns to the front to empty his abandoned box. The DUB student drops a deck of tarot cards on the counter and smiles.

"Was that a Bearsden Police officer asking you questions?"

I avert my eyes while I ring her up and don't answer. It's none of her business.

"What did you do?" She bends over the counter, snorting. "Kill somebody?"

I hand the items to her and answer in a sarcastic tone. "Yeah. With a knife I carry in my backpack."

"You don't have to be rude. I was kidding." She snatches her merchandise and leaves the store.

When the door shuts with the clank of the bamboo chimes, Shane approaches me with his hands in his pockets. "Darling, I am truly impressed with how comfortable you are in your new skin as a witch. But that?" He shakes his finger at me and laughs. "That will return to bite you in the rump. Not to mention it's not good for sales."

"She didn't think I was serious," I say, shrugging it off. "I'm sorry—tired of all the accusations, I guess. Did you hear the detective's line of questioning?"

"I did. Don't pay him no mind. He's fishing, and he caught a shoe. But I fear he'll be back."

"Me, too."

I stare out the store window at the Saturday shoppers strolling by. Somewhere out there, the curious detective is pounding the pavement, searching for more clues. But he'll not scrape any from me.

The afternoon drags on like fingers scraping on a chalkboard. Julia rings up another customer but scans one item twice—the fifth time she's done it. The man buying toys for his kid checks his phone and huffs. Tremors return to her hands and she stumbles over her words.

"I'm so sorry. I'll remove the extra item." She attempts to make the change but gives up. "I can't remember how to do it, Gwyn."

"Don't get upset," I say, removing the game. "Did you take note of how I did it?"

"Oh, yes. I remember now." She hands the bag of merchandise to the impatient customer. "Thank you for shopping at Mystic Sage."

He grunts and rushes out the door. Julia plops on the stool and frowns. "I don't think I'm ready to go solo yet. You must be so frustrated with me."

"No. You made a few mistakes today, but you're performing so well now."

Shane comes behind the counter and rubs her shoulders. "Pumpkin, you've improved so much. Don't let a few setbacks bother you."

"I appreciate your confidence," she says. "But how will I ever manage on my own?"

"Have confidence, Julia. The store is only open for another hour, anyway. Frankly, you may perform better without us hovering."

Shane embraces her. "Gwyn's correct. If you forget something, I'm right in the back doing inventory. Just holler."

A head of wavy, fire-red hair passes under the streetlight outside and enters the store. "Hey, Gwyn. Are you ready to go?" Skye asks. "I want to get back to the apartment for a movie. Zach dropped me off and will be waiting. You'll need to give me a lift home. Hi, Julia."

Shane's girlfriend flashes a smile and waves.

"Yeah. No problem." I put on my fleece jacket and grab my backpack. "Julia, you'll do fine. Remember, I stuffed cheat sheets under the counter if you forget anything."

"Thank you, Gwyn." She stands up and straightens her blouse. "I'm ready."

"You sure are, Pumpkin," Shane says. "I'll be in the back. Goodnight, ladies."

"Good luck, Julia," I say. "You'll do fine."

"Thank you, Gwyn," she replies, folding her hands. "Have a wonderful evening."

Skye and I stroll to the Celestial Gardens under indigo skies, twinkling stars and a luminous moon lighting our way. The temperature has dropped with the setting of the sun, but the warmth of the day lingers. We arrive at Mitchell Hall in record time and enter through the gate after checking for stray Unremarkables. The Seelie Fae children haven't crossed over yet, so we approach the mound and yell at the opening.

"Shailagh? Aonghas? We're here to play for a couple of hours."

We stand back, preparing for them to cross over. But only the sound of scampering squirrels breaks the silence.

"Maybe they aren't coming tonight," Skye says. "I mean, they've got those changelings to play with over there now."

"When has that made a difference?" I ask. "This would be the first time they didn't cross over." I glance at my phone in the dark. "It's still early. Why don't we rest on the concrete bench near the fairy fountain?"

"Sure. Why not? We haven't hung out in ages. Once you started your master's degree, we didn't have any classes together. All the shit that's gone down in the last couple of years hasn't allowed much leisure time, either." Her phone dings and a playful smile erupts. "And Zach came into my life."

"I'm happy you found someone who can love you for who you are. Or should I say, despite what you are?"

"Right? He's amazing. When I told him I was a witch, he didn't doubt my confession for a second. He scratched his chin and asked me if I could change the grade on his last final. I answered yes, but it would be highly unethical, and I wouldn't do it. He laughed at me and said he hoped I would answer correctly. After the witchy sex that night, he said he didn't want to share me with anyone else. I agreed, largely because he was comfortable with me practicing witchcraft."

I chuckle. "I bet he was. Have you thought about what you're going to do once you finish your doctorate? You have another year left."

"Well, I don't know. The department is in shambles right now. Archie must have told you."

"He said Leslie is worried about the department because the Dean won't renew Nick Evans's position. He's not sure about the visiting professor position Seamus has, either. Of course, he is going home in June."

"It's worse. Dr. Duffy is bagging Spring Semester now. Once he finishes teaching the two Winter Session courses, he's done."

"What?" I ask, gaping at her. "He told me he was going back at the end of the semester."

"I was waiting outside Dr. Hughes's office today when he bailed on them. I tried not to listen, but...it's hard not to. She flipped out. He kept telling her he couldn't commit any longer due to some sort of impending doom. He said he wouldn't be available after Ostara, so he can't teach in the spring."

"Is Archie aware he is returning to North Ireland?"

"Beats me. I'm a lowly TA—not supposed to know he's leaving. But you and Dr. Duffy have a...special relationship. I thought I should tell you."

I rub the palm of my hand. "Thanks. I won't say anything to Archie, in case Leslie hasn't told him yet." But for damn sure, I'm going to ask Seamus.

We chill for another hour, calling on the pranksters a few more times, but they still don't show. We meander around the sculpted shrubs guarding the refurbished fairy statues and fountains, re-calling past events in the Celestial Gardens: the Sluagh attacks and banishment, my exit from the coven, the time the Seelie Fae pulled Councilman Corey Jones through the portal, the failed attempts at closing the mound, and sending the Dearg Due back to the Otherworld. Living in Bearsden hasn't been a walk in the park, but I wouldn't change a thing. This is my town and my family.

Skye reads the time on her cell phone. "It's eight already. I gotta go, and you should, too. We can't wait all night for the Seelie Fae."

"Yeah. I'll send a text to Trinity and Leslie. This was odd." I check the time on my phone again as we pass through the iron gate. "I wonder how Julia fared. She was so nervous. But Shane limited her work to a couple of hours. She's probably on the way home now."

We stroll down Main Street and descend the steps to the Green. For once, I struggle to keep up with Skye as we meander through the red paver walkways. The movie they're watching tonight must be outstanding, or could there be another reason? A chuckle es-capes me.

"What are you laughing about?"

"A funny idea passed my mind."

My intuition spikes inside and I stop in my tracks. I turn my head to find Shane's girlfriend entering a DUB building. My body buzzes, and Skye gapes at me.

"Did you feel that?" she asks in her husky voice.

"You felt it, too?" I survey the area for hints of a witch spying on us, but the sensation has dissipated.

"Why did Julia go inside Menzies Hall? It's 8:15 p.m. on a Saturday night."

I glance back at the red-brick building. "I don't know."

CHAPTER SEVENTEEN

CAT SITH SECRETS

BY THE TIME TUESDAY rolls around, Archie hasn't shared the news about Seamus leaving. I won't betray Skye's confidence. There has to be a reason he won't reveal the news. Maybe they're trying to convince the Irish professor to stay? Or they can't tell students yet? But the prospect must be hanging over their heads like guillotines ready to drop. All of them—Leslie, Archie, Seamus, and Ashley—are spread as thin as butter on too many slices of toast.

The premonition of the Fomorian hasn't returned to my slumber in days, despite the presence of the clear quartz stone on my nightstand. I've put off talking with Seamus for as long as I can. He may have insight into why his personal crystal enhanced my sixth sense, but is now dead as a piece of coal. When I slip on my puffer jacket, Archie shuffles into the foyer, chatting on his cell phone.

"Aye. I understand, Quinn." He peers up at me, his eyes twitching, and turns around. "I can't talk now. Gwyn's on the way out. We'll chat again later. I want to chat with Dad myself." He shoves his phone into his jeans pocket.

I slip on my gloves, preparing for the frigid blast that moved in. My long-sleeved tee and jeans may not be enough for the chill. "Harris not doing well?"

"Naw. He's not improved even a wee bit. They're so concerned, Hamish Brown moved into a guest bedroom."

"Wow. How did your father feel about him moving in?"

"Not happy at all. He's complaining he bought Hamish's flat and now he isn't living in it."

"Well, at least your dad hasn't lost the will to complain. Take it as a good sign. If he loses his spirit, that's when you start to worry."

"Aye. You're right. This is my home, but my family lives in Edinburgh." He flexes his jaw. "This is pulling me apart."

I wrap my arms around him and caress his back through his DUB sweatshirt. "What can I do?"

He kisses me and swipes my cheek. "Nothing, Gwyn. It's not your problem to solve."

And his father's recovery isn't the only issue. I sense the troubles stacking like bricks and weighing him down. Why can't he confide in me regarding the staffing issues in the Celtic Studies department? I step away and grab my backpack from the oak hall tree.

"Anyone report on Shailagh and Aonghas?" I ask.

"Naw. Quite strange, though. They could have left for good."

"Without saying goodbye? I got so used to them being here. Maybe we're going too early. Skye and I will drop by again when she's able to go around midnight."

"I told Seamus I would meet him on campus at noon on the dot. He has very little time between his Winter Session courses, so I'm meeting him for lunch. His treat."

"Aye. He's covering my class so I could spend the month in Scotland. Now I'm here. The teaching assistantships don't cover Spence and Skye during Winter Session. Leslie and Ashley are teaching, too. I should help them with grading. It's the least I can do under the circumstances."

"Yeah." I pause, hoping he'll elaborate. But he doesn't. "Don't forget, I'm stopping by the farm to sift through some of Agnes and Leslie's grimoires. See if I can find advice on detecting the sources of magic."

"You won't let it go, will you?" He shakes his head. "Gwyn, there is no way that sweet old woman is a witch, certainly not a malevolent one."

"But Archie, I did an internet search of her name. No results. Everyone has a former address pop up at least, but not her—*poof*. She appeared out of nowhere. Don't you find that odd? We may not be sensing witch magic. Skye and I both felt the warning buzz, which is strange. Other than Seamus, I'm the solitary witch who usually picks up on its presence. When I searched the area, Julia appeared. When she went into Menzies Hall, the sensation disappeared."

"Aye, but you need more proof than a one-time occurrence, Gwyn. Most likely, it's a coincidence. If Shane discovers you've snooped into her past, you'll lose his friendship, especially after what happened with Cordelia Davenport. Tread carefully."

"True, but I was right about her," I say, blinking. "Plus, you don't believe in coincidences, remember?"

"You win. Promise me you won't report this to Leslie or Trinity, though. It's solely speculation."

"No. Skye and I are sitting on that information for now." Along with the secret of Seamus's leaving.

I kiss him. "Have a fantastic afternoon, honey."

"You, too, my love."

He kisses me on the cheek and I venture out into the chilly air. The brisk walk to campus takes around ten minutes, and I rush up the steps to the double door entrance of Stewart Hall. It's been ages since I met Seamus at his office. I descend the stairs to the musty basement and dart past Leslie's office down the hallway, turning the corner at the end.

I arrive at the visiting professor's office and raise my hand. An aura overwhelms me as a memory of Nick Evans flashes in my brain—the first time I met him here. The door opens as my fist hovers above my groggy head. Seamus is wearing a DUB polo shirt and dark dress slacks, his typical teaching attire, his long, jet-black hair gathered behind his head as usual.

"Gwynedd, are you OK?" Seamus asks.

I lower my hand. "Yeah. I was recalling the first time I came to this door. The memory startled me."

"Not a pleasant memory, I'm certain. Please, come in. Lunch is served on the veranda," he says, gesturing to his messy desk.

"Thank you for bringing lunch for me. You're so busy. I could have brought us something to eat." I remove my puffer jacket and hang it on the back of a chair.

"Nonsense. Let me spoil a...good friend while I'm able."

I sit down in the chair at the front of his desk and Seamus limps without his cane to his seat on the other side. I take a bite of the wrap and pull out my water bottle to wash it down.

"Mmm. What a yummy hummus and spinach wrap. Thank you."

"You're most welcome." He bites into his club sandwich and chews. "What brings you here, Gwynedd? Archie shared what happened in Edinburgh. I am deeply sorry his father is recovering from a wicked hex. I hope this witch from Dean Village can hasten his recovery. He also told me you left before you could find the grimoire you sought. Is Gorawen ill?"

"Nooo. She's fine. But Ellie Jones?" I down some water and swallow. "Not so good. She walked in on us performing magic and hightailed it up the hallway to the front door. The hand blocked her from escaping before we could explain ourselves."

He drops his sandwich on the paper plate. "Oh, my. Gorawen must have panicked."

"I mean, Ellie flipped out. But Aunt Gorawen and I calmed her down. Convinced her we were good witches. She's going to continue to care for my aunt, hiding her secret." I roll my lips inward. "That's not why I'm here."

"Please, continue then." He takes another bite.

"I've had more premonitions, and they've expanded. But I didn't use the grid. Archie keeps a clear quartz crystal on his bedroom dresser in Edinburgh. I woke up our first morning there to an expanded vision. The stone was glowing."

A wide grin seizes his face. "I hoped you would acquire the skill."

I stop mid-bite. "What skill?"

"Step three, of course." He wipes his face with a napkin, a look of accomplishment glimmering in his glassy, sea-green eyes.

"You mean the cat sith top step?" I place my hummus wrap on the plate. Suddenly, my curiosity replaces my hunger.

"You have continued to practice focus with the amethyst geode and the clear quartz, yes?"

"I had, yeah. Until we left for Scotland. It was going well."

"How have the visions progressed?"

"They were expanding, one in both directions. Nothing for days. The last one occurred during my sleep with your crystal on the nightstand next to me. Now...zilch."

"Have you worked with the geode and clear quartz since your return?"

"No. I haven't had time. Why?"

Seamus leans on the desk. "Gwynedd, I hesitate to bring up the training you completed with me because—"

"You kissed me?" I glance at my hummus wrap, begging for consumption.

"Exactly. But if you recall, you had difficulty with your concentration. Regular practice with the two crystals in tandem increased more than your intuition. It improved your focus. The natural progression to tap the clear quartz crystal to enhance your visions took hold. You had a few successes, but the focus was lost when you stopped practicing with the stones. I also believe these murders of the witches in nearby covens are invading your thoughts. Hence, your diminished focus."

"Wow. You make so much sense. Why didn't I come and talk to you sooner?"

"Why did you wait so long? I was here." He finishes his sandwich and drinks tea from his DUB mug.

"One more thing. While we were down in the vaults, I had an eerie sensation, like the magic of dead witches still occupied the chambers. Could the presence of unfiltered roaming witchcraft have heightened my senses somehow?"

"Interesting theory. All things are possible."

"Good to know." I shift in my chair, staring at the cat sith painting on the wall behind his desk.

He tilts his head to the right. "You can ask me anything, Gwynedd."

I peer up at him, suppressing the urge to divulge what Skye told me. I promised not to say anything. "Nothing. Thinking about how I should proceed from here."

The yearning still burns in his eyes. "I believe you have all the knowledge you need. But I'm always here for you, Gwynedd."

I finish my wrap and shove my water bottle into my backpack, hitting the dirk as I push it in. "Thanks for your advice and for giving up your valuable space between classes."

"My time is yours...always."

How do I respond to a statement of devotion like that? I put on my puffer jacket, throw my backpack over my shoulder, and open the door.

"Will I see you again?" I ask, doubt invading my thoughts.

A faint smile curves his mouth. "I am certain of it."

But I'm not.

Agnes leans back in the chair across the table from me in her upstairs library. Relaxed in her black sweater and loose knit pants, she sucks on her joint and expels the fumes with a hiss. I hack at the smoke, flapping my hand all around me. But the act is futile.

"Do you have to blow your pot in my face? I'm trying to research here." I summon my witch energy with a chant and a grimoire floats across the room to the table.

"My house, my library, my rules," she says, inhaling again. "No one is forcing you to fucking stay. Don't let Leslie catch you doing that."

"She won't, and come on. You know how pot affects me. I can't concentrate if I inhale too much of it." I open the old tome and flip a few pages.

Mr. Yeats scuttles in, transforming into his human form. He wheezes and waves his hand back and forth. "Ms. Pritchard, must you smoke while we are working?"

"Yeah, I must. And don't fucking call me that. You make me sound like someone's granny." Agnes blows another stream at the familiar and laughs.

Leslie strolls into the room dressed in her usual administrative attire, a long-sleeved blouse and skirt. How does she brave the icy temps?

"Good afternoon, Dr. Hughes." Mr. Yeats adjusts his spectacles. "We didn't expect you."

"I needed a personal reference for a class. This Winter Session has been extremely taxing. Hello, Gwynedd," she says, approaching her designated bookshelf. "Agnes said you were coming by. What are you looking for?"

"Hi. I'm sifting through a few grimoires with general directions on implementing the craft. Hoping to find some hints to identifying specific sources of magic."

She pulls a book off the shelf the old-fashioned way and turns to the appendix. "You want to determine if the magic is witch-produced or fairy?"

"Identifying the source would help us prepare for an attack, wouldn't it?" I ask.

Agnes bends over the table and snuffs out her joint. "You're ruining my buzz."

"Sorry, but thanks for stopping. The smoke gave me a headache."

Mr. Yeats examines the contents of a book and places it next to me on the table. "It's not good for your lungs."

"Aww, fuck you," she replies. "I'll do as I please. And by the way, I am still kicking."

He turns around, pursing his lips. "I'm simply trying to be helpful."

"Why are you smoking marijuana in the middle of the afternoon, Agnes?" Leslie asks. "You said you were going to dust off the shelves."

She guffaws, slapping the table. "Woman, you think I actually dust them?"

"Oh, Agnes. If you don't want to do the work, say so. I will gladly do it."

"Nah. I'll dust them after Gwyn leaves, sweetheart. All the tension around these witch murders is stressing me the fuck out. What if we're next?"

Leslie walks to her partner and wraps her bony arms around her shoulders. "Dear Agnes, don't worry yourself over the prospect. We will discuss how to prepare ourselves at the circle on Thursday evening."

Wow. Even Agnes isn't impervious to the threat. Now I'm concerned. I've had four encounters—the evening on the Green when I ran into Seamus in the alley, New Year's Eve on the way to meet with Riley, outside Ronnie's house, and the night Skye and I saw Julia on the Green. I dismissed the incident on New Year's Eve because I figured Riley was nearby. Was I wrong?

Leslie kisses her on the cheek. "I understand the pot helps with the stress, but shouldn't we be on our toes? Perhaps refrain from your recreational pastime until this issue resolves and we're safe."

The hedge witch grimaces. "And stay stressed out? Fuck no."

Mr. Yeats passes me another book, and I continue to flip the pages silently; I am not getting in the middle of this argument. Leslie bends down and gazes into her lover's pale-gray eyes. Agnes's glower melts like butter on a hot day.

"OK. I'll do it for you, sweetheart."

"Splendid. I must get back to campus. Gwynedd, good luck with your search, but I doubt you'll find anything." She starts toward the doorway but turns around. "Is there another reason for your research you haven't mentioned?"

Oh, fuck. I swallow. "No. I had the time, so I thought I'd check."

Agnes crosses her arms on the table and stares at me like a huge pimple has sprouted on my nose. I shift in my seat.

"Well, thank you for taking the time, Gwyn." Leslie smiles at her love. "I'll see you when I get home, dear."

"Bye, sweetheart," Agnes says, never moving an inch.

Leslie's footsteps dwindle away as she descends the stairs. The front door shuts with a bang. As my mentor continues to spy on me, I flip a few more pages and scour the grimoire for clues. But the hedge witch hasn't budged.

"What the fuck are you doing?" I ask, slamming the book shut. "Are you so high you can't move your eyeballs?"

She squints at me. "You're fucking lying."

"Why would you say that?" I plop back against my chair and glance at the familiar. "What am I supposed to be lying about?"

"I don't know yet. Why don't you tell me?"

My gaze drops to the closed grimoire, realizing I can't lie to my mentor. Leslie? Sure. I can spew a white one to her. She wasn't forthcoming with detrimental information about the Tuatha Dé threat. But Agnes? She has never lied to me, *ever*, because that's who she is. Love her or hate her, she's the real deal. I earned her trust. She deserves the same.

"Mr. Yeats, you're so helpful," I say, buttering him up. "Would you mind getting me some tea? I need the caffeine boost."

"Of course, Ms. Crowther." He turns toward the hedge witch. "Would you like a tea...Agnes?"

She snickers. "Sure, but make an herbal peppermint. I don't want the caffeine to ruin my buzz."

Mr. Yeats transforms into a cat as he scuttles through the doorway. I peer up at her and lower my voice.

"I have a hunch, but you can't tell Leslie. Not yet, anyway. In fact, don't mention this theory to anyone. I asked Skye not to say anything until I have more proof."

She rubs her hands together like a praying mantis, one covered in tattoos. At that moment, I'm grateful not to be her mate.

"OK. Hit me. What have you got?"

"Skye and I went to check on the Seelie Fae Saturday night, but they didn't show."

"Old news. They still haven't. That's no secret."

"I know. We walked back to the house through the Green, and I felt a buzz, the warning I get when I sense magic near me. I scanned the area and saw Julia Harding entering Menzies Hall. It was around 8:15 p.m."

"Well, no wonder you didn't find the Seelie Fae playing in there. Too early for them."

"Did you hear what I said about Julia?"

"Oh, for fuck's sake, Gwyn. I've talked with the woman. If she were a witch, I'd know it."

"What if she isn't? Could you identify a fairy? A Tuatha Dé Danann? Courtney Erickson was here for a couple of years and joined the coven. *No one* noticed. Ditto for Alys Morgan. And of course, there was Nick Evans. I did an internet search on her. Her name doesn't show up anywhere. She isn't who she says she is."

She twists the side of her mouth. "You think she's the dangerous woman Riley Shaw warned you about? A member of Nuada's family."

"I don't know. I said it's a hunch. If so, she doesn't appear to recognize I'm the one she's after. Archie made me promise not to tell Leslie or Trinity yet. But he didn't mention your name."

She snorts. "You know fucking well he meant to include me. You're fucking around with his intent. Don't be surprised when this comes back to bite you in the ass."

"Please, don't tell Leslie. I found nothing in these grimoires to guide me. I'll have to do my own snooping."

She shakes a finger at me. "That could get you into trouble, too."

I chant an incantation and send the grimoire back to the shelf with a wave of magic. "I'm going to ask a few invasive questions, nonchalantly, of course, so she doesn't suspect anything. Meanwhile, I'll update the coven on my visions on Thursday. They've expanded. I think I know how to increase them this time. You can tell Leslie about them. I would have mentioned it, but I didn't want to keep her from work. They're overloaded."

"Yeah. Fuck DUB. I'm tired of sharing her. I support her desire to teach, but the schedule this year has sucked balls. Fifty years we were apart. Am I wrong to want more time with her?"

"No. You want to spend the precious days you have left with her." I put on my puffer jacket and grab my backpack. "Agnes, has Leslie mentioned anything about the woes of the Celtic Studies department?"

"Not much. I know she's not happy with the Dean of the College. And they're all overloaded. Why do you ask?"

I'm a dick for asking her this, but I can't stop myself. "Did she mention how Seamus is doing?"

"Nah. You know that cat sith witch. He's a loner. He'll finish out his work at DUB in the spring and go home without a how do you fucking do to any of us. Except for you." She winks hard at me and pushes up from her chair. "Whoa...I may need some coffee to dust those shelves."

Mr. Yeats walks in carrying a tray with tea and sets it on the table. "You're leaving?"

"I'm sorry. I totally forgot I have to be somewhere." Is it wrong to lie to a familiar? "Agnes, I don't tell you enough. I love you, you ol' hedge witch. Thanks for always having my back."

"Hmph. Get the fuck outta here."

The familiar straightens his suit and glares at me.

"Don't feel slighted. I love you, too, Mr. Yeats."

He fluffs his tie. "I appreciate the sentiment, Ms. Crowther."

"See you on Thursday, Agnes."

On the way to my car, it occurs to me. Leslie hasn't told her partner about Seamus, either. What is she hiding?

CHAPTER EIGHTEEN
A WINTER CHILL

THE BITTER WINTER TEMPERATURE continues through Thursday with a threat of snow. Thick, dark-gray clouds blanket Bearsden, threatening a heavy snowfall. Not the most enticing weather for a midnight visit to the Celestial Gardens. Skye reluctantly agreed to meet me there to test my theory of why they haven't appeared for our visits. Fortunately, Mystic Sage provides a toasty refuge from outside elements—at least until Ashley Lewis and Courtney Erickson enter the store. They're bundled up like mini snow persons in puffer jackets, beanies, and mittens.

I shudder from the brief burst of frosty air and finish ringing up a customer. Ashley and Courtney head directly to the toy section. Courtney is beginning to show. Another half human, half fairy child is on the way. Never in any universe did I believe I'd develop a fondness for the Tylwyth Teg who betrayed Archie. Yet here we are.

"Thank you for shopping at Mystic Sage." The shopper exits the store, leaving the newfound friends alone with me. "Hi, ladies. I think we're gonna get snow."

Courtney glances at the window front. "Hasn't begun yet, but the meteorologist said some of the white fluff may show up by midnight."

"Greaaat," I say, my smile falling flat.

"How are you, Gwyn?" Ashley asks, setting a kid's puzzle on the counter.

"I'm OK. I don't have many more days left here. As soon as I finish training Julia, I'll clock out for the last time. Spring Semester, I have to concentrate on my master's thesis. I want to find a job in my area, but I will miss working here. It's bittersweet."

"Well, I know Jeff will miss you terribly."

I pass the bag to her. "I'll visit, if for nothing else but the herbs. Courtney, I have a question for you before an Unremarkable townie strolls in. Can you recognize other types of fairies besides your own?"

"Not really. I mean, sometimes I sense their presence, but I can't always discern who or where they are. I hate to dredge up the past, but like the Sluagh that Audrey Kenilworth summoned from the Otherworld. Before it crossed over, it found its way to you through the trees in the area. I sensed them there. Didn't you, too?"

"Yeah," I reply, my jaw falling slightly. "When I was near the host trees, bursts of icy air would chill my bones. A nasty odor would appear, too. Thanks for reminding me."

She laughs. "You're welcome, I guess?"

"It's OK, Courtney. I forgave you. Sincerely, thank you for the advice."

"We better go," Ashley says. "Jeff and John are waiting to go to dinner. Aidan, too."

"Tell him Miss Gwyn misses him."

"I'll bring him to the Imbolc party at Mrs. Pritchard's farm."

"I look forward to it. Once all of this mess is resolved, I should have time to babysit again."

"He would love that, Gwyn. He misses his friend with the *invisible hands*." She chuckles as they exit the store.

I'd nearly forgotten the sluagh's attempts to injure me—and its chilly air of death. At least I know it's not an evil Unseelie fairy after me this time.

Julia arrives at the store around six and I sit on the stool while she goes solo at the register. Her hands shake. She drops merchandise on the floor. Several purchases need voiding, and the customers tap their feet and huff. She starts from scratch. Archie may be right. How can this barely functional Boomer be a supernatural serial killer? I send a text to Skye.

Me: *I sensed nothing when she entered the store.*

Skye: *Could she be masking her magic when she's around you?*

Me: *True. But what about her demeanor? If this is an act, she deserves an Oscar.*

Skye: *LOL. Nick Evans fooled you, too. Remember?*

Me: *Ugh. Don't remind me. But he glamoured me intermittently. I've got protection.*

Skye: *Ask her some questions? Try to trip her up?*

Me: *Good advice. I'll brainstorm.*

Skye: *I can't go tonight. Sorry. I told Ashley I would help her grade for free.*

Me: *Well, shit, but that's nice of you.*

Skye: *Spence is going in my place.*

Me: *Oh. How did you convince him?*

Skye: *I gave him a choice. Grade papers or go with you.*

Me: *Hahaha. Sounds like Spence.*

Skye: *He'll meet you at Archie's.*

Me: *OK. Thanks.*

"Thank you for shopping at Mystic Sage." Julia passes the eco bag to the young mother. "Come back again for the Imbolc sale."

The door shuts with a clank of the bamboo chimes and Julia's hands drop to her side. Is her reaction relief or frustration?

"Are you OK, Julia?" I ask. "You seem...frustrated. Do you not want this job?" Or are you here to spy on me?

"No, I mean, a little. I want to do well so Shane doesn't fire me. I need this position."

"He wouldn't get rid of you. Why are you so nervous? It's retail. You aren't performing surgery. No one will die if you ring up the tarot cards three times."

Shane is in the back, accepting a delivery. This is my chance to be invasive. But how do I do that without creating suspicion? I'm not Jack Schmidt. I can't manipulate like he can.

"Julia, I am curious. You don't seem to be very techy. Are you online anywhere? Any social media sites? Employment sites? I tried to find you on one site to add you to my network so we can stay in touch once I leave, but your name didn't appear anywhere." *That was good, Gwyn.*

Her eyes grow round and white, and she kneads her fingers. "I...I...can't use any of them. I'm embarrassed to be so behind the times. It's why I want this cashier's job. I don't think I could find another position without a work history."

Another customer enters the store with a ding and Julia faces the cash register. "Welcome to Mystic Sage."

I plop back on the stool. No work history. Who doesn't have at least a short resume at her age? Could I be right after all?

I have so many layers on, I can barely move my arms and legs. If Spence doesn't arrive soon, I'm going to break out in a hot flash and soak my clothes. I've avoided them for months and would like to continue that winning streak. The mantle clock in the living room dings the first of twelve as I zip up my puffer jacket. Archie leans on the stair newel, dressed in a T-shirt and lounge pants, tapping. Someone knocks with a rat-a-tat-tat.

"Finally, he's here," I say, slipping on my gloves.

Archie shifts to the door and pulls it open.

"Hey," he says in his baritone voice. "Are you ready for our nippy stroll?"

"No, but it's necessary," I say. "Archie, I'll text you when we arrive. We'll stay for an hour, tops."

He grasps my hand through my glove. "Be aware and don't leave Spence's side. Promise me."

"Come on, Archie," Spence says. "Gwyn is a badass. She doesn't need me to defend her. We'll be fine."

"That may be true, but fairy magic is powerful. Don't forget Nuada's strength."

"I haven't." I tap the side of my backpack. "And before you ask, yes. I have the dirk."

"I'll be in bed when you return, but not asleep. No need to tiptoe up the stairs."

"OK." I kiss him on the cheek and step onto the front stoop. "Don't worry."

"Bye, Archie. Keep the bed warm." Spence waggles his eyebrows.

The temperature seems to drop with every step as the icy air penetrates my outerwear. We pick up our pace as we cross the maze of red paver walkways through the Green, our misty-white breath trailing behind us. Snowflakes trickle down like flecks of confetti, covering the moon in a hazy veil. By the time we reach University Avenue, the fluff increases, and I pull my hood over my head.

"Thanks for coming with me. Should we have canceled? The storm is getting worse."

"Nah. We're good, sis," Spence says, pulling his DUB beanie over his ears. "We don't have far to walk now, anyway."

While we continue across the Green toward Main Street, I mull over what could be going on in the Celtic Studies department. "Archie seems stressed about work. Have you heard anything?"

"Why should he be strung out? He isn't teaching Winter Session. But then, I'm not TAing, either. But Skye and I are helping Dr. Lewis with her overload."

"What about Seamus?" I ask. "Does he appear overwhelmed?"

"That dude never complains about anything. Cat sith witch vibes. Why do you wanna know?"

"Curiosity." Skye must not have told him what she heard when she was lurking outside Leslie's office.

"Don't you think Archie's stress is related to his dad? Sounds like he got walloped by an underground witch bitch."

A laugh spurts out. "You have a way with words, Spence."

"Wait until you read my thesis." He blows on his gloved hands and rubs them together.

We finally arrive at the steps at the end of the Green and ascend to Main Street. We proceed across to Mitchell Hall and stop at the iron fence. Jack Schmidt is exiting the gardens decked out in full winter gear.

"Quick. Run this way," I say, nearly slipping on a patch of ice as I head toward the right side of the building.

Spence rushes past, grabbing my hand, and pulls me against the rough exterior wall of Mitchell Hall. My heart pumps overtime; I can practically feel my cortisol levels rocketing sky-high. The snow collecting on my jacket and hood does little to cool the sweating, but my cheeks are numb.

My coven partner peeks around the corner, panting. "What the fuck was he doing in there?"

"I don't know, but let's wait for him to get out of sight."

"What if he saw the Seelie Fae children? Dr. Hughes will burst the crystal on her staff."

"Doubtful. They haven't shown up for days."

Detective Schmidt walks with a purpose in his step and disappears when he turns the corner. He must have parked on North Campus. I motion to my lanky partner and we dart to the iron entry gate. I can barely identify the mound through the clumps of wet snow, dropping at a steady pace now. The gardens are dark except for a security light on the back of the house. We approach the portal. I call out to the Seelie Fae.

"Shailagh! Aonghas! Spence and Aunt Gwyn are here. It's safe to come out."

We stand in front of the mound, shaking. Spence bounces from one leg to the other.

"You know, if you put a little muscle on your bones, you'd have more insulation for weather like this."

"Your body is hardly ready for a trip to Antarctica."

"No, but I layered. I'm actually hot underneath."

He snickers. "Archie would probably agree with that."

"Very. Funny." I move closer to the opening in the mound. "Shailagh? Aonghas? Please, come out."

A few snowflakes wet my nose and the portal lights up. The Seelie Fae cross over, dancing with delight. "Aunt Gwyn, you're here!" They run to us, clad in their usual attire of loose shirts and shorts. They rub their arms, shivering.

I bend down. "Where have you two been? My friends and I have been coming to play, but you weren't here."

"We crossed over, Aunt Gwyn," Aonghas says. "But the man with the mad face yelled at us."

Shailagh interjects. "We ran behind the mound to hide. Every time we crossed over, he was here, so we came later after he was gone."

Spence squats down. "What was he doing in here?"

"We don't know," Aonghas says. "He looked at the ground. Walked around. We hid until he left."

"Does he come every night?" I ask, wiping my face with a glove.

"We don't know," Shailagh says, shaking. "After the first two times, we waited until the moon was burning bright in the sky."

"Thank you for telling us." Spence and I exchange curious glances and I scan the gardens. "It's too cold for us to stay any longer, and this storm is getting worse. We'll come back again when this weather has passed."

"We're cold, too," they reply. "Bye, Aunt Gwyn. Bye, Spence."

"See ya later, kiddos," he says, waving a mitten.

The Seelie Fae fade as they enter the portal. Spence and I dart out of the gardens, stopping at the walkway to check for Unremarkables passing by. But we're alone under the hazy lamppost. We cross Main Street and run down the steps to the Green.

"Let's walk as quickly as we can," I say. "I can't feel my toes."

"I thought you were all toasty under all those clothes?"

"Not anymore. The temperature must have dropped."

A chill passes through my jacket as if ice cold hands have pierced through the down inside. I shudder from head to toe and my gut tightens. We pick up our pace as we cross University Avenue onto Central Campus. The wind whistles through the alleyways, resembling howling coyotes, sending swirls of white toward us. The Old Men oak trees appear menacing with their arm-like branches threatening from afar. An icy blast resembling a tornado shoves us up the slick paver walkway and I fall on my ass.

"Are you OK, sis?" Spence grasps my arms and pulls me up. "We should run on the snow-covered grassy area."

"Yeah. My lower back can't survive too many more of those falls."

We run across the fresh snow, leaving footsteps behind us, until we arrive at the alley to Douglas Street. I glance back to see the white stuff falling serenely in tiny clusters against a background of stillness. What the fuck?

"Spence, stop. Turn around and tell me what you see."

He spins on his boots and gazes into the distance. "What happened to the fucking blizzard?"

"I don't know. The snow doesn't even appear to have moved. There are no mounds or drifts from the gusts."

Spence rubs his eyes and looks again. "That's fucking weird."

"Yeah," I say, clutching my abdomen as a wave of dread overwhelms me.

CHAPTER NINETEEN

A COVEN'S PREP

THE *VROOM* OF SPENCE'S sedan driving off resounds up the road while I dash to the back of the house. Once I'm inside, I drop my backpack and strip down to my T-shirt and undies because my jeans are soaked. As I pass the basement door, the crystals call to me, begging me to practice. The mantel clock dings twice and rings throughout the house, reminding me how late it is. Practice will have to hang tight until tomorrow.

The upstairs hall light spills onto the stairs to direct my way. Still, I step carefully in my stocking feet. I flip the switch off and tiptoe into the bedroom. Archie is resting with his back against a pillow, his laptop resting on his thighs and his eyes firmly closed. The lamp on his nightstand shines on his face, highlighting the slight scar on his cheek. I wash up for the night, slip on some pajama bottoms, and climb into bed.

"Archie," I whisper. "Honey. I'm back."

He lifts his head. "I must have fallen asleep. I was trying to grade these papers for Seamus. How did it go?"

"Good. We figured out a few things. I'll tell you in the morning. I'm exhausted, and so are you."

"Aye. I need to apologize to Seamus when I wake."

He closes his laptop and places it on the nightstand. After turning off the light, he crawls under the bed linens and cuddles against me, and I feel not only our bodies entangle, but our worries, too. I tense up. How will I ever fall asleep now? I wish he would share his hidden apprehensions, but part of me doesn't want to know. My own issues are weighing me down, and I'm not sure I have anything left to help him.

I roll over and caress his chest through his T-shirt and kiss him. "I know you're overwhelmed by everything. Can I remove even a little of the worry? I love you, Archie."

"No, my love," he says, stroking my face in the dark. "Our life course does not travel the direction we want it to go all the time. But I'm grateful to the gods you are on that path with me. I pray you will always be there at my side."

"Of course I will. Where else would I go if not with you?"

He kisses me, and for these few brief moments, the burdens of our lives slip away. No ill parents, no witch murders, no threat of fairies. I remove my pajamas and undies, pushing them aside, and grab the elastic of his pants. He may be exhausted, but he's rising to the occasion. As I slide off his bottoms, his body shakes from the cooler night air. I summon my witch energy and pass my hand down his torso to warm him up.

"Ah, Gwyn. What would my world be without you? You're my soul."

I kiss him and shift on top, filling myself with his manhood. He moans in relief, as if I've banished the stress from within. We make love slowly, tumbling back and forth as if time stands still, until we purge our bodies of the unavoidable pains of our existence. I roll on my side and lay a hand on his heart. He rests his forehead on mine.

"I love you, Gwynedd. Stay with me always."

"Archie, I'm not going anywhere. You're my heart."

Archie and I stop by Tyler and Zoe's home in Archie's Tesla to give them a ride to the Fellowship meeting. Trinity decided the farm was a safer place to meet again, under the circumstances. The Pumpkin House is DUB turf, which means we can't protect it as well. Road crews have cleared the streets of the snow, leaving mounds of white slush piled on the shoulders. The local news made no mention of the "blizzard" Spence and I witnessed. It's baffling.

"So, let me get this straight," Tyler says. "You think there was a snow tornado?"

I toss my hands in the air. "I don't know what Spence and I saw, but we didn't imagine the phenomenon."

"Spooky." Zoe wiggles her fingers in my face. "Maybe it was a ghost from Imbolc past."

I chuckle. "Funny. I believe you're confusing holidays."

"What do you make of it, Archie?" Tyler asks.

"Not sure," he replies. "Did a gust of wind move their bodies? Yes. The ground was icy. Wouldn't take much."

"But what about the snow?" Zoe asks. "Gwyn said it didn't appear blown at all."

Archie turns his blinker on to turn onto Agnes and Leslie's driveway. "The snowfall was quite thick at times last night. It was dark as a dungeon. Hard to tell what happened, if anything."

"Well, at least we know what's going on with the Seelie Fae now," I say. "We'll discuss tonight what to do about Jack Schmidt."

Archie pulls up to the front of the farmhouse and parks. When we enter the house, Mr. Yeats is standing guard.

"Don't forget to remove your wet shoes. Ms. Pritchard does not want her floors damaged."

Zoe kicks off her boots. "If we have to take off our boots, why are you still wearing shoes?"

"She has a point, Mr. Yeats," Archie says.

He straightens his vest. "I'll have you know I *never* go outside. My shoes are always spotless."

Tyler places his boots on the mat and examines his shoes. "Not one scuff."

"Precisely," Mr. Yeats replies, crossing his arms.

"I think we're the last ones here." I pull off my boots. "We better get in there."

Everyone is chatting among themselves when we enter the living room. Elijah, Shane, Trinity, Leslie, and Agnes gather in front of the fireplace, organizing the agenda, I assume. As usual, the young witches squish together on the floor. Zoe and Tyler join them. Ronnie motions to me from behind the sofa. Archie and I find two empty seats next to her. My best friend leans into my ear.

"I haven't heard from you for over a week. Did I offend you?" she asks with a snort.

"No, I've been doing shit nonstop. I'll stop by tomorrow and catch you up." I peer at Archie out of the corner of my eye. "Not a good time to talk."

She pats my hand. "Gotcha. Come by for tea after breakfast. Derrick will have left already."

"Sure," I say. "There's a lot to share."

Archie nudges me. "What are you whispering about?"

"Catching up. That's all," I reply. It's not a lie.

Leslie taps her staff three times. "I call this circle to order. We have much to discuss this evening. Trinity will begin."

Agnes, Leslie, Elijah, and Shane find seats on the sofa and side chairs. Our coven leader remains standing, a fist resting on her hip.

"The first thing on the agenda is about the Seelie Fae. Spence and Gwyn went there after midnight. They have been waiting until the early morning hours to cross over. But the reason is disconcerting. Detective Jack Schmidt has been going in there. The children told them he's been coming in there consistently and snooping around. He caught them playing one night, and he yelled at them. They ran and hid—waited for him to leave before returning to the Otherworld. After that, they peeped through the portal opening before crossing over."

"Can we be sure about this?" Shane asks. "How do they know the man was Jack Schmidt?"

Spence shoots a hand up. "Because Gwyn and I saw him coming out of the Celestial Gardens through the gate."

Soft chatter fills the living room and Trinity waves a hand to calm the babble. But my fellow witch friends have a slew of panicked questions.

"Was he looking for clues to the murders in there?" "Why would he search in the Celestial Gardens?" "Do you think he saw the Seelie Fae cross through the portal?"

Tanner shouts out, "Yo! What we shouldn't be doing is losing our shit. That's not helpful."

"No, it is not," Leslie says. "But we can prepare for further investigations to occur. He's an Unremarkable who is doing his job. Nothing more."

Agnes growls. "Let him snoop in there. As long as Shailagh and Aonghas continue to wait for him to leave, we're fine."

I raise my hand. "But why is he going in there? None of the murders occurred in the Celestial Gardens. What is he searching for?"

"He must know the Fellowship visits the gardens to perform ceremonies," Skye says. "They're listed on the community calendar of events. Maybe he thinks we're hiding something in there."

Archie interjects. "We are, in fact, concealing a portal to the Otherworld. Let's hope he never finds it. With the murders in the other covens—pagan groups as far as he understands—he must be exhausting all possibilities. He's a smart man. To him, the pagan groups have the answers he is seeking. He let up when he was searching for Nick Evans. I believe he will not give up this time until he finds answers."

"Which brings us to Elijah's announcement," Leslie says. "Your turn, councilman."

Elijah pushes up from his chair, a crinkle in his brow. "John Erickson has heard a rumor that Jack Schmidt has requested assistance from the FBI. Apparently, the Wilmington field office has too many cases on its plate at the moment. It may take a while to respond, but they will be descending on Bearsden in the near future."

"Oh, fuck the FBI." Agnes blows a raspberry with her tongue. "They won't find the witch killer either. Because they can't identify the root cause of the deaths of these women. Even we're having trouble with that." She glances at me. "Let them come."

"I don't know, Agnes," Ronnie says. "I think it's a problem. They may not discover the killer with any more ease than we're capable of, but they can sure stumble onto things they shouldn't. If Jack or an FBI agent witnesses the supernatural, we can kiss the hidden nature of our coven goodbye."

"I imagine they will send a single officer to survey the evidence initially." Elijah shoves his hands in his pockets. "Which at this point in the investigation can't be much."

Tanner raises a hand. "Aren't we losing track of our original objective? These murders have sidetracked our search for a portal-closing spell. And let's not forget, there could be Tuatha Dé Danann fairies out there searching for Gwyn—and doing it through us. If they haven't arrived yet, we're missing our opportunity to close it for good, safeguarding Gwyn as well as the rest of the town."

"Important points, Tanner," Leslie says, lifting her chin. "Unfortunately, our progress remains limited to one very grim spell that would complete the deed." Her sullen eyes fall to Agnes. "I recommend we continue making protection pouches to repel glamouring." She shifts her gaze to me. "Especially Gwynedd. We must not miss a day. Our preparedness will save us."

"I *love* making protection pouches." Zoe rubs her hands together. "I can make extra if anyone gets too busy."

"I could help with that, too," Skye adds. "Until Spring Semester begins."

Trinity stamps the heel of her stiletto. "Here, here. Frankly, we don't know where this all will lead, friends. For now, continue moving in pairs after dark. I would even say watch your back during the day. So far, there have been no more incidents that we're aware of. The other covens are taking precautions. If you notice anything unusual, report the phenomenon."

Skye peers at me and shifts in her seat. We have suspicions about Julia Harding, but until we have solid evidence, we can't accuse her in front of Shane. So, we remain silent.

Our coven leader continues. "We'll visit the Seelie Fae when we are able after midnight, but you'll have to scour the area for Jack Schmidt before you enter the gardens. I'll let our Elder close tonight."

Leslie stands and scans our informal circle, deep concern etching her face. "I have one more announcement before we disband. This will come as a shock to most of you, as much as it affected me. After much thought, Dr. Seamus Duffy has decided to return to North Ireland earlier than planned, most likely by Ostara. Therefore, he will not be teaching Spring Semester."

"What the fuck?" Spence hops up off the floor. "Who's gonna teach his classes? If they don't replace him, I'll get behind."

Archie's shoulders stiffen. "I understand your concerns. We are all aware of how this will affect the students, undergrad and graduate level. We're reaching out to other colleges with programs in the region. They may have adjunct faculty willing to fill in for one semester."

Ronnie whispers in my ear. "Wow. Did you know this, Gwyn?"

I can't explain now where others may hear. But I am as shocked as everyone that Leslie is announcing it to the circle. This has to be adding to Archie's stress.

"In the morning. I'll tell you everything," I whisper.

Skye pulls on Spence's jeans. "Calm down. They'll figure it out for us."

"Why aren't you more upset?" he asks, rubbing his upper thighs. "This could ruin our graduation target." Because she knew, friend.

"Sit down, Spence," she replies. "Screaming at the top of your lungs won't change anything."

"Indeed," Leslie says, her gaze falling to the floor. "With that, I disband the circle. Be careful, my friends."

On the way to Tyler and Zoe's, we try to allay their concerns, but my son can't pack his worries away.

"They'll never find someone to replace Dr. Duffy this close to Spring Semester. Will they scrap his courses?"

"That's one option," Archie replies. "Please, don't make this your concern, Tyler. You and Zoe have enough on your plates."

"I think it stinks," Zoe says. "I can't believe Dr. Duffy didn't consider how this would affect everyone, especially the students."

Tyler hugs his love. "He's a cat sith witch. Thinking of himself first."

I twist and peer around my car seat at him. "Don't criticize Seamus. We have no idea what's going on in his personal life, and we're not entitled to know." But why is he returning to North Ireland? And why didn't he confide in me?

"Whatever," he says, rolling his eyes. "Zoe and I wanted to invite you guys to come for dinner on Sunday. Can you?"

Archie pulls up along the curb and parks. "Do you work on Sunday, Gwyn?"

"No. We'd love to," I say. "Can't wait to see what you've done with the old furniture, too."

"Yay!" Zoe hops out of the car. "Bring yourselves, nothing else."

"Love you guys. Night." Tyler slides out of the back seat and follows Zoe into their house.

I blow him a kiss and we drive one street over to our home. Once we enter the warmth of our abode and hang up our winter gear, we amble into the living room and sit, propping our feet on the steamer trunk. I lay my head on Archie's chest and he wraps a comforting arm around me. The mantle clock dings once for the half hour and continues to tik, tik, tik, following the slow steady beat of his heart.

Since selling my house on the eastside of Bearsden, I've bounced from one temporary living situation to another. Now, I finally have a place I can call home where I'm loved and wanted. I can't even remember the last time that feeling passed through this heart of mine. I hate to ruin this moment, but I have to confront Archie about the cat sith witch.

"You knew Seamus was leaving. That's why you were so stressed out."

"Aye. I couldn't tell you. Leslie said we had to wait until the last possible moment. Seamus requested our silence."

"What will happen if you can't find instructors to fill in?" I peer up into his icy blues.

"We aren't sure. Leslie fears for the department."

Palpitations sputter in his chest, reminding me he is as vulnerable as the next person—or witch. The distress over Harris's lack of improvement certainly doesn't help. No wonder neither of us can focus. I sit up and stare at the basement door.

"I'm so tired, but I have to make time to practice with the crystals. If Seamus is right, reviving my energy is all I need." I rub my lower back as I push off the loveseat.

"You go on, Gwyn." He stands and kisses me tenderly. "I'm going to sleep. Between the jet lag, your midnight Seelie Fae visit, and the lovemaking after, my eyes need toothpicks to stay open."

"Don't wait up for me, honey. I'll be up as soon as I have some success."

He heads up the stairs and stops. "Remember one thing, Gwyn. You can't save everyone."

"No, but I can die trying."

He leans over the stair railing. "I'd rather you didn't."

"Go to sleep, honey. I'll talk to you in the morning."

I blow him a kiss and dart down the basement stairs to the musty magic room. The hum of the dehumidifier grates my ears, so I flip the switch. I slide the amethyst geode and clear quartz crystal in front of me and attempt to focus my intention, but my eyes veer to the picture of my parents at the top of the table. They would want to know what's happened in these past few weeks, but I can't afford to spread my energy over too many areas. Mom and Dad will have to wait.

I hold each crystal in the palms of my hand, set my intention, and call on my witch energy. Magic spirals up from each stone and connects in a swirl of hazy white, intensifying with my focus—and collapses. After several more tries, my ears ring with an excruciating whir and the room spins like a gravity ride at the carnival.

What am I doing wrong?

Chapter Twenty

A Safe Haven

Baby Luna rests in my arms while I lay out everything that's happened since I last spoke with Ronnie. Her ears are glued to my explanation while she makes us tea—Jasmine Green for me, herbal peppermint for her. She surprises me when she chants an incantation and sends our cups to the kitchen table on a stream of amber magic. They drop on the surface with a pop.

"Look at you, witch momma," I say with a rise of my eyebrows. "I remember a day when none of us would have flaunted our magic, not even in our homes."

She cackles and sits down next to me. "You only live once, right? Or maybe twice?"

I admire the fairy-like hair of her daughter, a witch in the making. "She really is beautiful, Ronnie. A miracle of magic."

"Yes, she is," she replies, stroking Luna's wisps of blond hair. "She wouldn't have arrived healthy if it weren't for your quick thinking. When she's older, I'll tell her how you brought her into the world using your witchcraft skills."

"We've come a long way, haven't we?"

"Do you regret any of it? The coven luring you in? Discovering you're a witch?"

I glare at her. "Finding out Archie was a womanizer?"

She laughs again and nudges me. "Well, that worked out in the end, too, right?"

"Yeah." I glance down at Luna. "I love holding her, but she should really sleep in her crib. We can discuss more when you return."

"I'll put her down and come right back."

Ronnie takes Luna to the nursery and shimmies back into the kitchen, plopping into her chair. She sips her herbal tea and sticks out her tongue.

"I don't know if I can live without my death coffee, but Luna sleeps better if I avoid drinking it. Why didn't you call me and talk about all this? I'm your best friend, Gwyn."

"You also have a new baby. I didn't want to add my worries to your overflowing plate."

She squeezes my hand. "I always save a spot for you. There isn't anything you can do about Archie's dad or Seamus leaving. Unfortunately, he has to cope with both. I am surprised he didn't tell you directly, though."

"I almost asked him. If he wanted me to know, he would have told me." I sip my tea and set the cup on the table.

"What about the strange buzzing you've felt? Do you believe it's Julia? You should have probably told Trinity and Leslie. If your hunch turns out to be right, they will be pissed you didn't tell them."

"Archie thinks it was a coincidence. I'm going to do a little more snooping, but I have to be careful. I don't work on Fridays, so I won't see her today. Saturday night is a good time. That's when Skye and I saw her on the Green. I told Agnes what happened."

She slaps her face. "For fuck's sake, Gwyn. Do you think she'll tell Leslie?"

"No. I trust my mentor. She's one person I can always count on...besides you, of course. And Archie."

"I would hope so. The real question should be, what if Julia isn't the source of the warning signs? Who or what is the origin of them?"

I recall the unusual gusts of wind on the Green. "I don't know. But I'm working on increasing my energy to expand my premonition, like Seamus told me I should. Last night's practice didn't affect my dreams, unfortunately. If I can decipher enough of what's coming, I may avoid the worst of what could happen."

"Be careful, Gwyn. The last time you tried to influence your visions, you nearly lost your own life when the Dearg Due attacked you." She finishes her tea and chants, flying her cup to the sink.

"Except Seamus was there to stop her." As if he had access to the vision, too.

"Sure. But he's leaving soon. Who knows when the Tuatha Dé fairy will arrive? He may not be here to save you this time."

I stare down at the tea leaves settled at the bottom of my cup. In the center, a cluster of the dregs form a long line. Not having the skills to read them, I can't decipher all the remains. But for sure, they signal a lengthy journey ahead of me. I don't need a fucking witch reader to tell me that.

I meander around the store, dusting the merchandise and the shelves. Occasionally, I stop and observe how Julia is progressing on her own. She makes a few mistakes but jokes with the customers, making the needed corrections. Her confidence has grown exponentially in the last week—almost as if she was feigning ignorance all along.

Shane isn't working today and Jeff left at 6:00 p.m., leaving me to close the store. Since I have the dirk in my bag, I'm walking home alone—despite Archie's objections. He's still trying to lighten Seamus's grading load. Escorting me would cut an hour from his available time and add more pressure to his already anxious existence. Plus, I can handle any malevolent being. I killed a Tuatha Dé Danann. When the last customer in line exits, I stroll to the counter and fiddle with the pens in the skull mug.

"You're doing well, Julia. You don't appear nervous at all, even when you screw up. And we all do."

"Since I've been handling the register on my own, I find the work almost second nature now. Thank you so much for all your patience."

"You're welcome." I stare out the window at the melting snow mounds on the sidewalk. I hate small talk, but... "Some weather we had the other night, huh?"

"Yeah," she says, dropping her butt on the stool. "It was sooo cold."

"Spence and I walked back through the Green in that storm. My jeans were soaked when I got to the house."

"Mine were, too. Actually, I saw the two of you on my walk home."

Suddenly, her eyes grow big and round, exposing rings of white. A notification rings on her cell phone, prompting her to jump up and yelp like a toy dog. A customer enters and goes to the puzzles section.

Julia moves to the cash register, a tremor emerging in her hands. "I...I better get back to work."

"Me, too," I say. "Shout if you need anything."

"Let me know if I can help you, sir," she says. "I'd be happy to assist you."

I turn and head to the herbs section. For the next hour, customers pour in like the holiday season has returned and Julia rings up the customers one after the other without a break. While I restock the shelves, I process what she said over and over in my brain. If she saw Spence and me on the Green, that means she was near the Green at 2:00 a.m. What the fuck was she doing out in that weather in the middle of the night? Judging by her behavior, she clearly didn't mean to let it slip.

If she's a Tuatha Dé fairy—a member of Nuada's family—she must be the most bumbling one they have. But she could still be dangerous. How do I find out? An easy way would be to remove Archie's dirk from my backpack and ask her to touch it. She'd freak out.

I bend down on my hands and knees to stock the lower shelves. The entry door dings again and shuts with a clank. My phone reads 7:48 p.m. No chance of closing the store early tonight. An exchange of unintelligible words transpires between Julia and the shopper. Immediately after, I hear steps approach as I place the last jar on the shelf. I turn my head to find a pair of black wing tip Oxford shoes next to me. My witch's intuition tugs at my insides.

When I push up on my knees, I discover a dashing man in his late 40s standing directly under the ceiling light and staring down at me. He's wearing a black wool coat over a button-down shirt and crisp slacks. Nearly six feet in height, he has thick dark hair, a prominent square jawline, and the most enchanting hazel eyes—brown and green with flecks of gold. Not the same as mine, but they captivate me. So much so, I stare into those pupils long enough that I'm too embarrassed to say anything. The aroma of expensive aftershave makes me woozy. After a minute of him lifting and lowering his eyebrows, I finally break my silence.

"I'm sorry. May I help you?" I ask, dusting the dirt off my jeans as I stand.

"Yes, actually," he says in a warm, inviting voice. "The cashier said you're Gwynedd Crowther."

"That's my name. Who wants to know?"

"I'm Special Agent Andrew Blackwell." He flashes a badge at me. "With the Federal Bureau of Investigation."

I swallow and read the badge. Fuck. It seems authentic. "What can I do for you, Agent Blackwell? It's almost eight and we're closing in a few minutes."

"Yeah, I saw on the door." He gestures with a hand. "I thought you'd be open until nine. I'm investigating a series of unusual deaths of women in New Castle County. My assignment doesn't officially begin until tomorrow, but I decided I'd get a head start. A Detective Jack Schmidt gave me your name and said I would find you here. He says you were with the first victim when she died."

He steps closer and I step back, knocking into a shelf. The jars of herbs topple onto their sides and roll. "Shit." I scramble to catch two before they fall to the floor and set them on their bottoms. What is wrong with me? I turn around to find he has invaded my personal bubble even more. And I have nowhere to go.

I peer past him at Julia, who is ringing up a customer and out of ear's reach. "Like I said. I'm about to close, and the cashier is training. I have to help her log out of the register."

"No problem." He passes me a business card. "If you would give me a few minutes of your time soon, I'd appreciate your cooperation."

I stare into those captivating eyes again, thinking I'll do anything he asks. "Sure. I have time tomorrow." *Why did I agree so willingly? What is the matter with me?*

"Wonderful." He shoves his badge inside his coat pocket. "I look forward to hearing from you. Enjoy the remainder of your evening, Ms. Crowther."

I stand there frozen while he exits the store, my heart doing jumping jacks. The last customer follows the FBI agent out the door. I check my pocket for the protection pouch—still there.

Julia shuts the register drawer and tilts her head. "What did he want?"

"To ask questions about the woman who passed away on the Green."

"Shane said you were there when she died. Do you know what happened?"

Why is she asking me? To trip me up? "I'd rather not talk about it. It was upsetting. Go ahead and log out. I'll set the alarm and we can go."

Julia gets wintered up in her bright yellow jacket, hat, and gloves while I put on my black wool coat, grabbing my backpack from underneath the counter when I've zipped up. On the way out, I realize I forgot to set the alarm.

"Shit. Go on home. I forgot to do something."

"Have a good night, Gwyn."

Julia heads east on Main Street for her apartment. I enter the store to discover I had left a light on in the back. When I return to the front, I catch Shane's lady friend running past the storefront window, now heading west toward the Green. Is she going to Menzies Hall again? *This is my chance.*

I set the alarm, lock the door to Mystic Sage, and weave in and out through the townies until I arrive at the junction where Main Street opens up to the Green. I dash down the steps and run until I cross University Avenue. In the distance, I glimpse Julia's yellow jacket as she passes under a lamppost. I continue to hurry toward her. As I get closer, she turns to ascend the stairs of Menzies Hall and enters through its double doors.

When I arrive at the red-brick Georgian building, I stop. While my breath surrounds me in a cocoon of misty-white, I battle the urge to run inside. If Julia sees I've followed her, she will know I suspect her. If I don't spy on her, I can't figure out if she's meeting other fairies here at night. I dash up the steps and go in.

I attempt to sneak into the lobby, but the soles of my boots squeak on the gleaming terrazzo floors. After removing them, I shuffle across the rotunda to a large board displaying a sign with the words "Meeting in Room 117." I continue down the hall until I come upon the classroom. A poster taped on the door glass reads "Domestic Abuse Survivors Support Group." I peek through the window and find Julia consoling a crying woman. As she lifts her head, she makes eye contact with me. I jump back.

Fuck. She saw me. And holy crystals. I was so wrong. She was a victim of domestic abuse. I shove my feet back into the boots and squeak down the hallway toward the lobby. A door slams and a voice echoes after me. "Wait, Gwyn! Please, wait!"

I stop with the last squeak of my boots and turn around. Julia rushes toward me, huffing and puffing. She pats her chest as she speaks.

"I'm getting too old to run. Thank you for waiting. Why did you follow me?"

Shit. What should I say? Certainly not the truth—that I thought she may be the mother or sister of a Tuatha Dé fairy I killed a while back.

"Shane's last girlfriend turned out to be a monumental bitch and broke his heart. I thought you might be hiding a secret. I couldn't stand by and let someone hurt him again. Why hide this from him, Julia? He would support you."

Tears well up in her eyes. "I was told not to trust anyone. After I got to know Shane, I couldn't tell him." Her face twitches. "Because my name isn't Julia Harding. My husband beat me so badly I had to leave. A local domestic survivor's group showed me how to change my name and get a new social security number. If that son of a bitch ever finds me, he'll kill me. I lied to Shane because they said to never share my true identity with anyone. But now you know. He will hate me, and I'll lose the job at Mystic Sage just when I was putting my life in order."

"Oh, Julia." I embrace her. "You don't need to worry. I won't tell Shane." I clasp her hand in mine. "But you should. I promise you. He is one of the good guys." He has secrets, too. But it's not my job to divulge his witch secret, either. "I am sorry I spied on you. It was an invasion of your privacy. I saw you sneak in here one night and got the wrong idea. You also said you saw Spence and me early in the morning—a strange time for a leisurely walk."

"I take walks when I can't sleep. Your behavior wasn't very nice. I thought Bearsden would be a safe haven for me." She whips out a scowl and thrashes me with it.

"You're absolutely in the right to feel as you do. Bearsden was a fine choice. I was wrong." Oh, so fucking wrong thinking she was a Tuatha Dé, but I'm not so sure about the *safe haven* part. "Go back to your support group. Again, I am sorry, Julia."

"Thank you, Gwyn. I will tell Shane." She turns as if to go, then stops. "Please be careful walking home. The news says these unusual deaths of women in the area may actually be murders."

"I will. I don't have far to go. See you on Tuesday at the store."

Julia drags her feet down the hallway, wiping her face with a tissue. What a stupid mistake. My phone reads 8:37 p.m. In a few minutes, Archie will start texting, wondering where I am. I rush down the steps and take the first left on the paver walkway to the alleyway. As I sprint through the darkness toward Douglas Street, a gust of wind blows my hood back and a bitter chill burns my ears.

My body buzzes, and I snap my head around in all directions, searching for a witch, but I find no one. What if some other entity triggered the sensation? I fumble, trying to pull down the zipper of my backpack and grab the dirk. With a flip of my wrist, I tug it out and summon my witch energy, sparking amber magic to branch out like tentacles.

"Stay away! I can defend myself!"

A spiral of air containing twigs and leftover leaves whips to the left, then to the right, stopping as if to inspect me—and appears to cackle. It swims around me and flees up the alley toward the Green. I stand frozen with the dirk in my tight grasp, preparing for its return. But the entity is gone.

What the fuck was that?

Chapter Twenty-One

DUBIOUS DREW

I shove the dirk in my backpack and take off like a sprinter toward home. My heart thumps against my ribcage until I enter the mudroom. When I tug at my boots, I fall on my ass, but I jump back up and remove my jacket. "Archie!" I drop my bag on the tile floor and dart through the house. "Archie!" I find him in the living room, sitting on the loveseat with his laptop. He peers up at me.

"Why are you shouting? I'm right here."

I approach him and collapse on the cushion next to him. "So much shit happened tonight. I don't know where to start." I swallow to moisten my dry throat.

"At the store?" He closes his laptop. "Or on your walk home? You appear quite distraught."

"Both, and I am. I'll start with what happened at Mystic Sage."

For the next few minutes, I share my suspicions about Julia and the visit by FBI Agent Andrew Blackwell. Archie rubs his goatee while he listens intently, never interrupting. When I finish, he drops his hand.

"Detective Schmidt is determined to figure out what the actual cause of death was. You'll need to be extra careful with what you say to him."

"Yes. For some reason, I'm worried I'll spill the beans to him. I can't explain it."

"Why would you openly tell him?"

"I don't think I would. But when he asked to talk with me tomorrow, I said sure. Didn't blink once before I answered him. He made me nervous."

"What will you do about Julia? Confront her?"

"I kinda did already." I grimace and wait for him to flip out, but he doesn't.

"Well, do I have to pull it out of you like taffy?"

"No. At first, she went east on Main Street but turned around and walked the opposite direction toward the Green. So, I followed her into Menzies Hall. She was hiding a big secret, but it wasn't what I suspected." I clasp his hand. "Archie, Julia is a domestic abuse survivor. She changed her name, and she's afraid Shane will fire her if he finds out she was lying to him. Worse...not want to be with her anymore. I quelled her fears."

"Ahhh, I told you so, didn't I? You better hope she doesn't tell Shane you were stalking her, and that's exactly what you were doing."

"I know, but I told her she should talk with him. That she can trust him."

"So, you're back to square one, then."

I blink twice. "I'm not done. When I turned and entered the alley, a gust of cold air blew my hood back. But it wasn't the wind. Some entity swirled around me like a mini tornado and my body buzzed—the same as before, when I sensed a witch in the area."

"What?" He lunges forward on the loveseat and summons his witch energy, passing his amber glowing fingers over me to check for injuries.

"Except I saw no one." I push his hand away. "Stop fussing over me. I'm fine. The experience matched what Spence and I experienced on the Green during the snowstorm. Could my ancestral warning system be triggered by other magic?"

"You believe it's fae magic? Tuatha Dé? Tylwyth Teg?"

"I don't know. The one thing I'm sure of is that I have no idea what it was. We need to tell the others."

He shifts forward on the cushion. "Did you have the dirk with you?"

"Yes. I pulled it out and ignited its powers. I threatened the entity and it took off."

"Interesting." He lifts his head and gazes at the weaponry on his wall.

"What are you thinking?"

"Either fae or a witch could use magic to mask themselves. However, they would most likely have to appear in their actual form to cast harm. Flashing my family heirloom likely kept you safe."

"Would a witch fly away from an iron dirk, though?"

"Not sure. The threat alone may have done enough to scare any witch off. Whatever this entity is, apparently, it's been increasing in activity."

"But why stretch out the inevitable? Why not come and get me immediately? And why cast malevolent magic on these witches? To stop them from communicating with us? Or me?"

Tension gathers on his brow. "They say revenge is a dish best served cold."

I snort. "Are you trying to scare me? If so, you failed. I've been preparing for a visit from Nuada's family since I ended his existence."

"No, my love." He wraps an arm around me and pulls me against his firm torso. "But...if the entity is a Tuatha Dé biding her time, she's dragging this out to frighten you."

I raise my head and kiss him. "Well, whoever she is, she isn't doing shit. I don't scare easily anymore. Come and get me, bitch."

He chuckles. "You may get your wish. We can alert Trinity and Leslie tomorrow. No need to disrupt their sleep tonight. We could very well have extremely stressful days ahead of us." And he's already wound as tight as an old clock.

"Did you hear from Quinn today?"

"Aye. Dad has made no improvement. We're still hopeful."

I kiss him again and stand. "I'm sorry, honey. You can't lose hope. Get back to your grading. I'm going downstairs to practice with the crystals. My vision holds answers. I don't understand how the Fomorian fits in this scenario, but I will do my best to find out."

I spend the next hour connecting the energy of the amethyst geode and clear quartz stone, chanting my incantation over and over with an intention. But my head spins, prompting me to grab the edge of the wooden table. I stop for a few minutes to empty my brain of all the worries in my life, eyeing Archie's collection of grimoires and witchcraft tools on the shelf. I recall the evening he was training me in ancestral divination, the first time I made a connection with my mom. Archie told me he loved me that night after we drank too much Scotch whisky.

Concentrate, Gwyn—my super focus. I have to find it again.

I clasp the stones in each hand once more and set a focused intention, as Seamus suggested. Finally, after several attempts, I celebrate my success with fireworks of white and gold magic criss-crossing above me. I repeat the process until the neurons in my brain won't speak to my body any longer. When I'm tapped out, I place the gorgeous purple gem aside for the night. Seamus said all I needed was to revive my energy source and the connection to the clear quartz would emerge again. I grab his gift and go upstairs to bed.

Archie rests beside me, already deep in slumber, his eyes twitching. I lie on my left side, my gaze fixated on the clear crystal. Seamus said I needed to recover my focus. How do I concentrate with all the competing pressures clogging my brain like a backed-up toilet?

Where do I find the plunger for that?

Agent Andrew Blackwell grabs my arm, but I pull away and run. In the next moment, I'm in the Celestial Gardens, faceless people gathering in the distance. A man transforms into a magnificent fairy with platinum-blond hair, glowing green eyes, and full wings expanded. A blast of air rustles the limbs of the hawthorn tree, prompting me to spin on my feet. The enormous Fomorian approaches me, his boots disappearing into the mud. I pinch my nose to avoid his rank odor. People are yelling, and I look back, but the lacey fog hinders my view. At the portal, Leslie and Agnes scream as the blustery wind blows debris throughout the space. A cat roars as it jumps at the gray-skinned being.

"Nooo!" I sit up in bed and glimpse the quartz crystal on my nightstand. A halo of white seeps outward in a radius nearly a foot wide.

"Gwyn." Archie touches my forearm. "Did your vision return?"

"Yes." I glance back at the stone. The faint glow is dissipating. "Practicing the crystal connections finally revived my energy enough."

"So it would seem. I didn't notice when you got into bed. I couldn't keep my eyes open past eleven. What did your vision reveal to you?"

"The Tuatha Dé fairy who is coming after me is not female. I saw him in the gardens before the Fomorian crossed over. And Agent Blackwell was there, too. Or maybe it was another place. I'm not sure."

"Surely a female family member must be involved. Riley Shaw warned of a woman, not a man."

"If there is, she hasn't surfaced in my visions yet." I face him and entwine my fingers with his. "What if Riley was wrong?"

He tightens his grasp. "No way to know, Gwyn, unless your vision expands more. When will you meet with Agent Blackwell?"

"I told him I'd call today to arrange a meeting. Should I have him come here?"

"Aye, but why the fawk did you agree to meet him? You're under no obligation to."

I can't tell him I reacted like a school girl talking with her first crush. "He made me nervous. The words just spewed out of my mouth on auto. He was the last person I expected to run into in the store. It would reflect badly to change my mind now."

Archie scratches the back of his head. "Call him and get it out of the way. I'll get breakfast started. We can fill Leslie and Trinity in later. Remember, we're having dinner with Tyler and Zoe at the house."

"Shit. I almost forgot. Should we cancel? No. We can't. They were so excited about having us over."

"Gwyn, breathe. We'll discuss everything later with the others. The coven will meet and prepare for the inevitable, as we always do."

After a quick trip to the bathroom, Archie heads downstairs. I dig out Andrew Blackwell's business card and my cellphone from my backpack. While I sit on the porcelain throne, I call the agent—two birds, one stone. A few rings fill my ear and he picks up.

"Hello. Special Agent Andrew Blackwell."

My mouth falls open, but I can't respond. The words get tangled in the back of my throat like a cat's hairball took refuge there. I cough and clear my throat.

"Hello? May I help you?" he asks in a sultry baritone voice.

Suddenly, I'm embarrassed to be sitting on the toilet. I cross my legs. "Yeah. Sorry. Something was stuck in my throat. This is Gwynedd Crowther."

"Oh, yes. Thank you for calling. I have Detective Schmidt's notes, but I would like to hear what happened directly from you."

"Sure. If you want, I can give you my home address."

"Actually, I'd prefer meeting on Main Street. There's a quaint restaurant with a retro vibe...the Sunshine Garden Café? I'll buy us some coffees."

Shit. I hope Ronnie can pop in when I'm there. "OK. But I drink tea. What time?"

"Sure. Tea it is. How about one? I don't want to ruin your Sunday."

Like interviewing me regarding the death of an acquaintance won't do that? "I'll meet you there."

"Thank you, Ms. Crowther. I will arrive by one."

The signal disconnects and I set my cell on the floor and flush the toilet. As the whirlpool spins into the sewer, I imagine my existence descending into the abyss. Ask all the questions you want, Agent Blackwell, but I don't have to answer. I wash up and text my best friend.

Me: *I know you're on maternity leave. But any chance you could go to the café at one?*

Ronnie: *Why? Do you want to eat lunch?*

Me: *No. An FBI agent came into the store. He wants to meet me at the café.*

Ronnie: *Well, at least he has taste? LOL.*

Me: *Very. Funny. Can you be there? Please?*

Ronnie: *Of course. Derek can watch Luna. Are you scared?*

Me: *No. But I need moral support.*

Ronnie: *LMAO. Are you sure you want me? Haha.*

Me: *LOL. Yes, and thanks. See you in a few hours.*

When I enter the Sunshine Garden Café, Ronnie waves from a booth in the back, her crimson curls flopping on her shoulders. She's directly behind the seat where Agent Andrew Blackwell is sitting, pointing an index finger at his head. She flips around when he stands and motions to me. I smile and approach him, sliding onto the bench across from him. He flags a waiter.

"Can we get a coffee and a tea? Thanks." He pulls out a notepad and leans on the table. "Thank you for being so cooperative. You could have asked for a lawyer to be here—still can."

"I have nothing to hide." Holy crystals. I'm lying like a two-bit criminal, but one with a genuine smile. Is it a bad thing I've improved this skill?

He passes a finger back and forth on his notepad. "I've read through all the notes Detective Jack Schmidt shared with me concerning the three women who died. Says here these ladies were acquaintances of yours. Anything you want to add?"

"No. I can't think of a thing." Really? He's wasting my afternoon asking what he could have easily verified over the phone?

He gazes directly into my eyes. "Are you sure?"

I squirm on the booth seat, but I can't break his hold on me. Luckily, the waiter arrives with our order. He sets a cup of tea in front of me and places the mug full of joe inches from the edge of the table near him. If I don't answer him, he's going to badger me until I do. He is an FBI agent, after all.

I sweeten my tea and take a sip. "Agent Blackwell—"

"You can call me Drew," he says in his alluring tone of voice.

I gaze into those sexy hazel eyes while I reach for the stevia packs and knock his mug over, sending the java off the table.

"Whoa!" He shifts to the side of the bench and grabs a handful of napkins.

"Oh, my gods. I'm so sorry. I am a huge klutz."

As I sop up the coffee on the surface with a clump of napkins, he dabs his black dress slacks. When he's finished, he checks the contents of the mug.

"Don't stress over it. I didn't need the extra caffeine, anyway."

He winks at me and a warm aura overwhelms me. My face flushes.

"Why don't you just ask me what you want to know? I don't like games. Detective Schmidt does mind trips on people. I hate it." I drop my cup on the saucer.

A seductive grin crawls onto his face and he leans back. "Did you know Dr. Nicholas Evans, the Delaware University at Bearsden assistant professor who went missing?"

Fuck! At any minute, my heart is going to burst through my ribcage like a scene from a sci-fi movie. Why is he asking me about Nick? My jaw locks, and my fingertips tap the mambo under the table. His sexy smile falls flat.

"Here's what we know, Ms. Crowther. The third victim, a Laura Lovelace, was good friends with Dr. Evans before he disappeared. She used to be a member of a local pagan community group like the one you belong to in Bearsden. Now she's dead from…we'll call it unknown causes. You knew Nicholas Evans. In fact, you dated him for some time before he went missing." He checks his notes again. "Are you aware of anything new regarding his disappearance?"

I swallow and compose myself. This suave turd will not break me. "Jack Schmidt already spoke to me about his disappearance when it happened. The case was closed. He said Nick must have wandered off into the woods and got killed by the cougar that was running loose at the time."

"Except he didn't close it. He's been working methodically on the case since."

Shit. I finish my tea and push my cup aside. "That's quite an obsession, don't you think?"

"He merely wants to solve the case, Ms. Crowther." He flashes another smile at me and captures my gaze. "May I call you Gwyn?"

For a moment, I'm floating outside myself. What is wrong with me? The clammer of plates brings me back and I fold my hands on the table.

"Listen, Drew. I don't know what is going through Jack's curious brain. But I'm not responsible for what happened to those women. Riley and Elizabeth were close to our pagan group. I am heartbroken over their deaths."

"What about Laura Lovelace?" he asks, an eyebrow arching.

I clam up. Maybe I do need a lawyer?

A notification rings on his cell phone and he closes his notepad. "I have to go. But we'll talk again soon." He stands and throws money on the table. "I look forward to it. Goodbye, Gwyn."

Drew slips on his wool coat and exits the café. Ronnie jumps up from the booth behind and drops into the bench seat where the agent sat a few moments ago.

"For fuck's sake, Gwyn. What was the matter with you? You basically told him whatever he wanted."

"Not everything." I wipe my flushed face. "I don't know why I stumbled over my words." When I press on my pants pocket, the protection pouch lump pushes back.

"I mean, he is a hunk of a man. When Trinity said an FBI agent may show up, I was expecting a stone-faced authority figure." She leans over the table. "He is downright sexy."

"Who cares what he looks like? He asked about Nick. Despite what Jack told me, he's still searching for clues to Nick's disappearance."

"Oh, fuck. If he ever finds out Laura slept with Archie, he'll knock on your front door. Which is also Archie's now."

"We don't have time for Jack's stupid detective OCD. An unknown entity came after me last night and my vision expanded."

Ronnie bends over the table, her freckled face turning pale. "What do you mean? What the fuck happened?"

I lean in. "Something supernatural came after me in the alley next to Menzies Hall. The same thing happened to Spence and me, but we didn't realize what it was. I have sensed it other times, too, but I never saw anything. The being was threatening, but I scared it off with Archie's dirk. During my sleep, a Tuatha Dé appeared—a male fairy, not a woman. The warning signals I've experienced over the last month could be him. Also..." A tremor appears in my hand.

My best friend grasps my fingers. "What, Gwyn?"

"Agent Blackwell was in the premonition. I didn't think much about it at first, but..."

She gapes at me. "Fuck."

UNREMARKABLE REVELATION

T YLER AND ZOE COOK a wonderful lasagna for all of us—his grandmother's recipe. The garlic bread is so soft, it melts in your mouth. We reminisce about our visit to Aunt Gorawen's home and the time we spent with the Cockburn family, hoping Harris will eventually recover from the hex. But Archie and I wait until after dinner to share what's happened recently. Why ruin the meal? After a quick cleanup, we move to the living room. The sofa and chairs from my house on Mulberry Lane fit perfectly in the space. They're worn in, comfy, and familiar.

"We can't stay much longer," I say. "We're meeting with Trinity, Leslie, and Agnes at the farmhouse. An unknown entity came after me last night on the way home."

"What?" Tyler lunges forward in his chair. "Are you OK?"

"Yes. I'm fine, obviously. I had the dirk with me."

"We think it scared the being off," Archie says. "From the description, it resembles what Spence and your mum experienced during the snowstorm the other night."

Zoe shifts on the sofa. "What do you think it is?"

"We aren't sure," I reply. "I've had other encounters where my body buzzed, warning me of a nearby witch. Most of them,

I dismissed, attributing them to Seamus and Riley Shaw. Then that strange occurrence happened on the Green during the Storm—and last night."

"Why were you alone?" Tyler asks, frowning. "You're supposed to have a partner."

"I didn't have far to walk, and I had the dirk with me. But I won't make the same mistake again. To top things off, the rumors Trinity heard were true. An FBI agent was assigned to the cases. He met with me to ask questions about the witches who died." And about Nick Evans, but I can't share that information with my son now. He'll worry.

"Shit, Mom. Do you think they suspect you were involved in their deaths?"

"Why would they?" Zoe asks, throwing her palms up. "Unless they think you poisoned them somehow."

I jump out of my chair, my eyes bugging out as the realization hits me. "That's precisely what they believe. I'm fucked."

Archie grasps my hand as he stands. "Don't jump to conclusions."

"I was kidding, Gwyn." Zoe gets up from the sofa and hugs me.

"No. It makes sense. They can't find the true cause of death because they don't have the skills to test for negative magic. Some poisons are difficult to detect. What should I do?"

Archie caresses my back. "For starters, do not panic. They will never find proof to connect their deaths to you because you didn't kill them."

I glance at his comforting eyes, take a cleansing breath, and gather my thoughts. "You're right. I'll deal with the accusation *if* it happens."

"Exactly. Meanwhile, something is building in the supernatural world. We don't know what yet. But we must prepare. Take out the dirk, Gwyn."

I remove Archie's family heirloom from my bag. "Archie and I discussed this at length. If and when the Tuatha Dé fairy crosses over, he won't have the same radar to detect my scent that Nuada possessed. He'll sniff out magic use and possibly narrow down the search. But he may find you first. I want you to carry the dirk from now on."

"No fucking way, Mom," Tyler replies. "You need it."

Archie lays his hand on my son's shoulder. "Your witchcraft skills have developed amazingly well, but not nearly as far as your mum's progress. I wish I had two to share, but I don't."

"I want this, Tyler," I say. "Please do not argue with me. I couldn't live with myself if Nuada's relative got to you first and you had no way of defending yourself against him."

Zoe wraps her arms around him. "Please take it, Tyler."

He strokes her floppy brown hair. "OK. But I don't know how to use the thing."

"I will train you," Archie replies. "It will come naturally, being an ancestral witch. I'll stop over after dinner on Tuesday when your mum is at work. But you can try to initialize the power housed within its shell by summoning your witch energy. Set your intention."

I pass the dirk to my son and he pulls it from its leather sheath. When he grips the wooden handle, the gem glows. He raises the enchanted dagger as he chants an incantation, summoning his magic. An amber glow seeps from his hand onto the blade and tentacles splay from the tip.

"Wow. I thought I'd have to try multiple times," he says, gaping at his success.

Archie pats his back. "You'll do well. But you must practice how to call on its magic quickly. You will have little time to react should the Tuatha Dé come after you. Keep it somewhere safe. I recommend sleeping with it, actually."

Tyler lowers his hand and the amber glow dissipates. "I understand."

"Thank you," I say, hugging him. "You're doing this for Zoe, too. Remember that."

She pushes up on her toes and kisses him on the cheek. "Thanks for listening to your mom."

He flexes a side of his mouth. "I always do, don't I?"

"Yes," I say, grabbing my backpack. "We should go. Trinity has probably arrived at the farm already."

Archie and I head to the mudroom and put on our winter gear. On the way out the door, my son stops me.

"Keep me updated, Mom. Remember, I'm not a little boy anymore."

"I know. We'll be in touch."

The drive to the farm takes about fifteen minutes. We slide on a few slick spots on the way. Trinity's car is parked out front. We spend the next half hour explaining everything that's happened over the past twenty-four hours, including my interview with the FBI Agent Andrew Blackwell and the expansion of my visions.

Mr. Yeats sits on the wooden table in the magic room, his tail swaying like a pendulum. His head rotates back and forth as Trinity paces from one side of the room to the other, her burgundy hair bouncing on her shoulders. Leslie taps her fingers on the table while Agnes slouches in a chair, a who-the-fuck-cares expression on her face.

"Will you fucking stop, Trinity?" Agnes asks. "You're making me nauseous."

The coven leader stops and shakes her index finger at the hedge witch. "You know damn well I need to move while I think on what to do. Preparing for an unknown being's attacks, the coming of the Tuatha Dé and the Fomorian... We don't have time for these investigations by Unremarkables. They're muddying my brain."

"Indeed," Leslie says. "But we must prepare despite their invasive questioning. Do not allow their investigations to distract us from our goals."

"What should I do if the two of them keep badgering me?" I ask. "I've managed to stretch the truth and tell some white lies, but in the end, I'm a terrible liar. One of them is bound to notice. Especially this Agent Blackwell."

Agnes flings a hand downward. "Just tell him to fuck off—my go-to phrase for the cops. He can't make you say anything."

"And how did that response work out for you?" Archie asks with a raise of his eyebrows.

"Eh. Sometimes they threw me in a holding cell and locked me up. But they couldn't keep me in there. No charges to file."

Trinity crosses her arms. "Agnes, we're trying not to bring attention to the Fellowship."

Mr. Yeats jumps off the table, changing into his human persona when his paws touch the wooden floor. "May I make a suggestion?"

"No," the hedge witch replies, throwing him a side-eye. "You're always fucking meddling, and you don't even leave the house. How could you offer any advice on the cops?"

Leslie scowls at her partner. "I would like to hear your recommendation, Mr. Yeats."

"Thank you for your confidence," he says, straightening his gray vest. "I suggest you turn the tables on the authorities. Accuse them of violating your privacy and ask them not to bother you again."

Agnes snorts. "I rest my case."

"Actually, it's not a bad idea," Archie says, stroking his goatee.

Mr. Yeats bats his eyelashes at the hedge witch and the rest of us chuckle.

"Eh. Screw you and your mismatched eyes." Agnes sticks her tongue out at him. "Busybody."

Leslie glares at her love. "Oh, Agnes. Behave yourself."

Trinity grimaces. "Are you serious, Archie? They'll laugh at her."

"I mean, Gwyn shouldn't lob accusations against them, of course. But she could demand they tell her if she's a suspect. It would be advantageous to know for certain."

"If the cards were all on the table," I say, "I could plan how to respond better. But how do we prepare for all the rest?"

Trinity scratches her head. "The coven will meet here on Thursday evening to discuss potential solutions. I'll send a group text. Meanwhile, we should go visit the Celestial Gardens on alert—in groups of more than two witches, too. We don't know what we're dealing with. This supernatural entity could be a new being that's crossed over, or an old one using magic to mask their true identity. Either way, we must prepare."

"Indeed," Leslie says. "Archie, would you mind speaking with me briefly about the department? It won't take long."

His face becomes sullen. "Of course. I'll meet you downstairs, Gwyn."

I step toward the doorway and Agnes follows me.

"Come on, ladies," she says. "We're too good for the academics."

A sigh slips through Leslie's lips. "Oh, Agnes. We won't be long."

My mentor stops and motions at the familiar. "You, too, busybody."

Mr. Yeats transforms into his chimera cat persona and scuttles out of the room ahead of us. Trinity goes home and Agnes waits with me at the door while Leslie and Archie discuss Celtic Studies department issues.

"What do you think they're talking about?" Agnes asks. "Leslie seems more stressed than usual. Seamus's leaving has put her in a shitty spot. Fuck him. Why couldn't he wait until Spring Semester was over to return to Northern Ireland?"

"I don't know. He's a cat sith witch, so he sure as hell isn't going to tell us why." Not even me, apparently. "I hope they can convince the dean to approve a search for new professors. They're running out of time to find anyone decent to start in the fall. You think their schedule is bad now? Imagine it with the positions filled by adjunct faculty."

"That's what scares me. I barely have evenings with her now."

Archie runs down the stairs and slips on the bottom step. "Shite." He peers up at me. "Don't say one word."

Agnes leans over him. "Word." She guffaws loudly, filling the foyer with her witchy cackle.

We all chuckle as he stands, rubbing his butt. "You never let anything pass, do you?"

"Not if I can grab a hearty laugh out of it. But you make it easy. See you Thursday, witches. Get the fuck out of here."

On the drive home, Archie doesn't mention one word about his discussion with Leslie. But my witchy innards tighten and pinch. I wish he would confide in me, but asking him would be unfair. If he could share, he would.

When I wake on Wednesday, the spot in bed next to me is cold and empty. The clear quartz crystal rests peacefully on the nightstand. Skipping my practice with the crystals the last three nights was a poor choice. I would have gotten nowhere, though. My focus hopped on the train to the Otherworld and left the rest of me at the station after the interview with Agent Blackwell. No matter what I do, I can't rid him from my brain. I hop off the mattress, get cleaned up, and head downstairs.

Archie is standing at the stove in a T-shirt and sleeper pants when I enter the kitchen, preparing omelets. I recall the first time I woke up in his bed the morning following the Mabon Celebration. I discovered he had screwed Courtney Erickson in the study room when I saw the Horned God tattoo on his ass. He apologized for the indiscretion and made me breakfast.

I'm no longer that naïve Unremarkable woman who was reeling from the lies of a dead, cheating husband. And I don't need anyone to fight my battles for me anymore. But it's wonderful to have this gorgeous ancestral witch by my side.

"Good morning, honey," I say, wrapping my arms around him from behind. "Thank you for cooking breakfast."

He turns around and kisses me. "No vision, I assume, or you would have said so."

"No. I don't remember any of my dreams the last three nights. I'm waking too often. What's weird is…I used to have them during the days, too. Witchcraft and premonitions aren't an exact science, and I am hardly an expert. I got a late start at the age of fifty-three."

"Stop bashing yourself. Your skills have progressed so well since that first class where I ignited your powers. I let you sleep in, thinking you may have some success. Every day brings new possibilities."

"I suppose. I'll force myself to practice tonight even if my focus remains on vacation."

"What time does your shift at Mystic Sage begin?"

"Around 3:00. Remember, I'm going to the Celestial Gardens with Skye. I'll drive and park behind the store. Spence and Tanner will meet us there to be safe and walk us back to the parking lot, too. If I have an ounce of energy left when I return, I will work with the crystals."

"Sounds good. Get through tonight. The Fellowship meets tomorrow evening, and we'll figure out our game plan in more detail." He caresses my cheek. "Be careful. You don't have the dirk on you."

"I will." I kiss him to offer reassurance, but tension remains in his brow.

After I scarf down my breakfast, I drive to the parking lot behind Mystic Sage. When I enter with a ding of the bell, I find Jeff sitting on the stool at the cash register. Elevated voices seep from the back into the front of the store. While I unzip my jacket, I look at my young boss and gesture at the doorway. He shrugs.

"Hell if I know. When Julia arrived, she asked Shane to talk in private, and they went back to the inventory room. Not my business, but he has yelled out some rather spicy southern expletives a few times. Phrases like dang it, son of a biscuit, crapola…and my favorite, mother trucker. They must be having a lover's quarrel. A shame. They both seemed so happy."

"Fuck," I say, gaping at him. "This is my fault. I better go talk with them and clear things up."

I stuff my gloves in my pockets as I rush through the crystals room, Jeff shouting behind me.

"Are you sure that's a good idea, Gwyn?"

Shane and Julia snap their mouths shut when I enter. Boxes rest in piles, blocking the backdoor exit—a fire hazard. She must have caught him in the middle of a delivery. My boss glares at me with those emerald-green eyes, ready to attack me with a hidden laser beam. Lucky for me, he's a witch and not an alien.

"Well, I declare. Here comes the stalker herself."

My mouth falls flat, and I glance at Julia. Holy crystals. How do I fix this?

"I told him everything, Gwyn, like you suggested."

"Explain yourself," he says. "I'm madder than a puffed toad."

I swallow. "Shane, I thought she was hiding secrets, which she was. But she turned out not to be who I suspected. I didn't want you to get hurt again after—you know who. I'm sorry."

He hisses through his teeth. "After she confessed her true identity to me, I feel compelled to come clean regarding my own secrets—tell her like it is."

My eyebrows take a leap. "Uhhh...are you certain you're ready to cross that bridge, boss?" What the fuck is he doing? He didn't want Julia to be *in the knowing*.

"I am," he says, grinning at his love. "If she could risk her life by sharing her past, I'm ready to do the same."

Holy crystals. I glance at Julia. "She may flip out. You know that."

Her mouth quivers. "What? Are you secretly married?"

"No, sugar," he says, taking her hand in his. "But what I am about to confess may send you out the front door. I'm more than a pagan. I practice witchcraft."

She squints at him. "Like an actual witch who casts spells? I knew you sold this stuff, but I never imagined you believed anything in here was more than an illusion."

"Gwyn, perhaps I should show her."

"I'll shut the door." Because the minute he puts his magic on display, she's apt to dart out of the room screaming. I click the lock.

Shane grabs a small rose quartz crystal and passes it to his love. "This is but one example of what we can do. This stone contains healing properties. Your body and mind could heal much faster with its use. Place it in the palm of your hand."

"I understand you believe in the power of these, but I don't, Shane."

"Humor me, sugar." A loving grin spreads his whiskers.

Julia sets the rose quartz in the center of her palm and Shane rests his hand on top. He chants an incantation under his breath, calling on his witch energy, and his fingertips radiate an amber glow. Her lower lip falls and she begins to hyperventilate. I rub her back.

"It's OK, Julia. He's casting a healing spell."

"You're doing fine, sugar," he says. "Breathe with me."

She follows him, sucking in air slowly. After a few passes, she relaxes. "Oh, Shane. I haven't felt this calm in years. Thank you."

He cups the side of her face with his other hand. "You're welcome, sugar."

"Is this truly your secret?" she asks. "You aren't hiding a wife somewhere?"

"No, sugar. This is who I am. But I hesitated to reveal my true self."

"Since Julia knows the truth, I'll tell you why I was suspicious," I say. "I thought she might be a member of Nuada's family spying on me."

My boss pulls on his beard. "I understand, but I wish you'd trusted me enough to share your theory."

"You're right. I made an enormous mistake. Please, forgive me."

Julia's eyes dart from side to side. "Who's Nuada?"

"Oh, sugar. Take a seat on one of these boxes. There's so much more to tell."

"I should relieve Jeff at the register," I say. "Take your time, Julia. This is a lot to soak in."

She hugs me, an unexpected response to my invasive meddling. Smiling, I squeeze her gently before I dart to the front, remove my jacket, and stuff it behind the counter. Jeff finishes ringing up a shopper and logs off the register. He waits for the clank of the bamboo chimes before attacking me with questions.

"What happened back there?"

I slap my face. "Shane told her—everything."

Jeff's body goes rigid as a board. "Like she's *in the knowing* now?"

"Yup. He's filling her in on the Tuatha Dé fairy situation. I doubt he will tell the entire story today." I peer back through the doorway. "There's a lot of ground to cover."

"Wow. I didn't think he'd ever divulge his witch status to her."

"It's my fault. Why don't you leave for lunch early? I can handle this. How's Ashley?"

"She's great." He slips on his puffer jacket. "We're actually celebrating her new position. She got confirmation she can move over to the English department next fall."

I plop onto the stool. "Archie told me she applied. I'm happy for her. Give her congratulations from me."

"Sure," he says, opening the door. "Shane said the danger is getting worse for the coven. Be careful, Gwyn."

"Thanks, boss. I appreciate the concern."

He exits, and a few minutes later, Agent Blackwell strolls into the store. He's wearing his standard outfit—a wool coat over a dress shirt and dark slacks. Shane and Julia continue to talk in the back while I'm stuck alone in the front with this G-man. Few shoppers browse on Wednesday mornings. He approaches me, sporting a warm smile to manipulate me. Not today, agent. This is my territory—well, Shane's. I stand up, crossing my arms.

"Good morning. How may I help you today?"

"I've had an illuminating conversation with Detective Jack Schmidt. Perhaps we could meet again for coffee and have a discussion?"

"Not interested," I say, pinching my lips together. "The store is empty. Whatever you want to chat about, you can say to me here. Until a customer wanders in, anyway."

My gut pinches, and an aura builds inside me, creeping toward my heart. He pulls out his notepad and flips past a few pages.

"Jack Schmidt has done a bit of digging into Laura Lovelace, the third victim. Apparently, she once dated your current partner, Dr. Archibald Cockburn. Some have said she obsessed over getting him back. Care to comment on that?"

The aura burns and my face flushes. "No. Why don't you just ask me?"

"Ask you what exactly, Gwyn?"

His gaze seizes my attention and the room disappears. *Drew Blackwell grabs my arm, and suddenly, I'm in the gardens. The familiar scene flashes before my eyes, image after image, until the Fomorian blinks at me and the Tuatha Dé fairy's green eyes burn into my awareness.* I fall forward and catch the edge of the counter.

"Ms. Crowther? Gwyn?" Drew Blackwell asks, rushing behind the counter to check on me.

I sit down on the stool and clutch my abdomen. "I'm fine. A little dizzy, that's all. I must be dehydrated." I can't tell him the truth. That I had a premonition. But why is he in it?

"Ms. Crowther, should I call someone?"

"No." My eyes narrow. "Are you done? Because I have nothing else to say."

He stands and shoves his notepad into his coat pocket. "You know something, and I will find out what that is, eventually. This isn't the last time we'll speak, Gwyn."

He meanders around the counter and exits the store. I dig into my backpack for my cell and call Archie.

"Hi, Gwyn. Something wrong?"

"You bet your tattoo-free ass there is. Agent Blackwell just left. He knows you slept with Laura Lovelace and that she was trying to get you back. Jack Schmidt siphoned the information out of some witch."

"Fawk. Are you all right?"

"Yeah, but I had a daytime vision. A customer is headed into the store. I'll tell you more when I get home after work. Bye, honey."

"Love you, Gwyn." The phone connection goes silent.

I stare out the front window at the passersby. Drew Blackwell is a key to my premonition. I don't know how, but my witch's intuition is pointing an arrow at the invisible apple on his head.

Chapter Twenty-Three

NEFARIOUS MAGIC

Spence, Tanner, Skye, and I shiver in the darkness of the Celestial Gardens after midnight, lit dimly by a sliver of a waning crescent moon. Indigo skies twinkle with a splash of stars while we wait patiently for the Seelie Fae to cross over. We're bundled up in puffer jackets, hoods, and gloves like nine-year-olds on a snow day, but the glacial temperature has numbed my legs and toes. We huddle together while I finish sharing the revelations regarding Julia's past.

Spence leaps from one leg to the other, making me edgy. "I'm surprised Julia didn't scream bloody-murder and dart out of the store."

"She loves Shane," Tanner says. "And he's been so good to her. Why would his being a witch bother her? Sounds like her ex-husband was a brute."

I warm my face with my gloves. "Well, I almost screwed up his chance at happiness with this woman. I should have asked her directly instead of creeping around on her like a psychopath."

"To be fair," Skye says. "We both thought it was odd she went into Menzies Hall so late at night. And we both experienced that warning of magic in the area."

Spence stops jumping and cozies up to Tanner. "Well, now we know it's something nefarious—whatever was chilling out on the Green the night of the storm."

"Dude, you have to put some meat on your bones," Tanner says. "You're gonna get hypothermia."

"I can't help it if I burn all the calories I eat. No one should be hanging out in low temps like this, except polar bears."

Skye approaches the mound and yells into the opening. "Shailagh! Aonghas! Are you coming out?"

We join her and wait for the pranksters, but there is no sign of them. All we're doing is freezing our asses off. Jack Schmidt's visits must have deterred them. I mean, it's not a terrible consequence. We have to worry about their shenanigans less. A twinge snaps at me inside.

"I don't think they're coming," I say, expelling a puff of white. "We should go."

"I agree." Tanner scans the gardens. "It's dead in here."

The young men head toward the iron gate. Skye and I follow. When we reach the sidewalk, I spot someone walking in the distance, a man of medium height in a dark winter jacket. As he gets closer, I recognize the heavy eyebrows.

"Shit. Run toward the steps to the Green. Detective Schmidt is coming."

We dash across Main Street and descend the stairs. Skye walks back up a few to spy on the detective.

"What's he doing?" Spence asks.

She flings her hand at him. "Shhh...he may hear you."

Tanner joins her, whispering. "He's entering the Celestial Gardens again. What clues does he think he's gonna find in there?"

"He knows the Fellowship has ceremonies and celebrations in there," I say. "We reserved the space for Imbolc. He must think we're hiding something."

Skye comes back down, chuckling. "Well, we are. I hope the Seelie Fae remain on the other side. If they come out and he catches them crossing over, we'll have some explaining to do."

"Let's get going," I say. "I officially can't feel my feet."

We make our way across University Avenue and follow the red-paver walkway toward the Old Men oak trees.

Spence rubs his mittens together. "Why go in the middle of the night? Do you think he suspects the children were supernatural?"

"Nah," Skye says. "He's probably trying to catch them running around again, so he can file charges against the parents. He may have gone in there the first time searching for clues, though."

A whoosh of air blows past us, kicking up tree debris on the ground. Tanner stops abruptly and looks to the right. "Did you guys notice anyone walking next to the library?"

"No. Nothing," I say, but my abdomen snaps like a rubber band. An icy breeze bites my cheeks, worse than the existing bitter temperature, and an alarming dread overwhelms me. "We need to get the fuck out of here."

I take off down the angled walkway toward Menzies Hall. The others sprint to catch up with me. Tanner and Spence follow closely behind, but Skye is lagging.

"For fuck's sake, Gwyn," she says. "What's the matter?"

"My intuition." I scan the area. "And the sudden bitter cold."

Spence cracks up. "Sudden? Has your mind left your body? Because the temperature has been below freezing all night."

An icy gust passes by again and Tanner spins around, pressing against his cheek. "I felt it, too."

Debris kicks up and swirls around our bodies. We bat at splinters of wood that seem to be attacking us. Somehow, we're stuck inside the body of this sudden mini tornado. We attempt to run, but the wind is too forceful, trapping us within the spiral—more like a prison built of air.

"What is going on?!" Skye shouts. "We need to do something!"

Spence pushes against the force of the winds. "I don't care if we're on the Green. We may have to use magic to get out of this."

"I agree," Tanner says. A chunk of a branch cuts across his forehead, slicing open skin. "Shit!"

Skye loses her beanie and her fire-red hair gets caught in the whirlwind. "We should chant the incantation to break free from a stronghold."

"Yes!" I say, plucking twigs out of my jacket. "Summon your witch energy and let's do this in synchrony."

We chant, repeating the same phrase in unison, and an amber glow radiates from our palms. When we press back against the barrier, the surface gives like rubber.

"Keep pushing," Tanner says. "The surface is bending."

Skye's hand breaks through. "Yes! It's working!"

My hands pierce the barrier and Spence steps through. He grasps me by the torso and pulls me out. Tanner and Skye spread their arms wide and the mini tornado flees from us, landing near the Old Men oak trees. The figure of someone wearing a dark hooded cape appears and throws a ball of black and red vapor—unlike any magic I've ever seen.

Spence yells in a high-pitched voice. "Watch out, witches!"

We scramble, and I dart toward the alley after Tanner and Spence, losing track of my red-haired Zillennial friend. A blood-curdling scream erupts behind me. When I snap my head around, she stands frozen in a haze of green.

"Skye!" I run toward her, screaming. "Spence! Tanner!"

A large black cat appears and leaps at the mysterious attacker. But the person in the hooded cape disappears as the feline pounces. By the time I reach her, Skye has collapsed on the crunchy grass. Her lips part and she tries to form words. She flinches, arching her back, and moans in obvious pain.

"Don't try to talk, Skye," I say, covering her mouth. "It'll make things worse. That's what happened to the others. Fighting back may kill you."

She closes her mouth and tears well up in her eyes. I lay a hand on her abdomen. Tanner and Spence kneel next to me while the cat sith witch circles us.

"What the fuck did they do to her?" Spence glances at the enormous feline. "Is that Dr. Duffy?"

"Yes," I say, panting. "He must have sensed I was in danger. I think the stranger cast the same nefarious magic on her that was used against the other witches who died. Did you recognize the person in the cape?"

Tanner quickly scans the area. "No sign of them now. Did you get a glimpse of their face, Spence?"

"No," he replies. "The hood hung over and cast a shadow on their face."

"We have to get her to the farm, where we have easier access to the spell database and the grimoires," I say. "Something similar happened to Archie's dad, Harris. But we couldn't help him. An old witch removed the hex from him." I wave to Seamus. "I'm OK. You can go back. Could you meet us at Leslie and Agnes's house in case you can assist with her recovery?"

The cat sith witch roars and sprints down the alley.

"I'll carry her." Tanner slides his arms under Skye's body and lifts her off the frosty earth. "I've got you. Hold on. You're gonna be OK."

We head down the red paver walkway toward the alley, and my intuition stabs me. I peer back to see a man in a winter coat standing on this side of University Avenue. Holy crystals. I dash to the alleyway to catch up with the others and call Archie.

"Hi, Gwyn. Where are you? You were supposed to get back by now."

"Oh, my gods," I say. "Whoever the malevolent person or being is, they attacked Skye. She's under the control of malevolent magic. I think we should take her to the farm in Spence and Tanner's SUV. We need Agnes's expertise."

"Fawk. I'll get changed and meet you at the car." The phone goes silent.

The walk to the parking lot seems to take hours. As we approach the SUV, I spy Archie at the rear. Spence unlocks the car with his fob and lifts the hatchback.

"You're going to be all right, Skye," Archie says, placing a comforting hand on her shoulder. "I'll get in the back with her." He crawls in and gestures to Tanner, who lowers Skye to the carpet. Together, he and Archie slide her in farther, resting her head close to Archie.

We all hop into the car and Spence drives like a NASCAR racer to the farmhouse. Archie chants an incantation softly in the back, attempting to heal her. He peers up at me and shakes his head—the same as Harris.

Spence speeds up the gravel and dirt driveway, kicking up dust, and slams on his brakes. I jump out of the car, run up the steps, and bang on the door repeatedly.

"Leslie! Agnes! Wake up!" After a few impatient seconds, I remove my glove and knock again with my bare knuckles until they turn red. "Agnes! Leslie!"

The door finally creaks open to reveal the hedge witch in her purple robe. She rubs her eyes. "What the fuck are you doing, banging on my door at this hour? It's almost 3:00 a.m., Gwyn!"

Archie starts up the steps, holding Skye in his arms. Tanner and Spence bring up the rear. Agnes notices Skye's limp body and her demeanor turns sullen.

"What the fuck happened? Get her the fuck in here and put her on the sofa."

We follow Archie into the living room and he places her sleeping body gently on the cushions. Mr. Yeats scuttles in and transfers into his human persona.

"Oh, my. What has happened to Ms. McGowen?"

"I think a witch cast a hex on her," Spence says.

"Never you mind, familiar." Agnes motions with her thumb. "Get Dr. Hughes. She was dead asleep when I left, but she must be awake now. Go on!"

He wrinkles his nose at her. "As you wish." He darts up the stairs, transforming into a cat as he scuttles up.

"We were at the Celestial Gardens checking on the Seelie Fae," I say. "They never crossed, so we left. On our way back via the Green, we got trapped in an enchanted whirlwind and couldn't break free at first. We had to resort to using magic in public to get out of the trap."

Tanner continues. "When we broke through the barrier, the mini tornado swirled across the Green toward the Old Men oak trees. Then it transformed into someone dressed in a black hooded cape. They threw a red and black vapor ball in our direction and we ran. Seamus showed up as a cat sith and jumped at the attacker. But Skye was behind us and got struck."

"Fuck!" Agnes hobbles over to the sofa and lays a hand on her body, chanting to summon her magic. She gets zapped like she's touching an electrical current. "You tried to heal her?"

"Aye," Archie replies, brushing fingers through his locks. "I may have given her body a boost of energy, but I had to contend with the same pushback you experienced just now. It resembled what transpired when Riley Shaw was attacked. And..." He strokes his goatee. "The witch who attacked my dad used similar magic."

"Yeah," I say. "I remember you describing her and her strange witchcraft. Could it actually be the same hex?"

Leslie comes rushing down the stairs with her robe flying open. "I overhead all of you. This is dreadful. We can't lose Skye."

Mr. Yeats scampers in and sits on the floor, swinging his tail. The front door swings in and Trinity rushes into the living room in sweats and a pink puffer jacket.

"I got here as quickly as I could. Scared Charlie out of her knickers getting a phone call this late. I sent an emergency group text to the others. How is she?"

"Not fucking good," Agnes says. "I think she's been hexed. It's definitely not fairy magic. Archie thinks it's the same hex that a witch cast on his dad."

I send a quick text to Tyler and Ronnie, letting them know I'm fine and will contact them later. They must be freaking out.

Archie gestures at our coven leader. "I contacted Trinity after Gwyn called. Explained everything that transpired on the Green." He turns toward Skye. "I couldn't reverse the hex or heal her—same as my dad. But I was able to cast a sleeping spell. She should stay unconscious. As long as she's not attempting to speak or communicate with us, I think we have time to remove it."

"But how?" Trinity asks. "Archie, you said a homeless witch hiding in the caverns hexed your dad. Could we remove the hex the same way?"

"An old witch who lives in Dean Village came to the house to remove the hex. I don't know how he could help us from over there, but I sent Quinn a text. He should wake soon."

"Thank you," she replies. "Agnes, do you know of a spell?"

The hedge witch scratches her cheek. "I don't remember one. But at the least, we should light a black candle. In fact, I've got two in the magic room. We should use both."

"I'll grab them," Spence says, darting out.

Mr. Yeats transforms into his human persona and follows him out. "I'll help you, Mr. Huxley."

I squat next to the sofa and swipe Skye's hair off her face. Spence and the familiar return with the black candles. Leslie removes the lamp from the end table at our red-haired witch's feet.

"Place one here," the Elder says. "Put the other one on the floor next to her head."

Mr. Yeats sets a candle on the table while Spence places the other according to Leslie's directions. They pass their hands over the wicks and ignite them. The flames flicker with eternal hope for our friend.

Trinity crosses her arms. "They will need to burn until the wick runs out. That could take a couple of days. We'll have to watch over her the entire time."

Mr. Yeats straightens his suit jacket. "I do not need sleep. I will gladly remain at her side."

"Well, I'm not fucking going anywhere," Agnes says. "This is my house. In fact, I think I will head back to bed."

"How can you sleep, Agnes?" our coven leader asks. "With one of our own in danger?"

She twists the side of her mouth. "There's a fucking evil witch out there trying to kill us for some fucking reason. Is she mentally ill? I don't fucking know. But for sure, we won't have the power to fight her if we aren't at our strongest. We all need to sleep. Take turns watching her and get some shut-eye. Meanwhile, maybe Archie's brother will contact him by sunrise. Come on, Leslie. Let's go to bed. The younger witches can fill the first shift."

"I agree," Trinity says, throwing off her jacket. "Good call, Agnes. Before we decide who's going to keep watch, is there anything you haven't told me?"

Tanner slides the candle on the table a little closer to Skye's feet. "I don't think so. Spence?"

"Nope," he replies. "Gwyn and Tanner explained everything."

I recall Detective Jack Schmidt standing on the sidewalk at University Avenue and gasp. "In all the commotion, I forgot to say anything."

Archie squints at me. "What did you forget?"

"When we were on the way to the alleyway after Skye was attacked, my witch's intuition kicked in. I glanced back toward Main Street. Jack Schmidt was standing on the Green, where it intersects University Avenue. I think he may have seen us."

Mr. Yeats clutches his chest. "That's alarming."

"Fawk, Gwyn," Archie says.

Trinity's jaw drops. "Did he observe you performing witchcraft in public?"

"Maybe?" I grimace and brace for the Elder's explosion.

Leslie flinches. "This is horrendous. If he glimpsed even a portion of what transpired, he'll be knocking on all our doors. Our city council allies will have something to say. We need to talk with Elijah when he arrives later this morning."

"Who fucking cares," Agnes says. "No one will believe him."

I fiddle with an earring. "Also, Drew Blackwell knows Archie had a relationship with Laura Lovelace."

"The affair happened a while ago," he adds. "But to the authorities, it's likely a wee suspicious."

Spence snorts. "You think?"

Trinity glares at Archie. "Your prior relationships come back to bite us in the ass too damned often."

"Hmph, you all worry yourselves over nothing," Agnes replies. "They have no actual evidence because none of us killed her. Leslie, we need to get some sleep."

The Elder shuffles out in her slippers. "I won't be able to close my eyes."

"Eat an edible. You'll be fine." Agnes cackles as she leaves the room.

"Sometimes I don't understand what runs through that hedge witch's mind," Trinity says. "But we'll deal with Jack later."

Tanner moves next to me. "Why don't you and Archie get a few hours of rest? Spence and I will stay up."

"I'm wide awake," Spence says, kneeling next to his good friend and classmate. "No way I will be able to sleep."

Archie offers his hand. "We can rest in the spare bedroom upstairs. You'll be worthless to her without your full power."

"OK," I say, standing. "Please, wake us if she stirs."

Our coven leader slides a chair next to the sofa and props her feet on the coffee table. "I'm gonna sleep right here. I sent a text update to the other witches. Told them Skye is stable for now and to stay in bed. Mr. Yeats, you can rest here next to me."

The familiar transforms back into a chimera cat and lies on the floor next to the chair. Archie and I drag our fatigued bodies to the spare bedroom and collapse onto the mattress. My other half rolls over and finds his slumber in a matter of seconds. But I can't shake the image of Cro-Magnon forehead man staring at us. Did we fuck up this time?

My eyes finally droop and a final thought trickles in. Why didn't Seamus come to the farmhouse to help us?

Chapter Twenty-Four

TO SAVE A WITCH

Drew Blackwell leans into me and I stumble back. He's speaking, but in my dream-state, someone has hit the mute button. My heart rate spikes while he explains his actions and I panic, darting to the front door of the house. I run out as if my life has moments left of its precious existence...

"Gwyn!" Archie shakes me by the upper arm. "Wake up! You were screaming in your sleep."

When I lift my lids, he's only inches from my face, a crease embedded between his eyes. Sunrays splay through the curtains, causing me to squint. I slide up against the old oak headboard, panting.

"Drew Blackwell. I think he's the one, Archie."

"What do you mean?" he asks. "The one who figures out who the witch killer is?"

I swallow. "No. He's a Tuatha Dé—the member of Nuada's family searching for me. My vision doesn't explain who the nefarious witch is, or why she's after us."

"How can you be sure? Does he tell you who he is in your dream?"

"I don't know. I can't hear what he's saying. But after he talks to me, I lose it and run out of our house like I'm running for my life. You shook me too soon. Didn't get to view the rest of the premonition."

"Quite disconcerting. Avoid him for now. Ridding Skye of this hex is our priority. We'll address your concerns regarding Agent Blackwell once she's safe."

My phone vibrates on the surface of the chest of drawers next to the bed. Texts from my son and best friend are waiting patiently on the screen.

Tyler: *I hope Skye is OK. See you soon.*

Ronnie: *OMFG. I can't believe this shit! I'll be there around nine.*

"Tyler and Ronnie replied to me. They're concerned about Skye. We should splash water on our faces and go downstairs. Have you heard from Quinn yet?"

"Haven't checked." He grabs his cell from the nightstand. "Aye. He said to call when I'm awake. It's around nine o'clock. Why don't you go ahead? I'll talk to him up here."

After a rushed visit to the bathroom, I make my way to the living room. I discover Seamus bending over Skye. She's lying comfortably on the sofa in the exact state she was in during the early morning hours. Agnes and Leslie stand at her feet, looking more aged than usual. Tanner and Spence must be sleeping. Trinity leans forward in the chair near her head while Mr. Yeats paces back and forth in feline form. The black candles continue to burn. Nearly two-thirds of them remain. The cat sith witch pushes up, leaning on his cane.

"I've tried every hex removal I am aware of. Unfortunately, I was unsuccessful."

"You finally made it," I say. "I wondered what happened to you after the attack on the Green."

He averts his eyes from me. "My transition back to human took much longer this time. I drove here as soon as my human form stabilized."

"We always welcome your help, Seamus," Trinity says. "Thank you for trying."

Leslie lifts her chin. "We will have to pursue another course of action."

"What fucking approach do we have left?" Agnes asks. "We've exhausted every spell we know of."

The steps rumble and chatter echoes in the foyer. Tanner, Spence, and Archie shuffle in, discussing something.

"I spoke with Quinn," Archie says. "After discussion of the similarities between my dad's symptoms and what Skye is experiencing, we believe the same hex removal may work on her. How is she doing?"

"The same," Trinity replies. "Wouldn't this old witch need to advise us?"

Agnes snorts. "They'll never get an ancient fart witch on a plane."

"Dr. Hughes got you on a plane," Spence says, crossing his arms.

Leslie chuckles. "Indeed, I did."

Tanner shoves his hands in his pockets. "Does it matter? He probably doesn't have a passport."

"No. Most likely not," I reply. "But we could use video chat. Hamish Brown—that's his name—could direct us. From the mixing of the paste to the slicing of our skin. We can figure out the incantation."

Seamus slips in a few words. "I would be happy to help with its implementation."

"Thank you, Dr. Duffy." Trinity shifts her gaze to me. "What's the paste for?"

"Forget the paste." Spence's head snaps left and right. "Why the fuck are you cutting us?"

Archie chuckles. "You'll be fine. I'll explain later once Quinn gets back to me. He's already setting things up with Hamish. I hope he says yes, because he has never used modern technology—may be leery of it."

"He likes me," I say. "I'll sweet talk him. Where are the others? I thought they'd be here by now."

As if on cue, the front door opens and footsteps approach. Tyler and Zoe rush in. My son dashes in my direction and wraps me in an embrace.

"I am so glad you're OK." He releases me and turns toward Skye. "But I wish that evil witch had missed her, too."

"What are we going to do?" Zoe asks, pouting. "She's one of my best friends."

The door swings in again. Ronnie, Shane, and Elijah walk in. My best friend rushes to her red-haired, witchy twin. She drops a heavy bag on the floor and kneels next to her. We brief them on the plans to reverse Skye's hex.

Ronnie grits her teeth. "We have to find this bitch witch who did this. And eliminate her."

"I've updated our allies on the council through John Erickson," Elijah says. "They've been told about the dangers of both the rogue witch on the loose and the Tuatha Dé fairy. Mayor Devine flipped her lid, but she sends her thoughts concerning Skye. I truly believe she cares."

Shane twists his beard. "Jessica is stuck between a rock and a hard place. Being an Unremarkable, she understands her limitations in helping us—a terrible spot to govern from when you're the mayor watching out for so many residents."

"Elijah, why did you tell her about the Tuatha Dé?" Trinity asks. "We don't have confirmation he has crossed yet. He's only appeared in Gwyn's visions."

"Actually, I think he has," I say. "My premonition expanded during my sleep. It's Drew Blackwell, the FBI agent. I'm almost certain."

Tyler gapes at me from across the room. "Fuck."

Agnes smacks her hands together. "Makes sense, too. He can ask you a trillion questions and you wouldn't become suspicious because it's his job."

"Indeed," Leslie replies. "Gwyn, avoid him at all costs until we figure out how to proceed. But first we must treat Skye."

Archie's phone rings. "Hi, Quinn. Will he do it? Brilliant. Send me the incantation and the list of ingredients. We'll prepare for the chat. How's Dad? I know. I'll talk to you later about it." He ends the call, rubbing his temple on one side of his forehead. "This may get a wee bit messy. I recommend we spread a blanket on the floor and move her to it."

We spend the next twenty minutes rearranging furniture and laying a thick blanket on top of the rug. Elijah and Tanner lift Skye off the sofa and transfer her limp body to the soft cotton. The young witches gather the herbs and other items from the magic room. After placing them on the coffee table nearby, Seamus directs them in the concoction's preparation according to the incantation. We wait impatiently for the video call from Archie's brother. His phone rings and he touches the green icon to accept.

"Hey, Quinn. Everyone, this is my brother."

"Nice to meet you all." Quinn's face fills the screen. "Wish it was under much lighter circumstances. I'd like to introduce Hamish Brown. He's the expert who rescued my dad from the hex that dreadful witch in the vaults cast on him. Here. Take my phone."

The old Dean Village witch pushes his face into the camera so all we can see is his big schnoz. "Fawk the pleasantries. From what I noticed, the candles have little wick left to burn. Where is your young witch who's under the affliction?"

"Back off a wee bit, Hamish," Quinn says. "Aye. There you go."

Archie props the cell using a few books and adjusts the camera so Hamish can view her entire body.

"What a beautiful young lady," he says. "May the wicked witch who cast the hex on her freeze in the Otherworld. Is the mixture ready to go?"

Archie puts his face in front of the camera. "Everything except the sacrifice."

"Sacrifice?" Spence shouts, his voice jumping into his falsetto range. "Oh...OH. That's what the slicing is for."

"Aye," Hamish replies. "The blood of her loved ones must be added to the mixture to bind her to all of you. That should purge the hex from her body. But do it quickly. The spell needs time while the candles are burning."

Spence runs to the kitchen and returns with a knife in his hand. He clenches his teeth and cuts across his palm, dripping blood into the bowl. "That fucking hurt, but I'd do it a thousand times for you, sis."

He hands the knife to Ronnie and covers his palm with a rag. One by one, we give our blood, sharing the love we have for our most devoted witch. Seamus leans against the fireplace mantel, observing us. When we've all finished, Hamish reminds us what the next step demands.

"Time to strip her down," he says matter-of-factly.

Spence's eyebrows take a leap. "We have to strip her naked? I'm pretty sure she'll be pissed if we do that in front of everyone. I mean, not that she's a prude. But..."

Agnes makes a prune face. "Too fucking bad. It's not like she has much choice."

"I agree," Leslie says. "We must follow the spell exactly as Hamish directs us to."

The front door opens with a bang and Skye's boyfriend Zach runs into the living room, panting. He darts to her and drops to the floor. "What the fuck?! Are you going to save her?" He bends over her and strokes her face. "Do something."

Ronnie kneels on the floor next to him, rubbing his back. "I called him. Told him what happened."

"For the love of the gods," Trinity says, wiping her face. "Why would you tell him?"

Shane steps forward. "Because he has a right to know even if he's an Unremarkable. He loves her."

"Actually, he should be part of this." I take the knife and bowl to him. "The spell needs the blood of her loved ones. You're the most important one, Zach."

He snatches the knife from my hand and slices across his palm, squeezing droplets of blood into the bowl. "What now?"

"You must remove most of her clothing and spread the paste on her exposed skin," Archie says. "Do you want help, Zach?"

"No," he replies, grabbing the bowl. "Except for Ronnie. Can you help me take her shirt and pants off?

"Of course," she says. "Is this allowed, Hamish? He isn't a witch."

"Aye. He's the best one to apply the paste," he replies. "Because he loves her with his whole heart."

Once they've removed all but her bra, panties, and socks, Zach spreads the mushy concoction all over Skye's skin. When he's done, you would swear she's just received a mud facial. He lies on his side as close as he can get to her, clasping her hand. Not being a member of the coven, Seamus continues to observe us from afar.

We gather in a circle and chant the incantation, setting our intention to reverse the hex, the same as Archie and his family did with Harris. Except this time, it's our made family—our Fellowship. When we've chanted the last words of the spell, we bandage our wounds and huddle around Archie's phone to thank Hamish.

"You're most welcome. The Cockburns have been very good to me since I saved Harris. I would gladly help all his family. The candles should burn out by evening, but I will be deep in slumber by then. I hope to hear positive news when I wake."

Quinn takes the phone. "I'll call you tomorrow, brother. I wish you all the best."

"Thank you," Archie replies. "Talk to you in the morning."

Agnes peers at Skye, trying to mask a visage of sorrow. Every so often, my mentor lowers her rough exterior and the caring woman buried deep inside seeps through.

"This is going to be a long fucking day," she says, frowning. "Come into the kitchen. I'll make coffee and tea."

Tanner sits in the chair Trinity slept in overnight. "I should stay with Skye and Zach."

"OK. I will bring some coffee, hon," Spence says.

We amble out of the room, hesitant to leave our fellow witch in such a state. But what else can we do? Ronnie picks up her bag and approaches me.

"Archie, go on," I say. "I wanna talk to her."

"Of course, my love. I'll make you a cup of tea." He continues into the foyer.

My best friend hugs me. "Skye has to come out of this. I can't imagine a world without her. Why would someone want to hurt her?"

"I don't know," I say, pulling back. "Like Unremarkables, witches can be psychopaths, too. What's in your bag?"

"Oh, my breast pump. I'll have to pump a few times while I'm here, or my milk may deplete a little."

"Great idea. But you should have stayed home. You're a new mom and Luna needs you."

"She has a father, too, Gwyn. If I didn't come and Skye failed to survive this...I would have always blamed myself for not sacrificing a few hours with my daughter to increase her chances."

We join the others in the kitchen and I realize Seamus must have remained in the living room. I pick up the tea Archie made for me and walk back, but he isn't in there. When I check the hall tree, his long black coat is missing. He snuck out without us noticing. So like the cat sith witch.

Throughout the day, we monitor Skye's vitals and eat in shifts. But who has an appetite? Not me. My stomach growls like a bear for an hour before I relent and force down half of a cheese sandwich. Ronnie said she couldn't fathom not being here to help. My mind replays the incident on the Green and guilt clenches my heart. Why was she lagging so far behind me? Did the deranged witch call out to her?

By nightfall, the black candles have but a few flickers left. We gather around her, waiting anxiously. Archie, Leslie, Agnes, Trinity, and Shane huddle together near the fireplace, whispering about the unwanted outcome, I bet. In a corner of the room, Elijah talks on his cell, most likely updating the Ericksons. Ronnie sits on the sofa and shares pictures of Luna on her phone with me. What an enchanting infant she is.

On one side of Skye, Tanner, Spence, Tyler, and Zoe sit on the floor and chant an intention of removal. Zach rests next to her on his bottom with his legs crossed, glued to her hand. He raises his head and stares at the flames.

"They're almost out. What happens if she never wakes up?"

Trinity shifts closer to Skye. "One step at a time, young man."

Ronnie throws her phone down and leaps up from the sofa, clutching her chest. "Oh, my gods!"

"What?!" Zach shifts to his knees and inspects Skye's face and body. "Did she move?"

Everyone darts to our hexed friend's side; I spring from the sofa.

"No." Ronnie lifts her hands, revealing wet spots on her shirt above her boobs. "I forgot to pump an hour ago. My milk let down."

She breaks into an uncontrollable cackle and the rest of us burst out laughing. Suddenly, Skye sits up like a vampire rising from her coffin, flailing her arms and screeching.

"You fucking bitch! Come here and try that again!"

Everyone shouts, a chorus of cheers resounding as we stamp our feet on the floor.

Zach leaps at her, wrapping her in an embrace. "I thought you wouldn't come back from this."

Archie rubs his jaw. "My dad woke up yelling similar words. Curious."

"Well, they were both attacked by similar deranged witches," Tyler says. "Makes sense."

"Why am I in Agnes's living room in my undergarments?" She notices the paste on her skin and squints. "Oh, my gods. I remember now. That witch nailed me with a hex. You reversed it."

Ronnie drops to Skye's feet. "We weren't sure the incantation they used on Archie's dad would work on you."

"But it fucking did," Agnes says. "We owe Hamish Brown a giant-size thank you."

A wide grin sparkles on Shane's face. "Darling, this world would have suffered without your existence."

"Not to mention what we would have told our allies on the city council and Mayor Devine." Elijah lifts his cell phone. "I'll let them know you survived. What an amazing miracle to have you back."

"How do you feel, Skye?" I ask. "The hex reversal left Harris weak."

Standing with Zach's assistance, she attempts to balance. She falters a bit but takes a few steps alone and holds her own. "I think I'm OK. But I could eat a dozen donuts right now." Her stomach roars like a lion.

"Let's get you some dinner, then, my dear," Leslie says.

Spence hugs her and chuckles. "Maybe breakfast and lunch, too. I'll help."

"I'm not gonna lie." Trinity rests a fist on her hip. "I don't know what we were gonna do with you if you didn't return to us. So, thank you for coming back."

Skye chuckles. "You're welcome. Can I have a robe? I'm freezing, but I want to clean this shit off me before I put my clothes back on."

"Oh, yeah," Ronnie replies, passing her Leslie's cloak from the hall tree.

While Skye slips the hooded cape over her, she stares at Ronnie's chest, a crinkle in her forehead. "Why are your boobs soaked?"

CHAPTER TWENTY-FIVE

PERSISTENT DREW

ALTHOUGH THE FELLOWSHIP CELEBRATES Skye's revival, we have to acknowledge the realistic threat of the witch killer who targeted us. We have a working incantation to reverse the effects of the hex, so the threat is less worrisome. But what if it fails to work for other witches? Despite the acquisition of a successful hex reversal spell, Leslie has advised the coven to remain on guard as well. For the time being, Skye is living at the farmhouse. To my surprise, Agnes invited Zach to stay with her while she regains her full strength. The Fellowship will need her if the psychopathic witch attacks again.

Trinity contacted all the local covens and warned them to avoid evening outings. After sharing how to avoid its trigger of death, she offered our assistance to implement the spell should the deranged sorceress attack again. As dangerous as this situation is, we have another mountain to climb—the revelation of Agent Drew Black-well's true identity and what Detective Jack Schmidt may have seen on the night of the assault.

By Saturday, I've received several phone calls and emails from the agent, but I refuse to answer any of them. I let the voicemails collect dust online. Despite one night of regeneration with the crystals, my premonition hasn't expanded. Life doesn't stop for supernatural drama, so I go to work. Soon, Winter Session will end and I'll have to concentrate on my studies. But how, with the divergent threats afoot?

"Archie!" I peek into the living room. He's not there. "Where are you? I have to leave for work."

The basement door opens. "Did you call me?"

"Yeah. Gotta get to Mystic Sage. Jeff wants Shane and me to work the daylight hours and get home. He'll close the store every night this week."

"He can't keep that up forever. Who knows how long it will take us to root out this witch?"

"And we don't even have a plan. We lost our circle this week. Saving Skye was more important, of course." I zip up my puffer jacket and grab my backpack.

"You never asked how Tyler's training went last night."

"I assume he's doing well or you would have said something."

"He is. Like his mum." He wraps his arms around me. "He worries about you. Not having the dirk in your possession leaves you vulnerable."

"If Drew Blackwell is the Tuatha Dé who's after me, he hasn't figured out I killed Nick—Nuada. He would have taken me to the Otherworld by now...or killed me. Someone would have to tell him. The Bearsden Coven and Seamus Duffy are the only witches who know. As long as we all carry protection pouches to repel glamouring, he'll never find out, either. I'm safe."

"Does your witch's intuition confirm your theory?"

"My skills aren't advanced enough to recognize what it points to yet...until it's almost too late. Sometimes I think I'd be better off not having the ability at all."

"When we gather for Thursday's circle, we'll discuss a plan of action for going forward and what to do about the Imbolc Celebration. The Fellowship received the permit to celebrate in the gardens, but it may not be wise under the circumstances."

"Lots of decisions to make. Have you spoken with Quinn since you told him about Skye? How's Harris progressing?"

"Aye. Dad has improved, but he remains quite weak."

Dare I ask about his load for Spring Semester? "You've not mentioned what's happening in the department. Have you had any luck finding instructors to fill in for Seamus?"

"It's above my paygrade. With the threat of this unknown witch hanging over our heads, I've been afraid to ask her."

"The semester begins in a little over a week. If she can't find instructors, what are you going to do?"

"You better be on your way." He kisses me goodbye. "The steady rain could slow you down."

The change of subject nearly gives me whiplash. "I'll be home by dinner."

I step outside and flip open my umbrella. As I make the trek to Mystic Sage under gray, gloomy skies, I'm relieved the wet stuff is rain instead of the ice and snow from the prior week. When I enter, my sneakers squeak, squeak, squeak across the industrial vinyl floor. Julia is behind the cash register. A couple of DUB students are perusing the tarot cards.

"Hi, Julia. How are you today?"

"I guess I'm fine." She peers at the campus locals, then back at me.

"You don't look OK," I say, hanging my wet jacket on a low hanging hook.

The two young women come to the counter, Julia rings them up, and they exit the store. She closes the register and motions for me to move closer.

"I'm so worried for Shane, Gwyn. He finally told me everything the coven is dealing with...and you. Please tell me he'll be OK."

"If any of us gets attacked, we have a remedy. I don't want to say we should lower our guard. We have to root her out somehow and deal with her."

She lays her hand on mine. "What about this fairy Shane mentioned? Will he harm you?"

"Don't stress yourself out over the rare possibility. I can defend myself." I check for the protection pouch in my pants pocket. "We're all prepared. The truth is, we have no idea if we have the power to fight off a Tuatha Dé. I gave myself to Nuada freely in order to save my son."

Julia hugs me. "Oh, Gwyn. I am so sorry you went through that."

"I'm OK," I say, pulling away. "We...I took care of him. But his family may come looking for him. He could be here already. As a coven, we are strong. We watch out for each other."

"What a family should do." She clasps her hands together. "I have a daughter. But I haven't seen her for a long time. She's worried my ex, her stepfather, will follow her to Bearsden. I hope you can meet her someday."

"Me, too," I say, patting her shoulder.

Shane shuffles into the front of the store with a box and sets it on the floor. "My ears are burning. Have you two been talking about me?"

I chuckle. "Of course. You're the boss. We always talk behind your back."

"Only good things, Shane." Julia grins at him, her eyes twinkling with affection.

"So I suspected. Gwyn, would you mind helping me restock the shelves? I don't want Jeff to bother himself with it when he's here alone tonight."

"Sure," I reply.

For the next few hours, Shane and I replenish the shelves, tidying up as we go. It's wonderful how much the locals love and support this Occult store, but why are they so messy? Shoppers have tossed the tarot card sets aside and placed several herb jars in the wrong slots. Either Archie's sense of order has rubbed off on me, or some witch has cast a spell on me. He'd probably welcome the change, although he never complains.

When the time on my phone changes to 3:00 p.m., Shane and Julia leave. Jeff won't arrive for thirty-five minutes because he's watching Aidan while Ashley and Courtney go shopping for maternity clothes. By summer, we will welcome another half fairy, half human baby to the town. The store quiets down and I'm able to rest on the stool for a while.

I flip through the online news to catch up and happen upon an article regarding the death of a local man in New Castle. As I read, I discover the New Castle police found the body in Battery Park near the Delaware river. I skim the first paragraph until I read the name Gareth Thomas and my heart stops like it hit a brick wall. If I'm remembering correctly, he was one of the young male witches who helped us banish the Sluagh to the Otherworld along with Riley Shaw, Elizabeth Wang, and Laura Lovelace.

I scroll down to the last paragraph. Cause of death is unknown. There was another young male witch who helped us that night. What was his name? I rub my temples as knots wind in my stomach. The door dings and my intuition signals me. My heart switches to tachycardia mode as I peer up at Drew Blackwell.

"Not busy this afternoon?" the FBI agent asks.

"Not today," I say while sticking a pen into the skull jar. "January doesn't attract many shoppers late in the month. All the holiday clearance sales have finished. What can I do for you? We do have a sale on candles. Perhaps a blue one?"

"Sure. I like to burn them occasionally."

He ambles over to the candles display and lifts a few to his nose, sniffing. After choosing a chunky light-blue pillar, he returns to the counter and sets it down. My heart is about to burst through my chest, but I can't allow him to sense my fear. *Remain calm, Gwyn.* He has no way of finding out who you are. I ring up the candle and wrap it in tissue paper.

"That's $22.95," I say, placing the pillar in a paper bag.

He grimaces. "Pricey. Why does it cost so much?"

"It has herbs mixed in. This type of candle is used in casting spells. Mystic Sage is an occult store."

"Do you believe in witchcraft, Gwynedd Crowther?" He flashes a flirtatious smile at me. "Are you a witch?"

Wow. He's being direct. Drew must be tired of searching for me. I refrain from answering, tucking my secret into my brain's vault. He stares into my eyes with those oddly colored irises, and an aura builds in my abdomen like before. But my focus remains. I touch the lump in my pants pocket. The pouch is secure there. *Your glamouring won't work on me, agen*t. He picks up the candle, averts his gaze, and takes out his notepad. Here we go...

"I called your phone numerous times and sent you a couple of emails. You never replied. Did you not receive them?"

"Yeah. I'm not under any obligation to reply to you, agent."

"True. But avoiding me brings an air of suspicion, and I have more questions." He glances at his notes. "Someone reported observing you and a few others on the Green in the early morning hours on Thursday. They said a woman collapsed and a man carried her away. Sounds freakishly like the deaths of the other women. What happened, and who was the young female?"

Fuck. Jack Schmidt saw us. But did he witness the attack by the deranged witch? My face flushes. I snatch an ad flyer from underneath the counter and fan myself. "Sorry. Hot flash." But it's absolutely not. I'm burning like a specimen under a magnifying glass. I need time to fake a story. "Skye drank too much and needed a ride home. I knew I couldn't carry her if she passed out, so I called two young men in our community pagan group to meet me there. Good thing, because she did." I grind my teeth, hoping karma is on my side today.

"She's alive, then?" he asks, cocking his head.

"Of course," I say, smirking. "Did you actually think I killed one of my best friends?"

He arches an eyebrow. "It's been known to happen."

I cross my arms and glower at him.

"Would you give me her phone number to confirm these facts? And the two men in your pagan group?"

I hesitate because I have to talk with them first—get our stories straight. "I don't feel comfortable giving you their phone numbers, but I can have them call you. Skye got sick. She's staying with a couple of our older members. They're nursing her back to health."

"They need to call me as soon as possible. You don't want this tainting my notes in the investigation."

The door dings and Jeff Williams enters the store, waving to me as he walks past us to the back. As he rushes by, his brow crinkles. I return my attention to the agent.

"I'll send a text to them as soon as I get off work."

He closes his pad. "Thank you, Gwyn. Have a great evening."

Drew picks up his candle and heads for the exit. He pauses and turns around. "You never answered my other question. Are you a witch?"

For fuck's sake! He's determined! I swallow and force a smile. "I just work here, Agent Blackwell—for one more week, anyway. Spring Semester begins soon and I won't have time for this job."

"Good to know," he says with a nod.

The door slams with a clank of the bamboo chimes as I drop onto the stool. Jeff dashes into the front and inspects the sidewalk through the store glass.

"Are you OK? I can't believe he asked you outright about being a witch."

I puff air through my pursed lips, displacing my bangs. "Yeah. I remember a time I froze at the thought of coming eye to eye with another Tuatha Dé Danann. Now I just want to finish it—send him back to the Otherworld so I can live my life."

"He must be desperate. What are you going to do now that you're sure he's the one?"

"The coven is meeting on Thursday to discuss a plan of action for both the nefarious witch and Drew Blackwell."

"I overheard Courtney telling Ashley she wished she could help you all this time, but she's afraid the Tuatha Dé fairy may be too powerful for her."

"No," I say, shaking my head. "She has to put herself and the baby first."

The late afternoon sunrays beam through the front windows, reminding me of the time. I put on my jacket and grab my umbrella and backpack.

"Yeah. You should go," Jeff says, logging in to the register. "The sun will set soon."

I dash to the door and stop. "Tell Courtney I appreciate her desire to help, but this time, it's not her battle."

When I enter the house, I rid myself of my jacket and shoes. The living room is dark, but the kitchen light spills into the hallway. As I shuffle in, the mantle clock dings the first of five. The aroma of freshly made pizza permeates the air. Archie raises his head from the laptop.

"Dinner will be done soon. I was finishing up some grading for Seamus. How was work? Uneventful, I hope."

"Not exactly." I collapse into the chair next to him. "Drew Blackwell stopped by."

"Fawk. What happened?" He shuts the lid.

"He came right out and asked me if I was a witch—twice. Because I refused to answer the first time. I told him I worked at Mystic Sage, and not for long."

He brushes fingers through his hair. "Your intuition is right, then."

"I suppose. Archie, that's not all. He says someone saw the four of us on the Green. He didn't say who, but I'm sure Jack must have told him. How else would he know it was me? I mean, the whole point of bringing in this FBI agent wasn't only to figure out who was killing those women. The detective is obviously upset he never solved the case of Nick Evans's disappearance. I'm worried he thinks the pagan groups are cults killing people."

"Did Agent Blackwell allude to the idea? Or is your witch's intuition signaling you?"

"No. Call it a hunch. I sent a text to Skye, Tanner, and Spence to give them a heads up. Our stories need to align to avoid further suspicion before they contact Drew. The Fellowship has to create a plan to send him back."

Archie strokes my arm. "There is another alternative."

"Eliminate him? Let's not discuss this anymore." I recall the article I was reading when Drew came into Mystic Sage. "Shit. There's something else. The agent walked in when I was reading the news. I'll find the article." I search the browser on my phone. "Here. Read the first paragraph."

His eyes move back and forth, becoming rounder as he scrolls. "Isn't he the witch from the New Castle Coven who helped us banish the Sluagh on the night of the Winter Solstice Celebration?"

"Yes. Do you remember the name of the one from Wilmington?"

He stares at his weapons display for a moment. "I'm fairly certain his name was Brayton Harris."

I snatch my cell from his hand and enter the Wilmington witch's name in the search bar. "Fuck. Fuck. Fuck." I peer up at Archie. "He's dead, too—cause of death unknown. Funeral was a week ago."

He pulls me against his chest and caresses my back. "We'll figure this out, Gwyn."

Later in bed, I find calm in the rise and fall of Archie's chest and mull over how to fight this Tuatha Dé fairy. Nothing comes to mind, but there's one thing I am certain of.

I killed once, and I can do it again.

Chapter Twenty-Six

An Onerous Decision

As I recount Saturday's events the next day at the farmhouse, Leslie, Agnes, and Archie sit motionless in their chairs. Mr. Yeats stands with his hands on the edges of his suit coat. Trinity leans against the library table, the heel of her black stiletto clicking on the wooden floor like a runaway tap dancer. When I'm finished, dead silence settles over the room while they process the revelations. Our coven leader walks across the room and closes the library door.

"Skye is resting and doesn't need to hear this yet. Well, what do we do, witches? This Tuatha Dé will never leave here, not until he learns the truth concerning the whereabouts of his missing family member. If we kill him, another would appear in short order, and we'll be back in the same place. We have to deal with the fairy issue first. Then we can root out this wicked witch who's clearly off her rocker."

Archie rests his arms on the table. "I think our best path forward is to send him back through the portal and cast a spell of banishment."

"There is no guarantee he wouldn't cross over again in the future." Worry wrinkles Leslie's brow. "Drew Blackwell and his family of fae would blast their magic at the portal for as long as it took to break the banishment spell. And the next time, he would bring his entire Tuatha Dé Danann relatives with him, returning with a steely heart of vengeance. Because he'd know where you are, Gwynedd."

"She's got a point," Trinity says.

Agnes sits in the chair and doesn't comment, an expression of doom and gloom on her face.

A past vision replays in my head—an army of Tuatha Dé Danann crossing through the portal and swarming the streets of Bearsden, their winged bodies slaying our loved ones with beams of white magic. The one-eyed Fomorian blinks at me. I gulp down the saliva caught in the back of my throat.

"Leslie's right, Archie. I saw it in a prior vision—one that hasn't come to fruition, I hope. Plus, how many times have we had to fight evil witches and supernatural beings crossing into our town, exposing Unremarkables to unnecessary danger? The Sluagh, the Kenilworth ancestral witch family, Nuada, the Dearg Due, Alys Morgan. And now Nuada's relative, Drew Blackwell. Hasn't this coven's entire existence rested on keeping the community safe from corruption and harm? It's time to find an actual solution...and fast, no matter what the costs."

"I understand there is always a possibility my plan could backfire," Archie replies. "But we have few choices, Gwyn."

Mr. Yeats steps forward. "I am aware my opinions rarely receive the respect they deserve, but I am presenting mine, anyway. You must find a way to close the portal in the mound. Everyone's lives depend upon it—the coven and the town."

"Well, it's gonna fucking rain rose petals," Agnes says. "For once, I agree with the annoying familiar."

"You could make the statement without being insulting." Mr. Yeats straightens his suit jacket.

Agnes sneers at him and gets up from her chair. She shuffles to a bookshelf, grabs a tattered grimoire, and lugs it back to the table. After dropping the tome with a thud, she flips a few pages and stops. She looks directly at her love, and the Elder nods, casting her eyes downward.

"Leslie and I have been talking seriously about how to end all this." My mentor gazes at her love and smiles. "We have a solution to close the portal."

"What?" I ask, hopping from my chair. "Why didn't you tell us?"

"Why was I not informed?" Mr. Yeats asks, adjusting his spectacles.

"Praise the gods," Trinity says. "Well, don't keep us waiting on pins and needles."

We're all elated with their proclamation, except Archie. He's stroking his goatee, his eyes narrowing at the open book. I return my attention to the grimoire and scowl at the hedge witch.

"We can't use that spell, Agnes," I say, exhaling. "We tabled it, and you know why."

Trinity shakes her head at Leslie. "And I can't believe you finally agreed to it. I won't sanction the sacrifice of anyone, even if it saves us all. We vow to do no harm. Or have you forgotten?"

"They haven't," Archie says, a crease settled between his eyes. "Tell them."

"Tell us what?" I ask, swapping my gaze between the Elder and my mentor.

Leslie joins Agnes in front of the grimoire and they clasp hands. My mentor gazes at us in earnest. Mr. Yeats moves closer, turning his ear toward them.

"These fucking threats have escalated to the point we can't ignore, and the solution is smacking us right in the face. No, Trinity. Even I refuse to do harm to another now. I never believed in a thousand years I'd actually care about anyone again." She smiles affectionately at her love. "But all of you welcomed me into the coven, knowing how fucking difficult I am. That's why I'm going to sacrifice myself so you can cast the portal-closing spell and put an end to all this bullshit."

"What?!" I ask, moving towards them. "The fuck you are!"

Trinity stamps her heel on the floor. "You have had some insane ideas in the past, Agnes. But this is the looniest thing in the universe you've ever come up with. And you're giving her your stamp of approval, Leslie?"

The Elder squeezes Agnes's hand. "Yes. Because I'm crossing over to the Otherworld with her."

"Well...this explains...why you didn't share your plans with me." Mr. Yeats transforms into his feline persona and scuttles to a corner of the room.

"You must be joking." Trinity scratches her head. "Right? You're messing with us."

I examine their expressions, full of sincerity. "They aren't." I turn toward Archie. "Why are you sitting there in silence? Or did you know about their plans?" I squint at him. "Is this why you've been stressing over Spring Semester? Because you knew both Seamus and Leslie would be gone?"

He rises from his chair. "No, Gwyn. Of course not. I'm hearing this for the first time as well." He slips his hands in the pockets of his jeans. "But I understand their decision. Sometimes we have to sacrifice ourselves for family."

"Well, thank you, Dr. Cockburn," Agnes says. "Leslie and I made this decision rationally. But you don't have to be a fucking academic to arrive at the conclusion that this option is our best choice—for Gwyn, the coven, and the town."

"Indeed." Leslie raises her chin. "I was upset at first when Agnes proposed giving herself over to implement the spell. After being apart for decades, I can't imagine a life without her now. When I recognized she was determined to follow through with it, I decided I would go with her."

My eyes well up. "I don't want you to do it. There has to be another way."

Archie strokes my back. "I don't want them to go either, Gwyn. But we have to respect their decision."

"You're forgetting one thing, ladies," Trinity says, anger stirring in her jade-green eyes. "The coven has to agree to cast this spell using you as a sacrifice. No way any of them will vote to implement this spell."

"Exactly." I wipe a tear from my cheek. "You can't expect us to send you to the Otherworld willingly."

Agnes approaches me and takes my hands in hers. "You can, and you will. You won't be saying goodbye, Gwyn. Just...see ya later. Use that ancestral divination you're so good at and meet with us once in a while. One day, we will all be together again."

"We're telling the select few of you," Leslie says, "because we need your help to convince the rest of the Fellowship this is our best choice. We can banish the Tuatha Dé and seal off any future crossings of supernatural beings into our town—at least through this portal."

Trinity's flaming eyes become wet. "Leslie, this goes against every fiber of my being. But if this is what the two of you want, I won't stop you. Archie, apparently, you're all on board the train. That leaves you, Gwyn."

There was a time I was so angry at Leslie, I would have gladly laid a path for her to the Otherworld. As I gaze at her weathered, wrinkled face, framed by silver hair, I realize she's become the closest living person I consider a mother figure. I step back and scan their eyes, full of self-determination. Don't we all want control over our own destinies?

"OK. I promise to back your plan."

"Thank you, Gwyn." Trinity pats my shoulder. "Convincing the others will be easier if there is no dissent."

Archie wraps an arm around my shoulder. "This could change the future from the one Gwyn has viewed in her dreams and visions. If we do this now, we may very well stop the Fomorian from crossing over at all."

"Fuck, yeah," Agnes says. "He sounds nasty. Let's keep him out of Bearsden."

Trinity crosses her arms. "When do you want to attempt this casting? You must have some idea."

"Yes, we do," Leslie says, lifting her head. "Imbolc. We already have a permit to use the space. We will ask Elijah to chat with the city regarding a change in timeframe. If he needs to, he can get our allies on the council to help secure the necessary permissions."

Trinity's shoulders fall. "I guess it's done. When do we inform the rest of the coven?"

"Thursday night," Agnes replies. "Our usual circle."

"Should we tell them so close to Imbolc?" Archie asks. "That doesn't give us much time to prepare."

"Doesn't allow them the space to change their minds, either," Agnes says.

"Indeed." Leslie motions to her familiar. "Mr. Yeats, please come here. I need to address your concerns."

The chimera cat scuttles back and pops into his human persona. "What will happen to me once you're gone? I cannot go with you."

"You can become my familiar," I say, touching his shoulder. "If you want?"

He trips over his words, a rare show of emotion overcoming him. "I...I...would be honored, Ms. Crowther."

Leslie approaches him. "Once I am no longer of this world, you will transfer your loyalty to Gwynedd Crowther of Bearsden." She chants an incantation and waves a splash of amber magic. "So be it."

A slight tapping on the door resonates in the room. Mr. Yeats turns the key in the lock and pulls on the handle. Skye is standing there, her eyebrows arched.

"What's happening? Did I miss a meeting?"

Archie and I say nothing, averting our eyes from our friend.

Trinity glances at the Elder and the hedge witch. "No. Preliminary planning for our circle on Thursday. You were resting, and we thought you needed the sleep."

An awkward silence ensues as Skye observes our darting glances. Her gaze drops to the floor. "Okayyy...I'm going back to my room. Zach is supposed to call me in a couple of minutes." She turns and walks down the hallway.

"Phew! That was close," Trinity says, shaking her head.

We scatter around the room and shove chairs under the table. Mr. Yeats drops to the floor, changing into a cat as he falls, and zips through the doorway. Agnes carries the grimoire to the shelf and slides it into the space between two tomes.

"I'll send a reminder about the circle on Thursday night," Trinity says. "We'll meet here again. Safer, anyway. Until then, take care."

On the drive back to the house, the secrecy eats at me inside. Or is it my intuition sending another warning? I can't decipher the difference between my emotions and the signals anymore. Imbolc is six days away. How do I reconcile all of this with so little time left?

Thursday afternoon, I putter around the front of Mystic Sage, dusting off the shelves even though I passed a duster over them yesterday. Since this is my last day and Julia no longer needs my help, I'm searching for tasks to earn my pay—ways to avoid talking to Shane. When push comes to shove, I've become a better liar to save my ass and others. But I could never lie to him. Thankfully, I only worked two days this week.

As I meander past the candles and incense, the aroma of lavender, rosemary, and lemon balm tickles my nostrils. I will miss the smell of this place, but not how it triggered my allergies. A notification dings on my phone.

Drew Blackwell: *I heard from all your friends. They corroborated your story.*

Drew Blackwell: *But I have more questions.*

Ugh. What could he need to ask me now? He must be desperate for more clues. But I'm not going to tell on myself.

Julia organizes the mess under the counter, wipes off the surface, and motions to me. I walk over and pass the duster to her. She stuffs it in a nook below the cash register.

"I can't thank you enough for all your help. I would have never learned this job without your patience."

"You're welcome, Julia. I'm glad you and Shane worked things out, too. With no help from me, of course."

"We all make mistakes. I'm happy to call you a friend. I don't have many since...you know."

"If you ever need to talk to someone other than that white-haired boss of ours—well, yours—I am a phone call away."

"Good luck to you on finishing your master's degree. I wish you the best."

"Thank you, Julia. I appreciate the sentiment."

The time changes to 4:30 p.m. on my cell. Archie will arrive soon to pick me up. We plan on catching dinner before going to the farmhouse. Jeff enters the store, bringing a blast of icy air with him. The temperature has plummeted, sending Bearsden into a deep freeze. At least the skies are clear with no threat of snow. Luckily, the weather will be warmer for Imbolc.

I slip on my puffer jacket and gloves, preparing for Jack Frost to attack me the second I hit the pavement. "Hi, Jeff. Feels like the arctic out there."

"Worse," he says, removing his DUB beanie. "So, this is it—your last day."

"Yeah, it's bittersweet. I'll be shopping here as usual, though. Best herbs in town."

Shane ambles in, his hands stuffed in the back pockets of his cargo pants. "It's the end of an era. Gwyn, I can't thank you enough for working for me these past few years. I'll miss your face gracing this place every week."

I chuckle. "You act like you won't see me in about two hours."

"I know, darling." He averts his gaze for a moment. "We'll chat more at the meeting. You and Archie have a wonderful dinner."

Suddenly, I'm nauseous. I move toward the door. Shane will be furious I kept the plan to myself. I glance through the window glass. Archie has pulled up in his Tesla and parked at a meter. My perfect excuse to exit.

"My ride is here! Have a great evening, Jeff."

I slip out the door into the bitter wind and dash to the car. Once inside, I relish the heated seats. "Ahhh. My ass froze in the few feet I ran to get in here."

He drives west on Main Street. "Well, warm up. Would hate to lose your fine arse."

I throw him an icy glare. "It was hard to say goodbye to Mystic Sage. Shane gave me a job when I needed a change in my life. He's going to be so angry when he discovers I kept Leslie and Agnes's plan from him. And he will have every reason to be. I don't know how Tyler will react, either. But I think he'll understand because he respects the Elder."

"As he should. We'll cross that proverbial bridge tonight. Where would you like to eat, my love?"

"I don't know if I can. My stomach is doing backflips. You pick the place. I'll order a small serving of something."

As he turns on South Main Street at the curve, I rub my abdomen. How will I convince my fellow witches to go along with Leslie and Agnes's wishes when I'm barely able to force myself?

When we arrive at the farm, several cars occupy the parking area in front of the porch. Everyone must be here already. I check the time on my phone. It's half-past six.

"I thought the meeting didn't start until seven?" I ask. "Why did everyone come so early? I was hoping to chat with Trinity to solidify our course of action when we announce this to the others."

"No idea." Archie squeezes my hand. "Don't feel compelled to follow through with this. Do what you can live with because, in the end, they'll be gone. But you'll have to survive knowing you helped to send them to the Otherworld."

"I know. You can't argue with their reasoning, though. Leslie and Agnes must have been discussing this plan for a few days—maybe longer. I wouldn't be shocked if my mentor made her own decision months ago."

"Aye. Extremely possible. Time to face the music?"

"I suppose so. The Dies Irae from the last movement of Berlioz's Symphonie Fantastique is ringing in my ears."

We run up the porch steps and shove the door open. Angry voices are shouting over each other in the living room. "This is absurd!" "You had no right to keep this a secret!" "We won't do it!" Agnes spews a round of fucks at everyone, and Leslie attempts to calm them down. It appears this quarrel has been escalating for a while, and the volcano has erupted into a lava flow of expletives. Mr. Yeats scuttles to us and pops into his human self while we're hanging our jackets and removing our shoes.

"Where have you been? The others arrived early. Apparently, Ms. McGowen overheard your conversation with Dr. Hughes and Ms. Pritchard. *She told everyone.*"

"Fawk," Archie says.

My face flushes. "Holy crystals."

I dart into the living room, Archie trailing close behind me. The elevated bickering fades to a muttering of dissent. Leslie and Agnes are standing in front of the fireplace, their faces twisted in obvious anguish. Skye is resting on the sofa near them.

"They all know you, Archie, and Trinity agreed to back this preposterous plan," she says. "I'm not shocked except for you,

Gwyn. I never thought you would ever agree to something like this. After demanding we all be transparent."

"Yeah, sis," Spence says, crossing his arms.

Trinity peers at me. "We thought she was sleeping."

Agnes shrugs. "Apparently not."

Ronnie glares at me. "You didn't even tell me, your best friend."

"Come on, friends." Elijah moves next to Leslie. "We've already expressed our displeasure to Trinity and the Elder."

"Yeah," Tanner says. "Let's not rehash that."

Leslie adds, "Very wise. We do not have the time for regurgitation."

Tyler catches my gaze. "Mom, I'm not mad you didn't tell me. You had to honor the coven leader's decision to wait until tonight to reveal this. But seriously. You actually agreed to their ridiculous plan?"

Vexed eyes spear me in place from every direction as I scan their reactions. What do I say? They're right. Archie rubs my back.

Shane locks eyes with me. "Your mom was following Trinity's direction. Frankly, I'm shocked, because she has bucked the rules herself in the past. But she must have her reasons, and I am certain she will share them with us. Personally, I'm waiting with bated breath."

"We kept this secret because Leslie and Agnes asked us to," I say. "No, I wasn't on board at all initially. But this idea of theirs didn't drop into their brains out of nowhere. They had been discussing the plan at length. I don't want them to sacrifice themselves, either. But it's their decision. We should respect it."

Zoe pouts. "There must be another option."

"We already discussed what all the options are, witches," Trinity says. "None of them are good."

Archie steps forward, irritation burning in his eyes. "Hypocrites, all of you. When we had to fight the Sluagh, Gwyn stepped forward to sacrifice herself to bait that evil Unseelie fairy. You were fine with her risking her life in that situation. I, too, am divided. I want a better option. But it's not presenting itself."

"Well, I'm fucking touched," Agnes says with a snort. "I figured you'd all be happy to watch me cross that threshold. In fact, I imagined some of you might point the way." At the smattering of offended gasps, Agnes waves her hand. "I'm messing with you. I know you care. But don't be sad. Leslie and I will be fine because we'll be together on the other side. The fact is, we fucked up. We caused the problem fifty years ago. It's our responsibility to fix it."

Leslie's eyes tear up, an emotion she seldom shows. "My inferior witchcraft skills and a wandering mind prompted the spell to take a different course. Since then, I have watched Bearsden suffer from my incompetent actions. No more. The portal must be closed."

A quiet sorrow seizes the room while reality sets in. The expressions on my friends' faces tell me they're finally understanding the predicament.

Trinity sighs. "We should vote. If you're in favor of the plan, raise your hand."

One by one, my fellow witches slowly push their hands up, weighted down by the gravity of their decision. Archie raises his arm, and I follow—the final vote. Leslie scans our eyes, wiping a tear from her cheek.

"It is done. On the night of Imbolc, we will gather in the Celestial Gardens once more to close the portal. How should we lure Agent Blackwell there?"

"I'll do it," I say. "He already said he has more questions and wants to meet with me."

Leslie smiles warmly. "Splendid. I am so incredibly proud of you all. For always putting the needs of the town above all else. That has been the Bearsden Coven's primary goal from its inception."

Spence shoots his hand up. "Wait. What about the witch who has some kind of vendetta?"

"One problem at a time," Trinity says. "Once we banish the Tuatha Dé fairy and have closed the portal, we can concentrate on reining in the evil bitch. We'll meet up at Mitchell Hall at 10:00 p.m. to prepare for the casting. Carry a fresh protection pouch to repel glamouring. For now, I disband the circle. Take care until then."

We leave the house without one word muttered by any of us. What is there to discuss? On February 1st, we will say goodbye to the Elder and the hedge witch, sending them to their deaths at the hands of their own coven.

Emotionally, I may not survive.

CHAPTER TWENTY-SEVEN

FAIRY GOODBYE

On the drive back home from the farmhouse, I stare out the window at twinkling stars in the indigo winter sky, a sliver of moon keeping them company. By Imbolc, the illumination of the waxing crescent should be close to fifty percent—enough to work by. But what about tonight?

"Archie, drive me to Mitchell Hall," I say.

"Why?" he asks. "We should avoid going there until Imbolc, Gwyn."

"I have to say goodbye to Shailagh and Aonghas. Please, take me. I need to do this."

"What if they don't cross, Gwyn? They haven't shown themselves for some time."

"Then I'll take the risk and go every night this week until I coax them out. I won't have the opportunity on Imbolc because I have to meet with Drew Blackwell at the house."

Archie turns onto University Avenue and heads east. "All right. I can't park for long in front of Mitchell Hall."

"Thanks, honey. I'll hang there for five minutes, tops."

He loops around and drives west on Main Street until the mansion comes into view, pulling up into a metered space. "Should I go with you? The witch could be anywhere."

"No. You could scare them away. My chances of coaxing them to cross increase if I'm alone. My intuition appears to be working. I will dart out of the gardens at the slightest twitch."

"All right," he says. "If you aren't back in five minutes, I'm running in there."

I exit the car and dash into the Celestial Gardens. In the blackness, shadowy figures project from the ground. I stumble into concrete benches and fountains to get to the mound, belatedly realizing I left my cell phone in the console. I bend over and whisper into the opening.

"Shailagh? Aonghas? Aunt Gwyn is here. I want to talk to you."

The aperture remains dark as I dance to stay warm, channeling Spence's moves. A slight breeze kicks up and I cover my ears. Maybe I should chant an incantation of invitation?

I raise my hand and recite. "With open arms and a warm heart, I call on Shailagh and Aonghas to come; take part."

A spot of white emerges in the center of the mound, growing until the bright light fills the opening. Shailagh and Aonghas hop through the portal.

"Aunt Gwyn! Aunt Gwyn! You're here! We've been waiting for you to call us."

"I'm so happy you crossed over. When I was here before, I called your names. You couldn't hear me, I guess."

"I am so cold," Shailagh says, rubbing her arms.

Aonghas hugs himself. "We were afraid to come. There was a scary witch in here."

"Did you recognize her? Had you seen her before?"

"No, Aunt Gwyn," Shailagh replies. "She covered her face."

"But she was mean." Aonghas pouts as his eyes scan the gardens. "Shailagh, let's go back. She could scare us again."

"Wait. Before you return, I need to say goodbye. We are closing the portal in a few days. You won't be able to cross into Bearsden again."

They grab at me. "No, Aunt Gwyn. We don't want to say good-bye."

I remove my gloves and grasp their tiny hands. "We have to. There is a Tuatha Dé fairy here who wants to harm me and my friends. We have to send him back and close this portal so he and others can never invade Bearsden again. You must stay away. I don't want either of you to get hurt. I will cross over someday and we'll see each other again."

Their glowing mint-green eyes well up with tears and a sadness tears at my heart. I didn't think it would be this hard.

"We will miss you, Aunt Gwyn," they say, wiping away green tears.

"I'll miss you, too, Shailagh and Aonghas." I embrace their diminutive bodies. "Goodbye."

"Bye, Aunt Gwyn," they say, waving.

The mischievous pranksters cross through the portal and the aperture whooshes shut. A small whirlwind kicks up in the corner of the gardens, sucking up limbs and other debris. But is it the criminal witch? I observe as the mini tornado builds in strength, resembling the whirlwind I recall on the Green until it's expanded twice its size. A slight twinge nips me in my abdomen. I dart like a sprinter through the gate and slam the door behind me once I'm in the car.

"Get the fuck out of here," I say. "I think the witch was trying to materialize in there."

Archie speeds away. "If that is true, we may have an issue on Imbolc. Did the children appear?"

"Yes. They won't cross over again. I said goodbye. Plus, they fear the witch. They confirmed she's appeared to them."

"Knowing she's in there could complicate our task."

"As Trinity always like to say, 'One step at a time.'"

I open my eyes, squinting. The sun's rays beam across the bedroom and bounce off the empty glass case where Archie's family heirloom usually rests. I peer at the clear quartz crystal on the nightstand. No signs of energy radiate from its clusters of spires. Meditation with the stones the past two nights has accomplished nothing. My visions have hit a brick wall, as if someone inserted a mental barrier. At least my intuition continues to send me signals. Too bad my skills aren't advanced enough to identify what they're pointing to.

No matter. It's February 1st and Imbolc is upon us. We have to prepare for the casting. Once I've washed up and changed my clothes, I drag my body down the stairs. As I drop into the chair, Archie brings me a cup of tea. He kisses me on the cheek.

"Good morning, my love. You tossed and turned all night."

"I don't remember. Can't even vaguely recall my dreams. That ship sailed. I know enough to deal with Drew Blackwell. Hopefully, we're closing the portal and changing the trajectory of my premonition, anyway."

"No problems with convincing the agent to meet with you so late tonight?"

"I told him I didn't want anyone in the neighborhood to observe him coming into our house and that you wouldn't be here."

"Didn't he ask why? 10:30 p.m. is quite late."

"I said you had to work on grades for the end of Winter Session at your office on campus and wouldn't return until then."

"Brilliant, my love. But a part of me is a wee bit concerned with how adept your fabrications have become."

"Merely for the sake of our survival, honey," I say with a chortle.

I'm too fatigued to grab my spoon, so I chant an incantation and sprinkle a dash of amber magic. The spoon flips, landing in the tiny bowl of stevia, and scoops up the white fluff. It drops into my cup and twirls like a dancing ballerina, floating onto the saucer when it's done. I glance at his laptop. "More grading for Seamus?"

"Making sure my access is solid. Winter Session finals are today." He breaks an egg into the frying pan. "He asked me to double check his grades and enter all of them for him by Wednesday."

"Why did he ask you to submit the grades? Or did you offer?"

"A little of both." He turns around to face me. "Seamus is flying home tomorrow to North Ireland. He asked me not to share his plans with anyone."

I gape at him. "Yet you are?" A sudden sorrow overwhelms me. "Why didn't he tell me?"

"I think you're aware, Gwyn. He can't bear to say goodbye to you. He's still in love with you. Too difficult for him to face you. I'm breaking that promise because I know you have a special bond with him. I couldn't hide the information any longer. All I ask is, please do not go to him. Respect his wishes."

My eyes tear up. "I don't understand. We wouldn't be saying goodbye for good."

"Aye. But he is a solitary witch." He flips our eggs.

"You know...he appeared weak the night he came to the farmhouse to help Skye. He was so quiet that evening, and then he snuck out without speaking to anyone. Strange, don't you think?"

Archie sets our breakfast on the table and sits. "Aye. But he was always an odd one. Let's eat. We'll need our energy for tonight."

How can I allow Seamus to leave without a chance to say goodbye? I may have to break that promise and stop by tomorrow. But first, we have a task to complete.

Because of the meeting with Drew Blackwell, I plan to remain at the house while Archie, Tyler, and Zoe walk to Mitchell Hall. With that insane witch on the loose, we have to avoid an attack at all costs. The three of them can defend themselves against the nefarious witch should she go after them, but I plan to drive my

Prius and park illegally to be safe. An expensive parking ticket or towing is worth protecting myself, the coven, and my town. I'm relying on my intuition as a barometer to get me through this night. *Please, don't fail me.*

While Archie fills the afternoon grading the final exams, I read through my plans regarding Drew Blackwell and scroll through the images folder in my phone to rehearse the incantation to close the portal. How far back does this witchcraft go? Were the beings crossing into their village so bad they had to sacrifice one of their own, too? I skip the section on mixing the ingredients because I won't be there to help. The chant is simple yet gut-wrenching as I read it. *Within this circle we will cast, to close the portal of our past. Accept the blood of these mortal-hearted, to make our space safe once they've departed.* How can we follow through with this?

Archie cooks dinner, but I pick at my food. After we finish, we clean up and hang out on the living room sofa until it's time for him to leave. There's a knock on the door and I flinch. Tyler and Zoe step in.

"Hi, Mom. Archie." Second thoughts torment his face. "Are we really going to do this?"

"My stomach is doing somersaults," Zoe says, grimacing. "I don't know if I can go through with the casting."

"We're all doubting this plan, dear, but it's what they want." I caress her upper arm. "Leslie and Agnes are right. They created the mound and the portal in it. They are responsible. You can't argue with their reasoning."

"Tell me now if you're going to back out," Archie says, slipping on his gloves. "We can't complete the casting without a full coven."

My son and his love share heartfelt glances and nod. Tyler speaks for them both. "You can depend on us."

Archie pats his shoulder. "This act will be the most challenging task you'll ever complete, no doubt. Remember, we all make sacrifices. Your own mum selflessly put herself in harm's way many times."

"But she's still here, Archie," he replies.

A smile curls his mouth. "Aye. I am eternally grateful to the universe for making it so."

"Should Tyler give Gwyn the dirk?" Zoe asks. "In case Drew Blackwell gets suspicious and figures out who she is?"

Tyler pats the outside pouch of his backpack. "Yeah, Mom. You should have it."

He pulls on the zipper, but I stop him with a hand. "No, dear. You'll need to be prepared. Drew Blackwell could suspect something, but he won't hurt me. Going to the gardens is an opportunity to drag me through the portal, so he may use the opportunity to his advantage."

"But we'll be waiting for him," Zoe says, grinning. "Ready to smack him back to the Otherworld."

"I won't argue with you," Tyler says. "I know it's a waste of time. Archie, when should I take out the dirk? When we're ready to push Blackwell into the portal?"

"Naw," he replies. "Have the zipper open for easy access."

Zoe spreads her arms. "Group hug? I think we need it."

We huddle together in a long embrace while the mantle clock reverberates with a tick, tick, tick. I slink back, signaling to them it's time to go.

"Don't worry. I'm not scared. And I sense we're closing the portal before the events my premonition forecasts. Be confident. I am."

"Tyler, could you and Zoe wait outside for me?" Archie asks. "I want to talk to your mum alone."

"Sure," he replies. "Be careful, Mom. And good luck, not that you need it."

"Gwyn, don't fuck up." Zoe flashes her signature wide grin at me.

I chuckle. "Noted. Look for me around eleven."

They step onto the front stoop, their smiles fading as Archie closes the door. He moves close to me.

"What Zoe said—ditto." He kisses me and lays his forehead against mine. "I'll text you how to enter the gardens once we've outlined the steps. You'll have to wing the incantation."

"I read over the prose earlier. I'm ready."

The warmth of his erratic breathing heats my face. "Your last vision pointed to you running for your life. Gwyn, in case something happens—"

"Stop." I gaze into his icy blues, fraught with trepidation. "Not one pang of intuition has signaled the end of my life is connected with Drew Blackwell. I will arrive as close to the designated time as possible. Tell everyone to prepare."

"I love you, Gwynedd." He caresses my cheek with his gloved hand.

I stroke his goatee. "Ditto, but you need to go, honey."

Archie kisses me once more and exits the house, shutting the door behind him as he leaves. The room snaps into silence except for the irritating ticking of the mantle clock. But there is no time to fret over what could happen. I lower my jacket to a bottom hook and check the pockets for my gloves, nearly forgetting my keys and cell phone. I stuff them in, too.

Now, I wait.

Chapter Twenty-Eight

IMBOLC

For the next forty-five minutes, I pace around the house, replaying my latest vision in my brain. What happened when I ran from Drew? Did he dart out and follow me to the gardens? Clearly, he'll be there, because he was glowing brilliantly in his fairy form near the end of the dream. I check my phone for texts and find a list from Archie. They have prepared the spell.

Archie: *The concoction is mixed and we are ready.*

Me: *I received the list of steps. Anytime now.*

Archie: *Be careful, Gwyn.*

After another round of let's-visit-each-room, I interrupt my anxious traipsing to put on my shoes. When I've tied my second shoelace, I amble up to the fireplace, gazing at the painting of Mom. Standing in a field of wildflowers, she reaches toward the impending storm. Aunt Gorawen created these charmed canvases to spread across the world to attract protectors for my mother. The protection charm passed to me once she died and crossed into the Otherworld—all to keep me safe from the Tuatha Dé prophecy. Yet here I am, alone in the house, waiting like a sitting duck for his arrival—and at my invitation.

Why am I wasting my time trying to decipher the premonition? It won't happen now that Leslie and Agnes are sacrificing themselves to close the portal. I must concentrate on what I'm going to say to Drew Blackwell to convince him to go with me to the gardens without creating suspicion. The mantle clock dings once, making me jump and sending my heartbeat into overdrive. There's a tapping on the front door and I flinch. I tap my chest and walk calmly to the foyer, bracing myself one last time as I clasp the handle.

"Hello, Agent Blackwell. Please, come in." I pat the tiny bulge in my jeans pocket.

"Thank you, Gwyn," he says, entering. He removes his long, dark coat. "May I hang this on the hall tree?"

"Sure. Why don't we talk in the living room?" Yes, come into my lair.

Drew saunters in and sits on the edge of the loveseat. He's dressed more casually in blue jeans but wearing a long-sleeved button-down shirt. I sit down close to him, hoping my intuition gleans information from his presence. Meanwhile, he appears uncharacteristically nervous, rubbing his hands together. His notepad is nowhere in sight. I'm befuddled. Finally, he shifts on the cushion.

"Gwyn, I need to be forthcoming with the truth regarding this investigation."

He pauses, as if he knows what he's about to tell me may scare me off. Shit. Is he going to confess? Drag me to the gardens? I keep one eye on the front door. He gazes into my eyes, attempting to glamour me, I suspect. But his magic won't work. My protection pouch hides safely in my jeans pocket.

"What are you trying to say, Drew? For an FBI agent, you appear confused."

He moves closer to me. "I've asked to be removed from this investigation for personal reasons."

What? Is he trying to trick me? "I don't understand. Do you have family problems?" *He sure does. I killed Nuada. And how am I going to convince him to go with me to the gardens if he's off the case?*

His head quivers no. "My feelings have become compromised. I can't explain it. But…" He wavers on the cushion, falling toward me as he stares into my eyes and…attempts to kiss me.

I shove my hand between us, gaping at him. "What the fuck, Drew?"

"Damn." He jumps off the loveseat. "I am so sorry. I shouldn't have done that. There is something about you. I told you I can't explain it. I'm attracted to you—your eyes."

Weird. I felt the same way about his, and instantly, I question my entire theory. Fuck my lousy intuition skills. Holy crystals. The coven is waiting for me to bring the Tuatha Dé fairy to Mitchell Hall. What if I made a mistake? I have to poke him to find out.

"Why don't you ask me your lingering questions?" I push off the loveseat. "If you don't, Jack Schmidt will bang on my door, anyway."

"I can't. Another FBI agent has to be assigned to you."

Fuck. I wish I could trade in my intuition skills for a more advanced model because I was so wrong. I gaze into his magnetic eyes. "Do you think I killed those women?"

"I don't want to believe you hurt them. Did you?"

"Off the record? No, I had no reason to. Except for Laura Lovelace, they were close, respected fellow pagans."

"I'm not sure why, but I believe you." His eyes dart around the room. "Unfortunately, I won't have success convincing Detective Schmidt without proof. I am breaking every rule in the book telling you this. He's obsessed with this case."

"Yeah, I know. He never solved the prior missing person investigation concerning Nick Evans. I think he suspected me when it happened, but he let it go."

I glance at the mantle clock. It's ten of eleven. I make my way to the foyer, and Drew follows. He has to go. The others will panic if I'm late.

"Jack believes the deaths of these women are the key to discovering the professor's disappearance," he says. "I get the sense he believes your pagan groups have used these women as a sacrifice to your gods."

I guffaw at him. "No, we don't kill people as a form of worship. Please, try to convince him he's on the wrong path."

"I'll attempt to, but he is determined. You're hiding something, Gwyn. It's obvious. He won't stop until he solves the puzzle." He grabs his coat. "I overheard a few of the police officers gossiping. They said Jack moved to Bearsden for this detective job. He came specifically to investigate the Nick Evans case."

"What?" I ask, grimacing. "Hasn't he been in Bearsden for a while?"

Drew slips his arms into his coat sleeves. "No. Rumors around the department are he went after this position like a boss. Some say he was related to the missing professor—family."

My witch's intuition stabs me in the gut and I double over. Drew grabs my arm as an aura overwhelms me. Beads of sweat sprout on my upper lip. I stare at his hand grasping me.

"Fuck. Oh, fuck." I clutch my abdomen.

"Gwyn, what's wrong? Can I take you somewhere?"

"No, I gotta go," I say, snatching my jacket from the hall tree. "I can't explain right now. I promise I'll call you tomorrow."

He grabs my arm again and I yank it away. The pain increases inside. "Please shut the door when you leave."

I throw on my jacket as I run out of the house and hop into my car, speeding up the street as fast as I can. The vision continues to replay in a loop in my head. At the red light, my arm hits against the hard surface of my cell and I pull it out, trying to check for texts. Several are highlighting the screen, but the traffic light turns green. As I speed down Main Street, I try to read the texts, but I can't keep my eyes on the road. There's a reason Delaware passed a law banning the use of handheld devices while driving.

When I arrive at Mitchell Hall, I park my Prius and turn off the power. I read them one after another.

Archie: *save yourself stay away*

Tyler: *I love you mom*

The message from my coven leader is voice to text.

Trinity: *Gwyn... don't come to the gardens. (Yelling erupts and the audio goes silent.)*

Shit. I bang my head on the steering wheel. What the fuck do I do? I'll tell you what I won't do—leave them all in there to face that vengeful fairy alone. All my friends—my witch family. Ronnie, who's a new mom. Archie. My son. *Tyler. He has the dirk.* And, hopefully, a plan.

I exit my Prius, locking the door with my fob. As I approach the iron gate to the Celestial Gardens, my witchy innards remind me I'm in danger. But I grit my teeth and walk through.

The half-moon illuminates the gardens, occasionally broken by clouds that float across the sky and obscure the light. When I step, the ground squishes, releasing the aroma of melted snow and mud. In the near distance, owls shriek and hoot. As I approach the left corner of the garden, I recognize the backs of my fellow witches huddled together in a semi-circle. Nausea sets in as an aura builds inside me. I must remain focused, dismissing the sensation. They appear safe. On my next step, a twig snaps, and they separate.

And there he stands in front of the mound, glaring at me—Jack Schmidt. As I move closer, a dark figure standing next to him comes into view—a witch cloaked in a hooded black cape. The fucking deranged killer is with him. Why is she here? Leslie and Agnes stand at her right, their faces inflamed with fury.

"You should have remained at the fucking house, Gwyn!" Agnes yells.

Leslie shakes her head. "It's too late for scolding now, dear."

As I approach them, Archie's voice calls out to me.

"Gwyn. I told you not to come." Anguish distorts his face.

"Mom," Tyler says on my left. "Why didn't you run?"

Trinity shakes her head. "You disobeyed an explicit order."

They shout at me at random. "Run, Gwyn!" "Get out of here!" "We can fight back!"

I can't respond because they know the answer already. I couldn't sacrifice all of them to save myself when it's me he wants. When I arrive at the semi-circle, Archie shifts next to me and Elijah moves to my other side. Jack Schmidt steps forward.

"We've had quite the discussion, your friends and I, concerning the secrecy of your coven. I didn't possess the sensitivity to track your specific magic scent like my brother, Nuada, only the presence of witchcraft in the area. Every time I thought I'd discovered your scent, it would disappear, as if someone had set up a barrier." He scans our faces. "Perhaps a spell to confuse me. I knew I would find the witch of the prophecy if I was patient. But I never considered you would murder him. What is the phrase your kind likes to use?" He cocks his head and smirks. "Oh, yes. It's time to pay the piper."

"I don't understand," I reply, anger taking hold, not fear. "How did you figure out I was the one who ended his life? None of my friends would have ever told you."

Archie whispers, "We can fight them."

"Just give us the word, Gwyn," Elijah says in a muted voice.

Or am I wrong? I turn around and scan their expressions, searching for one guilt-ridden face. There is no way any of them turned me in. Seamus knows, but he helped me commit the deed. I mouth the words at my fellow witches, "Wait." They lay their hands on their hearts in understanding. Archie squeezes my hand. When I return my attention to Jack, he glances at the evil witch beside him. She nods once, and he continues with his arrogant speech.

"When Nuada didn't return to our kingdom at the expected time, I became concerned and tracked his essence to this portal in Bearsden. Knowing I needed a cover while I searched for him, I inquired about open positions in the town's police department. As luck would have it, a detective position was posted—the perfect cover to investigate his disappearance. I found the body of a John

Doe at the morgue and morphed into his likeness. After some glamouring, I got the job."

He smiles smugly and continues. "I spent the years since my arrival hunting for clues, following magic streams that ended abruptly. I must be close when a spell is being cast, or I can't identify the source. One evening, I happened upon an unusual trail of witchcraft I'd never encountered before and followed it into the gardens. I found no one, but I returned on multiple evenings. The night of the blizzard, I tracked that sorcery to the Green. And do you know what I observed?"

Spence eyes the woman in black. "You saw us fighting that bitch, whoever she is."

"Yeah, he was there." Skye points at the nefarious witch. "He watched her attack me and did nothing."

"Of course," Tanner adds. "Because he had a hunch she had information that would lead him to Gwyn."

"Perceptive, young witch," Jack says, glancing at the hooded witch. "She told me Gwyn was the witch who killed Nuada."

"But why did she murder all those witches?" Zoe asks.

Leslie lifts her head. "That is the key to the riddle, my friends."

I pull my hand from Archie's grasp and move forward.

"Where are you going?" he whispers.

"To confront the bitch."

As I approach the evil woman, I scour my brain. Who is this heinous witch who aided Jack in exposing me? My vision did not contain even a hint of her. When I'm merely a foot away, my insides pinch and a memory comes flooding back—nearly forgotten words spoken in a thick Southern accent flood my head like a tsunami.

"Where was I? Oh, yes. I performed a cleansing, but I sensed the young man who had lived in the space had suffered his demise there. In the bedroom, in fact. It makes me wonder why the police aren't calling it a homicide."

I jerk at the dark hood, revealing a face I know well—but it has deteriorated into a visage nearly beyond recognition—her skin is marked by deep wrinkles distorted not by age but by an extreme evil, most likely dark magic. Her eyes are black as obsidian and her long hair has turned white. But I recognize the narcissistic witch's blood-red lipstick and nauseating smugness—Cordelia Davenport.

I know my fellow witches recognize her too when I hear a chorus of expletives from behind me as they lose their shit.

"You fucking bitch!" Agnes shouts from the mound.

Trinity plods forward. "Go back to the slimy hole you crawled out of!"

Shane shifts to my side. "She cast a hex on our witch allies to inflict harm against those who helped the coven. And then she started on us. You learned nothing about rehabilitation, Cordelia! And to think I loved you."

"Your love wasn't true," she says in her deep Southern voice full of arrogance. "Or you would have gone with me when I left. You're as bad as they are and now you will all pay." She raises her hand, chanting an incantation. A black and garnet swirl of flame rises from her palm.

Archie stares at the familiar fire. "You've been to Edinburgh—specifically, the South Bridge vaults."

A light bulb flips in my head. "You've had access to the Book of the Dark Souls."

"Well, I declare," she replies, continuing to foster the flame. "Y'all aren't as dumb as I thought you were. I knew the only way to accomplish my revenge was to find a source of dark magic that would allow me to mask myself and apply a powerful hex. I flew to London to meet with an old crone I'd heard about. She told me of the Book of Dark Souls, and I took a train to Edinburgh. I snuck into the vaults and made a deal with the witch who was guarding the tome. She gave me one day to find a malevolent spell that would end in death. When I returned to the States, my face began to transform. At first, I was devastated, but then I discovered this." She raises her palm, the red and black fire flickering.

I glance at Archie and raise my palm at the others to signal them to stay put. "OK, Jack. You found me. I'll go with you freely, but don't allow this vile witch to kill my friends."

Archie grabs my arm. "I won't let you do this, Gwyn."

"No, Mom!" Tyler rushes toward me, his backpack hanging off his shoulder. He shoves his hand into the outside pouch. "We can fix this, right?"

A condescending smile erupts on Jack's face. "I owe this witch. I promised to help her in exchange for divulging the secret of Nuada's murderess. After all this, you think there is a way to avoid the consequences of your actions? According to prophecy, my brother had to spend years searching for you and earning your love. And for the privilege of becoming his bride, you murdered him."

"I never fell in love with Nick—Nuada. Because I was already in love with someone else." I smile lovingly at Archie. "The reason I offered to go with him to the Otherworld was because he threatened to kill my son." I lay my hand on Tyler's arm, the one grasping the dirk.

"Are you lying to me, witch?" Jack asks, his brow furrowing.

The Tuatha Dé grabs my hand and his eyes radiate a green glow. A burning sensation moves up my arm until it reaches my heart. Instantly, the night I killed Nuada replays like a horror movie in my brain, ending when I stab him with Archie's dirk. Jack removes his grasp and I return to the present.

"You are speaking the truth." He pauses while the years of bottled-up rage contort his face and body. "My brother...defied the prophecy." His tense shoulders relax. "Nuada was juvenile and arrogant. Taking you by force was wrong. You had every right to defend yourself and your son. I am done here."

I gasp. "Wait, what? You're letting me go?"

"Yes," Jack replies. "I cannot forgive you for what you did to my brother, Gwynedd Crowther, but I will not take you with me.

I will return to my kingdom in the Otherworld tonight. When I learned of your permit to use the gardens, I laid out a plan for my disappearance. I always cover my tracks."

I nod at Tyler as a sense of relief washes over me. He removes his hand from his backpack.

Cordelia's eyes blaze with a fervent hate. "No. You owe me!"

"I will not avenge my childish brother's wrongdoings," Jack says. "Perhaps you should reevaluate your own hatred, Ms. Davenport."

She waves her hands in the air. "I will have my revenge!" She chants, flinging fiery balls of magic at us.

While we scatter, Jack's body morphs into his fairy form, growing in height. His hair transforms into long, platinum-blond strands as his bulging muscles tear the fabric of his clothing. Large wings of black and pale gray sprout from his back. He leaps at Cordelia and tackles her to the ground.

"This is our chance, witches! We can send him back." Trinity corrals us together. "Leslie and Agnes..." She tears up. "We wish you a smooth journey. Begin the incantation!"

We raise our hands and summon our witch energy, chanting the prose from the spell we swore never to use. "Within this circle we will cast, to close the portal of our past. Accept the blood of these mortal-hearted, to make our space safe once they've departed."

The ground rumbles, triggering the soil to crumble like an earthquake has hit the Celestial Gardens. Jack and Cordelia continue to battle near the opening in the mound, striking each other with streams of magic as we chant. A gust of wind blows, rustling the branches of the hawthorn tree, and an aura overwhelms me. I turn around, floating outside myself.

The giant, gray-skinned monster stamps across the mud with his enormous boots, and I pinch my nose to avoid his putrid stench. The others scream at me to move as he approaches me, but I'm motionless as the white mist of my breath surrounds me. Leslie and Agnes shout at me to run. The winds increase, scattering debris everywhere, but

I stand frozen, watching the enormous being's one good eye draw closer with each step. A large black cat pounces on the giant, but the Fomorian smacks at the feline, sending it smack against the concrete fence.

"NO!" I'm jarred back into my body. "Seamus!"

While I steady myself, the coven continues to chant without me. The Fomorian veers off and grabs at the duo, still fighting. The Elder and the hedge witch move toward the opening.

Leslie raises her arms over her head. "Now is the time, Trinity!"

"Yes!" Agnes howls. "Do it, friends!"

"Now, witches," our coven leader yells. "Combine our power!"

I search for Seamus near the fence, but it's dark and debris is flying everywhere. So, I return to the circle, and we all raise our hands, radiating in full power with a bright amber luminescence. We aim our power at the Tuatha Dé Danann and the Fomorian, pushing them with all our strength toward the opening in the mound. The portal lights up, swirling left and right, and the three of them—Jack, the Fomorian, and Cordelia—get sucked in.

The earth quakes beneath us like a six on the Richter scale, knocking our bodies to the ground. In one fell swoop, the mound collapses into a mushy pile of mud and grass. We dart to the Elder and the hedge witch, who are lying flat on their backs.

"Fuuuck!" Agnes howls as she pushes off the ground, displaying the most epic scowl of the century. "Fuck you, Cordelia Davenport!"

Leslie is guffawing louder than I've ever heard her laugh as she struggles to get up.

I dart to my mentor and hug her. "Agnes, what are you screaming about? We shut the portal and you're still here!"

"Yes!" Ronnie rushes to them. "Why aren't you happy? Cordelia paid the price instead of you two."

"This was supposed to be a huge fucking historical moment. I was supposed to go out in a blaze of glory—a story told to covens for centuries. That bitch fucked up everything!" She flips the bird at the flattened dirt pile.

Leslie stands with my help and approaches her love, sporting a rapturous grin. "Oh, Agnes. Shut the fuck up."

The Elder embraces her partner as we gather around the collapsed mound. What starts as a single chuckle expands to an all-out laughing fest, celebrating our success. But even as I laugh, my eyes are scanning the gardens to my left, searching for Seamus.

Skye takes note. "Is this like the second time Dr. Hughes has dropped the F bomb?"

"Well, we don't know what she whispers to Agnes when they're alone." Spence waggles his eyebrows.

"There are appropriate times for its use," Archie says, hugging me. "Even for the Elder. Are you all right, Gwyn?"

"I don't know," I reply.

Seamus hasn't transformed back to a witch yet. I finally spot his limp cat sith body resting near the fence to the left of the mound and I panic. The others follow my gaze. Seeing him too, we rush together to check on him.

As we gather around his wounded body, blood seeps from his side. Bones appear crushed from the blow against the fence. Tanner squats and lays his hand on Seamus's white belly.

"His skin is warm," he says. "But I don't think for long."

The cat sith lifts his lids, exposing his sea-green eyes, and emits a faint roar. I drop to my knees and place my palm against his face. "What can we do, Seamus? Why haven't you changed back?"

He locks eyes with me and roars again. I raise my hand and chant, calling on my witch energy. As the amber glow seeps from my fingers, I press on his wound. But the injury remains unchanged. Archie squats next to me and caresses my back.

"You can't heal him, Gwyn," he says. "If he hasn't returned to his witch state by now, it's because this was his ninth transition. None of us can help him."

I remove my hand and the magic dissipates. "Why, Seamus? The Fomorian was after the Tuatha Dé."

"You know why, Gwyn," Ronnie says gently.

The cat sith witch roars one more time before his lids fall. Tears well up in my eyes and Archie holds me close. The others stand frozen in the chilly air, shocked as I am that we've lost a loyal friend. Elijah moves next to me.

"We must bury his body. If we don't, scientists will pick him apart piece by piece to analyze him."

"He's right," Trinity says. "Any suggestions?"

"The North Basin Creek Park," Shane replies. "A fine resting place for a solitary witch."

"I agree." Leslie pushes to the front. "Who can house the body until we can find a spot?"

Elijah scoops the cat sith witch up in his arms. "I will store him in the walk-in freezer at the shelter."

"You're a good man," Agnes says. "Seamus would be thankful."

Tears fall from Zoe's eyes. "Poor Dr. Duffy. He was a wonderful professor."

"Fuck that." Skye wipes her wet face. "He was a fabulous witch."

Spences sniffs. "Facts."

Elijah heads toward the gate, the body of the cat sith cradled in his arms. Trinity gestures to what's left of the mound.

"I know you all are sad, witches, but our allies on the council will be pleased with our success. And we closed the portal without harm to Leslie and Agnes. We should celebrate those accomplishments. Our friends remain with us for a few more years. Let's grab our witch tools and go home. We've earned an extended rest."

We gather in a circle to wish Seamus an uneventful journey to the Otherworld. After we collect our witch casting materials, Trinity and the Elder dismiss us. As we trickle through the gate, joy finds no home on my friends' faces. For me, I can't shake the guilt from my bones.

If Seamus had loved me a little less, he would still be alive.

Chapter Twenty-Nine

FAMILY PROMISES

I HAVEN'T SLEPT IN the two nights since Imbolc, haunted by Seamus Duffy's death. Sunday, the Fellowship gathered in a clearing deep in North Basin Creek Park to bury his cat sith body and pay our last respects. Jeff Williams, Ashley Lewis, and the Ericksons joined us, as well as all our Unremarkable friends, spouses, and partners who are *in the knowing*. I arranged for Aunt Gorawen to attend via video chat. Delivering the news about her long-time friend's death gutted me to the core.

But as they say, life marches on even though trauma will do everything in its power to fuck it all up. Despite Jack Schmidt's return to the Otherworld, there have been no articles in the news the last two days about him or any mention of our fellow witches who died.

Delaware University at Bearsden's Spring Semester begins today. My cell reads 7:00 a.m. Archie has a class at eight. I throw on my robe and drag my weary body into the kitchen. As I shuffle down the hallway, Archie's voice reaches me. He must be speaking with Quinn.

"Aye. Elijah and John Erickson delivered the good news to the rest of the city council and Mayor Devine. We're all relieved the portal is closed."

"Have you responded to the University of Edinburgh yet?" comes Quinn's voice over speakerphone. "They won't keep that visiting professorship open forever, brother. You must decide before they pass over you. I don't need to tell you again how much Dad needs you now."

"No. I understand my obligations, Quinn. I will make a decision soon."

With that last revelation, I stop. He applied for a position in Edinburgh? And didn't talk to me about it? Am I an afterthought?

The wooden floor creaks as I enter. "How is Quinn?

"Oh, Gwyn," he says, spinning on his heels. He sets his phone on the table. "I didn't know you were awake. He's fine, but Dad has made no improvement. Skye appears to have recovered from Cordelia's hex, but the one cast on him must have been worse. That, or his age is affecting his recovery."

"Could be." Do I mention the job offer he has conveniently kept hidden from everyone?

He kisses me on the cheek. "How do you feel this morning? You tossed and turned all night again."

"I'm tired, but I wanted to come down before you left for class."

"You can always go back to sleep for a wee bit."

I squint at him. "Before or after you tell me about the visiting professor's job at the University of Edinburgh?"

His shoulders deflate. "I was going to tell you eventually, Gwyn. I didn't believe I'd even get an offer. Quinn pressured me to apply. When I was granted an online interview, I thought I should at least go through the motions."

"What the fuck, Archie?" I say, flinging my hands up. "You had an *interview* and didn't think you should keep me in the loop?"

He swipes his fingers through his wavy locks. "I didn't want to add to your stress with the threat of the Tuatha Dé gripping at you. Sharing this information was unnecessary unless an offer was made."

"Sounds like they made one. And what about me in this equation?"

"You are the most important part of it, my love. But the college won't hire a replacement for Seamus. Leslie, Ashley, and I are left to pick up the slack. We don't even know if there will be a department next fall."

"What? Do they have the right to eliminate an entire program with no notice?"

"Aye. They can. According to Leslie, the Celtic Studies department has been operating on a thread for years. She's the one who made it thrive."

"I'm not happy with how you withheld this information from me. It's as bad as lying. Remember how you hid what a womanizer you were?"

"Aye. You have reason to be upset. I should have told you. I'm sorry." He caresses my cheek. "It's my instinct to protect you from hurt. I love you, Gwyn. We'll figure this out together."

"We can't plan our future together if I'm not part of the discussion."

"I know." He glances at his laptop bag.

"If you need to leave for class, it's OK."

"Naw. I have something to give you, but I don't know if now is the right time." He moves to his bag, removes an envelope, and passes it to me.

"What is this?" My name is handwritten across the front.

"I found the envelope in a slot of my bag this morning. When I stopped by Seamus's house the other day to go over some grades, he must have slipped it in there. Would you like to read the letter alone?"

"No," I say, falling into a kitchen chair. "I want you to be here."

I slide my finger through the flap and rip it open. A single handwritten note rests inside. I stand and read his final words as I wander around the kitchen.

Dear Gwynedd, if you are reading this brief note, I am gone, at least in the witch sense. With my last transition to a cat sith, I knew I would never speak with you again as a witch—either due to my permanent transformation or my demise. Like you, I had visions and understood fate demanded I protect you from the Fomorian.

After my connection with you during our crystal training, my own premonitions began to include you in them. I could see you did not need my protection at the time, so you saw me less. But the revelation in the library at the farmhouse revealed the Fomorian's existence and his crossing into the Celestial Gardens. He invaded my visions henceforth. It was then I recognized my destiny. I knew I would have to sacrifice myself to save you from the enemy of the Tuatha Dé by transitioning to a cat sith for the last time.

The difficulty you experienced in expanding your visions wasn't only due to insufficient focus. I cast a barrier spell to block you from seeing the entire scene play out. I had to be sure you didn't learn enough from the images to stop me from my task. I avoided interacting with you because I couldn't take the chance of revealing my plans to you inadvertently. Do not be sad for me, Gwynedd. I cared deeply for you. I will rest peacefully, knowing you are protected and the portal is closed.

Please inform Gorawen, I have left directions to transfer all my possessions to her name. A lawyer will contact her in the near future. You must not grieve over the decisions I made because I chose them freely. I am forever yours. Seamus.

Tears fill my eyes as I'm overcome with emotion. My hand falls as I pass Archie the letter. When he's finished reading, he pulls me against his chest.

"None of this was your fault, Gwyn. He said so himself. Don't let this eat away at you." He glances at his cell phone. "I wish I could stay here, but I have to leave for class."

He kisses me, picks up his laptop bag, and walks to the mudroom. I follow him, wiping my cheeks.

"Listen. I won't be here when you return later. I'm not leaving you. But I need to get my head straight. You withheld important information that affects my life, and I am too upset about Seamus to cope with it right now."

"Don't do this, Gwyn. I was in a difficult position."

"I know. You're worried about Harris. But you could have discussed the issue with me, and you didn't. You left me out. Spring Semester is gonna be horrible for me, too. I'm graduating. Give me two weeks to get started and clear my head. OK?"

He looks away. "All right. Whatever you need, Gwyn. Remember, I love you. That has never changed."

"I know. Good luck with your first day of classes."

He exits the house without muttering a word. I turn, head upstairs, and pack my bags.

By Tuesday, nature has surprised our town with early spring temperatures, a hint of the renewal to come. Agent Drew Blackwell has left several messages on my voicemail, so I finally call and agree to meet him at a local coffee shop on Main Street. When I arrive, he's sitting at a table for two dressed in a sport coat and jeans and facing the front window. He waves and I join him. I hang my hoodie and purse on a chair and sit down. He buys coffee for himself and tea for me. After mixing in some sweetener, he leans forward.

"Thanks for meeting me. I didn't want to put any of this in an email."

That's curious. "Am I in trouble, Drew?"

He gazes into my eyes, a trace of yearning still present. "No. It hasn't hit the papers yet. Please don't share this with anyone. The case was closed."

"What? How?" I ask. "Who made that decision?"

"Detective Jack Schmidt on Saturday, the day I met with you. He claimed the coroner's reports suggested the women died of natural causes—some sort of mutated respiratory virus. They were all pagans and must have had contact with each other. And get this. Jack Schmidt resigned without notice. Quit right after. Strange. I checked his apartment. He moved out and there's no forwarding address."

Of course not. "Weird, huh?" I bite my lip to quash my emerging grin.

"Very." He gulps his coffee. "I'm heading back to Philly today, but I'd love to stay in touch."

"I don't think that's a good idea," I say, taking my final sip.

Drew swallows his last gulp of coffee and stands. "I understand. It was a pleasure meeting you, Gwynedd Crowther."

He offers his hand and I stand to accept his kind departing gesture. His handshake is firm but warm. In another life, I could have fallen for this man, a searcher for truth.

"Likewise, Agent Blackwell."

Drew starts toward the exit and turns around. "You never told me what you were hiding. I guess I'll never know." He pushes through the door.

I slip on my hoodie and grab my purse. As I stroll down Main Street to my car, I think back on my reactions to Drew Blackwell. Holy crystals. Those weren't pangs of intuition. I was just attracted to him.

My phone plays *Don't Stop Believin'* as I enter the farmhouse. Tyler's name lights up the screen. I swipe the green icon and hang my backpack. Mr. Yeats scuttles up the hallway in his chimera cat form and enters the kitchen.

"Hi, dear. How are you?"

"Fine. Zoe wants to know if you're coming for dinner. She's worried you may have forgotten because of all the research you've been doing."

"Oh, I did forget. Can I have a raincheck? The library put some references on hold for me and I have to pick them up tonight."

I follow Mr. Yeats into the kitchen to find Leslie and Agnes having afternoon tea. I wave to them. The familiar jumps onto a chair and meows.

"Sure. She'll understand." He pauses and huffs into the phone. "Did I hear Mr. Yeats meow? Are you still at the farmhouse?"

"You heard him? Yes, I am. Please, don't start on me. I needed this time to myself while I started the semester."

"Sure, but it's been two weeks, Mom. I really wish you would get your shit together. I can't go through eight months of you in a catatonic state again, like when Dad died and you found out he cheated on you. This mess has bothered me so much, I told Nain and Taid about it."

"Come on. I'm not lying in bed all day. I've been doing re-search—working on my master's project."

"Suuure. Have you even spoken with Archie?"

Agnes drops her cup on the saucer and grimaces at me. Leslie raises her eyebrows and flips a page of a gardening magazine. Like usual, Mr. Yeats scuttles past, transforming into his human persona, and turns an ear to me—always the busy-body.

"No. I'm going to," I reply. "He sent texts asking me how I am. I replied."

"I understand it's your business," Tyler says. "But in his own way, Archie was protecting you, not unlike Seamus. I mean, I can't imagine how he got through these past months knowing he may need to leave Bearsden. He must have stressed over it the whole time. One thing I know for sure is he loves you. I knew it the day I spoke with him at the Raven Pub after you left the coven. I gotta go help Zoe with dinner. Talk to you later."

"OK. Bye, dear." I walk to the cabinet and get a cup to prepare some Earl Grey.

"You know Tyler doesn't talk shit, right?" Agnes asks. "I was OK with you staying here a couple of weeks, but all this going back and forth to DUB all day long is getting on my fucking nerves. Dealing with Leslie's coming in and out like a revolving door is bad enough." She glances at her love. "But that ends come May. Are you gonna tell her, sweetheart?"

"What?" I ask, setting my tea on the table.

"Gwynedd, I decided it's time for me to retire," Leslie replies. "Before you ask, yes. Archie is aware. Soon, the college will announce their decision to close the Celtic Studies department. For the moment, please don't share the news with Spence and Skye. It affects them majorly. With my retirement, Seamus's leaving, and Ashley Lewis's transfer to the English department, only Archie remains. The dean is using this opportunity to...how did he put it? To use the much-needed resources elsewhere."

I fall against the back of my chair. "Why didn't Archie tell me?"

"Because you're fucking here." Agnes downs the rest of her tea. "He's respecting your space. Gwyn, after all I've been through, I can vouch for one decision I'll never regret." She smiles mischievously at the Elder. "Making amends with Leslie. I would have died a lonely old bitch if I hadn't. Don't fuck up a good thing over his desire to spare you from worry."

Leslie closes her magazine. "Gwynedd, if I were Archie, I'd accept the offer in Edinburgh to be near his family, and you should go with him. Make a new life with your love."

"What about the coven?" I wave a sprinkle of magic and my spoon spins in the cup. "You wanted me to take over leadership one day?"

"As Agnes so eloquently likes to say, fuck it. Make the life you want, Gwynedd. The Fellowship will survive."

I chuckle at Leslie's colorful speech. "Agnes has had a terrible influence on you, Elder."

Leslie grins at her love. "A welcome change, don't you think?"

On Sunday, I pull up and park at the curb of Archie's small cottage—my home. But for how long? Once he sells the house, I'll have to move, too. I don't know if I can leave Bearsden. This town contains my entire life—my history, my family, my friends. I retrieve my bags from the back and stroll up the walkway, recalling the first night I came here. He kissed me in front of the fireplace and I burst into a hot flash, melting like a candle. A laugh spurts out as I push on the entry door.

I roll my suitcase into the foyer and hang up my jacket. Footsteps approach from the living room.

"Gwyn." He notices my luggage. "You're back?"

"Yeah," I say, dropping my backpack. "Yesterday, Leslie told me about the Celtic Studies department. Why didn't you call me? Tell me in a text?"

He shoves his hands in his pockets. "I wanted you to return on your own terms."

"What are you going to do?" I ask, approaching him.

He hesitates. "I already accepted the offer."

"Without talking to me?"

"What other option did I have? They're shuttering the department. Because I'm an academic, I must apply to positions where they're posted. I have no choice in the matter. I want you to go with me to Edinburgh. It's selfish of me to ask you to leave everyone you know here, especially Ronnie, Tyler, and Zoe. But I don't fawking care. I want you by my side for as long as you'll have me. Marry me, Gwyn. You would qualify for a fiancée visa, but we'd have to marry within six months of arrival."

My jaw drops. "Such a romantic proposal. But you researched all this."

"Aye. I never once imagined I'd leave without you, Gwyn."

I gaze into his clear-blue eyes. "But it's so cold in Scotland."

He chuckles and cups my face. "Aye. But I'll be there to keep you warm, my love."

When he kisses me, the concerns of the moment melt away. But the idea of leaving my son clutches at my heart.

"Can I think about it? I don't know how I can leave Tyler."

"Of course. I'll understand if you can't leave him. You showed me how important family is. But I told you I'm selfish. I want you with me."

"Before we left Edinburgh, Harris asked me to marry you."

His brow crinkles. "I wondered what he whispered in your ear that day—the scoundrel."

"Leslie told me I should go to Edinburgh with you."

He raises a corner of his mouth. "Well, she is a seasoned academic. You should consider her expertise."

I burst out laughing. "The woman who cared so much about opening a portal and keeping a secret that she pissed off her girlfriend and didn't make up with her for fifty years?"

"Maybe I'm a just a romantic?" He kisses me again. "I won't pressure you, but I'd be chuffed to have you come with me. You have to be content with your decision."

I lay my head on his chest. The steady beat of his heart reminds me he'll always be there for me. "Being with you makes me happy."

Later that night in bed, Archie reminds me how deep his love for me is as he peels back the covers and slips beneath the sheets. I recall the first night he crawled between my legs, grazing my skin with kisses as he moved closer to my most tender spot. After so many years of being cast aside by my cheating husband, he was fulfilling my desires. As I reach my peak, the memory of his panicked response when I yelled *stop* pops into my memories. I yelp and laugh between gasps of air, panting.

Archie inches up my torso and peeks his head out. "Why are you laughing? Suddenly, my love-making is humorous to you?"

"No." I pull him to my face, snorting. "I remembered how I acted on Mabon when you partook of my nether regions. I yelled stop because the dream I had of you flashed in my head—one of my first premonitions. You had such a look of panic."

He chuckles. "Aye. I was so worried you changed your mind—not that I would have pressured you to continue. I wanted so badly to make you feel again. Although I didn't realize it at the time, I loved you even then." He slides a finger across my lips and kisses me, igniting my flame once more.

"I can't live without you, Archie. I'll move with you to Scotland."

His face breaks into a smile and he kisses me. "We'll visit as often as we can between courses—as much as you need."

He enters me, and I wrap my arms around his torso, clinging to him with every ounce of my being. When we're lying next to each other, spent from our frolicking, I gaze at his sleeping body in the dark. His eyes flutter, a satiated smile on his face. A sudden ache clenches my heart.

How can I leave my son?

Chapter Thirty
GOING HOME

Spring Semester flies by faster than a hummingbird's wings flap. Between Archie's heavy course load and the daily research for my thesis, we barely cross paths, save for a few shared meals and collapsing into bed at night. Archie lists the house for sale in April, and an offer drops in the first week. By late May, the packing is done, and our personal items are on a ship to Scotland, along with his antiques and the family dirk. Archie sold the Tesla, but we're storing my Prius at Tyler and Zoe's home. I stop by Seamus Duffy's grave once in a while to place fresh lavender on the site. Today, I'm making the last visit for some time with Ronnie.

It's a sunny June day without a cloud in sight. The skies resemble blue cornflowers. I revel in wearing my T-shirt and shorts because there won't be many days like this in Scotland. When we're finished laying flowers on Seamus's grave, Ronnie and I hike back to town. On the way to Main Street, we talk about the experiences I had with Drew.

Ronnie snorts. "Oh, my gods, woman. You thought the FBI agent was after you because of butterflies in your stomach. You had the hots for him."

"Shhh." I scan the passersby. "Someone might hear you."

"You really think my voice carries that far?"

"Yeah, I do. You know you're obnoxiously loud, right?"

She cackles. "So Derek tells me."

"Do you realize how much I'm going to miss these walks with you?"

"Oh, stop. We'll video chat every day. Plus, Derek and I will visit for the wedding." She hugs me. "I'm so excited for you. I mean, I don't believe anyone has to get married. But Derek and I plan on it, eventually."

"I'm not sure we would have bothered, but Archie says it's easier for my visa. And it'll make Harris happy, but we're excited, too."

When we arrive at Mitchell Hall, I stop and peer at the entry gate to the Celestial Gardens.

"Do you mind walking back to the café without me?" I ask. "I want to stroll through the fairy gardens before I leave."

"Sure, Gwyn. I'll see you at the party tomorrow."

She hugs me one more time and heads to work. I stroll into the Celestial Gardens and meander around the fairy fountains, recalling the play times with Shailagh and Aonghas. I miss those mischievous pranksters.

While I rest on the bench under the blossoms of the hawthorn tree, a mother and two elementary-aged children enter the gardens. The young boy and girl dash around the fairy fountains, playing tag. Their mom sits on a bench and takes out a book. I amble over to the rebuilt mound and inspect the fake entrance, a replica of what once was. The curious kids stop next to me, panting.

"A friend at school told me the fairy mound is real." The boy bends over to inspect the opening. "He said they came out in the middle of the night when no one was around."

His slightly older sister frowns at him. "If nobody was here when they came out, how did anyone see them, genius?"

"You're jealous because none of your friends know about it." He pulls on my hoodie sleeve. "Do you believe in fairies?"

I recall my Unremarkable days, when I wasn't *in the knowing*, and squat down to speak to the young boy eye to eye. "I didn't used to think they were real, but now? Yes. I believe." I glance at his sister, who is turning her lip up.

"See." The boy sticks his tongue out at her and runs away. His sister darts after him.

I scan Alistair and Rose Mitchell's gardens one last time and walk through the iron gate.

The going away party at the farm is a blast and will probably continue once we leave for the airport. The Fellowship planned to have one last hurrah at the Pumpkin House, but the college made Archie turn in the keys—sort of a final *fuck you* from the Celtic Studies department. The shuttering of the department has screwed Spence and Skye. They want to remain in Bearsden so Archie recommended they apply to online degrees in the US and the UK. Surprisingly, Agnes is happy to have us celebrate with lunch at the farm. I think my mentor is actually relieved she didn't have to sacrifice herself after all. But she'll damn sure never admit it.

The entire coven is here, along with their loved ones, enjoying the food, drink, and friendly conversation. Jeff and Ashley have brought Aidan with them and the Ericksons accepted our invite, too. Courtney is nine months pregnant and about to pop any day now. Soon Bearsden will have two half-human, half-fairy Tylwyth Teg fae. Ronnie smiles as Derek passes Luna to Courtney, and she swoons over the infant as Elijah and Jasmine look on. In a corner of the room, Shane and Julia make googly eyes at each other. I am so happy for them both. Mr. Yeats remains in the magic room, avoiding the crowd.

The young witches are gathered around Leslie and Agnes, relishing in the failure of their demise. Archie remains by my side. We laugh and cry as we share memories, noting we'll make more in the future. But hopefully without the invasion of malicious beings. I survey the room, soaking in their joyous faces. I get a lump in my throat.

Our coven leader grabs a spoon and taps the side of her wineglass. "Quiet down, witches. I would like to share a few words."

"Shush, everyone," Spence says, snapping his fingers. "Our leader wants to make a speech."

"Thank you. I don't want to interrupt our jovial gathering for long. I ask you to join me in wishing our witches well on their new journey. When Leslie first told me she had invited a Scottish ancestral witch to Bearsden to help recruit young people into our coven, I wasn't too happy. I had my doubts about the flirty, attractive professor." She glares at Archie. "And most of them came to fruition."

He chuckles and raises his glass. "Guilty."

Everyone laughs and Trinity continues. "But then something magical happened. With all our help, he recruited a long-lost witch back into our fold—reluctantly, I might add. And then he almost screwed it all up. But she returned to us, making demands that made our coven better, stronger. This is not a permanent goodbye. We look forward to your many visits." She lifts her wineglass. "Here's to Gwyn and Archie. May you build a wonderful life for yourselves in Edinburgh. And keep a guest bedroom open."

The room explodes into celebratory exclamations of "Good luck!" and "Safe travels!" We clink glasses and sip our wine. Tyler glances at his cell phone and sets his soda on a nearby table—designated driver.

"Mom. Archie. We should get going in case the traffic gets bad."

"I can't say goodbye to each of you, friends." Their smiling faces warm my heart. "I'm trying to leave here without a wet face. How about making a circle?"

"That's a fabulous idea, Gwynedd," Leslie replies. "Clasp hands."

We squish together between the sofas in the living room, inviting our Unremarkable family and friends to join us. Archie squeezes my hand and I pass it on until the message of goodwill reaches the councilman.

Elijah fist bumps Archie. "Good luck, my man."

"Thank you," Archie replies. "Take care, everyone. We'll stay in touch."

My fellow witches shout their goodbyes as Tyler, Zoe, Archie, and I head to the foyer. Agnes hobbles behind us. The magic room door creaks open and Mr. Yeats scuttles up the hallway, morphing into his human presentation on the way.

"Oh, Ms. Crowther. Were you going to leave without saying goodbye?"

"No," I say. "But thank you for coming to the door. We have to get to the airport."

"It has been an honor being your assistant. I wish you and Dr. Cockburn all the best." He gives me an awkward hug."

"Thank you, Mr. Yeats," I say as he pulls away. "You were a wonderful helper, and I won't forget it."

Overcome with emotion, the familiar sniffs and adjusts his spectacles. He transforms into a chimera cat and scuttles back to the magic room.

Agnes peeks into the living room and whispers to us. "I don't suppose you'd consider taking him with you, would you?"

"I believe Dr. Hughes would have a strong opinion on the matter," Archie replies.

Tyler moves toward the door. "I'm going to turn the car around. Talk to you later, Agnes."

"Bye, everyone!" Zoe yells into the living room.

I glance at Archie. "Can you wait for me in the car?"

"Aye." He pats my mentor's arm. "Take care, Agnes."

"You, too, Archie," she replies.

He exits the house and I pause, attempting to maintain my dry eyes.

"I know you didn't want me to make a fuss in front of any witnesses. But I needed to say something to you before I go."

She scowls at me. "Don't get fucking sentimental on me."

"Well, you taught me I should always do whatever I want. Remember?"

She snorts. "Sounds like me."

"The day I lost it on your porch when you were refusing to train me until I'd painted your fence. I was so pissed at you, I didn't care if I ever talked to you again. But I'm glad I did. I would have never become the witch I am without you, Agnes. That should have been my mom's job."

Her eyes tear up and she clears her throat. "Well. Lowri did what she hoped would save you. And she may have if the coven hadn't fucked that all up."

"Well, if I had to choose a mentor in a different life, I want you to know I wouldn't hesitate to pick you again." I lean forward and embrace her. "I'm gonna miss you, you ol' hedge witch."

She squeezes me back, then pulls away and wipes the wet from her eyes. "Get the fuck outta here. You have a plane to catch."

"I love you, too, Agnes. Tell Leslie I'll be in touch." I step onto the porch and peer back at her.

"I will. Bye, Gwyn. By the way, when I was high, I may have snuck some Bearsden Poison into one of your bags."

An impish grin forms on Agnes's face as she closes the door.

Tyler pulls up along the curb and we hop out of the car. He darts to the trunk, helping Archie to remove our hefty luggage—two bags each.

"Give the realtor the keys once the settlement appears to be in the clear," Archie says. "I'll call you if any snags crop up."

"Will do." My son hugs him. "Have a safe trip. Try to sleep."

Zoe leaps at him with clutching arms. "Bye, Archie."

"Thank you," he replies, chuckling.

"Bye, Gwyn." She embraces me. "I'm gonna miss you guys." She blows us a kiss and gets into the car.

"The months to the wedding will go by in a flash," I say. "We'll chat often."

My son wraps his arms around me and tightens his grasp. I hoped to make it through without tears, but I become a blubbering idiot. How do I let go?

"I don't know how I'll survive not seeing you every week."

He releases me and laughs. "Maybe you'll have a life that doesn't require you to check up on me every waking moment."

"Like that will ever change." I smile and wipe my face with a tissue.

A car honks and an airport worker motions for us to move. Rushed goodbyes can bite me.

"We better get on the road," Tyler says. "Go live your life, Mom. Because you fucking earned it."

He hugs me one more time and gets in the car. As the sedan drives off, Zoe waves through the window. Before we check our bags, we search for the Bearsden Poison but find nothing—Agnes's last joke on us. Once we've made it through the TSA lines and we're seated on the plane, reality sets in. I'm moving to Scotland. Archie lays his warm hand on mine.

"Do you have any regrets?"

"Oh, yeah. I have lots of them. Not being raised as a witch. Missing decades with Aunt Gorawen. Living with a cheating husband who cared more about his own desires than his family. Missing out on raising Tyler with ancestral magic. Not being a part of the coven while I was existing as an Unremarkable. Missing out on years of friendships with some of the finest witches I know."

Archie arches an eyebrow. "And me? Do you regret anything?"

I squeeze his hand and gaze into his icy blues. "Not a thing. My life is forever changed because of you, and I'm thankful."

"But will you be happy in Edinburgh?" he asks, pressing his lips together. "Away from the only home you've ever known. Apart from Tyler and Ronnie. The Fellowship."

I smile warmly at his gorgeous face, a *wee* bit more weathered since we met in that first DUB class. "I'm content wherever you are, Archie. You're my home. Everyone else is merely a phone call away."

He kisses me and giggles erupt from the seats behind us.

"Gwynedd Crowther, I love you with every fiber of my being."

"And I love you, Dr. Cock-burn."

The End
Or is it?

About the Author

J.C. YEAMANS is an author of PWF Urban Fantasy and other paranormal fiction. A former public school teacher based in Lewes, Delaware, she writes about all things witchy to find the inherent magic in life's journey of discovery and love—all while making blunders along the way. As the owner of Reed Shore Press, she also publishes fiction and nonfiction works for others. Her prior career revolved around the performing arts. She is married and has two adult children. When she's not putting pen to paper (or more aptly, fingertips to keys), she spends time biking, hiking, and weightlifting.

Sign up for J.C. Yeamans's newsletter at jcyeamans.com to download A Trinity of Witches, a free backstory to The Bearsden Witch Series.

ACKNOWLEDGMENTS

Thank you again to my daughter for the help with the Welsh pronunciations in my books.

Thank you to my son for his continued help with my website and online store.

To my book cover designer Charles Clark. My books would be naked without you.

Special thanks to my editor Sarah Faeth Sanders. You always buff my books until they sparkle.

To my ARC Team. You rock!

OTHER BOOKS

The Bearsden Witch Series

Secrets of a Midlife Witch
Schooling of a Midlife Witch
Stalking of a Midlife Witch
Trials of a Midlife Witch
Intuition of a Midlife Witch
Resolve of a Midlife Witch

www.ingramcontent.com/pod-product-compliance
Lightning Source LLC
Chambersburg PA
CBHW030148310726
48970CB00005B/1638